Martha Whitmore Hickman

Martha Whitmore Hickman has written many works of non-fiction and books for children, but this is her first adult novel. She has three sons and five grandchildren; her daughter, Mary, died at the age of sixteen.

This book has been a long time in the writing and I am indebted to many people:

To the trustees and staffs of the Ossabaw Island Project, Yaddo, Virginia Center for the Creative Arts, and Ragdale Foundation for the inestimable gift of protected time;

To teachers who became friends, particularly to Anne Rivers Siddons, who saw the earliest pages of this book and has believed in it ever since, and to John Gardner who from the time I met him at the Bread Loaf Writers' Conference until his death was mentor, advocate and friend, and whose encouragement sustains me to this day;

To my agent, Harvey Klinger, for vision and persistence in calling this book into publishable form;

To my compatriots in the Tuesday evening writers' group – Rick, Alana, Madeena, K., Jim, Holly, Nancy, Squire, Mike, Alice, Phyllis, Linda, Sally, Catherine, Michael J., Michael S., Sallie, Ronna, Amy, Steve – for offering criticisms and sharing triumphs;

And beyond all that to my sons – Peter, John and Stephen – and their families for making the world a better place and to my husband, Hoyt, for unfailing love and support through all the years together.

Such Good People

Martha Whitmore Hickman

CORONET BOOKS
Hodder and Stoughton

Copyright © 1996 Martha Whitmore Hickman

First published in 1996 by Hodder & Stoughton
First published in paperback in 1997 by Hodder & Stoughton
A division of Hodder Headline PLC

A Coronet paperback

The right of Martha Whitmore Hickman to be identified as the
Author of the Work has been asserted by her in accordance with
the Copyright, Designs and Patents Act 1988.

10 9 8 7 6 5 4 3 2 1

British Library Cataloguing in Publication Data

Hickman, Martha Whitmore
Such Good People
I. Title
813.54 [F]

ISBN 0 340 65822 3

Printed and bound in Great Britain by
Cox & Wyman Ltd, Reading, Berkshire

Hodder and Stoughton
A division of Hodder Headline PLC
338 Euston Road
London NW1 3BH

To my Family

"We need, in love, to practice only this:
letting each other go.
For holding on
comes easily: we do not need to learn it."

Rilke

1

'Why would we want adults? Surely you're not thinking chaperones?' Annie queried her mother. She laid one hand on the blue Formica counter, as though bracing herself against a world suddenly bereft of reason. 'What could chaperones keep us from doing that we couldn't have done already?' Her dark hair swung forward and she reached up to tuck it behind her ears. She repeated her point. 'What could chaperones keep us from doing that we couldn't have done already – if we wanted to?'

'Nothing.' Laura set her near-empty soda can in its puddle of moisture – the accompaniment to an after-school chat that had begun pleasantly enough. She turned slightly on the blue and chrome stool and her leg brushed the knee of Annie's jeans. 'But suppose something happened? You might need help. An adult's judgment.'

'We're only going to the State Campground. We'll be ten miles from home. Gordon has a car.'

'I know Gordon has a car.' The spectre of Gordon's car had pursued Laura ever since, six months older than Annie, Gordon had got his license and an old Chevvy to go with it – a mobile secret interior space for carrying her daughter off. With Annie's permission, of course. 'I just don't like the idea. I'd feel better if you had an adult with you.'

'I'm sure you'd let Bart or Philip go,' Annie persisted. 'I bet they do all kinds of things you don't even know about.'

Laura smiled to herself. The thought of her two tall sons asking her permission to do almost anything seemed a bit ludicrous. 'When you're off at college you can decide what's right for you. Bart or Philip never went on overnight campouts without adult supervision when they lived at home.'

Annie's shoulders in the green cotton sweater rose and fell in a dramatic sigh. Her brown eyes narrowed and she leaned forward – a prosecuting attorney nailing a witness. 'Surely you're not concerned with what the neighbors would think!'

Laura was silent for a moment, considering. 'It's not the neighbors. It's me. I'm not,' she hesitated, 'I'm not comfortable with the idea. I don't like it.'

Annie shook her head, as though unable to believe what she was hearing. 'Surely you can't expect me to be stuck with your hangups.' She slid off the stool, her feet finding her shoes again, and swept past her mother. At the doorway she paused. 'I'll ask Dad and see what he thinks.'

'Mmmhmm,' Laura murmured. She heard the rise and fall of Annie's voice on the phone. Probably calling Gordon to report her mother's intransigence. The camping trip wasn't for several weeks – something to celebrate the end of the school year. She and Trace would talk about it. He was less likely than she to oppose his daughter, whether out of conviction or to win Annie's favor, she didn't know. As for her, Annie's favor hadn't been in the slightest jeopardy, until lately. Now she felt sometimes as though they were all walking on thin ice.

She pulled a cookbook from the shelf and began flipping through the pages for the risotto recipe. Frankly, she was tired of cooking. It had been all right when everyone was home and her life had been taken up with domesticity but now that, at last, they'd made the sunroom into a studio for her, the drafting table and paint brushes were calling.

A gust of wind banged the back door shut. 'Hello!' It was Trace, home from the college. She looked at her watch. Not quite four? Then she remembered – exam period. Still, it was unlike him to come home early.

'Hello!' He hurried in, dropped his books on the counter, gave her a quick kiss and turned on the radio. 'Hear about the storm?' His face was intent, brows drawn together, eyes

2

fixed on the dial as though it was a small TV and if he looked hard enough he could see the storm on its shiny black filament. Only the crackle of electricity came from the radio. 'What the . . .' he muttered, turning the dial.

'Storm?' Laura looked out the window. Dark clouds covered the sky. The young dogwood swayed sharply from the ground, its leaves upturned, silver, slapping against the air. 'I guess it's that time of year – spring storms in Tennessee. But I hadn't noticed. Annie and I were talking.'

'It's been on the news all the way home. A heavy storm front. Fifty mile an hour winds.'

'Hi, Dad.' Annie came into the kitchen. She'd taken off her contacts and her gold-framed glasses had slid down her nose so she had to hold her head back slightly to look at him. 'Dad, there's this camping trip . . .'

Trace continued to fiddle with the dial. 'What's the matter with this thing?'

'Dad?' Annie pushed her glasses back into place with her forefinger, levelled her gaze.

'Listen.' Trace nodded toward the crackling sound of the radio. 'There's a big storm coming.'

'Dad, for heaven's sakes. A little rain.'

'It's a heavy storm front. It's been on the news all the way home.' He put his ear close to the dial. 'All I'm getting is static,' he complained.

Annie looked from him to her mother, then back again. 'Well, whoop di do,' she said, and with a withering look at her father she left the room.

A huge clap of thunder and suddenly it was dark, at four in the afternoon. Another rush of sound and the rain began, lashing down in sheets of water that plastered against the windows.

'Good thing you got home,' Laura said. 'This would be a mess to drive in.' Trace had given up on the radio and was standing close to the window, trying to peer through the wall of water.

The refrigerator motor stopped, started again, stopped. Trace flipped a wall switch. No power. Another rumble of thunder. Almost immediately, a flash of lightning illuminated the room. Then a sharp, shattering crash.

Annie reappeared at the doorway. 'Wow! That was a biggie.'

'That one hit something.' Trace backed away from the window, moved toward the living room, Laura with him.

'Come on in here, honey,' she called to Annie, still in the kitchen. 'You don't want to be near a window.'

'I want to see the fireworks,' Annie called. Another clap of thunder, a flash of light, and she joined them in the living room, moved to the big picture window.

'Don't get too close,' Trace warned.

'You're a couple of chickens,' Annie said, but stepped back to stand by her mother and watch the trees sway and bend. The slender maple tree, newly planted a year ago after the mimosa finally died, angled over like an acrobatic dancer bending to the ground. Behind them the light from the kitchen flickered on, off, then back on.

For a minute the storm was quiet, catching its breath. Then another loud crack. The house shook. Lightning flashed into the darkened room.

At the bottom of the driveway by the telephone pole, a huge fireball flared, hung thirty feet above the ground.

'What's *that*?' Annie whispered.

They stared. No one spoke.

Again, a crash of thunder. Lightning shimmered in the room.

'Quick,' Laura said. 'The small bathroom.'

They hurried to it – an interior room, no windows – and closed the door, muting the sound. They huddled together in the small space, their knees pushing against the tan porcelain of the toilet bowl. It was Annie who lifted her arms to encircle them both, impulsively dart her head forward to kiss each of them on the cheek. 'I love you,' she said. As though this could be it, a final farewell, victims of disaster, the house falling down around them.

After a minute or two Trace opened the door a crack, letting in the roar of wind and driving rain. A strange scraping sound came from the living room.

'What on earth?' Laura said. The light in the bathroom went out. She felt Annie tremble against her shoulder.

They stood in the almost darkness for a few minutes, not

4

speaking, with only the narrow needle of half-light marking the crack of the door. Gradually, rumbling sounds replaced the crashes of thunder, the lightning preceded the thunder by several seconds.

'Well!' Trace pushed the door open, disengaging himself from the others. 'It's letting up.'

They stepped out into the hallway.

There was still some daylight. They hurried to gather candles, matches, a flashlight.

When the rain had all but stopped, Trace headed for the back door and the carport. 'I'll try the car radio and see if we can learn anything.'

In ten minutes he came back. 'The storm is moving east. They're calling it a tornado. I walked out to the street. That fireball was two power lines breaking – must have touched against each other going down. The church at the corner lost half its roof.' He stepped to the fireplace, stooped to peer up the chimney.

It was then Laura noticed the length of black chain in his hand. 'What's that?' she said.

'That scraping sound we heard?' he said, his voice muffled by the open fireplace, the angle of his lifted shoulder. 'The storm sucked the damper from the chimney and dragged the pull chain with it.' He stood upright again. 'The chain broke off on impact. The damper's lying in the driveway.' He stooped again, lifted the end of the chain toward a spot on the blackened fireplace wall. 'You can see right there. The pull chain's anchor's shorn clear off the chimney wall.'

'My God,' Laura said, the image of air, chain, household – their lives – being sucked into some gigantic vacuum, tossed into the air and thrown to the ground.

Annie stepped close to the fireplace to see. 'Wow!' she said.

'It was a close one,' Trace said, and the three of them looked at one another in the now returning light of early evening, as though they had not seen each other for a long time.

They lit the candles and improvised dinner, avoiding opening refrigerator or freezer – peanut butter sandwiches, cans of tomato juice and fruit. When they sat down to eat, their usual gesture of joining hands for a moment of silence was anything but perfunctory.

To Laura's relief, Annie didn't bring up the matter of the overnight campout, almost as though she, too, wanted to keep unmarred this time together. Instead, she talked on about school, about looking forward to the family vacation trip this summer. They would go first to Laura's family's reunion in Michigan.

'It will be sad without Grandpa,' Annie said.

'Yes, it will,' Laura agreed, her grief for her father a knot in her chest again. 'But it's important for Grandma, and the rest of us too, that the family all be together.'

They would go on from there to two weeks at a mountain resort in Colorado.

'Have I ever been to Colorado?' Annie asked Trace.

'No. A new state for you. A new place for all of us. Highly recommended by your travel guide.' He stood, bowed with a smile and a flourish of his hand, sat back down.

'Do they have horseback riding?' Annie asked.

'They do,' Trace said.

Annie went on. 'It'll be great to have Bart and Philip with us again. I really miss them.'

'I do too,' Trace said. His oldest son's coming graduation had made him sharply aware of the passage of time and, atypically, it had been he more than Laura who had pushed for the weeks in Colorado. 'Quality time, before they all get away,' he'd said to her, half joking.

She looked at him oddly. 'It's a little late for that, isn't it?'

He winced. Why do you think I'm pushing for it? he thought. But he made no comment. It was soon after her father's death and of course she was upset about that. He missed Will, a gracious man, a steady presence in Laura's sometimes volatile family. He loved them, and looked forward to seeing them. And Laura was right, her mother, her brother and sister, their families did need this time together after Will's death. But sometimes the commotion of her family gatherings got to him. It was his urging that put the time in Colorado after the reunion, not before. By then he would need a rest.

They did the dishes by candlelight and when darkness

settled in – their part of the city was black except for the lights of travelling cars and repair vehicles – they went to bed.

'It was nice in that bathroom, cozy,' Laura said, as she and Trace settled against their pillows. In her mind she saw the three of them huddled together, arms round each other, and Annie leaning forward to kiss them and say, 'I love you.'

Trace moved toward her. 'And since we've come to bed so early, we might as well make good use of the time.' His voice was light, his hand on her breast. 'I mean, it's a bit early to go to sleep, right?'

'Right.' She turned, lifted an arm to circle his neck. 'But not too fast, okay? A little pillow talk, maybe?'

'Sure. Anything special?'

'Just those moments with Annie – her reaching to us.'

'Mmm. What about them?' His hand was moving over the rise of her hip.

She closed her eyes against tears, glad of the dark. 'It's just that . . .' If he didn't know, how could she tell him? Or maybe it was more her problem than his, this threat of estrangement from her daughter. Annie was sixteen, after all. She had thought they could negotiate these straits better than most. But so far they weren't doing awfully well.

'*You* love me, don't you?' she said softly, his face above hers now.

'Believe me,' he said and slipped inside her and she wrapped her arms round him, tight.

In the morning the power was still off. They learned from the car radio that school was cancelled.

Trace gathered books and papers.

'You probably don't have power at the college either,' Laura remonstrated. 'You could stay here with us.'

'I'll find something to do,' he said. 'The power should come back soon.' He kissed them each in turn. 'Have a good day.'

Laura and Annie looked at one another and rolled their eyes. 'He'd probably be reading going over Niagara Falls,' Annie said.

* * *

7

Soon after lunch the refrigerator began to hum. Lights went on. It was a relief to have the power back, though it had been, Laura thought, adjusting electric clocks, turning off lights, in some ways a welcome distraction from things that had been troubling her – her father's death, the off and on tension with Annie, never knowing what her mood would be. Friend or foe? Confidante or recluse?

That evening her mother called. 'Are you folks okay?' Rachel wondered. 'It's been on the news about tornadoes in Tennessee.'

'We're fine,' Laura said. 'But it was pretty fierce for a while.'

'It didn't damage your house? The pictures looked awful. A wonder nobody was killed.'

'It pulled the damper out of the chimney.' The image still chilled Laura, as though all of their life blood was somehow being sucked away. 'The power was out for almost twenty-four hours.'

'You're still coming for my birthday, aren't you?'

'I think so. I'll check with Lillian and Howard. I know we tentatively planned to, when we were all home together.' She did a rapid calculation. Three weeks until her mother's birthday. Maybe by then she'd have preliminary sketches in to the publisher. It was her first commission, a small advertising brochure, but it was a start.

'They can come just for the weekend,' Rachel said. 'Can you stay a little longer?'

Laura drew in her breath. Lillian's library job. Howard's teaching. Her own time always expendable. 'I don't know. It's pretty busy here.'

'Oh?' Rachel said. 'What's going on that's so pressing?'

The question caught her off guard. What to say? I miss my father. Half the time I don't know my daughter. I have one commission and I'm trying to redo my old portfolio. My husband is so preoccupied that sometimes I want to scream. And besides that I'm getting age spots!

'Just a lot of things,' she said. 'I'll think about it. How are you doing?'

'Better, the doctor says. No more fainting spells. But I'm

not sure I want to stay here in the house. It gets pretty lonely.'

'Oh?' Laura's hand tightened on the phone. 'It hasn't been very long.' She tried to keep her voice light. 'You have to give it a chance. Is Nettie still coming?'

'Yes. A couple of days. The nights are lonely.'

'I'm sure. We'll talk about it, Mother, over your birthday.'

They said their goodbyes. Laura hung up. For a moment she leaned against the wall, her heart plummeting. Oh, dear. Maybe it wasn't going to work out for her mother after all. Then what?

She moved toward the next room. 'Trace?' she called. 'Annie?'

But they were watching television – pictures of the storm – and didn't look up.

2

The question of Rachel's future had lain like an undertow beneath the varied rises and falls, the whirlpools and surface calms of Will Taylor's long illness.

Laura had learned of his illness a few days before her parents were to have come for a visit. Her mother called. 'We can't come, dear. Father is in the hospital, a kind of dizzy spell. Maybe by Thanksgiving he'll be stronger.'

Several years ago he had had surgery for a growth in his chest. The report was encouraging – benign, all clear. Still, he had been coughing so, these last months. At their annual summer reunion at Lillian's home on Lake Michigan he had seemed frail. Laura and her brother and sister spoke of it quietly among themselves, not to worry Rachel or Will himself. They would stay in touch with each other, make visits to their parents as they were able.

After her mother's call, Laura made plans to go to Hadley.

On the way to the airport she said to Trace, 'If my father dies and my mother is left alone, what do you think? Could we offer to have her come with us?'

'I'd be happy to have her. It's mainly up to you, though. Most of it would fall on you. I know you've wanted to get back into art.'

'I know.'

They were silent. It had been a long-cherished dream, to pick up on the artistic career she had gladly put aside when Bart was born. Then Philip. And Annie. Three children in less than five years. Friends who'd known her in her brief years of working for the magazine had asked, 'Do you miss it?'

'No.' The answer was easy. 'This is my vocation now. Maybe later I can be a painter.'

But she'd kept putting off getting into it in any serious way. A few posters for the children's school events, the art council's annual show, some pastel sketches of her children. One spring she'd taken an advanced studio class in the adult education program at the high school but then was prevailed on to be in charge of programs for the fall PTA. She'd organize her time around painting and design later. When Bart left – the household down by one – she thought she would begin. Last fall, when it was Philip's turn to set off for college and there were only herself and Trace and Annie, surely then she would make a serious stab at it, maybe do some things for the spring sidewalk show in the Park. She mustn't wait until Annie was gone. She knew of women who went into severe depression when their last child left home, as though they had no reason for living. Either that or they got into a flurry of distractions – tole painting, club activities, volunteer work that kept them busy but didn't fill the void left by their children's leaving. She was determined not to let that happen. But she seemed to have less time for herself, not more, and now, with her father's illness, the possibility her mother might be left alone . . . Still, if she was disciplined about it, she could work with her mother here, couldn't she? Or wait a few more years?

She looked over at Trace. He was right of course. Most of it would fall on her.

They were almost at the airport when she said, 'Thanks. I'll tell her.'

That evening she and Rachel sat at the supper table after their first visit to the hospital and Will. 'Mother, if something should happen, if he doesn't get well, think about coming to live with us.'

Rachel, her shoulders bent with fatigue and age, looked up from the delicate Haviland plate, the vestiges of creamed codfish against the pale mottled roses. 'Thank you, dear. What about Trace?'

'It's from him too. We talked about it.'

Her mother stirred her tea again. 'That's very generous. We'll see.' She pushed back her cup and saucer and looked up. 'Well, let's get back to the hospital. Evening visiting hours have already started.'

Leaving Hadley after a few days, Laura hugged her mother in farewell. 'Of course we hope Father will be well. But if you should need to, remember what I said about coming to live with us.'

'Thank you, dear.'

But as time went by and Will did not get better, the prospect of having her mother come to live with them, finish her life with them, seemed more complicated, filled Laura at times with panic, at other times with a feeling of loving benevolence toward her and the prospect of caring for her, being close companions again.

Her father had been largely absent from her earliest years, working late, working Saturdays, not going with them on visits to her grandparents' farm in New York state. It was her mother who gave her life color and light, who was the lodestar and anchor in the world she shared with Lillian.

She had asked her mother once, lightly, so sure was she of the answer, 'You love Lillian and me more than Daddy, don't you?' It was early morning and they were in the back bedroom of her grandparents' home and her mother sat on the edge of the bed, looking strange and beautiful without her glasses, her long hair falling down her back, her white nightgown flowing from her shoulders. She looked amused at the question. ''I love you in a different way,' she said. Laura had been shocked, startled, more astonished than hurt. Who was he, that stranger?

But as she got older, Laura and her father grew closer. They were in some ways alike – even-tempered, given to jokes and attention to sunsets. Will was a gardener. He would take her on walks through his rows of corn, beans, tomatoes, then along the flower beds that edged the lawn. 'There's the iris. I tried some arbutus,' he said, 'but it won't transplant.' They recommended favorite books to one another.

She went back to Massachusetts several times that fall and winter. The growth in Will's chest had spread. It was growing very slowly. Perhaps he could have a few more years.

But he was failing and over the months their hopes seemed more contrived.

In mid-March Rachel phoned. The doctor had called her again. He said, 'Your husband is a very sick man. You had better alert the family.'

Laura went to Hadley again. Five days later, his wife and children around him, Will Taylor died peacefully in his sleep.

They arranged for the funeral, for burial in the family plot. 'I've always thought cremation,' Rachel said. They all agreed to it. Then, the decision made, she expressed misgiving. 'I'm not sure what Will wanted. We talked about it but I could never get him to say.' Her voice drifted off, as though if he happened into the room maybe at last she could get him to tell her.

The day of the funeral was warm for March. The snow was gone. They put sprays of evergreens on Will's grave. After the service, back at the house, circling the tables laden with platters of food the neighbors had brought in, sitting in the living room, their plates balanced on their laps, they spoke of Will, retold his jokes, his favorite stories, cherished the memories of his life.

The in-laws and the grandchildren went home.

Laura and Lillian and Howard stayed on for another week.

Laura had not repeated her offer – Come and live with us. The thought – What if she accepts? – suppressed during the crisis of her father's illness, returned now in panic. But her mother had said nothing. A woman came to help with housework and laundry. Rachel talked daily on the phone with her friends, with Will's sister who lived on the same side of town. She speculated about the coming summer, wondered whether to keep the car, spoke of the boy they hired each year to take off the storm windows.

One evening, after Rachel had gone to bed, Laura and Howard and Lillian sat in the living room, looking at old photos, artifacts of their parents' lives. Months ago she had told Howard and Lillian of her offer to Rachel. Now she blurted out, 'What if Mother *does* want to come and live with us? I should never have made the offer! I know I'm the only one who doesn't have a regular job. And I'd love to have her for a visit, or have her live with us half the time. But I can't give my whole life over, and I know that's what it would be.' She shuddered to herself. She hadn't even told them about wanting to revive an art career. Wait till it happens.

Howard took off his glasses, clasped the bridge of his nose, his fingers spreading out to rub his eyes, a gesture so reminiscent of Will that Laura almost forgot her anxious question. 'I don't think the matter will come up,' he said. 'She seems content here.'

Lillian pushed the sleeve of her blue sweater along one arm. 'You couldn't, Lou,' a nickname Lillian sometimes used when she was feeling protective or unusually tender toward her younger sister, 'but I'm sure it's been a security for her all these months. It has for me too, not needing to decide about making such an offer myself.' She drew in her breath. 'It wouldn't be easy. But I think we could handle it better. We have that great big house. All of our children are still home to help and be company for her. I'm home for lunch most days. I know it would be all right with Richard. I asked him.'

To their relief, the question, as Howard predicted, never came up. At the week's end they all went home. Maybe they would try to come back, all of them, for her birthday in May.

In April Rachel fell. She'd had a mild infection and got up suddenly. Nothing to worry about, the doctor said, but maybe it would be better if she could avoid having to climb stairs twice every day.

The cleaning woman and a neighbor helped her move her bed downstairs to the large bay window in the dining room. She was fine, she insisted, getting along fine, looking forward to seeing them. They weren't to worry.

But now Rachel seemed less sure of herself.

Her children, from their homes in Michigan and Tennessee and Texas, confirmed their plans to visit on her birthday – the last weekend in May. Laura was talking on the phone with Lillian about arrival and departure days when she spotted a small notation on the calendar. 'Wait! Annie hasn't said anything about it, but that Saturday is her school prom. I want to be here for that.'

Annie was in the next room. She called out, 'Forget it. I'm not going. Proms are a silly side show.'

'Hold on.' Laura cupped her hand over the phone. Had Annie and Gordon had a fight? Probably not. This must be part of Annie's rebellious streak. 'Okay if I go to see Grandma then?'

'Sure.'

But then Annie decided to go to the prom after all. 'Once in my life I should see what a high school prom is like,' she said, telling Laura and Trace one evening at dinner.

'Oh, dear. And I won't be here!' Laura said. She thought a minute. 'I wonder if the others could change our get-together in Hadley.'

'No, no!' Annie insisted.

'I hate to miss it – seeing you and Gordon off.'

'I'll be here,' Trace said.

'Will you take pictures?' Laura asked.

'Sure,' he promised. 'I'll be glad to. We'll be fine.'

'I'll get the camera all set up,' Laura said.

So that's how they left it. When the time came, Laura would go to Hadley. Trace would be here to take pictures and see Annie and Gordon off.

Annie bought herself a simple pale apricot-colored chiffon gown. 'Want to see it on me?' she asked Laura and Trace as they sat in the living room reading.

'Of course,' Laura said.

Trace put down his paper. 'Sure. Where is it?'

Annie laughed. 'I have to put it on first.'

In a few minutes she came back. 'Here I am.' She turned slowly in the light from the overhead chandelier, her eyes bright, cheeks flushed, her long brown hair curling at her bare shoulders, the skirt swirling round her long legs.

She put her hand to her throat, a string of pearls. 'I borrowed these, Mom. Is that okay?'

'Of course. I'd love to have you wear them. They were

my wedding gift from your father.' She looked over at him but he had already returned to his paper.

Annie backed up to her. 'Will you undo the clasp?'

'Of course.' She lifted Annie's hair, reached under, unfastened the pearls, let them fall into Annie's cupped hand.

'Thanks, Mom. I'll take this off now. Glad you approve.' Annie brushed her cheek with a kiss and walked from the room, the apricot cloth falling from her slim hips, floating behind her over the carpeted floor.

3

Over the years Laura Randall had watched her only daughter with a kind of tender awe. As the time for the birth of her third child drew near and her mother kept saying, 'Oh, I hope this time you have a daughter,' she had tried to reassure her, 'It's all right, whichever. Think of the hand-me-downs.'

Then Annie was born and in a rush of gratitude Laura remembered it all – the unconditional blind love she had felt as a small child for her mother. While that had moderated over the years, somehow there had been associations too rich to know, a kind of absolute *home* about her knowledge of her mother, about the train of life they carried, of eggs born in the womb, to wait, and wait, and sometimes combine with a chance flashing wanderer, the genes of a father, and become daughters and sons and, if daughters, like me, like me. And now, at her daughter's birth, in an elation no fatigue or residue of anesthesia could dim, I am the mother, and my daughter . . . she and I . . . we will be . . . a world.

It was that way through Annie's childhood, years of doing things together, of being the women in the family, of clothes and cooking and favorite books, so even the words, 'my daughter,' had the lift, sometimes, of a prayer of gratitude.

But the last year or two had been different. She didn't remember that the boys' growing up had been this hard. Bouncy and full of verve since her days in the womb, Annie was eager now to be making all her own decisions, wishing she didn't have another year of high school so she could be off on her own.

The thought of Annie's leaving overcame Laura sometimes like a final sadness. At other times – she hesitated to admit this even to herself – she knew it would be a relief to have her gone, to be free of the responsibility for her when they had so little way of affecting what she did.

Every week seemed to bring some new contest. Right now it was the camping trip. Before that it had been the clothing allowance.

For weeks Annie had been agitating. She wasn't getting enough clothing allowance. 'You don't realize how much clothes cost. This shirt,' she lifted the coarse cream-colored cloth of her sleeve, 'cost forty dollars. On sale! Do you want me to feel like an outcast at school?'

'We certainly don't,' Trace said. He turned to Laura. 'Peer approval is very important, I know.'

So they had agreed to an additional twenty-five dollars a month. 'Oh, thank you.' Annie had hugged them. Fifteen minutes later she was back. 'Can we make it retroactive to my birthday, or at least to the first of the year?' When they said no, they weren't prepared to do that, she left the room in a pout.

And there were the recurring jars to the sensibilities, though usually not what you could make a moral issue out of or fuss over without implying that you didn't trust her, which was unthinkable, since all your life with her had been built on mutual trust. Annie going into the room with Gordon and closing the door. Annie and Gordon entwined round each other while the family sat together and watched TV. When, later, she told Annie it was embarrassing, made them uncomfortable, Annie said, 'Would you rather we go somewhere else?'

'No, we wouldn't.'

There were times when Annie's bravura delighted her mother. Once when they were doing exercises in Annie's room, Laura, having quit first – 'That's enough for me, I'm hopeless, anyway' – lay back, her eyes half-closed, and watched her daughter stretch and twist, lift and turn, raise her head and shoulders in a perfect Yoga swan. 'It's beautiful,' she said.

Annie lowered her head slowly and turned to sit up. 'My photography class wants to do some studies of different ages and needs nude models. I wonder if you'd consider . . .'

Laura looked at her sharply. 'Me?'

'I think you have a nice figure.'

'Well!' Laura looked down at her body in the black leotard. 'It's done what I've needed. But I've never thought . . .' She looked up at Annie. 'Thank you anyway. But no, I wouldn't.' But after the exercise session she stood in front of the big hall mirror, pivoting slowly back and forth in the black jersey suit.

She saw Annie last Christmas at the party the college always gave for faculty families. She came into her parents' room to borrow Laura's curling iron. She was wearing a long red skirt and sleeveless rib-knit shirt that came high under her chin. 'I'll just do it here, okay?'

'Of course. You look lovely.'

'Thanks. So do you.' Laura was wearing a pantsuit of bright green silk splashed with white flowers, a long fitted jacket and flaring pants. Annie looked at her, appraising. 'I bet Dad loves that.' She took the curling iron, already warm from Laura's attempt to add some curl to her short auburn hair, leaned into the big mirror, scrutinizing her face while the metal rod of the curling iron, brown-wrapped with her hair, lay close against her cheek. She turned her head to the right, then left, lowered her chin, raised it, her eyes, squinting slightly through contact lenses, never leaving her own image. Laura, beside her, eyes brown like Annie's, a face with all its edges gone soft, combed her own hair and thought, how lovely she is but she isn't sure, and then, remembering herself at sixteen, we have all stood there. Am I pretty? I am a mystery. What will it be for me?

At the party, mingling among her and Trace's friends, she watched Annie circulate among the young people. Some of them she knew, some she didn't. But more than once she saw Annie surrounded by a circle of young men, her animated face turning from one, then another, saw their responsive laughs, their admiring glances.

Laura had not expected, or coveted, a daughter this beautiful, this successful. She had been pretty enough herself, growing up, but a much more timid adolescent than her daughter was. She had, in fact, said to Trace as the party drew to a close and Annie was saying a vivacious farewell to a trio of young men who stood in rapt attention, 'She's just the kind of girl I'd have found hard to take when I was sixteen.'

Now, her trip a week away, Laura's thoughts turned more and more toward Hadley. One evening she and Annie were at home together. Trace was at the college and Annie was doing homework in the den while Laura sat in the next room, reading. She'd been feeling sad, missing her father and, being alone, gave way to some quiet weeping, unaware that from where Annie sat she could see her mother's reflection in the dark window glass.

She didn't hear Annie get up from her chair but then there she was, her arms round Laura's shoulders. 'I miss Grandpa too,' she said, and for a minute they held each other, tears mingling on their cheeks.

'How do you think Grandma is doing?' Annie asked.

'Pretty well. I'll know better when I see her.' A wave of regret swept over her. 'I hate to be missing the prom. Such an event for you. For your mother, too.'

'Don't be silly,' Annie said. 'The only reason we're going is to see how klutzy it is.'

Laura smiled, thought to herself, and you spent a hundred dollars of your clothing allowance to see how klutzy it is? To Annie she said, 'Well, I'll see the pictures. And you can tell me all about it when I get home.'

It occurred to her the next day, as she threaded film in the camera for Trace, screwed in the flash attachment and left it all on his bureau, that while she'd miss the excitement, miss seeing her beautiful daughter at such an important moment, it had always been she, not Trace, who'd been first to cheer Annie on, celebrate her triumphs. This time, with her in Massachusetts, it would be just Trace and Annie. It would be good for them both to have this time together, without her.

4

Laura located her seat next to the window. 'Excuse me.'

The woman in the aisle seat tried unsuccessfully to retract her large bulk so Laura could pass. Then she stood and stepped into the aisle.

'Thank you.' Laura moved to her seat, sat down and leaned her head back, closed her eyes. She heard the woman reseat herself and reopen her magazine. Thank goodness. She did not feel like neighborly pleasantries right now. It was still quite new to her after so many years of family travel to be going somewhere alone and she wanted to savor the solitary adventure.

Outside the airplane window, rain beat a solid sheet against the glass, collected at the bottom in a churning run-off. She looked at her watch. Seven forty-five. Trace should be back home by now. He'd dropped her off at the curb, not waited, so he could get home in plenty of time to drive Annie to school.

Last night, when they'd heard the weather prediction, Trace had offered. Annie was studying at the dining room table and Trace called to her, 'Shall I drive you tomorrow, since it's promising to rain?' Laura had been pleased. She usually drove Annie in bad weather so she wouldn't have the long walk to the bus. She'd thought Annie's assent, 'Yeah, I guess that'd be okay,' could have been more appreciative. She did hope the two of them had some good times together while she was gone.

She picked up a flight magazine, opened it – not with the

intention of reading it but so that the stranger beside her would see that she, too, was occupied.

The magazine fell open to an article titled 'Reinventing Your Marriage', something to the effect that if your marriage was boring you could make changes – a romantic dinner in front of the fireplace, sex in different rooms, not always in the bedroom. Her own feeling was that your marriage reinvented itself with little prompting as children arrived, grew older, as circumstances changed. Like the old Russian five-year plans – every five years, give or take a few, a new agenda. You knew there was continuity, there had to be. But sometimes now, looking back, those first years with Trace seemed to have taken place in another lifetime.

She had met Trace at a party when she was visiting her brother at graduate school. 'Laura, I'd like you to meet Trace Randall.'

'How do you do?'

She looked up. A formality in the tone as well as the greeting. His dark eyes bright, dark hair falling forward, his head slightly inclined toward her in what her friend Magda, an expatriate from the Ukraine now working in NY, came to call his 'European manner'.

'Hi,' she said. A pause. 'You in geology too, like Howard?'

'No. Nothing that useful. Philosophy.'

'Ohh.' She'd been interested right away. 'I took a couple of courses in college. I thought I'd like aesthetics until I learned it was mostly math.'

'Well, not quite.' He smiled, excusing the oversimplification. 'And you? What do you do?'

'I work for a children's magazine in New York. Design. Layout. Sometimes a little writing. I designed a write-in column with this owl. Hootlet. Kids wrote to me. I answered them, sent them a picture.' She paused. 'Not of me. Of the owl I drew. Hootlet.'

'Hootlet?' His eyes behind his glasses widened.

'Sure.' She was beginning to feel slightly giddy in his presence – this intense dark-eyed young man so devoid of the studied nonchalance of many of the men she knew.

'An owl.' He didn't press her further, though a smile

crinkled the corners of his mouth. 'Want to get a drink of something?'

They headed toward the refreshment table, then went out onto one of the stone porches facing the quad.

'What aspect of philosophy are you working in?'

'Kant. You took philosophy, you said. Did you read him?'

'Yes, but I don't remember much. What were his,' she floundered, 'basic tenets?' and thought, I sound like a landlord.

'Do you remember his categorical imperative?'

'Well,' she searched her mind, 'no. What was it? Is it?'

'Basically, it's the idea that the good is only good if it's good for everyone. Something can't be good for one person unless it's a position everyone can espouse.'

'It sounds all right. Are there serious flaws?' Behind him, she saw Howard come to the door, his eyes scanning the porch. He'd wanted to introduce her to some other people. She turned away so he wouldn't see her.

'Well, yes.' Trace appeared not to have noticed her little maneuver. 'It might be good for society to have a group of total pacifists in it, but not necessarily good for everyone to be a pacifist.'

She pondered it. 'I see.' The juke box was playing a slow dance number. She turned back toward the door. Howard had gone. Inside, the shadows of dancers moved across a window.

He followed her glance. 'Would you like to dance?'

'Right here?'

He held out his arms. 'Sure.'

She moved to him. 'Is it good for everyone – dancing?' she teased, her words close against his cheek.

Two weeks later he came to New York to see her. When he left on the late Sunday train they kissed goodbye. Walking back along the station platform she felt her heart race. 'This one could be it,' she said aloud, her words swallowed by the hiss and chug of trains starting to move.

They got in the pattern of visiting one another every few weeks. In New Haven she stayed with Howard. In New York Trace stayed at the Y. In a darkened theatre, walking through a park, he would reach for her hand. When she entertained him at Howard's apartment, Howard tactfully staying away, they sat on the sofa, close, his arm slung round her shoulders. After they were engaged, their embraces became more ardent. But there was never any question but that they would wait for sex until they were married. Of course they knew people who weren't waiting, but it was not their expectation for themselves. They waited.

Within a year Laura gave up her job, gladly, and they were married. Sex was, they agreed on their honeymoon drive through New England, eyeing one another over restaurant tables, coming in from sightseeing and throwing their coats on the floor, worth waiting for.

While Trace finished graduate school she taught nursery school. When he got his degree they moved to Ohio – his first job. Within a year, Bart was born. Three years later, Philip. A whole new world – a marriage with children.

She got a letter from her old magazine. They were expanding to two issues a month. Was she freelancing at all? They could send her stories to illustrate. They'd love to work with her again. She wrote back. Thank you but no, the children kept her busy, she was happy with what she was doing and didn't want deadlines to cope with. With Annie's birth – a daughter now – her life felt complete. If at times the days were long and routine – by four thirty she could start dinner and after dinner she could get the children ready for bed and maybe then she and Trace would have some time to themselves – it was a small price to pay for the joy she took in her young family.

Her life with Trace seemed good, gratifying and full. Out for an evening with friends she would think, when we get home, Trace and I . . . The promise of his presence. Waking in the morning, she would turn to him.

They had minor disagreements, lapses of attention to each other. Trace was busy with his work, she was caring for the children. She would have liked to share more of her life with him. One day she attended a lecture at the Y – one of their 'Strengthening the Family' series – in which the lecturer, a round-faced beatifically smiling man with a fringe of dark hair round the white dome of his head, suggested that now that relationships were no longer held together by economic need, the criteria hinged on meeting one another's emotional needs. The primary exchange under this new god, Communication, could be expressed by, 'This is what it feels like to be me. What does it feel like to be you?' Listening, skeptical, she was surprised to feel her eyes sting. She told Trace about the lecture. 'We don't talk much,' she said. 'Not in that way.'

He seemed mystified. 'What would you like to talk about?'

'Tell me how you feel about things.'

He put his arms round her. 'I feel that I love you.' His hands slipped to her waist, reached under her sweater.

She clutched at his wrists. 'That's not always what I want!'

For a while he would remember to ask when he came in, 'How are you feeling? How was your day?' He would already be pacing around, putting things away, glancing at the newspaper headlines.

In despair she would say, 'I went to the store. I took the children to the dentist.' To his matter-of-factness she could not bring her tenuous feelings – delight at Annie's conversation with a cardinal outside the window, her ambivalence about career. Was it devotion to the children or inertia that kept her so tied to them? Her issues seemed suddenly insignificant, hardly there. It was too risky, knowing his eyes would grow distant, his attention wander off.

But if sometimes she felt she gave more to the relationship than he did, she also drew on his strength. Feeling often that she had no edges to define herself, only the needs of other people, she was reassured by his independence: if he existed, so could she. They fed one another. As they got into their thirties and then their forties and some of their friends' marriages began to crumble, they would look at one another with gratitude that they were, after all this time, still intact. When her father became ill, she relied on Trace's steadiness, was grateful for his comfort as, through six months, her father weakened, then died.

It troubled her that he wasn't closer to his sons and daughter. She told him, surprised at the intensity in her voice, 'They'll be grown and you'll have missed it!' A few years and it would be just herself and Trace again. Would he regret the decisions he had made? Would she regret hers?

A beam of sunlight – they were well above the clouds now – fell on her lap. She closed the magazine and looked out the window, remembering the day last fall – it was after Annie's sixteenth birthday and soon after Philip had left for his first year away – when Annie came in from school, flushed with excitement. 'My sculpture won first prize in the art contest!'

'That's wonderful!' Laura said. Annie had worked long hours on a figure of a young woman bent to a climb, a walking stick in one hand, a lumpy backpack strapped to her shoulders.

'There's going to be a reception the first night of the art show – that's when I get my prize. You and Dad can come!' She ran up to look at her wardrobe. 'I'll have to decide what to wear!'

At dinner she told Trace. 'I won a prize for my sculpture.'

'Great! Is that something you've been working on?'

'Dad!' Laura and Annie exchanged incredulous glances. 'I've worked on it for weeks. The girl hiking. With the backpack. I've had it home practically every night. Don't you remember?'

'Oh, yes,' he said quickly, trying to recover. But his eyes betrayed him. He didn't know what she was talking about.

Annie was suspicious now, expecting the worst. 'There's a reception next Tuesday night. You and Mom are invited.'

A look of consternation crossed his face. 'Let me look at my book.' He took a small black appointment book from his coat pocket, flipped the pages. 'I'm afraid I can't,' he said. 'But I expect Mother . . .' He looked toward Laura, his smile bright, expectant.

'*Why* can't you?' Annie demanded, leaning toward him, her hand a fist on the table. 'You got a speech to give or something?'

He seemed surprised. 'A department meeting. I have to present my courses for next year. It's the last meeting before the catalog goes to press.'

'Can't you have the meeting another time? Does it have to be Tuesday?' Her voice rose, querulous, piercing.

His expression was calmly contrite. 'The dean will be

there. It's been scheduled for months. There are a lot of people involved.'

Her hands flew into the air. 'Well, can't somebody else do it? Can't you write it down and give it to somebody?'

He shook his head, his composure unassailable. 'There may be questions. I need to be there. I'm sorry. I'll see the sculpture later.'

Annie jumped up, threw her napkin to the floor. 'You'll never see it. I'll smash it before I let you see it!' She stalked to the kitchen, her voice catching in a sob.

Trace followed his daughter into the next room. 'I'm sorry,' he entreated. 'If I could avoid this meeting, I would. But it's my job.'

Annie turned, eyes blazing. 'I know it's your job. But it's always something. It's always Mom who does things with me. It's never you. You don't even remember the damn sculpture! It's a wonder you know my name!'

Trace straightened as though from a blow. 'I don't get it. What's going on?'

'You don't know me! You never did!'

He was dumbfounded. He looked at Laura, back at Annie. 'What do you mean? I've always loved you.'

'You're never here for me! You never have been, not since I was a little girl. Not even then!'

Her anger seemed boundless. Laura watched them, her heart aching for them both.

No one spoke. Then Annie's voice cut through the silence. 'It's always been this way,' she said. 'But I've noticed it more with Philip gone.' For a second her eyes flicked away from him. 'I've only got another year and a half then I'll be gone too. I'd like us to do better before I go.' She was crying now, her anger spent.

'I'm sorry,' he said, his face white. But she had already left the room.

As the weeks went by, Trace tried to be more attentive to his daughter, talking with her about college choices, bringing home books to help with a school project on 'Tracing Your Family Tree', a subject in which he had a lot of interest. For a while things seemed better, then Annie complained, 'He's just going through the motions. I'm afraid it's too late for Dad and me.' She gave him back the genealogy books. 'Here. I changed my mind. I'm switching to another project.'

Trace, too, brought Laura his hurt and anger. 'I'm knocking myself out trying to be a better father. She's not giving me a chance.'

Laura's lip tightened. Impatience pushed against her rib cage. 'What did I tell you? You waited too long. She's complaining about a lot of years.' Seeing the stricken look in his eyes, she added, 'Besides, she's an adolescent, remember? It's not easy, establishing your independence. Believe me, I know.'

Which brought her mind back to the question of Rachel, and what the week ahead might bring.

She scarcely noticed when the captain announced, 'We have reached a cruising altitude of thirty-five thousand feet.' And when the woman next to her turned to her as the sound of the food cart drew near and said, 'Well, it looks like they're bringing our breakfast,' she was glad of the distraction.

Trace closed the door of his office, hung his raincoat on the coat tree in the corner, making sure the sleeves weren't dripping water onto the pile of papers jutting from the nearby shelf, then walked to the window and looked out at the pouring rain.

An airplane sounded overhead. Not Laura's. She'd be well on her way by now.

'Remember to tell me all about the prom,' she'd said, kissing him goodbye.

'I will. And I hope things go well with your mother.'

'Thanks.' She slid out of the car and, suitcase in hand, walked into the terminal. Watching her, he'd felt that familiar pang, *she's leaving*, as though he was cast adrift without an anchor. He checked himself. Just for a week, dummy.

Ordinarily he'd have gone right to the office, but he'd offered to drive Annie to school.

He was back at the house by seven thirty. No sound of Annie. He had breakfast and read the paper. At last he heard the shower, the whine of the hairdryer. He looked at his watch. Eight ten. Often she didn't eat breakfast, but even so it was getting late.

He went to the bottom of the stairs. 'Annie?'

No answer. He read the classified ads. At eight thirty he called again, 'Annie?' and started up the stairs wondering whether something was wrong.

She came charging down, looking ready for a movie audition – white sweater, coral skirt bouncing against her thighs.

'Aren't you afraid you'll be late?'

She stopped on the step. 'You here? I thought you'd gone. You're always gone by now.'

'We agreed last night I'd drive you to school.'

She seemed disconcerted, but only for a second. Then a look of dismissal. 'Celia called me. She's picking up two other kids. Then me. We have a field trip to the Bates Library. We're meeting there at nine.'

'The Bates Library is right next door to my building. I could easily take you.' Her expression hardened. Careful, he thought and shifted to, 'What's going on at the library?'

'Dad! Please, I'm in a hurry. It's something about a new computer system for research. They want us to know how it works. You know – nerd city.'

Yes, he knew 'nerd city', as she put it. He'd been on the committee to purchase that system for the college. It would facilitate all kinds of complex humanities research.

'I could easily take you,' he repeated, and thought, you feel I don't give you enough time? Here I am, offering. Instead he said, 'Isn't it silly to have Celia make an extra trip?'

'She doesn't mind.' Annie brushed past him without a word of goodbye.

He watched her go. He'd lost an hour of work for nothing, incurred his daughter's impatience once more. He threw the rest of his coffee down the drain and left the house.

It looked as though the rain would last a long time. He turned from the window, got some coffee from the outer office, said 'Hi' to Lutie Simpson who was busy at her desk, came back and sat down, waiting for his spirits to heal. He took a deep breath, inhaling the smells of coffee, books, a certain mustiness from being in the basement, even the faint presence of pipe smoke that seeped in from Jim Bloskin's office next door.

This office was his domain, his haven. He could come in here and feel in a world apart, in whichever world was engaging him – the Greeks, the German Romantics, the neo-linguists, the rationalists. Philosophy was his garden of earthly delights, heavenly delights, too, or whatever larger frame of reference you envisioned when you got into metaphysics.

He'd been content at Duke. Teaching, research, enough publication to boost him to associate professor at thirty-five. But when, a couple of years ago, Marsh had offered him, this job – full professor, tenure, an office of his own, 'Almost the biggest inducement,' he'd joked to Laura who'd known how he hated having to share an office with anyone but especially with a garrulous chain smoker – he was delighted to accept. Bloskin's pipe he didn't mind. It was far enough away, even companionable.

He knew Laura had made his immersion in his work possible. It was she who had borne most of the responsibility for the family. She'd assured him that was what she wanted. 'I'll get into other stuff when the children are older,' she'd said. In the last years she'd berated herself for not doing more with her art. He'd tried to give her what support he could. He was confident she'd find her way.

Sometimes he envied her the closeness she had with the children. As though they were a club unto themselves, and he an outsider. Jokes, glances they passed back and forth, allusions to experiences they'd shared, without him. A sense that, for them, he was somehow off code, missing the beat.

Perhaps they were right. He wasn't sure about his ability to relate to children, to girls even less than to boys. His own passion as a child had been history. History and astronomy. On his first visit to a planetarium he'd been so excited it was a wonder he didn't waft up through the dome. What was out there in that dazzling night? How to comprehend those distances, measured in light years? With his allowance he bought books, a small telescope, then a larger one. He spent hours poring over charts of the night sky.

His brother was too young to share his enthusiasms. Six years apart, they lived in different worlds, and pretty much on their own. Their father was a busy doctor, their mother a teacher of piano. Every afternoon after school sober-faced children, music cases in hand, filed in and out of his parents' living room. They had more access to his mother than he did. He turned to his books.

From time to time, a father himself, he made an effort to do something special with the boys, things fathers were supposed to do with their sons. He had been no athlete and was relieved when his sons showed no interest in Little League – all those hours of sitting on bleachers, cheering your children on, hoping they didn't get hurt.

He'd tried fishing. One morning when Bart was nine and Philip seven they'd got up at four, taken the fishing gear and a thermos of cocoa and driven to the oxbow on the river, where they rented a rowboat from a wizened old man who appeared to be barely awake himself. They strapped themselves into orange safety vests and rowed out into the middle of the large pond where they sat in the fog, chilled to the bone, their fishing poles projecting from the boat like turret guns.

Eventually Bart caught a fish. He looked at it, flopping on the bottom of the boat. 'Now what?' he said.

'You have to take the hook out of its mouth.' He grasped the fish, which immediately slithered from his hand. The boys sat there, mouths open, as he struggled to recapture it, yank the hook out, put the fish in the pail. 'There. When we're done, we'll clean the fish, take them home to Mother.'

Then Phil caught two, and Bart another. He himself brought in one.

The sun grew hot. 'Are we done yet?' Philip asked. 'I'm hungry.' They'd long ago finished the cocoa.

'Me too,' Bart said.

Back on shore, he got out the knife the sports store clerk had recommended. He'd seen his grandfather clean fish, back at the Iowa lake where they'd vacationed decades ago.

His first efforts ended with fragments of skin and entrails. Finally they got the five fish cleaned.

'Dad?' Philip said as they were approaching home.

'Yes?'

'I don't want to eat those fishies.'

'Me neither,' Bart said.

They buried the fish in the garden.

'How did it go?' Laura asked when they came in. Annie was with her in the kitchen. They were making cookies.

'Well,' he began.

Philip broke in. 'Guess what, Mom?'

'What?'

'We buried the fish.'

'That's fine,' she said, as though not a bit surprised. 'Here, a little solace.' She held out the plate of cookies, warm from the oven.

That night after the children were in bed she said to him, 'Just the same, it was good of you to take the boys. I'm sure they'll remember it.'

Recalling the look of distaste on their faces as he'd tried to gut the fish, he said, 'I'm sure they will.'

Sometimes he told them stories. Ready for bed, they would plead with him, 'Tell us a crazy story.' He would spin off fantasy tales of space travel, sudden drops through the center of the earth, adventures in which they had bizarre encounters with characters in books or remote historic figures. 'And then Christopher Columbus would swoop down to where they were hanging by their toes to the edge of the ring of Jupiter and he would give them all an earth-space ticket and they'd be home in no time, ready for bed.' The children would shriek with delight, jumping up and down on their beds. 'More! More!'

Laura would come to the door. 'Trace, you're overstimulating them. They'll never go to sleep.'

On summer vacations when he was free from teaching responsibilities they would go off on mountain climbing trips, sometimes with Annie and Laura. And once a year, when Annie and Laura went to the church's Mother-Daughter Banquet, he and the boys would have their annual 'boys' night', starting with the whole fat-laden works at

McDonald's, then a movie, the scarier the better. Sometimes they'd work in a round of miniature golf, getting home tired, grubby, and happy.

As a father to his sons, he felt he had been at least moderately successful. But with Annie he was less sure. Especially lately.

She'd usually been there when he told his stories. Did she remember her laughter and delight? Did she remember the times he had carried her up the mountain or stood at the side of the pool to catch her as, again and again, she jumped off into his arms? Or did her present mood have no room for anything but complaint and disappointment?

As a little girl, she would show him her pretty dresses, her newest achievements, bring him her school papers and report cards. He had a great interest in family history, and it was Annie, more than the boys, who asked about the old photos in the crumbling leather photo album, the framed marriage certificate of his great-grandparents that hung on the wall.

And then she grew up.

He had never had a sister, never been close to the home life of adolescent girls. As, month by month, his daughter changed from the slender stick of a girl with long brown braids to a beautiful young woman with breasts, hips, hair that curled and hung around her shoulders like a Mata Hari shawl, he found himself confused, unsure how to respond to this new being in his house. Her voice took on new lilts. She had a gaggle of friends who would come by – boys and girls. She would introduce them to her parents. Once he overheard one of her friends say, as he moved into the next room, 'Your father is very handsome.' 'Do you think so?' Annie had asked, but he could tell from the rise in her voice that she agreed, and was proud. He had smiled to himself, pleased too, but aware of his graying hair, the slight paunch he had begun to acquire.

At other times it seemed she could hardly stand to have him around.

And then, of course, there was Gordon, a nice enough boy but no match for Annie. Gordon's chief interest was in cars, and a small combo he played with under the name of

'That's No Momma'. And yet this slight young man who was barely out of a retainer was the star round which his daughter's life seemed to revolve.

Trace looked out the window, saw the Bates Library through the rain. Was Annie in there now, being shown the marvels of a system he had helped devise?

When the rain stopped he wanted to take the station wagon in to get the tires rotated, ready for the trip to Michigan and then Colorado. No rush, but easier to arrange with Laura gone and the demands on the car down to one driver. Maybe he could do it over lunch. In Colorado – a special family binge to celebrate Bart's graduation before he settled down in earnest to look for a job – they'd do some mountain climbing, ride the high trails. He had a colleague out there he might try to see. A red light went on in his head. This is vacation, remember? You'll get flack from the kids and Laura if you haul your work into it.

He turned to his desk calendar, his appointments for the day.

By coming in later than usual he'd missed the breakfast meeting on plans for a reception for the new faculty member – a specialist in Plato coming in from Tulane. He'd told Stoddard yesterday he might not be there – 'Family responsibilities. Let me know if you want me to do anything.' Stoddard had given him an odd look, as though he might be doing something subversive. Trace didn't explain.

He looked at his watch. Nine thirty. He had his intro course at ten and his graduate seminar on Aristotle at two. Then a talk with Jim Bloskins about the course they'd be teaching jointly next semester. Maybe he'd pick Annie up after school.

He gathered up his briefcase and a couple of extra books he was going to put on reserve, then headed off to his class. Unlike some of his colleagues, he really enjoyed his intro class; for some of the students it was their first real taste of analytical thought, the available playgrounds of the mind.

After the class he drove down to the filling station and left the car. 'Check it over carefully, will you, Louie? And rotate the tires. We'll be driving on narrow mountain roads – don't want any accidents.' He got lunch at the diner, then picked up the car, got back to the office in time to gather the stuff for his seminar.

There was a note in his box, from Stoddard. 'Call me over the lunch hour, Trace. It's about the reception for David Ignatius. I'll be gone all afternoon.'

Lutie was at her desk. 'When did he leave this?' he asked her.

'Just after you left for your class.' She shrugged in sympathy.

Trace winced. Stoddard liked to have his messages answered promptly. But it was too late now. He'd call him tomorrow.

After the seminar he talked with Jim, deciding what books they'd assign and who would have major responsibility for each of the units.

He made a few notes in his teaching diary and was about to leave when there was a tap at the door. 'Come in,' he called without looking up.

'Dr Randall?' A young woman's voice. 'Are you busy?'

It was Kate Morton. The question usually irritated him – no, I'm sitting here twiddling my thumbs, hoping something will show up to fill this empty space in my life. But not this time. Kate was one of his best students, a fine mind, a pleasing manner.

'Come in, Kate. Sit down. What's on your mind?'

She came in, blue eyes bright, dark hair held back with a purple scarf that matched the heavy sweater hanging over her jeans. She sat down and swung her book bag to the floor. 'Well, you know I've been thinking about staying on after graduation and getting a Master's?'

He shifted in his chair so he was fully facing her. 'That's certainly a commendable thought. I noticed your name on the department list of people who might want to do that. You're a fine student. You know we'd be glad to have you.'

A flush of pleasure rose on her face. 'Thanks. I kind of thought that, but it's nice to have somebody say so.'

She seemed, momentarily, at a loss for words and he said, 'Have you considered a topic you'd like to pursue, or even what branch of philosophy?'

She hesitated. 'I don't know whether it's academically

respectable, or obscure enough,' she looked up with a conspiratorial smile, 'but I'd like to do something with Aristotle and academia.'

'That seems a natural partnership,' he said. 'What particular aspect of academia?'

'Well,' she said, leaning forward, 'ever since I heard of it in junior high school I've been fascinated by the concept of the golden mean – of moderation – and now I'm interested in how that fits in with the way the academy conducts its life. I mean,' her voice took on an edge, 'we talk about it as though it's some holy precept but we don't carry it out at all in our work here. Moderation is a C plus. So is there a way it's germane to what we stand for or not?'

He nodded. 'Good question. It's one choice. It's not the choice most of us make, or perhaps should make.' He sat back in his chair and put the tips of his fingers together. 'When we get to the Romantics they're more for all-out effort, outlandish aspirations – cathedrals soaring into the sky and so on. And you're certainly right that academics give lip-service to the concept but they're not too good at carrying it out. Though,' he smiled wryly, 'if you'll remember from freshman year we do make our initial pitch about the well-rounded student, about academics not being everything.'

She laughed. 'Yes, and then you assign a hundred pages of reading a night and fifty-page term papers.'

'I know. We're victims of our enthusiasms. I'm as guilty as the next person.' He paused, the image of Annie's face distorted in anger shouting 'You don't know me!' almost obliterating the friendly, composed face of the young woman in front of him.

She went on, unmindful of his inner digression. 'But your enthusiasm is partly what makes the subject come alive. And if everyone practised moderation in everything, we'd never have the inventions, or literature, or the artistic things we have. People have to be almost driven to excess sometimes, don't they, to accomplish what they want to?'

'I guess so, Kate. Even moderation has to be exercised in moderation. Marie Curie was hardly moderate in her search for radium. Or Crick and Watson, trying to find the DNA code.'

She stooped and picked up her book bag. 'Well, that's the direction I'm thinking – exploring that balance of zeal and dispassion. I didn't mean to get carried away – no moderation there. But what I came to ask you is, if I decide to stay and do the Master's, would you be my advisor?'

He was startled, and immensely gratified. For a moment he didn't speak.

'If you have too many other students, it's perfectly all right. But your lectures are so clear and you really listen to the students.' She smiled ingenuously. 'You're my first choice,' she said.

He felt his heart swell. 'Thank you, Kate. I'd be delighted to be your advisor.'

'Good.' She proffered her hand, and they exchanged a warm handshake and she left. For a moment he stayed at his desk, basking in her approval, her trust. He'd gathered from what she'd said once in class – it was some discussion of personal ethics and she had made a joking reference to 'my difficult period' – that she'd had some turbulence growing up.

He got his coat and briefcase and started for the car. He still might reach school in time to pick up Annie. But by the time he got there the students appeared to have left. Maybe he and Annie could play Scrabble or something after dinner.

A pile of mail was on the kitchen counter, along with a note in Annie's handwriting. 'Dad, I'm going to Celia's for dinner. The casserole Mom fixed for us is in the fridge. Put it in the oven – 45 minutes @ 350.'

'Oh, great,' he thought, and headed out for Shoney's.

He was in the study, reading, when he heard Annie come in. It was nearly eleven. 'Hi,' he called. She must not have heard him because she went right up to her room and closed the door.

'Ready?' Howard stood by the doorway in his gray slacks and sweater, his hand on the light switch, ready to darken the dining room for the arrival of the birthday cake.

From the kitchen Laura called, 'Not yet.'

Then Lillian's voice, 'This is a major candle-lighting event,' ending in a giggle.

Rachel touched the front of her blue brocade dress in consternation. 'You don't have to light them all,' she called back. But of course they would.

'We're in no hurry.' Howard leaned over and touched her shoulder and for a minute she grabbed his hand before she let it fall.

She looked around – at candlelight glowing on crystal and silver, highlighting the sheen of damask, the gleam of the Haviland china, at the bouquet of roses and lily of the valley.

Such treasures her children were. They'd been busy all day, almost ever since they'd arrived yesterday, fixing all her favorite things – poached salmon in parsley sauce, tiny peas, spinach salad with walnuts, her favorite orange chiffon cake.

She settled back to wait.

It wasn't that she was afraid, being here alone. She'd been alone all those months Will was in the hospital. But it was lonesome. Even though he'd been in the hospital all that time, at least he was in the same world with her. It did frighten her a little too, this suggestion from the doctor that she should not live alone any longer. 'Why ever not?' she'd wanted to know.

'Because, Rachel, you fainted once. It could happen again, and the fall could be much more serious than an easy topple from the couch.'

For a while she'd thought him an alarmist, and that she'd be more content here at home than living anywhere else. She had people coming in to help. Her friend Mabel called her every day. She didn't much care for the idea of an old folks home. The children had their own lives to live – though Laura had made that offer when Will first got sick.

Will . . . He had taken such joy in the family, too. It grieved her that some of the grandchildren were too young to carry any memory of him into adulthood. Howard's children would remember him. And Laura's. And Lillian's girls. But probably not the baby. Not very well, anyway.

The baby was just the age – five – Laura was when she'd been taken sick. Today with all the new medicines that kind of infection could probably be cleared up in no time. But a whole year Laura had been bedridden – the first perilous weeks when they thought she was going to die, then months of recovery.

'Ready!' Howard snapped the light switch.

Behind her, the door from the kitchen creaked open.

'Happy birthday, dear Mother,' they were singing. 'Happy birthday to you.'

There was the cake, high and gleaming, circles and circles of small flickering lights and her name, Rachel, spelled in green letters on the pale orange frosting. Lillian set it down in front of her and Laura quickly distributed small bowls of ice cream – vanilla, with real vanilla bean, Rachel knew.

'We didn't have room to write Happy Birthday,' Laura whispered in her ear, 'but we knew we'd be singing it.'

'Of course. Thank you, dears. Thank you. Eighty candles.' She lifted her hand, put it back in her lap. 'I won't try to count. It must have taken you hours to get them all on.'

'Just a few minutes,' Laura assured her.

'Ready? Make a wish,' Howard said. 'Need any help?'

She looked up at them. They were all leaning forward, eyes fixed on the cake, lips slightly parted in vicarious expectation. Her dear children.

'Well, maybe,' she said. 'One, two, three.' She filled her lungs, leaned forward and blew, and they all joined in until, with the last circling whoosh round the edges, all the candles went out. They cheered and sat back, triumphant.

'Wait. Time for a toast.' Howard got to his feet and poured the last of the wine into their glasses. He raised his glass, and the others followed. 'To Mother, with all our love,' he said and then, mindful that this was her first birthday without Will, he raised it again. 'And with all our love, and our gratitude, to Father.'

Her eyes stung, though it was partly from happiness, to have them all here. They came and circled her chair, hugged her, hugged each other, too, for good measure, then returned to their places, to sip the wine and admire the cake for a few minutes before they cut it.

'Remember the first cake we made for you, Mother?' Laura asked. 'The frosting was so thin it sank into the cake and Dad brought daffodils from the garden to lay round the edges.'

'You worked on it all day long,' she said.

It reminded them of other stories.

'Remember that time we came home and the furnace had gone out and we made hot chocolate and sat around the fireplace all night until the house warmed up?'

'Remember how Dad used to take us on mystery rides – and they'd always end up at Howard Johnson?'

'Remember the time we got locked out and Dad had to climb to a second-story window while we all watched and cheered?'

Watching them, looking round the circle, feeling the warmth of the occasion, this hallowed room, she thought, 'It will be hard for them to give this up. It has been a special place for them, for the grandchildren, too.'

Last year on a college-visiting tour – before Philip had decided to go to college closer to home – Laura and Philip had stopped by. 'Hi, Grandma,' he'd said, giving her a hug that all but lifted her off her feet. 'We left home a day early, so we could be sure and see you.'

'He's right,' Trace had said. 'It was a pretty busy time, getting him ready. We thought we'd swing up and see you after we dropped him off. He wouldn't hear of it. We had to come here first.'

Will had been so touched. Philip had looked at his favorite location of ant lions under the back steps, tried unsuccessfully to fold his six-foot frame into the 'secret closet' that led off the upstairs linen closet, given the pulley line a few revolutions out over the back yard, recalling how he or Bart or Annie would attach a basket and send messages back and forth. After they'd had a round of Will's homemade rootbeer and her applesauce cookies, they left, waving from the car until they were out of sight. Then she and Will had sat on the glider on the side porch, in a kind of wordless contentment, relishing the lovely September day.

'Well.' She picked up the knife. 'I'd better cut the cake before the ice cream melts.'

'I'll hold the plates.' Laura moved a plate close to where her mother was lowering the knife and Rachel slipped a piece onto the flower-glazed surface. 'Who gets the first piece? Lillian, you're the oldest.'

'Don't remind me,' Lillian laughed, accepting the plate her mother handed her.

After the cake and ice cream, they had coffee. In the silence, a question hovered. Lillian broached it. 'How are you, Mother?' she asked.

They'd asked it before, a quick, for-the-moment question when they came in.

'I'm doing fine,' she said. 'I haven't fainted again, not since the first time. I've gotten along well. My friend Mabel calls me every day.'

'Is she still in her house next to the high school?' Howard asked.

'No. She moved to the Cramer Retirement Home.'

'Does she like it?' Laura asked.

'She says she does. I wouldn't like it. Alarm buzzers and hand rails everywhere. Only old people. I don't need that. I'm pretty healthy for someone my age.'

'Are you sure?' Lillian asked again.

'Let's not talk about it now,' she said. 'Let's just enjoy my birthday.' There was no hurry. They'd be here for several days.

5

The first thing Trace did when he got to his office was call Stoddard. 'Good morning, Ben. Trace here. Sorry I couldn't get back to you yesterday. I took my car down to get the tires rotated for our summer trip. By the time I got back you'd gone.'

'Yes.' Stoddard's voice was cool. He was obviously not interested in small talk about the trip. 'We missed you at the meeting.'

'Yes. I'm sorry. I told you I'd do what I could about the welcome for David Ignatius.' Stoddard did *not* like people missing department meetings, and that Trace had been gone at noon evidently made it worse.

'Since you've come most recently, you'd have the freshest memory of what it's like, being a newcomer.'

Was this a put-down, an additional reproof about missing the meeting?

But then Stoddard went on, 'We'd like you to do the welcome speech. Just a few minutes – five or ten. Can you do that?'

'Well, yes, that'll be fine.' Trace was pleased, told himself to forget the paranoia. He was a good after-dinner speaker. He'd had a reputation for that at Duke. Since he'd come here no one had asked him. A short speech. Some dry witty remarks. A gracious welcome. 'Yes, sure.'

'So you and Laura will be there?'

'Not Laura. She's up with her mother. What time Saturday?' He flipped through his black book. Uh-oh. Annie's prom. There it was. 'A's prom. 8 o'clock. Take pictures.' No mention of the reception for Ignatius, though he'd known it was likely to be this Saturday. He should have written it down. Now what? He wanted to be there for Annie. And he'd promised Laura. But this was important too. Maybe if worst came to worst Gordon's parents would take the pictures. 'What time Saturday?' He dreaded the answer. These things were usually at seven thirty or eight.

'Not till late. We're doing it as a reception after the string quartet concert. Both Ignatiuses play in community orchestra, so they think this is a great idea.'

He felt almost giddy with relief. 'Terrific. Sounds wonderful.' Stoddard might think his enthusiasm a bit much, but who cared? 'What time, then, do you figure?'

'We're estimating the reception will start at nine thirty. We give everybody a chance to get something to drink. I introduce you. You talk. Ignatius responds. Then we eat. Any questions?'

It was Stoddard's hallmark: 'Any questions?' He closed department meetings with it, always in a pompous tone, as though addressing a congressional inquiry instead of a collegial group. It usually annoyed Trace. This time he was amused.

'No questions. I'll be there.'

That evening at dinner – by now they were working on the casserole – he told Annie of Stoddard's invitation. 'I was really pleased,' he said. 'They haven't asked me to do anything like that before.'

'Saturday night?'

'It doesn't start until late. I'll still be here to see you off and take pictures.' He smiled at her fondly. 'I want to see Gordon's face when he sees you in that dress. And your mother's pearls,' he added brightly.

Annie's eyes narrowed. 'How late?'

'Not till after the concert. Nine thirty, maybe.'

'Dad!' She flung her fork down on the table.

'What's wrong? The prom's at eight.'

'Dad,' her voice registered scorn, 'nobody goes to a prom at eight.'

'When do they go? Eight is what I wrote in my book. That's what you told me.'

'That's what the ticket says. But nobody goes then. First, there's hors d'oeuvres. Then there's a barbecue. Then everybody has to change. *Then* you go to the prom.'

'So what time is it by then?' His mind was jumping ahead. How could he explain a second defection to Stoddard? Besides, he wanted to be there to welcome Ignatius. He'd already made notes for his talk.

'We meet at Celia's at five thirty. Her mom is fixing hors d'oeuvres. Then we go to Jeanine's for the barbecue at six thirty. The girls are all taking our stuff to Jeanine's, to change there. The guys go and change and pick us up about eight thirty. Then we stop by our folks' houses so they can see us. *Then* we go to the prom.' She was explaining it laboriously, laying down the terms, as though to a child.

'So what's the problem?'

She sighed, as though only a total idiot would ask such a question. 'It puts me under pressure and it's an important thing in my life and I don't want to have to worry.'

He recalled her acerbic comments about proms and how superficial they were. He did not remind her. 'I'm skipping the concert. I can get to the reception from here in five minutes. That's time enough, surely.'

'Who knows? It might be. It might not.' She sighed. 'It's just that you promised to be here, and now you've taken on work stuff and it's the same old story.'

Now *he* was irritated. 'Hey, wait a minute. You told me eight o'clock. Now I'm committed to do this talk. There should be plenty of time. In a pinch, I suppose you *could* even get Gordon's folks to take pictures.'

'Sure, Dad, sure!' She burst into tears, flung her napkin on top of her unfinished food and ran from the table.

He put his head in his hands. 'Jesus Christ,' he said.

After a while she came back downstairs. He was in the living room, reading. She sat in a chair across from him, her clipboard and geography book in her lap.

'Honey,' he began.

She looked up. Her eyes were red and swollen.

'I'm sorry, dear. It'll probably work out fine.'

'Mmmm,' she murmured. But she didn't protest further, and they both went back to their books.

Saturday night came. At six thirty he ate a light supper – leftovers of the tuna salad he'd fixed for lunch – and thought of Annie and her friends having barbecue at Jeanine's. He'd written it all down to be sure he got the sequence right in his mind and didn't make some gauche allusion and have Annie accuse him of not caring what she did.

After that he dressed for the reception – his good suit, the red paisley tie Annie had given him last Christmas. By now it was seven thirty and the girls were probably putting on their finery, Annie the loveliest of the lot, he was sure, smiling benignly at his fatherly pride as he pulled the tie through the loop at his neck.

At eight o'clock he put his light raincoat by the door in case the evening turned cool, studied the camera to be sure he knew how to work it, and went over his notes once more.

By eighty thirty he was feeling a little edgy. Surely she'd get here in time. He went over his notes again. He scarcely knew this man, Ignatius, but he came with good credentials and seemed pleasant. He'd probably be a fine colleague and it would be nice to have someone else be the junior member of the department, take some of the committee assignments.

By ten of nine he was pacing the floor. She could still get here in time. He thought of calling Jeanine's but Annie would never forgive him. Besides, according to the schedule she should already have left. It wouldn't take him long to snap the pictures. The reception was only five minutes away. He didn't like to rush in at the last minute, though. He'd need a little time to collect himself. And Stoddard would be frantic if he didn't show up a few minutes ahead of nine thirty.

At ten after nine he went out onto the front porch, leaving the door open in case the phone rang. Outside, the night was clear and starlit, perfect for a prom. Clusters of fireflies flickered near the big tree. A car approached, went by. Would they be in Gordon's car, or someone else's? Annie hadn't said. Two more cars turned at the corner, came toward the house, went by. *Where were they?*

His jaw felt wired. He went inside, brought his coat out

and laid it over the porch rail. He'd already pulled the car out of the driveway, parked it in front. He'd brought the camera out too, clutched in his hand, his fingers like a vise.

Once more he looked at his watch. Nine twenty. Where was she? Dammit, where was she?

Gordon gunned the motor. 'Get in!'

Annie was already in. Jeanine and Bill climbed in and slammed the door. The car pulled away.

Annie clutched in her hand the envelope containing her mother's pearls, the half-empty string trailing across her lap. 'I told you we should go to my house first,' she said. 'My father will be berserk.'

Gordon bent over the steering wheel, intent on the road. 'If you hadn't busted the beads or if you'd let my folks pick them up later, we'd have been okay.' His voice was dark.

'Oh, sure,' she said. 'By the time they got back from the movie your cat might have eaten the pearls.'

He snorted. 'Cats don't eat beads.'

'Well, scattered them all over. My mother would kill me if I lost her wedding pearls. And if I hadn't been in such a hurry I wouldn't have broken the string.'

The car cut round a corner. 'Hey, watch it,' Bill muttered.

'You made me mush my corsage,' Jeanine complained.

'I should have called my father,' Annie moaned. 'I bet it's already too late. I told him we'd go there first, then to your folks,' she hurled at Gordon.

'There should have been plenty of time,' he muttered, 'if you hadn't broken the beads.'

'Oh, shut up,' she said, her head craning as they turned the corner. The house came into view. The porch light was on, and the light in the front hall. But the car was gone.

'Just a minute, dear. It's cool for May, isn't it?' Rachel stopped partway through her mid-afternoon walk and pulled her blue sweater more tightly round her.

'Need some help?' Laura leaned over, fastened one of the buttons at her mother's waist. 'There. That better?'

'Yes, thank you.' Rachel steadied herself on her daughter's arm and they continued on their walk.

In the several days her children had been here they'd taken turns accompanying her on her walk – past Will's garden, then the Hollisters, the MacDonalds, the house where the new people lived. Up to the corner, then across the street, and back.

She wanted to tell Laura first – about her decision not to stay.

She had wakened early this morning, remembering the conversation last fall when Will first got sick. Howard and Lillian had made general comments about caring for her, helping her with whatever arrangements she chose. But it was Laura, that first time she came after Will was hospitalized, who'd spoken of her coming to Woodbridge to live with them.

It would be some kind of role switch, Laura caring for her, after all those months she'd cared for her daughter. Five years old. Six by the time she was able to go out and play like a normal child and even then they had to be careful – extra rests, no competitive sports. For years afterwards, when she was out shopping with Lillian and Laura and they would run into a friend and stop to chat, the question would come up, 'Which is the one who was sick?'

She would nod toward Laura. 'This one.'

The listener's gaze would follow hers. 'She certainly doesn't look sick now.'

Once she had observed Laura roll her eyes skyward at this and she had cautioned her afterwards. 'You mustn't let my friends think you're impatient at their questions. A whole lot of people prayed for you for a long time. Of course they're interested.'

Laura's face had flushed. 'That's all I ever am!' she said. 'The one who was sick!'

'Darling! You're fine now. It's just that you came so close to dying. If you hadn't had good care . . .' It hadn't been easy, those weeks of terror and then months of convalescence – trays, bed baths, all the rest of it.

Back then, forty years ago, she'd not anticipated she'd be the one needing care.

They had reached the corner, crossed, started back. In front of the Lewis house she said, 'Jane Lewis says they're going to put the house up for sale and move to Florida.'

'Hmmm,' Laura mused. 'You'll miss them. They've been here a long time.'

It was an opening. She could tell her now. But she hesitated.

Earlier, over lunch, finishing up their strawberry short-cake and coffee, they'd all talked about how she was doing, about possible options should she ever decide she didn't want to stay here.

'You might like to spend parts of each year with each of us,' Laura had suggested.

'That might work fine,' Lillian had said.

They mentioned the retirement homes. Yesterday Howard had driven them in the rented car around the city 'for old times', but also to give them a view of the three retirement homes, 'in case you'd ever want to consider them', he said. They knew she had friends in two of the three.

They assumed, as she had, that she'd be happiest staying here, in the home she'd lived in for fifty years, with her friends, her church, Will's sister and brother-in-law only a few blocks away. 'We could help you find a housekeeper,' Lillian said, 'if you don't want to stay alone.'

Their recital with its myriad of options all but made her dizzy, like the options the executor had listed for her after Will died. 'Consult with the children. Or do what you think best,' he'd said. 'I'm an old lady.' – she'd laughed, passing it off. But it was true, her head did get fuzzy if she had too many options to think about. She'd thought then that maybe it was time to let someone else handle the details of life. But that last talk with the doctor made it seem more urgent. 'You shouldn't live alone, Rachel. Consider getting someone in to stay with you.' A stranger? When she could live with her own daughter?

She'd taken her last bite of strawberry. 'Housekeepers aren't that easy to find,' she'd said. And then, 'Whose turn to walk with me?' She'd thought it was Laura's but she wasn't sure.

'Mine, Mother,' Laura had said gently. 'But don't you want a nap first?'

'After my nap,' she'd said.

Now there they were, the walk almost over and she hadn't mentioned it yet. Her heart beat a little faster. Not that she was frightened, but it was a big step, moving away.

They reached the edge of the garden.

'Stop here a minute?' she said.

'Of course.'

'Will would have had it all planted by now.' She looked at the weeds, the few wildflowers scattered across the brown dirt. 'I won't see it another year.'

Laura patted her hand. 'Of course you will. You're getting a lot stronger. The last time we walked up this way you were much shakier. You'll be bounding up and down the sidewalk in a few weeks.'

Rachel leaned her shoulder into Laura's. 'I don't want to stay on here. I want to come and live with you.' She felt Laura's arm beneath the blue sweater tense and stiffen.

'I'm not sure that's the best thing for you, Mother. You'll miss your friends.'

'My friends are dying off.'

'You wouldn't know anybody but us.'

She shook her head, dismissing it. 'You're enough for me. You and Trace and Annie. Bart and Philip when they come home. I'll love seeing them oftener.'

Laura had begun moving them slowly forward again. 'Let's think about it,' she said. 'You didn't speak of it at lunch.'

'I wanted to hear what you all had to say. And I wanted to tell you first.' The words, begun as shared confidence, turned sour in her mouth. What was the matter with Laura? She'd have thought she'd be pleased. Of course it would be an adjustment for everyone but last fall Laura had sounded as though she'd like her to come. 'I've already thought about it,' she said.

They approached the house. Through the ruffled net curtains she could see the table with the Japanese lamp, the brown chair by the window where she often sat to read, or knit.

They reached the door and went in. The cream and blue striped wallpaper in the front hall seemed reassuring. The small Hitchcock chair. She was tired, ready to sit down.

'Lillian, Howard,' Laura called, as though they were off somewhere instead of right here where they'd been twenty minutes ago.

Lillian looked up from the desk where she and Howard were going over some of Will's business papers.

'Mother was thinking some more about what she'll do next – maybe not live here in the house after all,' Laura said, her voice hushed, as if she was telling some guarded secret. She looked toward Howard and Lillian. 'Tell her,' she eased her mother onto the couch and sat down on the edge of the Windsor chair, 'tell her what you think.'

From her perch on the couch Rachel looked at her son and daughters. They were moving their chairs to form a circle round her. Oddly, she remembered those old pictures of covered wagons forming a circle to fend off the enemy. Howard spoke first. 'I thought you'd decided to stay on here.' His eyes swept the room, the wall of books, the Victorian sofa, her mother's carved rosewood chair by the fireplace, the French doors leading out onto the porch. 'It would be a wrench for you to move after fifty years. I'm sure we could get extra help.'

'I don't want extra help. I want to go with Laura. She invited me. I've decided.'

Lillian leaned forward. Her long strand of green glass beads swung across her lap. 'What about half the time with me and half with Laura?'

'I'm too old to be travelling like that,' she said. 'The rest of you can come and see me at Laura's.'

'But you're getting stronger,' Laura said. 'On the walk today . . . You've done so well on your own, so much better than any of us thought you could when Dad got sick. You'll be able to go out again, lots of places.'

'I'm not eager to, without Will. I'll be content to stay home, with you. I can read, help with cooking. I'll make friends there. I already know your neighbors.' She didn't understand all this effort to dissuade her.

She looked back at her younger daughter. Surely Laura would support her decision. But her face was distraught.

Laura leaned forward, her eyes wide, dark, and put her

hand on Rachel's knee. 'Mother, I don't think I can do it. I thought I could. This has been a hard year for us. I've just started to make my way again as an artist. We'd love to have you visit, or live with us six months of the year. But all the time . . .' Her voice faltered, she looked round frantically as though searching for help. 'I'm sorry,' she said. 'I know it's terrible, going back on my invitation.'

Rachel, stunned, moved her hand stiffly against her brown challis dress. 'But last fall . . .'

Laura's face, already pale, turned paler still. 'I know. I thought I could, last fall.'

There was a terrible lump in her throat. 'I took care of you when you were sick,' she said. 'You'd never have made it without me.'

Quickly, Lillian spoke. 'Mother,' her hand closed round her beads, 'you're welcome to come live with us in Michigan. We have a bigger house. There are more of us there, to keep you company.'

They were all looking at her, the same look of pained intent on each face. 'Thank you,' she said to Lillian. 'I'm glad someone wants me.' She looked over at Laura, then back at Lillian. 'Thank you. I'll think about it. Not now. Maybe later.' The truth was she didn't want to go to Lillian's. Too many people buzzing in and out all the time. Howard? Howard hadn't said a thing. If she were to go with him, a lot of it would fall on Irene. It wasn't a son's place to make such an offer.

After a supper marked by strained silences, they talked of it again. Laura reiterated her offer. 'I'd love to have you stay for six months. But I need some time to myself. And you – you'd miss everything you're used to. And,' she spoke as though it was some kind of a joke, 'what if we got to resent each other?'

'I never resented my mother,' Rachel said.

After another moment of silence Laura excused herself. 'I want to call home. Last night was Annie's prom.'

She was gone a while. When she came back she was dabbing her eyes with a handkerchief.

After a minute Howard said, 'How are Trace and Annie? How was the prom?'

She swallowed, took an audible breath. 'Trace is fine. He wanted to know what all we're doing. I told him.' Her voice caught. 'He sends his love.'

'And Annie?' Howard asked.

'Actually Annie wasn't there. Trace said there'd been a bit of a schedule crisis – he'd tell me later. He said she had a good time.' She managed a smile.

'Bring pictures to the reunion,' Lillian said.

'Sure,' Laura promised.

After a while Rachel stood up. 'I'm going to bed.' She looked toward Laura, then at the others. 'It's true I've been quite well,' she said, 'but the doctor doesn't want me to stay alone.'

During the next two days they made efforts to locate a housekeeper. Rachel, still reeling under this turn of events, thought of a woman who might suit her. 'Carlena Shaw. I've only met her once. I know her sister through the church. I think she's an LPN. She goes around taking care of old people. Maybe she could come.'

Laura volunteered to make the call.

From her bed in the next room, Rachel listened. 'Wonderful!' she heard Laura say.

Well. She did like Carlena. But . . . Her eyes filled with tears. She heard the children coming and turned toward the window.

Laura came into the room, Howard and Lillian with her. 'She'll be glad to come. She finished her last case two weeks ago. She'll come over tonight and we can talk.'

'I have a good idea once in a while,' Rachel said. Stiff in her pride she said, 'I have enough money. Though if we spend it all it won't go to you.'

Carlena came. They all liked her, a sturdy, ebullient woman, her voice loud from years of associating with the hard of hearing.

'When can you come?' Rachel asked.

'Tomorrow. I got nothing holding me back.'

The next day Lillian and Howard and Laura helped Carlena move into the room that had been Rachel's and Will's.

Back downstairs, Carlena asked, 'You got a bell? I'd like her to have a bell in case she needs me in the night.'

Laura found an old brass bell in the attic. Carlena set it on the windowsill by Rachel's bed. 'Now, you use it.' She shook her finger admonishingly. 'I don't mind getting up. That's what I'm here for.'

'I will.' Rachel gave it a practise shake before returning the bell to the sill.

In the morning Howard and Lillian and Laura stood in the hall with Carlena and Rachel. 'I'll take care of your mother, don't you worry,' Carlena said. She was holding Rachel's arm.

'You've called a taxi?' Rachel queried.

'Yes,' Lillian said. 'Remember, Mother, if you decide you don't want to stay here you're welcome to come to us.'

'Or share the time with us,' Laura said. Her eyes met Rachel's briefly, a pleading look, then she looked away.

'Thank you,' Rachel said stiffly.

The taxi came. One by one they kissed Rachel goodbye. 'We'll call tonight,' they promised.

Through the open front door Rachel watched them go down the walk and climb in the taxi, watched the taxi pull away, saw Howard's white handkerchief fluttering at the window.

She watched until the taxi drove out of sight.

She turned to Carlena. 'Do you have children?'

6

Laura took a cab home from the airport. Trace had classes all afternoon. Once inside the door she set her suitcase down and took a deep breath. Then she walked slowly through the house, relishing the quiet, the calm orderliness of the house, the soft blues and greens, the touches of peach and apricot, the symmetry of furniture and rooms, the gift of available solitude.

In her workroom, the sunlight slanting in through the western window, she found a single rose in a clear glass vase. A slip of paper lay beside it: 'Mom, I love you. Annie.'

'Oh! What a dear,' she said. And then an additional note: 'I have play rehearsal until seven. Don't wait dinner.'

She checked the freezer. She could put together a hasty ragout. In the vegetable drawer were fresh greens, enough for a salad. They must not have done too badly, Annie and Trace. She hoped they had had good times together.

She took her suitcase upstairs, put it on the bed. On her bureau was the accumulated mail from her absence – some circulars, a letter from her friend in Illinois, a letter from Walter Stone Company. She tore it open. Yes, they liked the preliminary sketches – go ahead. They'd need five double-page spreads, ten singles. She could map out the text however she wanted.

She sat on the bed, clutching the letter to her chest. Her first real contract. A quiver of anxiety went over her. What if she'd agreed to her mother's coming? How could she have done the work? Still . . . She saw Rachel's anguished face, heard her words, 'You invited me!'

She unpacked, then went to the phone and called Rachel. 'I'm home, Mother. How are you?'

'I'm pretty tired, but I'm all right.' There was a pause. 'How's Annie? How's Trace?'

'I haven't seen them yet.' She looked at her watch. Ten past five. 'Trace should be coming soon.'

Another pause. 'Tell Annie I want to hear all about the prom. Be sure you bring pictures to the reunion.'

'We will.' She thought to ask about Carlena, but it was too pointed, drew attention to her own default. 'It was wonderful to be there for your birthday, all of us.'

'It was nice, wasn't it?' Rachel's voice was a bit formal, but why not? They said goodbye and hung up and Laura sat in the chair in the kitchen and closed her eyes. *Mother!* she thought.

Trace came in. 'Hi!' He called from the door. She went to meet him. They hugged and she leaned against him, his familiar steady self. 'I'm so glad to be home,' she said.

He pressed the back of her head against his shoulder. 'Dearest,' he said, and stooped to kiss her closed eyelids. 'By the way, Annie has play rehearsal. She won't get here till seven. She said not to wait dinner.'

'I know. She left me a note. I thought we'd wait. I got out two sherry glasses.' She led him into the kitchen, poured the sherry and handed him a glass. 'To celebrate our being back together.'

They went into the living room and sat in the soft dusk of early evening, the smell of new-mown grass coming in the open window.

Laura sipped the sherry, relishing the soothing liquid as it slid down her throat. 'It was so good to talk with you that night after I'd told Mother. I felt so awful.'

He put his glass down on the lamp table by his chair. 'I'm sure it was hard for everyone. But it's not as though any of us deserted her. Lillian offered. You offered for six months at a time. She'd always be remembering what she'd lost, leaving there. She'd keep telling you. If she can manage in her own home I'm sure it's better for her, too.'

Laura breathed in his words. 'Oh, I hope so.' She took another sip of the sherry. 'How did you and Annie get along? Did you spend much time together?'

'Not a lot. It was pretty busy – for her and for me.'

'Your evening classes were over. I was hoping—'

'She was busy too.'

They heard the back door open, close. Annie hurried into the living room. 'Mom!'

Laura stood to embrace her daughter. 'Thank you for the flower, dear. It was a wonderful welcome home.'

Annie returned the hug. 'You're welcome. How's Grandma?'

'I think she's doing fine. We – she, actually – found a woman to stay with her. Her name's Carlena. Grandma's known her before. I called, just before Dad came home. She wants to hear all about the prom.' She smiled and sat back down. Annie collapsed onto the sofa. 'So,' Laura said, 'how was the prom?'

'It was fun. We had a good time. Gordon even sent me flowers.'

'Wrist bouquet? Shoulder corsage? I'm sure you looked gorgeous. I can't wait to see the pictures.'

The silence was palpable.

'There'll be pictures,' Trace said. 'But we don't have them yet. Gordon's parents took the pictures.'

'What? You couldn't work that simple camera? All you had to do was turn it on and push the button.'

'That wasn't it.'

'Well, what happened? Were you so dazzled by Annie's beauty you couldn't function?' She glanced at her daughter. Annie was staring at her father with a look of scornful resignation.

'Dad wasn't here when Gordon and I got home for the pictures.'

Laura turned to him. 'What do you mean you weren't here? Where were you? When we talked you said everything went fine.'

Trace's jaw was set in a grim line, his eyes dark, guarded. 'I didn't want to talk about it over the phone. You had enough going on up there.' He raised his hand to forestall further questions. 'I'd agreed to give a little speech to welcome Dave Ignatius. We thought there'd be plenty of time.'

'*You* thought there'd be plenty of time,' Annie burst in. 'I told you I didn't know.'

'We estimated the times. It should have been fine,' he said.

Laura flung up her hands. 'But how could you have planned to do *anything* else? This was her big evening. You know teenagers. A party like that can have all kinds of mixups.'

'I waited as long as I could,' he said. 'As it was I was late, which did not go over well with Stoddard.'

They heard the back door open. 'Anybody home?'

'Come on in,' Annie called. To them she said, 'It's Gordon. We're going to watch the movie on television.'

Laura sighed and sat down as Gordon walked into the room. 'Hi, folks. Like my new shirt?' He pulled at the bottom of his T-shirt, flattening it out so they could see the green and blue globe and the words 'Love your mother' arched above. 'Cool, huh?'

'That's neat,' Annie said.

'Yeah.' He tucked the shirt back into his jeans, straightened the belt round his slender waist. 'How is everybody?' He turned to Laura. 'How was your trip?'

'Fine,' she said. 'I hear you had a good time at the prom.'

'That's my girl.' He was looking at Annie, smiling, his brown eyes warm, glowing, oblivious of everyone in the room but her.

Laura glanced over at Trace. He was staring down at the table. He didn't look up.

Later, after a dinner eaten in haste, Gordon sharing a few bites of the ragout, Gordon and Annie went to watch the movie. Laura and Trace started to clear up the dishes.

Laura held a plate under the faucet. 'Was there some reason Annie and Gordon were so delayed getting here, other than that everything took longer than they'd thought?'

'I was about to tell you.' His voice was tense. 'They had to go to Gordon's first. Then, as they were leaving, Annie got something caught on your pearls and they broke and scattered all over the floor. They were already late, but that finished it.'

'Oh, my.' She had the image of the pearls falling, rolling under strange furniture, into corners of a house she had never seen.

'I've taken them to the jeweler to be restrung.'

'Thank you. I hope she got them all. She didn't mention the pearls breaking.'

'I'm sure she would have,' he said.

They heard a peal of laughter from the den. 'Well, I'm glad they had a good time,' she said. 'Even so.'

He was hanging cooking spoons on the pegboard. 'You didn't ask about my talk, how it went.'

'Your talk?'

'To welcome Dave Ignatius.'

'Oh.' She was wiping up the counter. Her hand tensed. 'Well, how did it go?'

'Very well. Actually, I was quite a hit. I wish you'd been there.'

She whirled to face him. 'I wouldn't have been there, remember? I'd have been home, seeing Annie off to the prom!'

In the next room Annie and Gordon sat slumped back on the couch, Gordon's arm round Annie's shoulder, her legs in their faded jeans slung across his lap, her feet dangling above the moss-green carpet. The room was dark except for the flickering images of the movie, a saga about some pets who miraculously found their way to a family's new home.

Annie reached for the remote and turned the sound one notch lower. 'God, you sure showed up in the nick of time. I thought my mother was going to blow a gasket!'

'Hunh?' Gordon was watching the picture – a child in a blue shirt, his face pressed against the back window of a station wagon, and a golden retriever staring mournfully as the station wagon drove off with the whole family inside. 'Cheer up, Poochie, they told you they'll be back.'

'She just found out my father wasn't here to take the pictures.'

'Pictures?' Now the footage shifted to the car interior, the three children tight-lipped and sad.

'The prom pictures, dodo.' She slid her hand in front of his eyes. 'You remember the prom pictures?'

He pulled her hand away. 'I'm sure my dad got some good ones.'

'Yeah, but that wasn't the point. The point was, my father had promised and then he went off to make a speech and my mom is in outer space because he was going to be here and see me off and tell her about it since she couldn't be here herself on account of my grandmother's birthday and sometimes I can hardly wait to get out of this house. Especially with my brothers gone.'

He didn't answer and she said, 'Are you listening to me?'

'Sure, baby. Your father couldn't take the pictures. Though there should have been plenty of time if you hadn't busted your beads all over the place . ...' His voice drifted off, and he chuckled softly.

Annie swung her legs off his lap, planted her feet squarely on the floor. 'Yeah. Wait up. If we'd come here in the first place like we were going to. But no. Your folks wanted to go to a movie. Like it was only our high school prom. A movie! Give me a break!'

'Hey, sweetheart.' He turned his attention to her now and patted her knee. 'Hey! I'm sorry we didn't get here before your dad left. If I'd known we'd be so late I wouldn't have pushed for going to my place first. We goofed on that part. But the prom was fun. You looked terrific. The music was great. What's the big deal?'

'The deal is my mom has this fond hope that after almost seventeen years my dad is gonna start paying attention to me. Then, whammo, it happens again – even though this time it really wasn't his fault – and she goes berserk. She should cool it and give up. You'd think he'd tried to murder me the way she was carrying on.'

She settled back against him, tucked her legs up beside her. On the screen two dogs were moving across a field and a cat watched from a high rock. 'It's just that home's not the greatest place to be now. I wish my brothers were still around.' She brightened. 'Though my mom said Bart and Paula might move here next year – to Woodbridge, not this house. Boy, would I love that. Mom would too. She misses my brothers as much as I do almost.' As an afterthought she said, 'My dad probably doesn't notice they're gone.'

For a while they watched in silence. The scene shifted to some dark woods, the pets trying to cross a mountain range.

'By the way,' Gordon said, 'I finally got around to asking my folks about our end-of-the-year camping trip. They said no dice. I kind of thought they would.'

Now Annie sat up, looked at him directly. 'Just like that. What did they say?'

'They said, "You crazy? That's nothing for kids your age to be doing."'

'No discussion? Like, what could happen that couldn't happen anyway? Did you stick up for your rights?'

He shook his head, his eyes back on the screen – one of the pets had fallen into a raging river. 'Are you kidding? In my family no discussion, period. You think you got problems. My dad says, "You do it our way or you get out."'

She sat back, sighing. He could at least have tried to talk to his parents. Parents were so obstinate, stuck in the Dark Ages. At least hers would talk to her. Sometimes too much, almost. Wanting to know what she was doing, how she felt about stuff. At least her mom. Maybe it would be better to be in a family like Gordon's. But she didn't think so. She just needed some space.

She looked back at the screen. That cozy family. Now they were going to put out an alert, see if they could find the lost pets. Her own family used to be like that. Even her father sometimes, like when they were all off on vacation. Then first Bart left, then Philip. One more year and she'd go too. Sometimes the thought was a little scary. But mostly she'd be glad to get to college, be on her own.

She thought of Paula again. They'd met her last fall on a trip to visit Bart. If they came down here it would almost be like having a sister. She wished they'd come right away but Paula's father had died of a heart attack right after Christmas and Bart said she wanted to spend the summer with her mom.

At the thought of Paula's father dying, her eyes stung with tears. If her own father should die she'd feel so awful. Worse because she knew he was a fine man and brilliant and somewhere in the back of his knotted-up head he probably loved her. But as for having the least idea what made her tick, forget it. It made her sad, all the years they'd missed and how soon she'd be going and they'd still be strangers to each other.

In the movie, a child had wandered off and was lost. One of the dogs found her and the pets all gathered round. The scene moved to her anxious parents out with searchlights, the mother weeping and the father calling her name. Now the retriever spotted them and barked, pointing with his head. The father heard the barking and turned. He called out his daughter's name and started to run.

Annie's throat tightened.

Gordon, who had been running his hand up and down her arm, reached to undo the buttons of her shirt. He leaned close, breathing into her neck. 'How about we go to your room and shut the door and turn on some music?'

She lifted his hand from her blouse. 'Not while they're in the house! Besides, I want to watch the movie.'

For as long as she could, Laura refused to consider the possibility that Annie was having sex with Gordon. As serious a step as that was, as much as she knew they wouldn't want her to? Annie wouldn't, would she?

One evening when Trace was at a meeting, she and Annie went to an old movie. In it a fluttery woman, her face blinking with the gray and white flecks of old films, told her importuning fiancé she wanted to wait until their wedding night. The audience of students laughed uproariously.

In the car on the way home Annie said, 'I suppose you and Dad waited – till you got married, I mean?'

'We certainly did. We didn't even consider anything else. Does that seem impossible to you?'

'Sort of, yes.'

'Well, we couldn't have done it differently, being us. And it seems to have worked out all right.'

'How about now?' Annie said. 'What would you do now?'

She'd wondered it herself often enough. 'I don't know. I think I'd still want to be married first. On the other hand,

I might – I suppose there's no way I can know. It's a different time.'

In the light from the passing street light Annie turned to her. 'I know you, Mom. I bet you wouldn't wait.'

Laura wondered what to say, she who had taken years of being married to feel comfortable about her own body, that it was not something to hide and when you did reveal it you hoped the one you loved would make the necessary allowances. Sometimes, still, it was hard for her to believe Trace found her as desirable as he said he did, that it was not only the indiscriminate urgings of his own body that sent him to her so often, it was also the drawing power of her own, the legitimate hunger of her own adequate flesh, given to him, fed from him, their games the games of allies and not of adversaries pretending to be lovers until they were found out and sent from the room.

'Maybe I wouldn't,' she said to Annie. 'I don't know. There's the whole issue of safety, too,' she added as an afterthought, and a lame one at that. The danger of disease didn't disappear just because you got married. She waited for Annie to challenge her.

But she didn't. They drove on a little further and Annie said, 'Sometimes I'd like to tell you other things about myself, but I don't know if I dare.'

Laura made a sound of assent in her throat. She didn't want to answer too quickly, too lightly. 'I don't know what to tell you, honey. I'm willing to risk it if you are.'

'I'll see.'

In a few minutes they were home. Gordon had called. Would Annie call him back? They talked for an hour. By then it was late. No more was said about the conversation in the car.

Later, when Laura and Trace were getting ready for bed, she said to him, 'I had a significant conversation with Annie, after the movie.'

'Oh?' He was running through some circulars and bills that had come in the day's mail.

'Could you put those down?'

'I'm listening to every word.' There was an edge of

impatience in his voice but he put the stack of mail on the dresser.

She recounted the conversation, then said, 'She was almost going to tell me something.' She paused. 'You don't think Annie is, do you?'

'Is what?'

'Having sex. With Gordon.'

'I hope not. But if she is I hope she's protecting herself.' He was scanning the mail again. 'I've read that, even today, a large proportion of our students who are sexually active don't use condoms. Or any contraceptive at all.'

'Trace! She's not "a large proportion of your students". She's your daughter!'

'I know she's my daughter. You wonder if Annie is having sex with Gordon. I hope she isn't. I don't know. I do hope, if she is, she's—'

'I'm sure if she is, she's using something!' she interrupted him. 'We talked about it tons of times, the kids and I. They didn't agree on premarital sex, but they did agree on no accidental children. And I'm sure they know the danger of AIDS. There! Do you feel better?'

'I don't get it, Laura. What's the matter?'

'How can you be so damn clinical about the whole thing?'

'But we don't even know,' he said.

And then Annie told her.

It was the week after the prom, the last week of school. They were only going half days and Annie had stayed home with bad cramps. Laura brought her the heating pad, rolled the television into her room, brought some soup in for them to eat together. After lunch Annie lay on her stomach on the heating pad and Laura sat by her, her fingers playing with Annie's hair, fanning it over the jungle print pillowcase.

'Mom?' Annie said, her voice muffled by a mound of sheet lying close to her face.

'Yes?'

'I'm on the pill.' She lifted her head. 'Gordon and I . . .' Her voice drifted off.

'Gordon and you?' Laura said, trying to hold it at bay for a minute.

66

'Yes. Four months ago I went to the Public Health Clinic.'

'You did?' The image of Annie sitting in a dingy glaring waiting room, going there on her own, to such a cold impersonal place. Among strangers. *'Oh, Annie!'*

Annie rolled over, put her hands under her head. 'I feel very good about myself as a woman.'

Laura nodded in mute agreement. To what? The truth only. 'What about AIDS?' She blurted it out – a desperate move.

Annie smiled, shook her head. 'Gordon has never messed around, Mom.'

She nodded, still stunned. She couldn't imagine Gordon 'messing around' either, but these days who could tell?

'I'm sure you're not pleased,' Annie said. 'But it's my body, isn't it?'

'Of course. It's always been your body. But it's a shock to me. I didn't know.'

'Well, we didn't exactly make a public announcement,' Annie said.

'No, I suppose you didn't.' The world seemed to be spinning, the room, the bed. 'I'm going to lie on the carpet a minute, okay?'

'You can lie on the bed with me if you want.'

'Thanks.' It was then she started to cry, quietly, covering her face with her hands. 'I'm glad you're being careful. Do Bart and Philip know?'

'Yes.'

'I suppose they think it's just dandy?'

'They didn't say. They respect my right—'

'They're not your mother. I respect your right too. It's the judgment—'

'I'm sixteen,' Annie said.

'Yes, I know you're sixteen.' Careful, something inside her warned. She trusted you to tell you this. Don't drive her away. She sat up. 'Well, darling, is it going all right for you? Sex, I mean?'

'Mmmhmm!' Annie said.

Later in the afternoon, back in Annie's room, she asked, 'What about Dad?'

'What about him?'

'Will you tell him yourself? I don't want to know and have him not know.'

'You tell him. If he wants to talk to me about it, he can.'

She told him. He went to Annie's room. In a few moments she followed him down the hall. The door was open. She heard him say, 'I'm proud of you, being responsible.'

'Don't worry, I won't disgrace you,' Annie said.

His laugh was forced. 'That wasn't exactly my first concern.'

'Well, I wouldn't want to disrupt your life.'

'Disrupt my life? You're an important part of my life.'

'Dad! Since when? It's a little late for that now, isn't it?'

Grimly, Laura retreated down the hall. In a few moments she heard Trace's steps leaving Annie's room. He came in.

'Well?' she said.

'I can't say I'm too surprised. She's been very mature, getting birth control pills, insisting on protection.'

'But she's so young! Our little girl—'

'Open your eyes, Laura. She hasn't been our little girl for some time.'

Their new knowledge of Annie cleared the air. From time to time Laura found herself talking with Annie about sex. Yes, it was a great experience. One day Annie said, 'The first time – it was in my room – I called your name.' Laura was inordinately touched.

But at times, gazing out the window, her pencil poised over her drawings, or going by store displays of schoolgirl dresses or musical jewel boxes with dolls that turned to the music of 'Dance, Ballerina, Dance', tears came to her eyes and she thought, what happened? How did it turn out like this?

All spring she had felt restless. Was it her age, her father's death, the children's growing up? Some hormonal or psychic clock that seemed wound too tight and was ticking away? She knew that her daughter's adventurousness made her want more for herself. More what? More professional accomplishments? To go back to school? More closeness with Trace? Better sex? The sensuality of the young was certainly a reminder of past options and passing time. Jealous? A little, yes, how beautiful they were, so much ahead of them.

Summer was coming, and with it vacation, a change of pace.

7

'Here you are!' Lillian stepped down from the back deck of the big stucco house overlooking Lake Michigan and ran toward them, her long denim skirt skimming the top of the grass. Her white shirt was tied at the waist with a red kerchief, and a pair of sunglasses dangled from one hand. She reached Laura and they flung their arms round each other, giddy with laughter and delight. Then hugs for Trace and Bart and Philip and Annie, then back to Laura and, arms linked, the two sisters, the others following, walked toward the house, under trees, past the rope hammock, then round the end of the house toward blue sky and dipping gulls, the glittering water of the lake.

'Is everybody here?' Laura asked, pulling sunglasses from her purse against the brilliant sun.

'On the porch,' Lillian said. 'Howard and Irene got here an hour ago. Irene is settling the baby for a nap. Everybody else is out there. I would have been too but I came in to take the cake out of the freezer. Then I saw you.' Lillian turned again, her smile white in her tanned face.

'Mother there too?' Laura asked, and without waiting for an answer, 'How is she?'

'She's fine.' Lillian gave her sister's elbow a reassuring squeeze.

They had almost reached the porch. The blue and white striped awning flapped gently in the breeze. In front of the house the carpet of grass extended toward the lake to the low slatted fence. Beyond that the bank dropped off and the stairway sloped down to the shore. A few sailboats bobbed in the water and at the distant horizon a long ore-carrier tug sat like a dark block of wood against the blue-green sky.

'Here they are!' Lillian called out, and Richard, and Howard and Irene, Richard and Lillian's girls, Elsa and Christine and Jennie, little Timmy, and Howard and Irene's ten-year-old twins, Danny and Carter, all moved toward them with hugs and greetings. There were exclamations about Bart's just having graduated and about Philip's having grown a beard, and how Annie was now taller than her mother. Soon Annie and Elsa, who were only a year apart and always best friends at these family gatherings, had gone off to one side, followed closely by Christine and Jenny who didn't want to miss anything the big girls were saying. Howard and Trace were starting on academia stories and Richard was asking people what they'd like to drink, 'Soda? Lemonade? Spritzer?' and there at the center of the porch, reaching for her cane and pulling herself to her feet, Laura saw her mother, shoulders bent with the effort of standing, a sweater covering her arms even on so warm a day, the hem of her dress lifting from the floor as she slowly straightened herself, her face intent on her task but already looking, looking through the crowd.

Laura went to her. 'Mother!' She kissed Rachel's cheek, put her arms round her in a hug, and then stood back. 'Mother,' she said again.

'Hello, dear,' Rachel said. 'It's nice to see you. Did you just arrive?'

In the ensuing days Lillian's lakeside home gave them lots to do – basketball, swimming, boating – lots of room to roam around or sit and talk endlessly. Laura soon found herself back in her mother's circle of favor, able to re-enter again the intimacy they had once known. Rachel seemed stronger than she had since before Will's death, mellower too, relinquishing them all, going to bed early, leaving them to their late-night revelries, letting some of the conversation go by without saying, 'Can't you speak louder, I can't *hear*,' while her unused hearing aids dangled from her ears.

'Grandma is turning into a sweet old lady,' Laura said to Annie one day.

'Oh?' Annie said. 'I don't know that that's better. I liked her before.'

One afternoon most of the crowd went off to ride on the dunes. Laura and Annie, in charge of the night's cookout, stayed home to get ready and to keep Rachel company. 'I don't feel quite bouncy enough for dune buggies today,' Rachel had said.

After her rest, she suggested they have some lemonade. As Annie brought the tray with three tall glasses clinking with ice out onto the porch where Laura was helping her mother into a chair, Rachel said, 'Oh, and those pictures from your prom, may I see them now?'

'Sure.' Annie distributed the glasses, returned the tray to the kitchen and came back, the sheaf of photos in her hand.

'Your father took these, I guess?' Rachel said, reaching for them.

Laura and Annie exchanged glances. 'No,' Annie said. 'Gordon's father did.'

'I see. Well.' Rachel slid her glasses down her nose and moved the first picture close to her eyes. 'This your young man?'

'I guess you could say that.' Annie smiled. 'I guess that would be all right with Gordon.'

'What a lovely dress,' Rachel exclaimed, squinting to get the best possible view. 'Was it white?'

'No, kind of pale peach. Apricot. Pale apricot chiffon,' Annie said, looking over her grandmother's shoulder.

'My wedding dress was ivory chiffon,' Rachel said.

'And mine,' Laura said.

Rachel turned to Annie. 'Did you know your mother wore my wedding dress. We made it over to fit her.'

'Mom told me,' Annie said. 'I remember seeing it when I was a kid. We were up exploring the attic. It's in a big blue box, right?' She turned to her mother.

Laura nodded. 'You wanted to try on the veil. I put it on you and you looked at yourself in the old mirror up there.'

Rachel smiled. 'Maybe some day you'll use the veil with your wedding dress.'

Annie shook her head. 'I'm never getting married.'

'Of course you will,' Rachel scoffed, 'a beautiful girl like you.' Her look was wistful. 'Though I don't suppose I'll be around to see it.'

Annie reached over and kissed her grandmother's cheek. 'Nonsense, Grandma. If I ever get married you'd better be there.'

They went on through the pictures, heads inclined together. Rachel exclaiming over each one, asking questions, Annie explaining that this was Gordon's house and those other two were Jeanine and Bill, friends of hers and Gordon's.

Watching them, Laura basked in the glow of their affection for each other. She recalled wryly the old saying that grandparents and grandchildren get along so well because they have a common enemy. Whatever the reason, she loved seeing her daughter and mother together. In fact, this whole reunion with the family was wonderful for them all. Lots of talk of Will, a few occasions for tears, but mostly joy in being together.

There must be healing in numbers too. The presence of aunts and uncles, of cousins, the pleasure of swimming and boating and good food, of having Bart and Philip with them, had had a good effect on their family, seemed to moderate the tensions of the past months. And without Gordon here to occupy so much of Annie's time, Laura felt they had, for a while at least, reclaimed their daughter.

At first Annie had written to him every day, eliciting curiosity from her younger cousins, Christine and Jenny, who would see her on the beach, suntan oil glistening on her body, the straps of her white bikini drooping on her arms, her head bent over the vellum pad, and ask, 'Are you writing your boy friend again?'

Gordon's first letter to Annie, addressed in a roughly-printed scrawl, arrived toward the end of the week. She had been complaining to Laura – 'He promised to have a letter waiting for me when I got here.' Annie was on a hike with her cousin Elsa when the mail came. When she returned in mid-afternoon to the house, Laura was in the small sun room, reading. 'A letter for you, at last.' She pointed to the envelope on the white wicker table.

'It's about time, the creep.' Annie picked it up and flopped down on the green and white couch near Laura's chair.

After a few minutes Laura looked up. Annie was gazing out the window and the letter lay on her chest. 'Nice letter?' she asked.

'I guess.' Annie picked up the single sheet of paper and flapped it in the air. 'I write him *volumes*. And what do I get? A whole page and a half, about a dumb baseball game.'

Laura suppressed a smile, remembering Trace's factual accounts of university doings and her own extended ramblings about the meaning of life. 'I used to think I wrote better letters than your father, too. Maybe boys don't express themselves as easily.'

Just then Elsa reappeared at the door, wearing her swimsuit. 'Ready?' she asked Annie.

'In a minute.' Annie stood up, letter in hand, and started for the stairs, but detoured to drop a kiss on Laura's head. 'Yeah,' was all she said and Laura returned to her book, feeling a cumulative ease about Annie that had been rare in recent months.

Rachel, too, seemed content, though Laura left it to others to ask how her mother was getting along with Carlena. One afternoon as a group of them were sitting on the porch overlooking the lake, Richard, seated beside Rachel, turned to her. 'I understand you have a gem of a housekeeper, Mother.'

Rachel nodded, apparently unperturbed. 'Yes, we seem to be managing quite well. It's not what I expected but,' she hesitated, 'lots of things happen to us in life that we don't expect.'

Laura was glad to be at a little distance. She caught Lillian's eye, a quick nod.

A silence followed. An awkward silence, Laura thought, or was it only her anxiety that made it seem so? She was glad when Howard, sitting on the glider on the other side of Rachel, said, 'Well, I stopped over on my way to a meeting in Boston and Carlena's a good cook. I'll attest to that.'

Happily a boatload of their young folks arrived back at

the dock then and swarmed up onto the porch, stopping to brush sand from their feet and ankles, shake sand from their beach towels. They were full of stories about their unsuccessful fishing expedition and nothing more was said about Carlena, or about Rachel's living arrangements.

But as they were all gathering for supper, Laura sought out Trace who had been chatting with Richard about the degree of insulation a lakeshore home needed, and said, 'Mother seemed okay about Carlena and being in Hadley, didn't you think?'

He put a quick arm round her shoulder. 'Very much so. I thought that too.'

The night before they were all to leave, Rachel made the rounds of the family, stooping over her cane, waiting expectantly until each one stood and kissed her goodnight. 'It's been a wonderful week together, hasn't it?' she said. Her eyes filled with tears. 'I want to thank you all for coming. Now I'm going to bed.' She left amid the murmur of further goodnights.

After a few minutes Laura went into her mother's room. Rachel was in bed, the light on, a book lying face down on the blanket. Her eyes were closed, her head drooping slightly to one side. At the sound of the door opening she started and looked up. 'Oh, hello, dear.'

'I just came to say goodnight again.' Laura bent to kiss her mother's cheek, the skin fine like a baby's but sagging into the hollow of her cheek like old cloth hung on the arched bones of her face.

'Goodnight, dear. I guess I just dropped off.' She picked up the book and passed it to Laura. 'Here, take this.'

Laura put it on the bureau. 'It's been a nice day, hasn't it?'

Rachel smiled. 'Didn't the little children love having Bart and Philip take them in the boat?'

'Bart and Philip enjoyed it too. Bart said it reminded him of when he was a kid and Trace would take them on vacation outings.'

'How your father would have liked that. Laura,' her mother looked at her, eyes entreating, 'something happens, like today, the boat rides, and I think, I'll tell Will. Then I remember.' She paused. 'I keep thinking, he must be *some-where* where I can reach him. You know?'

'I know.'

Rachel took off her glasses. 'Take these too.'

Laura fitted the glasses into the case and set it on the nightstand. 'Shall I put the light out?' She reached for it but her eyes lingered on her mother's face, the brown eyes turned gray at the edges, the slow fading of pigment over the years. 'I love you,' she said.

'I know you do. I can see it in your eyes.'

Laura, grateful, touched beyond measure, put her hand over her mother's as it lay on the bedclothes. 'You're easy to love.'

Rachel's eyes filled with tears. 'Am I?' she said.

In the morning the families dispersed. Rachel would stay on a while longer with Lillian, then return to Hadley where Carlena would be waiting. Howard and his family went back to Texas. Laura and Trace, Bart, Philip and Annie proceeded to Colorado. They had planned a leisurely trip, with stops along the way.

With the shrinking of the family to the five of them, or maybe it was the confinement of being in the car so long, some of the euphoria from the reunion seemed to fade. Annie didn't want to sit in the front seat when Trace was driving. It made her nervous. She didn't approve of his choice of radio stations. 'You choose, then,' he offered. She twirled the dial, couldn't find anything she liked. When Laura, trying to be conciliatory, expressed a liking for Kathie Mattea, Annie snorted. 'You never listen to that kind of music at home! It's always classical stuff.' Philip and Bart carried on their brotherly banter, their talk about colleges and job searches, apparently unperturbed, prompting Laura to think she would do well to follow their example – which worked for about twenty minutes.

In Kansas – they were digressing for a visit to a great-aunt of Laura's – they stopped for lunch at a Howard Johnson. Looking at the menu, Laura said, 'I'll have clam chowder.'

Annie looked up. 'You edgy?' There was an accusing tone

to the question. 'You always get clam chowder when you're edgy.'

She was glad for the understanding, irritated at having no secrets. 'It's my New England heritage. Security food.'

'What're you edgy about?'

'A lot's happened. Everybody growing up. You wearing that top when you know we're going to visit Grandma's Aunt Helen.'

Annie looked down at the red knit halter stretched across her full breasts. 'It covers,' she said. 'What's wrong with it?'

The silence was awkward. 'Just that today,' Laura began, then stopped.

Trace was studying the menu, oblivious. 'What's everybody having?'

'Hamburger surprise,' Bart said. The smile around his lips went back to the previous conversation. 'She looks okay, Mom.'

'Think of it this way,' Philip said. 'Maybe Grandma's Aunt Helen is blind in one eye.'

'She's still got the other one,' Bart said, and winked at Annie.

The visit was pleasant and uneventful. As they were leaving, Aunt Helen, who had boasted when they'd inquired about her state of health that she didn't even need glasses except to read, looked at the three young people waiting politely on the porch and said to Laura, 'You have a handsome family.' She turned to Trace, a hint of mischief in her eyes. 'They must take after your side.'

The next day, almost at their destination, they stopped in a college town for ice cream and to wander through a row of shops. After the ice cream they separated, to meet again in an hour.

Laura was in a bookstore when she heard the bell over the shop door tinkle.

Annie came over. 'I've found something else I'd like for my birthday. It's just right for my room. Can you come look?'

Something *else*? Laura thought. In less than a month it would be Annie's birthday. She had a long list of requests

– a telephone for her room, a new camera, money to supplement her clothing allowance.

'Well, all right.' She would at least look.

The store was an art shop, with hammered silver, turquoise, art objects formed with string and yarn. Annie led her to a large yarn sculpture hanging from the ceiling. It was an intricate piece done in shades of blue, the yarn wound round crossed wooden dowels to form a three-dimensional tier of shaded blue diamonds.

'It's beautiful!' Laura said.

'Think how great it would look in my room.'

That was another thing, Annie wanted to do over her room. When she'd broached the subject Laura had thought, but you'll be off to college in another year. She hadn't said it, one doesn't write off a year as unimportant. She picked up the white tag hanging from the piece. Yes, it was expensive. Still, it was beautiful.

'All right. We'll get it for your birthday. I don't wonder you like it.'

'Oh, thank you!' Annie gave her a quick hug.

'It'll be clumsy to carry in the car. Maybe we could have it shipped home.'

'Good idea.' Annie put her arm through Laura's. 'I love it, Mom. Thanks a lot.' They went to find a clerk.

The woman came back with them and took down the hanging. 'This is a beautiful piece, one of my favorites.' They watched while she shrouded it in tissue and wrote out the sales slip. 'It's all handmade, of course.' She handed Laura the slip to sign.

'Does it have a name, this kind of piece?' Laura asked.

'It's called an Eye of God,' the woman said. She looked at Annie. 'Is it for you?'

'Yes, for my birthday.'

'How old will you be, dear?'

'Seventeen,' Annie said.

8

Laura sat on the cabin porch, sketchpad on her lap, her legs in dark blue slacks stretched in front of her, her feet resting on the long railing. Across the valley Long's Peak thrust into the sky, its crest shrouded in snow, snow curling in sweeps and crescents down the black rock. She pulled her blue sweater more tightly round her. The Colorado mountain air was cool.

This afternoon thunderclouds would roll among the high mountains, another in the series of daily storms they had come to expect this past week, the first of their two weeks at this family resort not far from Estes Park. The trail signs reflected the daily pattern: 'All climbers must be off the mountain by 2 p.m.' But now the sky was clear. Below her, on this side of the valley, a pine-needled trail sloped through the pine forest, past the barricaded riding stable to the sheer turquoise rectangle of the swimming pool. Further down the slope and barely visible through trees was the shingled roof of the main lodge.

She heard their voices before she saw Trace and the boys climbing the hill toward the cabin, a tall trio advancing, slightly out of step, Bart the tallest, his hair dark as Trace's had been before it started to gray. Philip was almost blond, Trace's height, perhaps still growing.

They reached the steps, climbed onto the cabin porch. 'Hi, Mom,' Philip called. All three went inside.

In a moment they were back out, Trace flipping through a magazine, Bart and Philip carrying bunched-up sweaters.

'Bart's going to show me a cirque,' Philip volunteered, fitting an arm into the sleeve of his blue cardigan.

Bart pulled his tan sweater over his head. 'Geo 314. A college education wasn't wasted on me.' He straightened the sweater round his waist, nodded toward the stable. 'If you see Annie, tell her I'm still interested in riding after lunch. You want to come with us?' he asked Philip.

Philip shook his head. 'I saw some weird tree frogs behind the lodge. I'm going to take my camera and wait. Very quietly.'

'Okay, Mr Audubon,' Bart said.

'You're talking birds,' Philip protested. 'I said frogs.'

Bart gave Philip a playful jab as they stepped off the porch. 'Come on. Let's go rock hunting.'

'I love seeing them together, don't you?' Laura reached a companionable arm to Trace, behind her. She didn't connect. She twisted in her chair. He was sitting against the porch rail, reading.

'What's so engrossing?'

He held up a journal. She recognized *Philosophical Review*. 'A piece on linguistics I'm going to use with my honor students. I'm loaning it to a man at the lodge. From Grinnell.'

It's vacation! she thought.

He stood. 'Actually, I came to ask if you'd like to go to town in an hour.'

Her impatience slipped a couple of notches. 'Yes, I would. Thanks.'

'You think any of the kids will want to go?'

'I doubt it. The boys won't be back and Annie'll be with Roger, as soon as he gets out of a student staff meeting.'

'With Roger *again*?'

'Be glad it isn't *still*. I talked with her this morning about coming in so late last night. She promised to keep better hours.'

He started down the path and she called, 'Trace?'

He turned. 'Yes?'

'Will you check the mail? There might be a letter from my mother. Or Lillian.' He nodded and went on.

She picked up a stick of cerulean blue from the wooden box of pastel chalk open on the wooden chair arm and began to darken the underbranches of the far trees, her glance moving quickly from paper to mountain and back again.

Pine needles scrunched on the hillside. This time it was Annie, her long strides covering the ground, brown hair swaying, her yellow sweatshirt hung round her shoulders and bouncing against her dark jersey.

She stepped onto the porch. 'Where's everybody?'

'Dad's found an academic colleague. They're talking shop.'

Annie gave an exaggerated sigh. 'Doesn't he *ever* quit work?'

Laura lifted her shoulders. 'Who knows?' She went on, 'Bart and Philip are hunting rocks. Bart said to tell you he'd still like to ride this afternoon.'

Annie glanced down the hill toward the stable. 'You can come if you want?' It was a question but she didn't wait for an answer. She leaned over to examine Laura's work. 'Nice,' she said.

'Thanks.'

Annie moved toward the door. 'I came up to change. I'm going to swim with Roger, or at least lie in the sun.' She looked toward the sky. 'If it stays out, that is.'

'Dad and I are going into town. Anything you want?'

'You might get me the new *Seventeen*. And some shampoo – Clairol, Medium. I'll pay you back.' Annie went inside.

Laura breathed in the smell of pine woods. Riding? She might try it while they were here. Annie was always urging her to new adventures, like the ferris wheel they'd gone on together last summer. At first she had demurred but Annie had persuaded her. High in the air, at the top of the circle, the wheel stopping and starting every several feet to let on new riders, she had suddenly panicked and covered her face with her hands. Annie had laughed, touched her arm. 'Open your eyes, Mom!'

The screen door opened and Annie came back out. 'Is this all right? My new one's still wet.' She was wearing last year's bathing suit, a lavendar bikini she had made herself. It was cut lower in front than her new suit. A triangle of white skin dipped deeply into the cleavage of her breasts.

'It looks pretty seductive,' Laura said. 'You look gorgeous.'

Annie looked down at her body. 'Me? Actually, I'm fat.' She leaned over and took the muscle of her thigh between finger and thumb. 'Look at that. Flab!'

'I know,' Laura said. 'I don't know how you live with yourself, looking so awful.'

Annie looked at her fondly. 'Well, anyway, I'll get a shirt. The air's cool.'

She went into the cabin and came out, her rose-colored gauze shirt buttoned to the start of her tan. 'That better?'

'It looks good to me.'

''Bye. I'll be with Roger.' Annie stepped off the porch. Laura watched her, her bare feet picking their way along the path, the long lines of her legs angling over the pine-needled ground. She disappeared through trees.

Laura returned to her sketchpad but her hand was still. First it had been Gordon. Maybe it still was Gordon. But for now, certainly, it appeared to be Roger.

It had begun a week ago, their first night here.

After dinner they'd gone to the auditorium for a show the student staff were putting on. At first Annie sat with the rest of them, but then she moved forward to an empty front row and sat, chin in hand, a faint smile on her lips, watching with undivided attention the young man named Roger who directed the show with a line of jokes and stories, sang 'Old Man River' with a flourish and power which caused Laura, too, to lean forward in her chair, then led the audience in a closing round, keeping time until to the surprise of all they came to a harmonious conclusion and he bowed his congratulations. He was easily the most attractive man on stage. Annie watched him, all the time.

Of course he noticed. After the show, as audience and performers mingled and walked away, he came over to Annie. Soon they were talking and laughing, Annie's brown eyes shining, her smile wide in her slender face, her long arms gesticulating, Roger leaning forward, his hand cupped to his ear in exaggerated response to the noisy room, his other arm resting lightly on Annie's shoulder.

After that, Roger spent much of his off-duty time with

Annie and, in his capacity as head waiter in the dining room, came to their table at least once a day to stoop close, smile at them all and say, 'Is everything all right?'

They would smile back and nod and one of them would say, 'Thank you. Yes. Everything's fine.'

Last night Laura and Trace had come back after a movie to find Annie and Roger on the couch in the living room. Roger sat with his back braced against one end and both his feet in Annie's lap, his shoes and socks on the floor. Annie was moving her hand back and forth over his foot and ankle and under the folded-back cuff of his slacks. An uncapped bottle of lotion stood on a chair beside them.

'Getting a foot massage,' Roger said.

'So I see.' Laura tried to keep her voice even, not to appear startled. After a few more exchanges about the evening, the movie, that this was Roger's second year on the student staff, she and Trace said goodnight and started toward their room.

'I'll be going soon,' Roger said.

'Good,' Trace said. They all laughed.

In their room Laura said, 'Well, that was a surprise. What next?'

'Your guess is as good as mine.' He was looking through the magazines on the bureau. 'Have you seen the new *Harper's?*'

In bed, he drew her close, his hand easing across her shoulders and down her back. She heard Roger and Annie get up and go out.

'Oh, Trace, listen. She's gone with him.'

'She'll be all right.' His tone was dismissive. 'We have to let her live her life.' His breath came faster. He pressed against her hip.

Moving to him, she thought of the pair who had just left, and of Annie's hand moving over Roger's ankle, languorous, back and forth, beneath the crumpled cuff. Then her own blood crested.

Afterwards she lay still. Trace slept. She heard Bart and Philip come in, go toward the room they shared.

She dozed off, then woke up to the sound of steps on the porch, the front door opening. In the moonlight she looked at her watch. It was past one o'clock. Annie was humming softly. Her footsteps came to the bedroom door. 'Yoho. Mom, if you're awake, I'm home.'

'Thanks.' Relieved, she'd dropped off to sleep. But not before deciding to speak to Annie in the morning.

She had. 'It makes Dad and me uneasy, your coming in so late. Besides, you don't want Roger falling asleep in the dining room.'

Annie scoffed. 'I'm sure that's what you're worried about.' Still, she'd promised to be in by eleven.

A sound drifted up from the pool. Laura looked down. A swimmer poised on the high diving board was calling to someone. Annie appeared out of the trees and approached the deck of the pool. Roger was already lying there on a lounge chair. She pulled a chair close to his and stretched out in it and they turned to one another, talking. He reached under his chair, handed something to Annie and she leaned forward, began applying sunscreen to her long brown legs.

A light breeze rustled the pine branches. Halfway down the hill a humming bird, its wings a blurred fan, poised at a blossom of columbine. Butterflies drifted against the low brush.

There was a splash. The woman from the high diving board had entered the water.

By the time Laura and Trace returned from town it was one thirty. A note in Bart's handwriting said, 'We've gone to lunch.'

They left their packages and went to the dining room – no sign of the children.

'Phil's probably gone off in search of flora and fauna,' Trace mused, smiling. 'Bart and Annie were going riding – wasn't that it?'

'Yes.' Laura felt an edge of disappointment bordering on resentment. Annie invited me to go. Not that I wanted to but they could have waited to ask.

Trace swung an arm round her shoulder. 'Well, how about just you and me?' he said and, to the hostess, 'Two, please.'

She led them to a table by a window where they could

look up at the mountain, its snow-covered peak almost blinding in the sunlight. But already a cluster of clouds was moving in from the west. Further down the mountain, a cleared strip of chair lift and ski trail marked a forested lower slope. Empty chairs swayed with the ratcheting of the cable. A few, occupied with summer sightseers, advanced steadily against the dark ground.

'Ski team, anyone?' Trace said.

Laura smiled. Last week they'd all taken the chair lift ride, enjoyed the view from the higher elevation. But she was glad to get back down. 'I will if you will,' she said, knowing she was perfectly safe. It was one of their joys in one another, an early discovered compatibility, that they had almost no interest in organized team sports. 'But I might have tried riding.'

'Fine,' he said. 'You still can,' and they both turned their attention to the menu.

After lunch they went to the lobby, stood by the big picture window. By now storm clouds covered the tops of the high mountains, though it was still clear on the lower slopes.

'I think I'll try a nap,' Laura said. 'We were up pretty late.'

'I'll hang around here for a while.' Trace spotted the man from Grinnell. 'Maybe I'll see if Don's read the article. If the kids come back in time we could take a trip to the museum. We haven't done that yet.'

Laura moved toward the door. 'I'll be at the cabin if anything develops.'

She was propped on the bed, reading, pillows pulled from under the dark chenille bedspread, when she heard Trace's footsteps on the porch. They were heavier, faster than usual.

He came into the room. 'Laura! A girl has been badly hurt and taken to Estes Park by ambulance. She was riding. They think it's Annie.'

'Trace!' Her stomach like a vise, she reached for her shoes, fear thick in her throat.

'Philip is waiting for us in the lobby. Bart went with the ambulance.'

Her hands shook as she tied the laces. She picked up her

purse, her blue raincoat – it might be a while and the air was cool.

'Why do they think it's Annie?'

'Her horse came back.'

They hurried to the lodge, grasping each other's hands, stumbling as they went.

A small crowd had gathered. Philip came to them, his face white, immobile. Laura reached to him. 'Philip.'

The lodge proprietor explained to Trace where the clinic was located. Roger was beside her, his face stark. 'It's on the main street,' the woman said, 'beside a gas station. I don't think you'll have trouble finding it. There's a sign, "Medical Clinic".'

Laura looked at Roger. Their eyes met, acknowledging their fear. 'Do you know where it is?' she asked him.

'Yes.'

'Maybe you could come and help us find it.'

He looked at the lodge owner. She released him. 'Go.'

Trace drove, Roger in front with him. Laura sat with Philip in the back seat. Her eyes consumed the road ahead. Faster. Annie, I love you. She tried to counteract the mushrooming panic that enveloped her. They seemed to be driving into it, it surrounded them, clung to them, viscous against their skin. We've been through other alarms that turned out all right. That time they lost Annie at the beach. The time Philip cut his wrist and they had to rush him to the hospital. Don't anticipate the worst! 'Badly hurt,' Trace had said. But maybe it was less serious than it seemed. Maybe it wasn't even Annie at all.

'It could be another girl,' Roger said. 'Some others went with the wrangler.'

'Yes,' Laura said. But Bart had gone with the ambulance. Annie. I send you my energy. Receive it. It will go into your fingers, it will curve with the curve of your skull. Annie, I pray for you, I fill your body with my life. For a moment she thought they were interchangeable. She knew it was Annie who had fallen.

She was thinking, what if she is broken and maimed? How shall we deal with that pain? There was another thought that darted by the corner of her mind: I don't want it. I don't want to give my life to an invalid. She turned from it in horror. This was her daughter, she would give anything to save her. Annie, however you are, receive my strength. Annie, be well.

The mountain road wound on. They came to the edge of town. 'Keep going straight,' Roger said. Then, 'Turn left. It's past the gas station.'

They saw the clinic sign and, at the edge of the parking lot, they saw Bart, his hands jammed into the pockets of his tan windbreaker. With a nod of his head he motioned them in.

They got out of the car. 'It's Annie?' Laura asked.

'Yes.'

'How is she?'

'I don't know. They're working with her. In the ambulance she seemed to move her head.'

'It's her head that's hurt?'

'Yes.'

They started toward the clinic. Roger hesitated, looked toward the clinic, then toward the road. 'I'd better go back,' he said. 'I'll hitch a ride. You'll call the lodge when—' His voice broke.

Laura hugged him quickly. 'Thanks for coming with us. We'll call.' He started toward the road.

They went into the clinic. The nurse directed them to an interior room. 'The doctor will be with you soon.'

On a white enamel table glass tubes stood in a wooden case. A blood pressure indicator rested beside them, its rubber tube a black curve on the white table. To one side was an electrocardiograph, its handsome teak surfaces gleaming.

They sat in chairs. The room seemed crowded, with four pairs of knees jutting into the empty space.

They turned to Bart. 'Tell us what happened.'

He leaned forward, his elbows braced on the knees of his tan chinos, hands clenched in front of him. His knuckles were white knobs. 'We were riding our horses. She was in back. Her horse turned away, onto a path they sometimes take. The wrangler came back and redirected the horse. We started out again. It turned a second time. It galloped out of sight. She called out. The wrangler went to help her. By the time we got there she had fallen. No one saw her fall.'

Laura sucked in her breath. 'You got there?' she said.

'As quick as I could. She was lying on the ground. She was unconscious.'

For a minute they did not speak. Trace gripped the chrome arms of the chair, shifted forward on the grained leather seat. 'The ambulance?'

'A passing car saw and phoned. The ambulance came quickly. I helped them lift her in.'

'*Ohh!*' Laura said. 'In the ambulance, how did she seem?'

'I was in front. I looked back. Once I thought I saw her head move. I didn't see her when the men took her out.'

Philip stirred, moved his foot against the chair leg.

They waited. Still the doctor didn't come. What could be taking so long? Surely someone could tell them something.

A family was milling around the desk in the main waiting room. A boy had an arm in a cast. They were all laughing. How strange that they were here – such a slight affliction. They were taking energy from the care of Annie. Why don't they go?

The doctor came in – a young man. He appeared shaken. 'Mr Randall?' he said to Trace. 'I'm Dr Baldwin.' He looked away from Trace toward the middle of the room. He did not look at any of them.

'She's unconscious,' he said. 'She's been thrown, dragged. Her skull is fractured. Her jaw is broken. I've given her shots to stabilize heart, breathing, everything we can do. I've sent her on by ambulance to the hospital in Boulder. A neurologist will be waiting. You can go there.' He paused. 'I'm sorry, I don't think . . .' He started again. 'I don't think she has a fifty-fifty chance of making it.'

Laura sat forward in her chair. The blood was leaving her head. She heard a harsh wail. It was her own.

'Do you want something for her?' the doctor asked Trace, as though Laura was an object to be tended to. She snapped up in her chair. 'I'll be all right. Can you give me some smelling salts?' She knew what to ask for. She had always been a fainter – standing too long before breakfast to have her hair braided, standing in the sun at Junior High Memorial Day exercises, waiting in a hospital while the doctor sewed up Philip's hand. For a minute she put her head between her knees, noticed for the first time the dulled swirling green and white of the floor tile, like ocean spray against rocks.

'The nurse will get you something.' The doctor's voice was cold. Anger restored her. She did not faint.

The doctor brought a map of Boulder and showed Trace where the hospital was. 'We'll find it.' Trace took the map.

The nurse handed Laura a cylinder of cotton wrapped in paper. 'It's smelling salts. You have to break it open.' The nurse's eyes were kind.

'Thank you.'

The doctor stepped forward again, a paper bag in his hand. He gave it to Laura. 'Her shoes and jacket.' In the next room on the floor under an operating cart Laura saw Annie's wine-colored jersey. 'Her shirt?'

'I had to cut it off her.' He handed her a folded tissue. 'I took out her contact lenses.'

She opened the tissue. There was blood on the discs. She stared into her hand, then folded the tissue in, like the petals of a flower, closing.

This time Bart drove, Philip in front with him. Trace and Laura were in back, one by each window, hands clasped across the open space between them.

'Tell us again,' Laura said to Bart. Maybe there was something they'd missed. Maybe he could prove the doctor wrong.

He told how the wrangler had called 'Hold on!' and gone after her but she was out of sight and when Bart reached them a few minutes later she was lying on the ground and the wrangler was kneeling beside her.

'She was already unconscious?' Laura's voice was faint. She wanted Annie not to have suffered.

'Yes.'

'The ambulance?' she prompted.

'A passerby called.'

'Then what?'

'He waited. I sat there on the ground with her. I covered her with my jacket. I kept patting her back, telling her she was going to be all right.' His voice was low. 'I didn't want her to be alone.'

'Oh, Bart, thank you.' Laura broke into fresh tears. Philip was sobbing quietly. She reached out to put a hand on his shoulder. But it was also Annie she reached for.

Annie at two, sitting with her on the rocking chair and turning the pages, telling the words phrase for phrase, her voice mirroring the inflections in Laura's own. 'His mummy didn't know him, she really and truly did not know him, because, you see, she had never seen a rabbit with red wings in all her life.'

She is braiding Annie's hair for her recital. The braids fall onto the Irish lace collar of the green velveteen dress Rachel made. Annie hurries to the piano to run through her piece one more time – 'To A Falling Star'. She plays it fast. 'I'll go slower when I get there,' she says. She is eight years old.

O Thou that takest away the sins of the world grant us thy peace. O Thou that hast walked through the valley of the shadow of death and feared no evil, I am afraid, fear is all I know, fear is who I am.

It was a long ride into Boulder. The road wound among mountains. The shadows lengthened, laid dark patches across the highway. The air turned cooler. There would be thunderstorms in the mountains. It was why the climbers were urged to be down by afternoon. They had always done that. They had abided by all the rules.

They watched the signs, the diminishing mileage to the city. Still Laura held Trace's hand. They did not look at one another. Their eyes were on the road.

She thought, if Annie dies . . . But wait. Don't anticipate it. Those other times disaster had threatened . . . 'I don't think she has a fifty-fifty chance of making it.' She saw Annie this morning walking to the pool, her long legs stretching over the pine-needled ground. She saw her at home, perched on the blue kitchen stool, her guitar propped in her lap. 'I live one . . . day . . . at a time,' Annie sang, her voice sweet, clear. 'I dream one . . . dream . . . at a time.'

At Boulder they found the hospital – a long low building,

tan stucco. Trace spotted the red Emergency sign. 'That way.' Bart had already turned.

The reception area was light, spacious. Long corridors led away. A woman sat behind a glass partition, the space in front of her a wide clear arc. Trace went to her. 'We're the Randalls. Our daughter—'

'Yes, we've been expecting you.' She was deferential, apologetic, asking the questions. 'Name of company? Policy number? Name of insured? Age? I'm sorry to have to ask you these questions.'

Laura watched Trace, astonished at his composure.

'Come this way.' A nurse led them to a small waiting room ringed with orange-upholstered chairs, a few benches. Tattered magazines rested on a low round table. A vending machine stood at one side. Nearby a coffee-maker held a black residue of coffee in a ringed glass pot. An elderly couple looked up from a bench as the four of them filed in.

'The doctor will see you as soon as possible,' the nurse said. She eyed the stale coffee in the pot. 'Would you like some fresh coffee? Or a soft drink?' They shook their heads and sat down, Trace and Laura together on a bench, the boys in separate chairs close by.

They waited. From where they sat they could see the admitting desk, the nurse bent over her papers. White-clad figures came and went in the hallway. Carts rolled by. The sounds of voices. Bart picked up a magazine, put it down. The elderly couple exchanged a few words with one another. Laura noticed that Philip's foot was wound round the chair leg, like a child too long at school.

She turned to Trace. 'Can't we go to her? Surely—'

He gripped her hand. 'I'll ask.'

He went to the desk. His words carried back to her. 'May we see our daughter? My wife and I . . .'

The nurse shook her head, said something.

Trace came back. His voice was weary, strained. 'It's best not to now. The doctors are working with her.' He sat down. A shudder went through his body and he reached for Laura's hand. She took it and for a moment they clung to each other, then let go.

She looked at her watch. An hour. Where was Annie?

Down what corridor? Behind what door? What could possibly be taking so long? Surely someone could tell them something. She didn't want to know.

She glanced at Trace again, his hands knotted, white-knuckled, in his lap, his shoulders bent forward, head bowed. He is praying. We are all praying in our own fashion.

She thought of the song Annie sang, 'I live one day at a time,' and she was glad with a fierce gladness that Annie strode into her life with such determination and courage. She remembered how Annie fed herself so young, holding the spoon in an infant's overhand grip, raising it deftly to her mouth – and not one year old.

She thought of another song Annie sang, 'Had I a golden thread, and needle so fine . . . And I would sing the courage of women giving birth.' Once she had said to Laura, 'I don't know if I want to have children or not. I don't know if I'd be a good mother.' Laura had thought of her mothering her dolls, fussing over her brothers when they were sick, and thought, you? If there is such a thing as a born mother, you are one. She thought again of her own motherhood and of Annie, an infant in her arms, and her chest contracted with pain and she leaned over and put her head on her knees. When she sat up again she was aware that the muscles of her womb were moving in rhythmic contractions. She felt no pain, only astonishment, and then no astonishment, as though it was to be expected that at this moment of Annie's extremity she should be re-enacting her birth. She thought, if she is being born into death let it be without pain for her, and she thought Annie must be dying and her shoulders arced forward over her empty body, surrounding that which she did not hold in her arms, not now, not ever.

A nurse came in. 'Will you come this way? The doctor will speak with you.'

They stood, Trace, Laura, Bart, Philip. Fear dragged like chains from their ankles, their elbows, their shoulders, fear pushed against their chests as they forced their way through it.

They followed the nurse down a corridor and into a small chapel – a simple wooden altar, candles, two windows of pale stained glass. The room was carpeted. Facing the altar were a few benches, an open area with upholstered chairs. They sat down.

A man came in, of medium height, thinning brown hair. He wore a tweed sport jacket.

'I'm Dr Winslow. I have bad news. I am sorry to tell you that Anne has died.'

There were guttural sounds, intakes of breath. They did not move. They were creatures of stone, children flung into the air in a game of statue. But they had known it.

'It was a massive injury to the brain. We have done monitorings. She never regained consciousness. There has been no blood to the brain. The heart is still pumping. It is just a question of time.'

Laura watched his face. Who was he to be telling them this? Not even a doctor's coat.

He went on, 'I wanted to ask you, would you have any interest in having her heart used for a transplant?'

Laura and Trace looked at each other. Yes, of course. Laura looked at the boys. 'You?'

They nodded. Anything – kidneys, heart, whatever could be used.

'I don't know if we can do it,' he said. 'We'd have to get her body to Denver. But we'll try. I'll be back in several minutes.'

He left and they moved into a circle, their arms round each other, heads bowed close. Panic rippled the muscles along their shoulders. They were leaning over a whirlpool. It was voracious. It would suck them in. Their sobs were random, without form, the cries of children waiting for someone to come and comfort them.

The doctor returned. 'We couldn't do it. We couldn't keep her heart beating.' Their faces, stunned, reflected additional pain. Not even *that*. Still, it was one less thing.

He motioned them to sit. 'You drove out here?'

'Yes.'

'Someone will have to fly, to accompany the body home.'

They looked to one another. It was a new affront. Now? When they needed each other? It was unthinkable.

Laura began, 'I've wondered . . .' Her hands were shaking and she clamped them together. 'We could have her body cremated . . . like we did with my father.' She saw again the small white urn being lowered into the ground. 'We could have them ship . . .' her voice broke; she bit her lip but forced herself to say it, 'her ashes . . . home.'

'Good,' Trace said. 'Then we can drive home together.' He looked round the circle. The boys nodded their agreement. A gram of calm descended on them all. They had made a good decision.

The doctor leaned forward, eager now. They had touched some moment of his own life. 'I had a young doctor friend who died of cancer. When he knew he was dying he asked that his body be cremated and his ashes scattered over these mountains he loved.' He paused and for a minute his eyes were bright. 'You might want to do that, leave her out here where you brought her.'

No, Laura thought, we can't leave her here. We need her with us. 'Thank you,' she said. 'That's an idea.'

'We can decide later,' Trace said. A look of relief crossed Philip's face, and Bart's.

'The coroner will come.' The doctor's voice was professional again. 'He's also a mortician. You can talk with him.' He stood. 'Would you like to see the x-rays?'

They followed him into another room. He picked up a pointer and showed against a brightly lit screen a series of pictures, outlines of a skull, gray, with deeper gray lines running through. 'You can see there is no blood moving in the brain. It happened immediately. You wouldn't have wanted her to live.'

They murmured their agreement, desperate to convince themselves he was right. 'Look.' Laura pointed to one of the pictures. 'Her wisdom tooth, not even descended yet.'

The coroner came, sandy-haired, smelling of aftershave. He was kind. He had seen the body. Yes, he would take care of it. Trace explained that they wanted cremation – no casket, no embalming. They would decide later, when they got back to Tennessee, what to do about the ashes – bury them, scatter them somewhere.

'Do you want to take the ashes with you?' the coroner asked. 'Or would you prefer I ship them?'

They pondered it, the spectre of Annie's ashes in the car. Philip said, 'I'd feel kind of funny having them in the car.' They agreed. 'Ship them.'

'I'll need the name of a funeral director in your town.'

'Not ship them to us?' Laura asked.

'It's the law,' he said.

They shrugged. They had no knowledge of these laws. They gave him the name of a Woodbridge funeral home.

'Would you want to see the body yourselves?' the coroner asked.

They looked at one another. 'I think so,' Trace said. 'Yes.'

Bart and Philip agreed. Laura was not sure. The skull fractured. A broken jaw. 'I don't know.'

'I think it's important that we see her,' Trace said. He turned to Laura, put a hand on her arm. 'It's up to you. But I want to. If we don't,' – tears brimmed in his eyes – 'we won't believe it.'

'I'll go,' she said. 'But I may not look.'

The coroner handed Trace a card. 'Here's my address. Give me an hour and a half.' He gave directions to the funeral home and left.

Trace turned to the doctor. 'We need to make some calls. Is there a phone we can use?'

'Of course.' The doctor led them across a hall, opened the door to a consulting room. 'In here. You'll have privacy. No one will bother you.' He stood at the door. 'I'm going to leave now.' He extended his hand. 'I'm sorry.'

'Thank you.' One by one they shook his hand.

Laura watched him go. Panic dug at her chest. How can he go? How can he leave us?

Trace called his parents in Maryland, his brother in Connecticut.

'I'd like to call Paula,' Bart said. 'She's at her mother's in Ohio.'

'Of course.'

He came from the phone, tears streaming down his face. 'Paula sends her love. She'll come down as soon as we get home.'

Laura called Lillian. 'I have very bad news.' She told her. Lillian's voice rose in a hysterical cry. 'I'll get Mother.'

Rachel came to the phone. 'Darling!' They talked. They would talk again tomorrow.

She called Howard. No answer.

'What about Gordon?' Philip asked. They didn't have his number. It would be in Annie's things. They would call him later.

Trace said, 'I want to call Matt. Tomorrow's Sunday. I want them to know.'

Tomorrow Sunday? Laura saw the small congregation, singing, talking, going about their business, not knowing. *Matt* – tall, sandy-haired, leaning forward over the pulpit, his face intent. She had talked with him when her father died. 'Tell me about your father' – compassion in his voice.

Trace called. 'Matt? Trace Randall.' He talked, then handed the phone to Laura.

'Matt . . .'

'Laura, I'm so sorry.'

Her breath caught. All afternoon, like a buzzing gnat, her mind had been searching, batting against windows, bouncing off. Had there been clues, indications? Matt was a minister, acquainted with the borders of the known world. 'I want to tell you something.' She told how Annie had said to her last spring, 'I wouldn't mind dying young. I wouldn't be afraid at all.' Even now she remembered her astonishment. And how just last week they'd been sitting round the table and Annie had looked down at her and said 'out of a clear blue sky, Matt' – and her voice was puzzled and she wanted to believe it meant something and she wanted Matt to believe it too – 'she said, "I've had a full life already". For no reason, Matt.'

'Oh, Laura. Thank you. I'm glad you told me.' His voice was heavy with his own grief for Annie. 'We'll all be waiting, when you get home.'

'Yes, when we get home.' Home . . . A wave of revulsion moved toward her. How can we go home? She saw the door of Annie's room, swinging open.

They started to leave. 'Wait,' Laura said. 'We should call the lodge.'

Trace called. He came away from the phone, his arms

hanging limp against his sides. 'I told the proprietor. I couldn't reach Roger. They'll let him know.'

A slow drizzle fell as they left the hospital. The air was cold. Across the highway, lights from a McDonald's blazed and blinked.

'Maybe we should eat something,' Laura said.

'I'm not hungry,' Bart said.

Philip agreed. 'Me neither.'

Trace demurred too. 'I wouldn't have thought of food.'

She persisted. 'I think we should eat something.' It was her primal task, seeing to it that her family was fed.

They drove across the road and got milkshakes and hamburgers. The cold of the milkshakes and the air made Laura shiver. She couldn't stop trembling. Trace put an arm round her and after a while the trembling eased.

They found the funeral home, pulled into a curved driveway between banks of evergreens. They got out of the car and went in.

The director greeted them. He indicated an archway to a room. They saw a long table covered with a white sheet mounding slightly in the center. 'This way,' he said.

Annie's body was lying beneath the sheet, drawn up under her chin. Only her head was visible. They walked toward the table, staying close to one another.

At first Laura looked with her peripheral vision only. The face was swollen along the jaw. The mortician had put a dark lipstick on Annie's mouth. She never wore that color. Her hair was parted in the middle. It should be on the side.

She wondered, shall I touch her? She stepped forward and laid her hand on the ridge of leg beneath the sheet, felt the bone. Inexplicably, it was a relief that she had done it. She turned her palm up, looked at it. See? Death was terrible, but the body was not terrible; she had felt it, as of old. the feel of it was on her hand. A sudden pain surged in her throat and with a cry she pressed her hand against her cheek. Bart, beside her, put his arm round her. She felt his sob against the crush of her blue raincoat.

The others stepped forward, touched the body, and stepped back. After a time, they murmured their consent and, together, they turned away, moved out into the hall.

Trace went to talk with the funeral director. He came back and once more they went to the doorway and looked again at the body on the long white table, the dark hair framing her face.

Outside, it was still raining. Cars swished by against the wet pavement. Trace drove. They left the city and drove into the mountains, through dark valleys and deeply shadowed roads. They reached the town of Estes Park and drove along the main street, past the darkened clinic, past the drugstore where security lights revealed the shelves of sundries and magazines and pink plush animals and remedies for all those ailments the flesh is heir to save this which carried them slowly by in a car in which in the back seat a space wider than the world cried out for its missing occupant and two brothers stared into darkness.

By the time they reached the lodge it was past midnight and only the lobby and a few random lights were still lit. The surrounding cabins had disappeared into darkness.

They drove up the hill to their cabin and turned into the parking space. The car lights played over a figure huddled on the steps.

They stepped from the car as the figure came toward them, a dark silhouette against the moonlight.

Trace recognized him first. 'Roger,' he said.

9

At her daughter Lillian's house in Michigan, Rachel Taylor sat in the blue velvet chair and stared out the window. Lights were still on upstairs in the Thompsons' house, though the rest of the street was dark. Barbara Thompson had been over for coffee – was it yesterday? It seemed a very long time ago, another world.

Noise came from the other room – some of the children still up. Probably none of them could sleep, except maybe the little ones.

During supper they'd all sat there, Lillian, Richard, the three girls and Timmy. Rachel had picked at her bluefish and baked potato, drunk some tea. The others didn't do much better – Richard trying to be kindly, fill in the silence, telling at length about his difficulties finding a parking place so he could buy an evening paper.

It was all Rachel could do to look at the girls. Three of them. The oldest, Elsa, Annie's age, was audibly sobbing. She and Annie had been best friends at reunion, doing everything together. Then Christine and Jenny. Jenny started to talk about a Brownie meeting. 'We're going on a campout, out by the horse farm,' she said.

'Shut up, Jenny,' Christine said. 'Not *now*.'

'It's all right if she wants to tell about Brownies,' Richard defended her, putting down his forkful of green beans.

'See? We are too going!' Jenny turned to her sister, taunting.

'So what do I care?' Christine retorted. She swallowed a sob.

Finally Elsa said, 'At least she died doing something she liked to do.'

Lillian shook her head, her mouth tight.

It was all right. There was nothing to say. Or nothing not to say, either.

Timmy was five, a sensitive child. When he'd come in this afternoon, his hands covered with mud from playing in the yard, Lillian had said, 'Wash your hands, Timmy. Then I have to tell you something.'

He didn't balk, which he usually did, about washing his hands. Something in his mother's voice, Rachel suspected.

When he came out of the bathroom Lillian took him on her lap. 'Something very sad happened,' she said, stroking his hair.

She told him. He was wide-eyed, incredulous. 'Our cousin Annie? That we just saw? Last week?'

'Yes,' Lillian said. 'Aunt Laura and Uncle Trace's little girl.' She corrected herself. 'Not so little,' she said.

Timmy slipped from his mother's lap, went to Rachel in the kitchen rocking chair. 'Grandma.' She took him up, and they rocked, and rocked. He slipped down to watch the last of Sesame Street.

At supper he looked up from his glass, a milk moustache across his lip. No one was saying anything. 'I'm sure the horse didn't mean to,' he said, wanting everyone forgiven so they could be happy again.

Lillian came into the living room, turned up the light by the desk. The dark parchment shade glowed red and blue like stained glass. 'Thank you. That's better,' Rachel said.

Lillian came and smoothed Rachel's rose-colored shawl. 'The children are watching TV. Do you want to join them? It would take your mind off it for a while.'

'No.' She stroked Lillian's hand. 'Maybe I'll read.' She picked up a book from the table by her chair, turned it over, laid it back down.

'Anything I can get you, Mother? You want to talk?'

'I was just thinking,' she hadn't meant to say it, 'you have three daughters. She had only one.'

'I know.'

'You don't mind my saying that?'

'Of course not. It's so *awful*!' Lillian's eyes darted to the bay window, here and there, frantic. 'Some day I've got to shorten those curtains. I don't know what to do about anything!' She strode to the window and came back. 'I think I'll get a book and come out here and read with you.'

'All right, dear. I won't stay up much longer though.'

Rachel picked up the book, one of Lillian's Agatha Christies, and opened it. And closed it. She was remembering how thrilled she'd been for Laura when Annie was born. It was wonderful to have sons. But daughters were such company. Growing older, it mattered even more to have a daughter's care.

For a moment the hurt dragged at her heart again. Why hadn't Laura wanted her? Might things have gone differently if she'd gone to live with them? Maybe they wouldn't even have gone to that place in Colorado. 'We want some time together,' Laura had said. 'It might be our last chance, once Bart gets a job.' And now . . .

She glanced down at her watch. Nine thirty. Maybe if she got into bed and read she'd get sleepy. 'I think I'll take my sleeping pill,' she said. She called into the next room where the children were watching TV. 'Whose turn is it to get Grandma's drink of water?'

Lillian sighed. 'I'll get it, Mother. No need disturbing them tonight of all nights.' She went to the kitchen, turned the water on full force. She brought the glass, still dripping, to Rachel. 'Have you got your pill?'

'Yes, right here.' She took it from the small reticule she always carried. 'All right. Help me up.' With a grunt she pulled herself to her feet and they walked haltingly from the room.

At the doorway to her bedroom she paused. 'You know, it's the first time I've been glad your father's gone,' she said. 'He'd have taken this so hard.'

Lillian nodded, tears in her eyes again. 'I know. I was thinking of him.'

Rachel looked out the window into the drifting dark. Oh, Will! Why Annie? Why couldn't it have been me?

*   *   *

In the night Laura woke from sleep. The heaviness came to her first, the drag of something ominous and full of pain. Then, a sharp arrow in the midst of it, she remembered. Annie was dead. 'Ohh . . .' A whimper only, no more than that of a child rebuked for walking on wet grass. The events of yesterday went by, particular moments stopped, distended, timeless, then jumbled together again like stones rolling down a chute.

'Trace?'

'Yes.'

She moved to put her arms round him. 'Have you slept?'

'I don't think so.'

They lay together, strangers to themselves, strangers to the bed they lay on, strangers to the embrace in which they clung to one another.

A sound came from the boys' room. A sob. 'Have you heard the boys much?'

'No. Off and on. They talked some.'

The sound came again.

'It's Bart.' She wondered how she could tell. A slight cough and she knew immediately which of them it was. But how did she know their tears? They didn't often cry, her sons, grown to manhood. 'I'll get up and go to him.'

'Would you like me to come?'

'Whatever you want.'

She slipped from the bed and went in the stream of moonlight to the hallway, steadying herself with her hand on the panelled wood. 'Bart?'

A murmur.

She went in and stood by his bed. On the far side of the room Philip was asleep. Bart lay on his stomach, his face turned sideways on the pillow, his bare shoulders wide above the rumpled edge of the sheet. Since they'd been grown they'd slept in their undershorts – a strange custom. Pajamas would be more comfortable, wouldn't they? She wondered if he owned any that fitted him. Maybe they'd give him some for his birthday.

She sat down on the edge of the bed. The dizziness came

over her and she bent forward quickly and then sat up. 'Have you been to sleep at all?'

'No.'

'Is there anything you want to talk about? Anything I can do for you?'

He sniffled. His head moved against the pillow. 'You could rub my back.'

She put her hands on his shoulders, moving back and forth, a slow rhythm. She used to rub their backs, singing to them, easing them off toward sleep. Singing the longest song they could think of. One year, all through the spring, the hot summer and on into fall, she sang 'The First Noel' to Philip – his nightly choice, the longest song he knew.

And Annie. Sometimes, alone in her room at night, Annie would call out. 'Mom?'

She'd go into Annie's room. 'Scareyitis?'

'Yes.' It would be noises, or shadows on the wall, being alone in the room. 'Everybody else has somebody to sleep with.'

'I know. We're right in the next room.' Laura would lie down beside her, on top of the covers, the child's body hardly a ripple under the blanket. She would sing, stroke Annie's hair. When she was sure Annie was asleep she would ease off the bed and go back, weary and cold, to fall into bed beside Trace. 'Everything all right?' he'd say, his voice thick with sleep. She used to wonder whether he minded – or was he relieved? – that Annie didn't call his name.

Trace came in. He squatted down beside the bed. 'Anything I can do?'

Bart groaned, shook his head, no, against the pillow.

After a while Laura said, 'I wonder if it isn't harder for you because you were there when it happened.' In her mind she had seen it – Annie, the horse, the trail, some trees. But there was a haze between her and the image. Maybe it filtered out some of the horror.

'I don't think so. If anything I think it was easier, being there.'

Trace murmured, 'I'd like you to show me the place before we go. I want to see it.'

Laura turned her head away, her hands suddenly stilled. Why? A shudder of revulsion went through her. Why would he?

In the morning, hungry at last, they went down to the lodge. The breakfast hour had passed. They'd had a call from the owner, 'Come down when you want to. Someone will be waiting.'

They walked close together, through a world that called out for Annie. The flowers, the pine needles on the path, the water of the swimming pool. So freshly remembered – the mirrors of her life everywhere.

Roger was there. He brought them tea, rolls, juice. They ate and drank, the rolls in their mouths like cotton, chewed over and over, hard to get down. He hovered close. 'Can I bring you something more?'

'No, thank you.'

They finished eating. Laura looked at the clock on the wall. It was only eleven. The day was already too long. They'd been up less than two hours.

In the lobby a man approached, eyes sad, mouth drawn beneath his gray moustache. He extended his hand to Trace. 'Say, I'm so sorry.'

Trace introduced him. 'This is Don Hetzl, from Grinnell. My wife, Laura. My sons, Bart and Philip.'

'I'm so sorry,' he repeated. They acknowledged his condolence. The boys wandered off.

The three of them stood awkwardly. At a small writing desk a woman addressed postcards. Two children leaned over a jigsaw puzzle. At the main desk the clerks were busy at their work.

'You want to sit down?' Trace asked.

They sat. Don Hetzl said, 'This whole place was stunned last night when we heard.' He paused. 'You were right there when it happened?'

'Actually, we weren't,' Trace said. 'My son Bart was.' He began to recount the whole thing, the ride to the clinic, the first wait, the statements of the clinic doctor. Then the drive to Boulder, the wait there and, finally, the nurse summoning them. 'The chapel was a giveaway,' he said. 'If we'd had any doubts before . . .'

Laura listened in mounting horror – every detail, but delivered as factually as the evening weather report. She felt as though a giant shell was closing down on her. She would be crushed. She could not breathe.

'Excuse me.' She stood and hurried out onto the porch, ran the length to where it became a balcony overlooking the pool. She sat down and leaned her head against the railing. The sound of laughter drifted up from below. A woman's voice, 'Don't you want to come get some lunch?' Laura raised her head to look. A girl of about ten, her dark braids wet from swimming, came running. 'There you are, Mama. I was looking all over for you.'

In the afternoon, up at the cabin, Trace came to her. 'Bart is taking me to see the place where Annie fell. Do you want to come?'

She drew in her breath. 'No, I don't. I think it's bizarre.'

'It's not bizarre to me. Not at all. I want to see the place.' His jaw was set, tense, his arms crossed over his tan plaid shirt.

She shrugged, retreating. 'Well, I don't want to go. Don't tell me about it.'

She went to Annie's room. She might as well start. She took Annie's blue cosmetic case from the closet shelf and began to fill it with the clutter of tubes, jars, flat plastic boxes. Her eyes fell on a box of tampons and she remembered – Annie was having her period. Nobody should die in the middle of her period! She sat down on the edge of the bed and opened her mouth and screamed, a long harsh cry. It was an astonishing sound. In the mirror her face looked grotesque, her eyes too big, pouches of flesh wrinkling under them, everything swollen and shapeless from crying. Horrified, she heard steps in the next room and Philip's anxious voice. 'Mom?'

Standing up, steadying herself, she said, 'I'm here, Philip. Did you want something?'

'No.' He stood at the door, his fingers pushing through his hair. He stared at her, his eyes guarded.

'I'm sorry,' she said. 'I didn't know anybody was here.'

'It's okay. You scared me, that's all.'

She went to him. 'Philip.' She hugged him. He was so slender – a tall, slender boy. He'd not yet achieved Bart's bulky manhood.

A sob shook his chest. 'I came up to read some stuff,' he said. He went back to his room.

She continued to sort through the things. Only this time, packing the tampons, she remembered Annie telling her last spring about the birth control and having sex with Gordon.

Well, they had adjusted to that. And she was glad of it too, since Annie had had so little time.

Damn! She closed the case with a quick thud. *Damn* such considerations. *Damn* that they were ever fitting and proper, ever in the world. At the thought of putting the words 'fitting and proper' next to Annie having sex at sixteen she began to laugh, only her laugh cracked in the middle and she dropped down onto the broad white bed. The cremation was today – that was part of it. Annie had already left her body, they'd seen that with their own eyes. But . . . *Oh. God!* She drew her legs to her chest and pressed her teeth against the hard bones of her knees.

On the mountain road Bart slowed the car to a stop. 'Over there, Dad. That's where she came out, that pathway just past the pine trees.'

Trace followed his son's pointing finger. 'Where? I don't see a trail.'

'It's not a trail. It's a narrow pathway. The trail joins the road a hundred feet down the highway.'

It was impossible. 'How could a horse and rider fit along that path, the way the tree limbs hang down?'

Bart sighed. 'They think the horse must have turned onto the wrong path, then got frightened and started to run.'

Trace's anger flared. He leaned forward in the car, his face almost against the windshield. 'They shouldn't have skittish horses at a public stable. They don't know how much experience people've had. Annie had ridden before, but she'd be no match for a temperamental horse.'

Bart was looking at him strangely. 'Dad,' he said, 'do you want to get out?'

'Of course.' What was he trying to do, prove it couldn't have happened? He stepped out of the car and for a moment leaned against the curve of the roof, then straightened.

Bart was walking along the edge of the dirt road to the spot he'd been pointing to. When he reached the path he turned in a few feet. Trace followed him. Sunlight filtered in through the overhanging branches onto the forest floor, onto the narrow path covered with pine needles. Wild flowers grew low along the sides, clambered up to cover the rocks that protruded here and there through the earth. The rocks.

Once again the vise grabbed at his gut. Had her head hit one of these rocks? If she'd fallen on the pine needles, would it have made the difference? A little softer maybe? Enough to cushion a head. Some people wore helmets to ride. Why weren't they wearing helmets? 'Can you show me the exact place where you found her?' he asked Bart.

Bart moved a few feet. He was wearing those chinos again, the same tan sweater he'd worn the day Annie died. Yesterday.

'Right about here,' he said. The hand he gestured with trembled and he shoved his hands back in his pants pockets.

'I see.' Trace looked down at the mountain pathway – dirt, gravel, stones, a few pine needles. Nothing to tell a passerby a mortal wound had taken place here. 'Where was her head?'

Bart stopped, flattened one hand against the ground. 'Here.'

'Her body lay from there toward me?'

'Yes.' Bart stood. 'Can we go now?'

Trace stooped down, ran his hand over the ground. Panic jumped at him, closed on his throat. He stood up again. 'And where was the horse when you found her?'

'I told you. The horse had already started back. We met the horse as we were running to find her.'

'I'm sorry. I forgot. And which direction had they come from? Does the path branch back there in the woods?'

'Dad! Yes, the path branches. But not close to here. They're sure she fell after the path turned. What difference does it make?'

'I don't suppose it does.' He heard the stiffness in his voice. 'I was wondering how close the trees were. Did she try to jump? I mean, to save herself?'

Bart raised his hands in a gesture of despair. 'God, how do I know? It all happened so fast. I tried to reach her. If I'd stayed behind her instead of riding on ahead, or if I'd . . .' Bart's voice caught. He turned and stalked away, then wheeled round and came back. 'We're just torturing ourselves, coming out here.'

Trace nodded, and moved toward the car. At the car he took from his pocket the card the lodge manager had given him. He held it out for Bart to read: 'Arthur Long, Attorney at Law'. 'I talked with the manager earlier this afternoon. I raised the question of negligence. Since the horse had tried to turn from the path once before, shouldn't the wrangler have stayed with her? He was very sorry. He gave me this card.' He put the card back in his pocket. 'We'll talk with our own lawyer after we get home.'

Bart opened the car door and for a moment they stood facing each other. Then they got in and drove away down the mountain.

Trace put his head back against the head rest and closed his eyes. He tried to visualize Annie in these woods. Was she terrified, falling? In his shoulders he felt the pull of arm muscles wanting to move forward, to wrap themselves round her, keep her safe. She would have let him, wouldn't she, if her life had depended on it? Because what kept emerging out of the gray mist in front of his closed eyes were images from the spring, the week Laura was away and Annie had stood in the kitchen berating him: 'This whole week you've hardly said ten words to me!' When he had tried, repeatedly, she always had something else to do. And earlier, when he couldn't go to the sculpture exhibit. 'You're never here for me, not since I was a little girl. Not even then!' For a while he had made extra effort, sharing his books with her, helping with her geneology project, trying to tell her about his work, what his life was like. At first it seemed to go better, he was hopeful.

Then she'd withdrawn. 'Don't hug me,' she said. 'You know you don't feel like it – you're trying to be a good father. You don't have to. It's better if we keep our distance.'

'If that's what you want,' he said, his arms hanging stiff at his sides.

His own family hadn't been very affectionate. He knew the hug of greeting and farewell from his mother. A handshake from his father – that was all. He knew the embrace of passion. But he wasn't so easy with the in-between stuff. The Affection Revolution. He liked it, the feel of other bodies, the charge of energy. Hug everybody. But not your own daughter. 'Okay, if that's what you want,' he'd said, trying to pass it off with a smile, covering the clench of pain at his heart.

He had told himself that surely in time she wouldn't be so standoffish, telling him self-righteously, 'You don't have to. It's better if we keep our distance.' Anger in her eyes. And now . . . Even with Laura sometimes Annie had been distant. It wasn't all his fault. Was it? *Was it?*

That was the question that buzzed in his head, that lurked behind his need to come out here to see just how it was, his need to tell – he knew he was sometimes tedious and compulsive – just how everything had happened, one detail after another, exactly, exorcizing his demons.

Because what if she could have stayed on the horse? What if she was so angry with him that at the moment of testing she had chosen to leave, or just had not had the will? What if she was so angered that the fraction of energy that might have saved her wasn't available when she began to slip, or tried to pull her feet loose from the stirrups?

That was why he'd wanted Bart to show him the place, tell him everything. Everything. How fast was she going? Was she leaning forward when you saw her? Could anyone tell if she had tried to leap free?

He looked toward Bart. But Bart was intent on the road ahead, and tears were falling from his chin.

Trace stood at the main desk at the lodge, Laura beside him. 'I'm Mr Randall,' he said to the clerk who appeared to be new, or at least one they hadn't seen before – bright makeup, hair very short, a red silk tie at the neck of her crisp white shirt. 'Our reservation goes through Saturday, but we'll be leaving tomorrow. Cabin Number Four.'

She looked perturbed. 'I'm not sure that with a late cancellation we can deduct that from your bill, sir. It's too bad you didn't let us know earlier.'

'Our plans have been uncertain,' Trace said.

The clerk pored over the registration notebook, her finger with its red nail polish flicking through the succession of lined yellow pages. 'What did you say your name was?'

'Randall. We came in nine days ago, on a Saturday.'

At the name Randall one of the other clerks who'd been working with his back to them jumped up. 'I'll handle it, Jody,' he said.

The young woman stepped back. Her glance darted from Trace to Laura, then back again. 'I'm sorry,' her voice was barely audible, 'I didn't catch your name.'

Laura hooked her arm more tightly into Trace's. 'It's all right,' he said. The young woman retreated into the inner office.

The young man picked up the pen. 'Tomorrow then? I'll make a note of it.' His hand shook, writing it down. 'Don't worry about the cancellation, Mr Randall. We'll handle it.'

Trace shrugged. 'Thank you.'

They were moving away when the boy called, 'Mr Randall? Mr Randall?'

They swung round. 'Yes?'

'I–I'm so sorry. All of us are.'

'Yes,' Trace said. 'Well, thank you, you've all been very kind.'

Laura said, 'Oh, by the way, we'll be gone most of today, in case we get any calls.' There had been a stream of calls, telegrams of condolence, since word had reached Woodbridge and, through the competent operations of the funeral director, other towns where they'd lived.

'You won't be here for lunch then?' He reached for a pad.

'No, we ordered box lunches. We'll be hiking in the gorge.' She lifted the sack to show him the lunches neatly packed in a bag with a carrying handle.

They went to the porch where Bart and Philip waited.

'Ready?' They headed for the parking lot, their feet crunching on the gravel.

When they'd learned they'd have to stay over until tomorrow – Trace wanted to talk with the lodge's lawyer – they'd decided to hike in the gorge again. Last week they'd gone there together, the five of them, revelling in the rocks, the waterfall, the clear mountain air. 'This is the most beautiful place I ever saw in my life!' Annie had said. They remembered now. They would go back.

At the lodge parking lot they picked up their car and drove to the beginning of the trail.

Bart led the way, then Philip, Laura following, Trace behind her. The sun was bright, the air cool. The trail ran along a shallow, glittering stream. Trees laced and spiked against the mountains and the sky. In the open meadows, birds sang.

At first the trail ran through flat ground. Gradually the terrain became hillier, rockier, bent at sharp angles round high rocks. Ahead of them they saw the high cliff rising. Occasionally, they stopped to catch their breath.

Laura, watching Bart and Philip move confidently along in front of her, thought, relish these, they are what you have. Might she even forget, for a moment? The space in front of her yawned, empty.

Suddenly, the trail angled steeply up, narrowed. They heard the water thundering down before they saw it.

The trail stopped against a rock face. To their right lay the gorge, the waterfall crashing into the pool far below. Just as they remembered. Those few short days ago. To the left a narrow path led up round the huge boulder to a flat plane overlooking the gorge.

Bart turned. 'Shall we go on up?'

They nodded, and started up the steep climb, single file, holding to the rocks to pull themselves along.

They got to the top – Bart first, then Philip. 'Need a hand, Mom?' Philip held his hand out to her and she took it, climbed the last step. She turned to Trace. 'You okay?'

He was already beside her on the high table rock.

'Here?' Bart said, indicating a flat space safely away from the edge.

They sat, put their lunches aside and gave themselves over to sound and water and sunlight. The noise and sight of the water seemed an anesthesia, drawing into its sunlit plunge all anxiety and pain, losing it in the white spume of the pool far below.

Birds flew about, a few butterflies.

A single orange butterfly drifted from the high trees. Laura watched as it flew, languid and hovering, above the gorge. Slowly it dipped, circled the deep pool, rose in an upward cone and landed on a rock twenty feet from where she sat, mesmerized. It stayed a long time, its wings lifting and falling, lifting and falling, a slow blur of black and orange glittering in the sunlight. Philip turned and caught her eye, inclined his head in a nod toward the butterfly and smiled. He turned back and her mind went with him again to the preening wings in sunlight. I, too, am thinking, is it Annie, come to us?

Then the creature lifted, poised, and apparently weightless, fluid as air, arced over the haze of water and over the high rocks and disappeared among the trees. She remembered the words of the doctor. 'Maybe you'd like to leave her out here where you brought her,' and thought, if we were to scatter her ashes anywhere, I could believe in this place.

They ate their lunches and after a while, with a questioning lift of the shoulders from Bart and nods of acquiescence from the rest of them, they started back down.

On the path, picking their way along the tumbling lower stream, the terrain gentler, Laura reached out to touch Trace's arm. He was walking ahead of her now.

He turned. 'Yes?'

'That butterfly, did you notice that orange butterfly on the cliff near us? It stayed there a long time.'

'No,' he said. 'I can't say that I did.'

'How could you have missed it?' She was impatient, grieved, that he hadn't seen it.

He shook his head distractedly. 'I was thinking of Annie,' he said.

Back at the lodge, a clerk handed Laura a note. 'A telephone message for you, Mrs Randall.' She opened it. From Virginia Thayer Shaughnessy. In Massachusetts. She'd left a number. Would Laura call back?

Trace looked over her shoulder. 'Recognize the name?'

'Indeed I do. My best girlhood friend. I dated her brother a few times. I've not talked with her in years. My mother told me she'd moved back to Hadley. They'd had a family tragedy – a car accident, I think. A little boy . . .' She put a hand to her mouth. 'I'll call her.'

She dialed the number. A woman answered. 'Hello?'

'Ginny. This is Laura Randall.'

'Laura, dear! I read about it in the paper. Oh, Laura. I'm so sorry.' Her voice broke, choked off. 'Excuse me, I've been crying all day.'

'Oh, Ginny.' She had begun to sob herself. 'Does it get any better? I mean, are you all right, you and Tom?'

'Sure it gets better. But it's hell for a while.' There was a sniffle at the other end of the line. 'When are you coming to Hadley?'

'Sometime in the fall, I'm sure, to see Mother.'

'Call me, Laura. I'll meet you at the airport. Promise?'

'I will. Oh, I will!'

When she left the phone booth she was smiling. Trace was waiting. 'It was as though I saw her yesterday! We'll get together when I go to Hadley.'

'Good.'

They went to dinner. As they left, Laura said to Trace, 'I actually tasted my food!'

The next day the boys packed the car while Trace met with the lawyer. 'He was noncommittal,' he said when he came back. 'The stable is a separate operation. We went and looked at the place again. I'll speak with our lawyer when we get home. He can pursue it if it seems a question of negligence.' He took a paper from his pocket. 'I have any information we might need.'

Laura turned away in revulsion. 'Please. Not now.'

Bart opened the car door. 'Let's get out of here,' he said.

10

Driving along, Trace took in the barren landscape, his hand curling tightly round the steering wheel. Two days they'd been on the road, hours of driving through terrain newly unfamiliar as though all sights in the world would now be viewed as for the first time, and scarcely worth anyone's attention at that. The weather notable only if rain lashed across the window or darkness came early.

They'd had breakfast at a Bob Evans restaurant. The sprightly red and white, the indomitable cheeriness of the waiter seemed a detour into a surreal world. They'd scarcely spoken to one another – ordered their food, eaten in silence. He was glad to leave.

'Whose turn to drive?' one of the boys had asked.

'I guess it's mine,' he'd said. They started out, travelling through the Arkansas scrub. He'd broach the subject soon. He'd been thinking about it during the last two days, trying to find some way through the darkness that pushed into his mind, filling his brain bone to bone, so even the skin over his skull felt tight. After a while he said, 'Would this be a good time to talk about the memorial service, what we'd like to include?' After conferring on the phone with Matt they'd agreed on a service in the early evening, three days after they got home.

No one answered. He took their silence for consent. 'I know it's not an easy subject, but we have more time now than we will when we get home.'

Still, none of them said anything. The silence was

awkward, as though he had broken some tribal rule. In his peripheral vision – he kept his gaze straight ahead, on the road – he saw Laura turn and look out the window. Cars passed, going the other way. Finally Philip said, 'What do you think we should have, Dad?'

'The traditional Scriptures, certainly. Some favorite hymns. Matt will have some kind of message, I suppose.' He avoided the word 'eulogy' – that was for old people, wasn't it? With accomplishments, descendants, a long life to review?

Laura said, 'I suppose we'll want a time for people to say something if they want to.' He heard an edge of impatience in her voice. Still, she was trying to help him. He was grateful.

'Yes, that too.' He waited. He wished the boys would speak. 'Some hymns?' he said. '"Amazing Grace?" "Precious Lord"? Do you like those?'

Silence.

'They're all right,' Philip said.

'Yeah, I guess,' Bart said.

Exasperated, he said, 'It's important that we decide, and you're no help!'

The tension in the car thickened. 'I don't feel like talking about it,' Bart snapped.

'You plan it, Dad. It just doesn't matter to me,' Philip said.

He slammed his hand against the wheel. 'Well, it should matter! These are important symbols. We want a service that's helpful, that expresses something. Other people will be there too.'

A truck rumbled by. Dust from the road flew up against the windshield. 'Is it some kind of public show?' Bart's voice was scornful. 'You afraid your colleagues won't think you're doing it right?'

He felt the heat rising in his face. 'No, I'm not, I want it to be right for us. And for Annie!'

'She couldn't care less. She wasn't even going to church,' Philip said.

Laura turned in her seat. 'This is terrible!' she said. 'All

118

we've been through and as much as we need each other, we're fighting over the memorial service!'

'Who's fighting?' Trace said. 'I'd just like some help. Matt is going to ask us what we want. I'm trying to suggest options.'

'Options!' Laura burst out. 'What is this, a stock exchange? A multiple choice exam?'

Trace shot a glance at her. She was staring straight ahead, her chin thrust forward. 'Calm down, Laura. I'm just trying to start the discussion. I made a few suggestions. Is that so bad?'

'What's bad is you sound like you're planning a meeting for some board of directors.'

'Damn!' he said. 'I'm opening up the subject so we can make some decisions about the memorial service. Hymns, readings, whatever. Matt will have ideas too. I want to be prepared. What do *you* want?'

She made a strained sound in her throat and threw her hands in the air. 'I want my daughter back.'

'Join the club,' he said.

Silence hung like a dagger.

They came to a toll gate. 'Where's the ticket?' Trace asked.

'Here.' Laura produced it from the glove compartment. He paid, and they went through.

'Here.' He handed her the change. She shoved it back in her purse.

Half an hour further down the road, Philip said, 'I guess "Amazing Grace" would be okay.'

Trace felt a lump rise in his throat. 'Good. A start, at least,' he said.

Signs for Woodbridge began to appear. As they got closer, the heaviness in the car shifted. They'd get home and the shock of Annie's absence would confront them all over again. He could put it off a few minutes. 'When we get there,' he said, 'you want me to go by the post office and get the mail?'

'Sure,' Bart said. 'Might as well.'

Soon they were at the turnoff. He took the main trunkline to the center of the town, found the post office and drove into the familiar parking lot.

He got out of the car, turned to look back through the window. 'I'll be back in a minute,' he said.

The same crew stood behind the counter. One of the men was a lookalike for Joseph Heller. Trace had thought of telling him but the fellow probably wouldn't recognize the name.

He went to an open window – a clerk he didn't recognize. 'I'm picking up the mail for Randall,' he said.

The man went back, returned with a long canvas basket full of mail. The yellow HOLD card was on top. The clerk picked it up. 'You want to resume delivery? It says here hold a few more days.'

'Please, yes. We came home early.'

'Well, it's always nice to be home,' the man said. He glanced at the card again. 'Wait, there's a package.'

This time he returned with a long rectangular box. He read the label. 'That's a new one, "Strings 'n' Things" – some craft shop in Colorado.'

'I don't know,' Trace said. 'I'll return the basket.' He took it to the car, the box lying precariously on top.

'What's the box?' Laura asked.

'A craft shop in Colorado,' he said.

For a minute she looked puzzled. Then she said, her voice breaking, 'That's Annie's birthday present. The Eye of God.'

Trace turned the front door key. They went in in silence, fearful, expecting some new terror to lunge at them from behind a corner or a door. Or that the doors and windows had changed places, in acknowledgement of the dislocation of their own lives.

Astonishingly, it was as it had been. The afternoon sun laid its customary windowpane patterns on the buff and blue vinyl of the kitchen floor, eased onto the green carpet, the dark mahogany of the dining room furniture, covered now with a fine layer of dust.

For a while they wandered, each of them, from room to room, reacquainting themselves with once-familiar places.

Neighbors came. Friends called and dropped by. By mid-afternoon the kitchen was full of food – platters of red tomatoes, tureens of chicken and beef in a savory sauce with vegetables. A friend came bearing two pies, balancing them on her open hands like an ancient priest offering prayer. Another held up a large canvas bag – 'I came to get your laundry.' She brushed away tears. 'I'll bring it all back tomorrow.'

Gordon came, on his way to his summer job at Burger King. He hugged them each in turn. 'I loved her,' he said, weeping. 'We were gonna get married.'

Laura and Trace nodded. Why demur?

Leaving, he said, 'I love you guys. I'll come back.'

'Oh please do,' Laura said, touched, grateful for this slender boy who had known Annie more intimately than anyone else.

Matt came. They converged in the living room. He hugged each of them wordlessly. He brushed his hand over his eyes, his line of sandy hair. 'Can we sit down?'

Laura and Trace sat on the couch, the boys on chairs flanking the window, mottled now with shade from the maple tree on the front walk. For a moment they listened to one another's breathing, to the ticking clock. Then Matt said, 'Before we talk about the service or any of that, tell me about you, tell me about her, and about what happened.'

At first no one spoke, then Trace sat forward, 'Well, as we said over the phone, she and Bart had gone riding and I was in the lobby of the lodge talking to a colleague and I noticed a boy rush in and go into the inner office and—'

Laura stood abruptly. 'Excuse me, I'll make some coffee.'

'I'll come help you.' Philip followed her out.

In the kitchen she blurted, 'I can't bear to hear him go through all that again – that flat voice, every agonizing detail.'

But Philip was occupied with the clatter of getting down cups and saucers and didn't answer.

The coffee made, she took the tray to the living room.

'We were talking about the service,' Trace said. She passed round the steaming cups then sat down on the sofa beside him.

'Yes,' she said. 'We talked about that some on our way home.'

The next day they made trips to the airport to pick up

Trace's parents, Ron and Doris. Howard and Irene and Trace's brother were coming in tomorrow, the day of the service, and would stay with friends who'd offered hospitality. Bart went alone to pick up Paula.

In the afternoon Lillian called – 'just to talk with you a minute, Lou.' Laura had talked with her and Rachel several times, from Colorado and on the way home. To her question, 'What about Mother?' Lillian had said, 'I don't think she should go down for the service. Let her stay here with me. Wouldn't that be best? I'll come down later, dear, when the flurry is past. But for Mother, now – the least confusion tires her. And she needs a lot of waiting on. It would be hard for you both.' In a way, it had been a relief. To her mother's repeated question, 'Do you want me to come? I feel I should be with you,' she had said, needing to be strong for Rachel's sake, and for her own, 'Not now, Mother. There'll be too much going on these first days. In a week or two. Or I'll come to Hadley. I need to be with you soon.'

Trace called the funeral director. Yes, the ashes had arrived. No, they didn't want to use the facilities of the funeral home, the service would be in the church. Yes, they would come over. He turned from the phone to ask Laura, 'Can we go over now?'

She snapped a plastic lid on a box of green beans. 'Yes,' she said.

The funeral director sat behind his desk, its surface color lost in the gleam of reflected light. Beside a small bouquet of white chrysanthemums a box of tissues nested under a dark shiny cover, a tissue hoisted like a white sail.

'You have several choices,' he said. 'You can bury the ashes, of course. Do you have a plot in any of our cemeteries?'

'No,' Trace said.

'We could help arrange that. Or you could scatter them – or have them scattered. I could help you secure a permit.' He looked up, deferential, waiting.

Laura leaned forward. 'We don't want to scatter them. At least, not now. If she'd been an *old* person . . . But sixteen?' How could she tell him why they needed Annie's ashes in one place, even a marker with her name? There was so little to declare she had been here, to insist on her having lived. 'But we don't want to bury them here, either. We've only lived in Tennessee two years. We've no feeling for this ground as *home* yet.' Trace shifted uneasily in his chair but she continued, 'You see, we never expected . . .' Her eyes filled with tears.

'I understand.' The director's hand moved forward, sliding the box of tissues toward her a fraction of an inch. She took one and held it to her face.

Trace began, 'We've talked about it, my wife and I, and our sons. I guess we've not yet made a decision. Perhaps we can defer it for a while?'

'Yes, some people do that too.'

Laura appealed to the director again – surely he must be sad too. Maybe he would share the burden with them? 'Could we leave them here, with you?'

'For a day or two only, Mrs Randall. Our insurance . . .'

She looked at him, incredulous. 'Theft? Does anyone steal ashes?'

'It has happened.'

'It stands to reason they couldn't keep them here indefinitely,' Trace said.

Reason? Laura thought. What had reason to do with any of this? Still . . . 'I suppose people would never decide,' she said. In her mind she saw rows of square boxes, like shoeboxes lining the walls of the shoe store in Hadley where every fall her mother took her to buy shoes for school. Row on row. And carpeted aisles, and a brass staircase, and cylinders in vacuum tubes clanging along the ceiling.

'You could leave them here until after the memorial service,' the director was saying, his voice gentle. 'Or you could take them with you now.'

Now? Take their daughter's ashes with them in the car? When it should have been Annie herself sitting beside them? Or leave them here subject to the vandalous acts of strangers? Already Annie's ashes had passed through the hands of strangers, handled casually, maybe tossed from truck to truck or into the cargo bin of some airplane, journeys of which they had no knowledge at all. What to do?

In a panic she looked toward Trace. 'What do you think? I don't know what to say.'

He leaned forward, rested a hand lightly on her knee. He turned to the director. 'We'll take them with us,' he said.

The director nodded. 'Just a moment then.' He slid back his chair and went into a back room and Laura put her hand over Trace's, grateful.

In a moment the director came out, carrying a box, six inches square, wrapped in brown paper and tied with a cord.

Laura held out her hands. 'I'll take it.'

He gave her the box. In the upper corner of the mailing label was the name of the crematorium in Colorado.

'The papers are inside the outer wrapping,' he said.

Laura and Trace stood, moved closer together. 'Thank you. You have been very kind,' Laura said.

He took their hands. 'I have children myself.'

They walked to the car. 'You want me to carry it?' Trace asked.

'No.'

He opened the door for her and she got in.

He started the car. Laura clutched the box against her breast, remembering the time when Annie was less than two weeks old and, at her mother's insistence, she'd taken her to the doctor. 'I don't like the looks of that cord,' Rachel had said, eyeing the tiny stump, the circle of dried blood.

Annie was sicker than either of them had guessed. 'It's a general infection,' the doctor said sternly, as though Laura had done something wrong. He gave Annie a shot of penicillin. 'She'll be fine.' He shook his graying head. 'We lost these babies before we had antibiotics.'

Walking to the car, shaken, grateful, Laura had held the tiny baby so close against her chest that a woman passing by had stopped suddenly, startled, and said, 'Oh, look. She's holding a baby!'

The car slowed. They were approaching home. They had ridden in silence but now Laura said, 'I'll put the box on the shelf in her room. Is that all right?'

'Yes.'

'I don't want the ashes at the service, do you?'

124

'No.'

There was silence again for a few minutes and then she said, 'I wonder what we'll do with them, eventually.'

At first he didn't answer and she wondered if he had heard her. Then he said, 'When the time comes, I think we'll know.'

The service was to be at seven thirty. After the embattled discussion in the car they had agreed on a few songs, a reading from Scripture. Matt would give a brief meditation. A youth advisor Annie had been fond of would play his dulcimer. Some silence. Prayers. At Matt's urging, Holy Communion. 'I think you'll find it helpful,' he'd said.

In the afternoon Laura and Trace set out for church, taking with them mementoes of Annie – a poster, a photograph, a favorite sand candle, the yarn hanging they'd bought for her birthday. In the car Laura said, 'I want to stop at a florist shop and get a flower for her.'

Trace slowed the car. 'What?'

'A flower. Just one.' They had discouraged the sending of flowers, though a few bouquets had come – from the neighbors, from Trace's colleagues, from Aunt Ella and Uncle Jackson in Massachusetts. 'In lieu of flowers contributions may be made to Woodbridge Community Church.'

Annie hadn't been to church much since Philip had gone to college. Before that they'd gone together, and to Sunday evening youth meetings, parties at somebody's house, weekend retreats. From the retreats Annie would come home, radiant and preoccupied. For weeks thereafter letters would come, plain envelopes with adolescent masculine scrawl or frail pastel tissue with outlined flowers and smiling faces. But not lately. 'Church isn't for me right now,' she'd said. Still, she wouldn't mind, would she – contributions to the church?

Trace frowned. 'I thought we agreed on the memorial fund. We have several bouquets there.'

'I want to have something from us. A single flower.'

'Won't that look odd, a single flower? If we're going to do it . . .'

'Who cares? If that's what we want.'

He shrugged. 'What *you* want. It's nothing I would have done.' Still, he turned in at the mall and stopped near a florist shop. 'You want me to come with you?'

'Of course.' She was fighting back tears, as much at the emotional cost of this conversation and that they did not see eye to eye when they needed each other so terribly as, at the moment, her grief for her daughter.

In the shop the fragrance of flowers seemed all but over-whelming. A young woman approached. 'What can I do for you today?'

'We'd like a rose,' Laura said. 'A tea rose. Just one.' It was Annie's favorite rose, one of her favorite colors. Suddenly Laura had an image of Annie modelling the prom dress, her slender body turning in a flow of pale apricot chiffon.

The woman reached into the case. 'How's this?' She brought out a tea rose in a clear glass vase. Laura took it. 'That's nice.' She turned the vase slowly. The blossom was perfect, golden, tiny veins of crimson running through the petals.

She looked at Trace. His face was expressionless, no more involved, it seemed to her, than if he'd been waiting at the grocery store. 'What do you think?'

'If that's what you want.' He pulled out his wallet. 'How much is it?'

'Just the one?' the clerk asked. 'I have more in the back room.'

'Just the one, thank you.' They paid the clerk and when she returned with the change, they left the shop and resumed their journey, Laura gripping the flower and vase, wrapped now in green tissue, against her chest, and drove the rest of the way in a tense silence.

As they started to arrange their artifacts on the table at the front of the empty sanctuary – its rows of chairs, its buff walls, its easy access to the street – a small girl in rolled-up faded red pants and a striped T-shirt came in. She stood by the plain glass window, a small dark outline of head, stubby braids, shoulders, against the panorama of houses, telephone poles, the adjoining street. 'What you doing?'

'There's going to be a service here, for a girl who died,' Laura said. 'We're fixing the room.'

The child's eyes widened. She looked at the photograph on the table. 'That her picture?'

'Yes.'

'Did you know her?'

'Yes.'

The child sat down, put her hands in her lap.

A second child peered in at the door. 'Evie?'

'I'm here.'

The second child joined her friend. They whispered to one another. They appeared to be waiting.

After a few minutes Laura said, 'The service isn't going to be until tonight.'

The child named Evie asked, 'You gettin' ready?'

'Yes. We're fixing the room.'

Evie looked toward the long table. 'Ain't there going to be a body?'

Laura glanced at Trace. He held the candle in his hands, action suspended for the moment, a look of sudden panic in his eyes. 'No,' she said, and moved toward her husband.

The girls looked at each other. They shrugged their shoulders. 'Okay,' Evie said. They stood up and walked to the door, closing it quietly behind them.

Laura put her hand on Trace's arm. 'It's all right,' she said softly. They went on with their work.

Bart and Paula were in the kitchen getting supper when they got home. Approaching the kitchen, Laura went by the door of Annie's room. Panic seemed to come up from the ground. For a moment she leaned against the doorway, light-headed, her heart beating erratically. Maybe I, too, will die. Maybe this will take me away. She went on, into the kitchen. Paula looked up. 'Oh, Mrs Randall.' She came and put her arms round Laura.

They ate dinner, their conversation confined to passing food around, to the generosity of neighbors and friends. Dinner over, they dispersed to change, to clean up the kitchen.

Laura and Bart and Trace's father, Ron, were still in the

127

kitchen when Trace strode into the room in his dark slacks, his tie and summer jacket. 'Everybody ready? We should be going.'

Laura was hanging up a towel. Her hands stopped in mid-air. 'Why? It's only quarter to seven. It just takes fifteen minutes to get there.'

'The service is at seven thirty,' he insisted.

'Don't you think I know that!' Her voice rose. 'Why do we have to be so early?'

'People may want to talk with us. I want to get there.' He began to pace, his step agitated.

Ron and Bart had turned away, busy with kitchen tasks.

'I can't go yet,' Laura said. 'They can talk to me later.'

Ron Randall cleared his throat. 'There are seven of us. We'll have to go in two cars anyway.'

'Paula and I could go with Dad,' Bart said.

'Go ahead,' she snapped. 'I'm not leaving till later.'

'Suit yourself,' Trace said, his jaw tight. He stalked from the room.

By the time the second car got to the church – Philip driving, Laura beside him, Doris and Ron in the back seat – people were filling the doorway, moving into the rows of seats. They stepped back to let the family pass, their faces a montage of sympathy and grief. Laura felt hands reach out to touch her, heard voices speak her name. She saw Bart and Paula at one end of a long front row. Just behind them were Howard and Irene and Trace's brother, Theo. Trace was at the back of the church, talking to Matt. With a nod to Laura, Ron moved forward down the aisle, Doris following, then Philip, then Laura. They moved in beside Bart and Paula and sat down. 'One more?' Philip whispered and slid onto the next chair. 'A place for Dad.'

'Of course.' Laura moved over, turned to look. He was still engrossed in talk with Matt. Her throat tightened. Was he never going to join them? She turned resolutely forward. A stir beside her and Trace sat down. Their shoulders touched. In a moment he reached for her hand. His fingers lay stiff on top of hers but she did not move and he withdrew his hand and folded his hands together in the wide dark hollow of his lap.

The pianist began to play.

Laura looked down at her lap, the skirt of her best summer dress. She had made the dress two years ago, covered the buttons, made the looped closings at the jacket neck. She had bought the cloth when she and Annie were shopping. 'It's kind of dull, Mom,' Annie had said. Blue print, blue on blue. Her colors, not Annie's. A wave of regret surged close. Should she have worn something else? Maybe the yellow dress Annie liked, with the wide coral belt? Would Annie mind that she had chosen this?

She looked up at Annie's picture – the eyes slightly averted, a smile playing around her lips. Darling, she murmured and tightened her hold on her white linen handkerchief.

Matt walked up the aisle. Passing the end of the row he stopped to put a hand on Laura's shoulder, moved on.

The congregation stood to sing. 'When the darkness appears and the night draws near,' they sang. Laura had thought of this hymn when her father was so ill, and now they were singing it for Annie. 'Hear my cry, hear my call, hold my hand lest I fall . . .' Her thoughts flew back to Annie in the emergency room. Was there someone there for you, to hold your hand? What is it like, the crossing over?

They sat down. Matt began to talk. Laura scarcely listened. She remembered Annie walking toward her through the trees on one of those mornings in Colorado. She had been startled – Annie had borrowed her terry cloth swim robe without asking and she had noticed the robe before she recognized its wearer – a robe just like mine! But it was Annie.

She heard Matt say, 'So what are we to make of the death of Anne Randall? Is there some answer to the question it puts to us?' He picked up the Bible and read, 'The Spirit intercedes for us with sighs too deep for words.' She thought, that's all very well but tell me something that makes sense to me, and she listened, and watched him, and time moved without passage, a frame at a time, without attachment or continuity, only this instant of her hand on her best summer dress, only Philip's brown loafer against the rung of the chair next to hers and Trace's shoulder touching her own – they leaned ever so slightly together; only Annie's candle burning on the table by her picture and above it the yarn sculpture called the Eye of God.

The friend they had asked to sing pulled his chair forward, laid a dulcimer across his knees. 'I live one day at a time, I dream one . . . dream . . . at a time,' he sang, his voice light and clear. 'You ask how long I plan to stay, it never crossed my mind . . .' He finished the song and his voice lifted into the first notes of 'Amazing Grace'. The people began to hum, and then to sing. '. . . And grace my fears relieved,' they sang.

Matt was holding the loaf of bread. 'It is my body, given for you.' They passed the loaf from hand to hand, passed the chalice. 'For you.' Trace handed her the bread. 'For you, Laura.' He handed her the chalice. 'Yes,' she said, and dipped the bread, put it in her mouth – its taste a sweet intruder on her tongue. 'Yes,' she said, again and felt her heart lift. For this moment anyway, in this room, they were gathered close. They were held in love. They were safe.

'Will you stand?' Matt was saying. They joined hands round the room. 'Shalom,' they sang. 'I'll see you again. Shalom, shalom.' It was over.

Laura and Trace turned to each other. They embraced. They looked at one another in astonishment, for how could it be, even yet, that they should go to a service to mark the death of their child? People came forward to greet them – hugs, words of sympathy, tears – then to move on, as in a rhythm of slow dancers, past the picture of the girl, past the candle and the chalice and the single yellow rose veined with red, narrowing into green stem, resting in a blown-glass vase, the water not halfway up the glass.

They went home. Already a small crowd of family and friends waited. They went in and ate food and drank tea and punch. They spoke of the service, of how fortunate that the weather was pleasant. They stood close to one another, loathe to have this gathering over. If they could be together, they could live. For this hour at least, they had evaded despair. 'Another cookie?' 'Another glass of punch?' 'Yes, please. I'd love some.'

The phone rang. Trace answered it, whispered to Laura, 'It's your mother and Lillian.'

She lifted the phone. 'Hi.'

Lillian said, 'How are you, dear? Mother's on the other phone.'

'Darling,' Rachel said. 'We've thought of you all day long. And of Annie. Such a wonderful child. Such a wonderful daughter. How did the service go?' Her voice trailed off.

Laura steadied herself, 'It went well, Mother. We're doing okay, considering everything. How are you?'

'About the same,' Rachel said. 'I wish I was there with you. I don't know how you stand it.'

'We don't have a choice,' she said, and swallowed hard.

There was silence. 'No, I suppose not,' Rachel said. Another several seconds of silence. 'Well,' she said, 'we'll talk again soon.'

'Yes. Thanks for calling. Give our love to everyone there.'

'Love you, dear. Goodbye.'

''Bye, Laura,' Lillian slipped in. They hung up.

Slowly Laura replaced the phone on its hook, then buried her face in her hands. Oh, if I could bring it to you and put my head in your lap and you could make it all right.

Returning to the living room she heard Paula saying to a neighbor, 'I'm Paula, Bart's friend. We're going to be finding an apartment in Woodbridge.'

'Oh, is there to be a wedding?' the woman asked archly.

Silence. Then Paula, her voice bright with courage, 'No. Not now.'

Laura went and put her arm round Paula's shoulder. 'We're so grateful to have Paula here,' she said.

11

The summer began to cool. The days grew perceptibly shorter. In department store windows mannequins of children wearing plaid dresses and chino slacks carried schoolbags in their hands. The rush hour traffic thickened. The Community Symphony and Chorus began its weekly practise. The college readied itself for a new fall term.

In the Randalls' white house on Hinsdale Road the members of the family proceeded through the days and nights of early fall, each moving as they were able in lives in which the strange and the familiar danced in a delicate *pas de deux*, the score unknown, even to the dancers. They talked often with one another, walked and ate and slept in a house and a world in which the loss of their daughter and their sister was a constant presence. If for a moment they forgot, as in sleep or some occasion of delight, some excursion into fantasy or absorbing work or the gaiety of friends, the reckoning awaited them on their return. For each of them the task of learning the unacceptable absorbed much of the random energy of their lives as well as that which they offered in their search for her, their still persistent habit of knowing her. Only now it was in a mirror, glimmering, distant, that they saw her: they reached up to touch her and saw their own hands.

Gradually, Laura sorted through Annie's clothes, the textures of her daughter's life – sweaters, jeans, bikini underpants, blouses in prints of trellised flowers. Trace would take them to the collection center at the college where they maintained boxes both for the area's homeless and for overseas relief.

'Here.' She showed him three large pasteboard boxes.

'Did you save anything?' he asked, anguish plain on his face.

'Yes. In the drawer.' She opened it and showed a pair of worn, faded jeans Annie had embroidered with flowers and a setting sun, a favorite robe, a khaki fatigue hat she had worn on camping expeditions with her brothers. 'I thought we'd keep these for a while.'

He nodded, 'Good,' and turned his attention to the boxes against the wall. 'I'll take them over some day next week.'

'You could put them in the back of the station wagon,' she said.

'No, I'll wait.'

She offered Paula the hand-knit mohair sweater. 'I'd like you to have it, unless you'd rather not.'

'It's beautiful, I'd love it. You don't mind if I don't wear it for a while?'

'Of course not.' Laura hesitated. 'Would you want any of the furniture from her room? You and Bart? The dresser maybe? The waterbed?'

Paula shook her head. 'I don't think so. Thank you, though. I'll ask Bart.' She went to ask him, came back. 'He feels the same way. Thanks, anyway.'

What to do with it, this symbol of Annie's independence, her lunge into adult life?

Philip, who had been leaning against the doorframe during this exchange, suggested, 'Maybe my friend Ziggy? He's counterculture, and poor. And a nice person,' he added quickly.

They smiled. 'Good idea.'

On Saturday he drained the water, took the frame apart and put it all on the station wagon and drove off. Laura and Trace, Paula and Bart stood at the doorway watching until the car was out of sight. Back in the house, Laura ran the sweeper over the matted rectangle of carpet where the bed had been . . . *'The first time, it was in my room . . .'*

'The first time . . .' When would desire return to her life, and to Trace's? Once, still in Colorado, she had moved toward him, unsure. He did not respond. Guiltily, she had reproved herself. How can you take pleasure in your body when she is dead? But she would want me to. I must be her skin, her body, since she has none. No, you are only your own.

Since then, she had felt no desire. Had he? They had not spoken of it.

One afternoon she went to the recreation center to swim. She had not wanted to go until now. In the spring and early summer Annie had often gone with her, sharing a locker – their one padlock. They'd swim for a while, then drag lounge chairs out and lie in the sun.

In the locker room, ready to swim, she put her clothes in the locker, reached for the padlock attached to her gym bag. The combination – what was the combination? If she forgot, Annie always remembered. Laura couldn't recall the combination. What was it? Sweat broke out on her hands. She began to turn the knob slowly. Would her fingers remember? To the right first – was it 32? No, 23, then left to 15, ahead to 27. She pulled on the lock. The shank slid down, the lock fell open. She leaned against the door, her heart racing. She threaded the lock through the handle and went to swim.

The water was cold. Then the heat of her body warmed her. She swam a few lengths, lay back on the water and floated. She swam again, slowly at first, then faster, her arms cutting through water, pulling her forward, her head turning, reaching for air.

In the shower she turned the water on full. It stung her shoulders. The water sluiced over her, the cluster of shampoo foam slid over her hip bone, down her thigh. She raised her arms up into the water, felt it spray against her underarm, run down the side of her breast. She lifted her face to it, opened her mouth, felt the water against her tongue and swallowed.

When Trace came home she met him at the door. 'I went swimming today,' she put her arms up for his hug, 'for the first time.'

At night she climbed into bed beside him, moved close. She ran her hand over his hair, her finger over his eyebrow, down his nose, along his chin, slowly circled his ear. His arms were round her, his hand ran down the side of her rib cage, over the rise and fall of her hip, moved back to cup her breast in his hand, his eyes watching her. He raised himself on one arm and reached over and put his mouth on her nipple. She made a small cry. He looked up.

'I'm sorry,' she said.

'Do you want me to stop?'

'No.'

They continued, slowly. When he entered her she sucked in her breath and felt her eyes fill with tears. If I were younger I could have another baby. If I were younger I could begin all over again.

She is at the back of the church, ready to take her father's arm. The music is playing. She is wearing her mother's wedding dress. They have remodelled it for her. Standing before the long mirror in the front hall she fingered the seed pearls edging the pointed sleeve, the hand-made lace collar. Her mother sat on the floor beside her, holding the cloth in place with one hand, with the other weaving pins in and out, securing the gathers of satin. 'There, how is that?' Laura turned. In the mirror she was slender, beautiful, the cloth lying folded against her hips, the panels falling away to the floor. 'It looks fine. I like it.' Her mother sat back. 'I was a lovely bride too.' Rachel smiled, remembering. After the fitting, she helped Laura take off the dress. 'Be careful taking it off. It's old silk, it could tear.'

Now Howard has seated her mother in the front pew. He is coming back up the aisle. Laura turns to her father. His profile is incredibly dear. He is looking ahead, soberly, like a child at a recitation. At the front of the church, Trace has come in, his brother Theo with him. Lillian passes her the bouquet – white stephanotis, clusters of gardenias, starpoints of babies' breath. Beneath the flowers the bouquet handle is solid, a single column wrapped in tape. Her fingers close round it. It is thick and firm. Will it feel like this, his shaft in my hand? The flowers tilt forward. She moves her hand along the shaft, straightening the bouquet. She looks at her father. 'Ready?' They move together along the aisle. Trace is waiting. She is beside him. Their arms touch.

Now she is changing to go away. Her mother comes into

the room to help her take off the dress. As they raise it over her head the cloth tears at the seam. Her mother gasps. 'What if it had torn sooner?'

'It didn't. It lasted.'

Downstairs Trace is waiting. As she comes down the stairs his eyes consume her – the blue velveteen suit, the fine blouse of china silk.

They say goodbye to everyone and drive away. Halfway to the hotel, they stop to shake confetti from their clothes.

At the hotel the elevator operator says, 'Congratulations.' They are embarrassed. How did he know? She has slipped the corsage, detached from her wedding bouquet, into her handbag so it will not give them away.

In the bathroom she puts on her white gown, the flowing peignoir. As she comes from the bathroom, he is sitting on the edge of the bed and he stands to meet her, his arms outstretched.

In the attic she has saved her wedding dress, its seam torn. Still, she saved it, for Annie. The lovely lace collar, the seed pearls, could be used on another dress, the ring of orange blossoms circle another veil.

The ring of orange blossoms. The gold wedding ring on her mother's finger, and on her own. The broken circle of farewell, the ring of the womb broken open. The circle they moved toward in their grief . . . 'I am sorry to tell you Anne has died . . .' their arms round each other's shoulders. The empty zero and the rim of the well.

If I were younger I would have wanted him, I would have wanted them, I would have wanted her. But not this. Not to have it turn out like this.

She fell asleep, an old nursery rhyme playing through her head . . .

> Ring around the rosy,
> Pocket full of posy
> Ashes, ashes
> We all fall down.

In her sleep she moved closer to Trace.

*   *   *

Trace set the three cartons down on top of a low bookcase at one side of the college Commons and scanned the room – clusters of easy chairs, tables with reading lamps and an occasional tattered journal or student newspaper, in one corner a grand piano, on the walls the huge archetypal portraits of past presidents and deans, their features lost under the glaze of varnish. It was before eight thirty and he'd come early so he could deposit the contents of the boxes before the room got crowded. At the moment there was no one else in the Commons but he could hear a buzz of voices – returning students registering for classes in the Great Hall. They'd be through here soon, on their way to check out mailboxes, bulletin boards, all the announcements of start-up events.

But where were the repositories for used clothing? They were supposed to be in here somewhere. Strange how things could escape your notice until they became part of your agenda. When his family had had used clothing to dispose of before, they'd just put it on a shelf until the next time the Retarded Citizens' Association or the Disabled American Veterans called saying their truck would be around and would they please put anything they had in a clearly marked bag on the front porch. But this time, having sorted through the things, Laura didn't want to delay passing them on, getting them out of the house, and he could understand that.

Then in one corner of the room behind a couch he saw a couple of large brown barrels, plastic liners hanging over their rims. He pushed his boxes back on the shelf as far as they would go against the wall – they were balanced a bit precariously – and walked over to see if, indeed, those were the barrels for used clothing. By now the first stream of students was coming through the Commons, but he threaded his way through them and arrived at his destination. Yes, these were what he was looking for, one marked LOCAL and one marked OVERSEAS. Then, above the low buzz of conversation, he heard a thud and a definite 'Oh, shit!' He turned and, through the spaces in the moving parade, saw a young man in tattered jeans and long scraggly

138

hair stooping over a pile of clothing on the floor and shoving it into a box.

For a moment Trace stood, frozen. Annie's clothes! Then he pushed his way through the now swollen line. 'Here, I'll get that. My fault.' He forced a laugh. 'I didn't set that very securely, did I?'

'Not very. Sorry, I just bumped against it.' The boy looked up. On his face was the stubble of a day-old beard.

'Please, let me get them.' Trace stooped to help. 'I was looking for the used clothing barrels. I shouldn't have left these here.'

'Wow!' In his hand the boy held a blouse of crinkly multi-colored knit. 'These are nice duds. I should send my girl friend over.'

Trace smiled lamely. 'Please, let me finish. I'm sure you were on your way to somewhere.'

'Okay.' The boy dropped the handful he was holding into the box, straightened up and joined the trail of students moving into the corridor.

Trace's heart raced. He had wanted to transact this particular piece of business quickly and as inconspicuously as possible. Furthermore, he had this feeling he had almost lost Annie's clothes, lost them to some casual student who would put them on some lovely young woman and they would carry on their lives as though nothing terrible had happened. He might even, sometime, see this young woman in one of his classes or at some college event and she might be wearing Annie's clothes.

The surge of students had passed and the room was all but empty now. He took his boxes over to where the two barrels stood, each partially filled with mounding multi-colored fabric – a rough khaki blanket, a bright green sweater, a crumpled pair of men's pants. He stood back to be sure of the labels again, then upended his boxes, one by one, into the OVERSEAS barrel, nested his boxes as best he could – he would take them back home at the end of the day and put them in the attic – and went on to his office.

When he reached the office Ben Stoddard and Dave Ignatius were standing talking by Lutie's desk – she hadn't come in yet. They looked up as he approached. 'Hi, Trace,' Ben said, then, taking in the nested boxes, added, 'You're not moving out on us, are you?' his jovial face settling into a smile, his chin sinking over his bow tie.

'I sure hope not,' Dave said. 'The idea of working with Trace Randall was one reason I came.'

The remark startled Trace, took him off guard. He was touched. He liked Dave Ignatius well enough, had welcomed him to the department, but he'd gone away so soon on their trip and since he'd come back he'd had little heart, or time, for getting to know a new colleague. All of the department people had come to Annie's memorial service. He'd expected the others but was grateful that Dave and his wife had come, never even having met Annie or knowing the family well at all. In the flurry of exchanges of sympathy after the service, each of his colleagues had proferred their sympathy. 'Let me know if there's something I can do.' He'd nodded, grateful. What could anyone do? But it was nice of them to offer. Since then none of them had spoken of his loss. Nor had he. He sensed their sympathy, their diffident concern. Once he had seen Lutie wiping her eyes after they'd had some exchange about changing a classroom location or some minor administrative matter. She didn't say why she was crying, but he knew. Their reticence was to spare him. He'd have done the same thing.

He hesitated. 'As a matter of fact, I just took some of my daughter's clothes to the used clothing barrels in the Commons,' he said.

And knew he shouldn't have. Silence. No more than a few seconds. Silence. But enough to make them all uncomfortable. He should have said he'd had trouble parking, that he'd forgotten where he was going, made some joke about leaving. But not this, plunging them into this awkward moment, shock registered on both of their faces.

Ben Stoddard reached up to straighten his red bow tie. Finally he blurted out, 'You like to know things are being put to good use.'

Dave Ignatius adjusted the sheaf of papers on his hand. He moved toward his office door, his arms in his tan linen jacket clutched tightly to his sides. His lips worked, as though struggling for what to say. 'Guess I better get to work,' he muttered, and slipped through the door of his office.

Trace stood there a moment, alone, then escaped into his office. Quickly, before he could sink into a morass of gloom, he began to go over his student lists for the fall term. But the names marched in columns down the page and he kept seeing in his mind's eye the pile of Annie's clothes spilled out on the floor of the Commons and he and that young man bending over them, stumbling over each other, trying to amend the disarray.

He picked up an issue of *Parabola* but he had no heart for that either. He was about to give up and head for home when there was a knock at the door. He wouldn't have answered it except that his light was on – a giveaway for his presence.

He splayed his hand out over the computer sheets and magazine and started to stand but said, 'Come in,' and sat back down.

'Dr Randall?' A young woman stood there, satchel in hand, a long knubby pink sweater hanging over jeans, on her feet those clumsy-looking running shoes everyone wore. Blue eyes, short brown hair. 'Kate! You had your hair cut over the summer!'

'Yes, I did,' she said. She appeared shaken, her blue eyes glistened. In one hand she held some yellow registration forms. 'I was bringing these by to have you approve my class choices.' She swallowed, took another breath. 'And maybe talk about my thesis project a little. But . . .' Her voice trailed off and she stood there, tears brimming in her eyes. 'Oh, Dr Randall, I just heard about your daughter. I can't tell you . . . I can't tell you how sorry I am, how terrible that is!' Her voice, sharp, rose in outrage.

'Sit down, Kate.' He gestured toward the chair and she sat, perched on the edge, leaning forward, and with the palms of both hands wiped the tears from her cheeks. 'Ohh, I don't know what to say,' she murmured, and wiped her face again. 'Excuse me, but it's just so awful.'

He waited while she composed herself, his heart aching with an unfamiliar gratitude and yearning toward this young woman who had been bold enough to speak of his heart's pain.

'It is awful, Kate,' he said, 'but bad things happen to people. We'll get through it. We have a lot of support from family and friends.'

'I'm glad for that,' she said, her voice rough and uneven. 'It's still awful.' Her glance darted around the room, almost frantic. 'Do you have a picture of her?'

He did have a picture of the children, and one of Laura, somewhere, but they had got shoved out of sight. He stood, reaching behind books, to see if he could find them. Finally his hand struck a hard plastic frame and he pulled out the children's picture from behind a stack of *American Philosophical Reviews*. He handed it to her. It showed Annie and Bart and Philip standing together on a mountaintop, the open sky behind them.

'Here she is, with her brothers. On Mount Mitchell. We were on our way south and stopped off to hike. It was a very hot day,' he continued, hardly thinking, the words rolling out. 'There were other hikers behind us and when we got close to the top this cool wind began to blow and one of the kids overheard somebody say, "It's just like air conditioning." It was quite funny.' He stopped, uncertain, gave a faint chuckle.

Kate's head was bent, her eyes intent on the photo. 'She's beautiful.' She sighed, and handed it back to him and he put the picture on the shelf and sat down.

He saw her watching him and then she said, her brow furrowed, 'Do you want to okay these courses now, or shall I come back another time?'

'I'll do it now.' He took the pages from her, glanced at the list – they'd talked about it in the spring – Jim Bloskins' seminar in contemporary philosophy, an advanced course on Aristotle, a seminar on moral philosophy and of course her thesis tutorial with him. Quickly he signed his name on the line for Advisor, and noted that his hand shook.

She took the papers and seemed to hesitate, as though she would say more. But he stood and moved toward the door. 'We'll talk soon, Kate, and meanwhile I hope your term gets off to a great start.'

'Thank you, Dr Randall.' Again, her eyes searched his face. She turned and left.

He closed the door behind her.

Then he sat down at his desk and put his head in his hands, his shoulders in the brown tweed jacket shaking with sobs.

12

Rachel lifted the window shade to look out at the night sky. Not that she could see, from this window, any of the constellations she used to know. Without her glasses she couldn't see the stars very well at all. Or was it the time of year? Not full dark though it was almost eight o'clock. She'd gone to bed early to get away from Carlena's chatter. But she wasn't sleepy yet.

She'd stayed on at Lillian's longer than any of them had planned, almost a month. She'd been home now for more than a week. Her own bed. Her own things. Her friends to talk to on the telephone. But it was all wrong, all over again. Tears filled her eyes. Annie, that lovely spirited child, not safely home in Woodbridge with her family. She couldn't get used to it at all.

Carlena kept trying to cheer her. 'There, there, dearie. You mustn't upset yourself. Want me to get something on TV? Want me to make you a cup of tea? Why don't I get a good mystery book for you to read?' Treating her like a child, as though she couldn't see Carlena was trying to change the subject, bring up cheery talk.

She reached over and found the right bottle and took another pill. She might be groggy in the morning but she had nothing to be alert for anyway. Except more of Carlena's talk. Carlena was a good woman. But she had her limitations. Furthermore, she didn't upset *herself*. It was life that upset her. She'd lost too many people not to be allowed a little sadness. 'Old age must have its liberties,' she often

said. And the children so far away. She longed to see Laura.
Since she'd been home from Lillian's the need to see her
younger daughter was almost a bodily hunger. If she could
hold her, comfort her, maybe some of her own heartache
would ease. They should have let her go to the memorial
service. They could have managed somehow, couldn't they?
She shifted her position, trying to get comfortable, pulled
the electric blanket loose from where it had got caught under
her shoulder. There. She would call Laura in the morning.

Laura and Trace were in the kitchen when the phone rang.
Laura answered.

'It's my mother,' she whispered, her hand covering the
mouthpiece.

'When are you coming home?' Rachel asked.

'Philip's leaving in two weeks. I don't want to go while
he's here. Why don't you come for a visit?'

'I offered to before. You didn't want me.'

'Mother!' Laura protested. 'It was too frantic then. Things
are quieter now. You could see Philip before he goes, and
Trace and Bart. You and I would have some time together.'

'Bart's girl friend, Paula. Is she still there?'

Laura hesitated, not wanting, now, to get into what might
be the delicate issue of Bart and Paula. 'Yes. She's staying
with us before they – before she moves out.' She grimaced
at her own duplicity.

'Well, would I be too much? Could you take care of me?
Would I need to bring Carlena?'

'I'm sure I could, for a couple of weeks.'

'Only for a couple of weeks?' There was silence on the
other end. 'Laura?'

'This time, yes.'

'Well, I'll think about it. Goodbye.'

Laura turned to Trace, standing by the refrigerator, drink-
ing a glass of milk. 'I can't do it.'

'Can't do what?'

'Have Mother for an indefinite period. Not now.'

'You don't have to,' he said.

In the past Rachel had usually set her own schedule. A
letter would come – 'I'd like to visit you. I'll stay two or

three weeks. Is that all right?' Laura would answer yes, they'd like to have her, it would be fine.

She would come. They'd have the house shined and ready for her.

With her grandchildren Rachel was an endless source of delight. On her visits she read to them, sang songs to them. She folded the corners of a handkerchief into the center, then with a flip and a turn rocked it back and forth in a Babies in a Cradle. She taught them to knit yarn rope on a spool. She showed Annie how to cross-stitch, holding the loose end of the thread against the back of the cloth with her finger.

'Like this, Grandma?'

'Yes, that's just right.'

Ten years ago Rachel had spent three months with them, convalescing from a fractured foot. She'd fallen when they were on vacation together. 'It's a bad break,' the doctor said. 'You'll be on crutches for two or three months.'

Laura and Trace had conferred with the children. 'Come stay with us,' Laura said. 'You can have Bart's room on the ground floor. He'll move upstairs with Philip.'

They went home and when Rachel was able to leave the hospital Will drove her the hundred miles to their house. They hurried out to greet her. She was in the back seat, her heavy cast propped on pillows. They'd rented a wheelchair and they stood by as, with Laura's help, she negotiated the move from car to chair.

In the house, Trace and Will lifted her onto the twin bed by the window. She was tired from the trip, relieved to be with them at last. Her eyes filled with tears. 'It's good to be here.'

Will left to go home.

In the mornings Rachel and Laura lingered over coffee. In the afternoons Rachel rested and read. They drank tea out of the best rosebud cups as Rachel recalled old stories, old times. She told of summers in the mountains with her mother, of an ocean crossing when she was seven, of visits with cousins and aunts.

She retold stories of Laura's childhood illness, of fevers, of late-night visits from the doctors, of their all but abandoned hope for her, then the emergency surgery, the daily visits to the hospital. 'We felt you were saved for a reason,' she said.

Laura took her mother to the doctor, to the hospital for x-rays. Will made frequent phone calls. 'Stay as long as you want,' he assured Rachel. 'I miss you but I'm managing fine.' The neighbors came to visit. Laura began to long for time alone with Trace and the children. 'Is it getting too much for you?' Trace asked.

'It's partly that she's my mother. Nothing is casual between us.'

One day Rachel said, 'You're awfully good to me. I know I'm keeping you from other things.'

'I wanted you to come. I can do other things later.'

But now, with Annie dead, Laura could not re-enter that world of old securities, old stories told again and again, old adaptations.

Rachel called again. 'I think of you all the time. If I come for a visit how long should I stay?'

Laura hesitated. Surely her mother remembered. 'Two weeks,' she said. 'I'd love to have you stay two weeks.'

Her mother's tone turned querulous. 'I don't like to think of having such a definite time. What if I don't feel like coming back then?'

'You can stay an extra day or two. We won't put you out.'

Rachel was not amused. 'I took care of my mother a lot when she was old and sick.'

'I know. That was very good of you.' But your daughter hadn't just died. 'This is a hard time for us.'

'I should think you'd want to see me.'

'I do. I'd like very much to have you come, for two weeks. It's just that,' she hesitated, 'I need to take care of myself right now.' There, she had said it. She leaned against the wall, her hand clutching the phone. The blue stripes of the wallpaper seemed to slip and then straighten. I need to take care of myself. If I don't, now, I will be paralyzed in my grief for ever. Please understand.

'If you came here how long would you stay?'

'Probably about a week.'

'You stayed longer than that when Father was dying.'

'Mother! You're not dying. Trace needs me. We need each other.'

'Well, I'll think about it.'

On Friday Rachel called again. 'It's too much for me, making the trip there. If you want to see me you can come here.'

'I will. After Philip goes.'

In the weeks before Philip left, Trace plunged into his work, Bart and Paula looked for jobs and an apartment, Philip prepared to return to college. Laura attended to family and household, any vocational efforts of her own far from her mind.

One late afternoon she and Philip were in the kitchen. She was working on the seafood gumbo she had learned to cook since coming south, and he stood by the sink, in jeans and green T-shirt, fixing his special salad – a variety of greens, mushrooms, nuts, tiny orange sections.

'In a way I hate to leave you guys,' he said.

Her heart dropped. She dreaded his leaving, diminishing the family again. She looked toward him, tall under the sink canopy, his head inclined, brown hair curling at the back of his neck. 'Any special reason?' she said.

He was lifting greens out of the salad spinner. 'I worry whether you're going to be okay, you and Dad.'

It was dear of him, and like him. Since he'd been a small baby he'd been attuned to other people's moods. 'With each other, or just with life?'

'Both. You have such different ways of reacting to stuff.'

'I know.' She gave the soup an extra stir. 'Sometimes his matter-of-factness drives me crazy, the way he talks about Annie's accident.' She felt a surge of regret to be talking to Philip in this way. 'I know society makes it harder for men.'

Philip was tearing lettuce into the large wooden salad bowl. 'I have the feeling sometimes that's the only way he can keep himself from coming unglued, to keep a tight lid on stuff, put the feelings in a barrel and then just keep talking so you won't notice they're pounding away trying to get out.'

'Oh dear.' She felt tears coming on, moved by Philip's

understanding and sharply aware how much she was going to miss him. 'I, on the other hand,' she attempted a laugh, 'am a wet sponge of feeling. Touch me, and get out of the way.' She reached for a tissue in the pocket of her apron, one Annie had given her, the words 'Laura's Lunchroom' in red block letters over some disreputable-looking characters lined up at a bar. 'Oh dear,' she said again.

Philip wiped his hands on his pants, came over and put his arms round her. 'Mom,' he said. 'It's okay. You don't scare me.'

For a minute she clung to him, letting the tears come. Then she stepped back. 'What about you? Going back there. Everything different, with her gone. Everything having to be learned all over again, in new terms, almost a different language.'

Tears fell unabashedly from his cheeks. 'I don't know what it will be like. I have good friends there, close friends. I need to move on, and I love college.' He stopped and a long shudder went through him. 'But there won't be a day that I won't miss her.'

'Oh, Philip,' she said, and they hugged one another again, and returned to their tasks.

The days went by. Laura saw her husband's sadness and did not know how to help him. She loved him. But she was angry, too. Since Annie was not here she would assume Annie's anger as well as her own. Had she not told him long ago, you're too caught up in your work, they'll be gone and you'll have missed it? Had she, too, not found his preoccupation with his work infuriating? His bereavement now was for a child he had never troubled himself to know until it was too late.

She and Trace needed each other, she knew that. If they were to find any life in the future, they must find it with one another. Anything else would only compound the grief of Annie's death and they had as much grief as they could bear already. Yet nothing fitted together as it should, as it used to. Sometimes their efforts seemed only to widen the distance between them, like parabolas that swing close, travel a distance together, then veer off in opposite directions.

One evening at home – Bart and Paula and Philip had gone to a movie – she went by the bathroom and saw Trace struggling to replace a lightbulb over the mirror. The light shield was held in place by small fasteners, hard to handle. He was stretching, one shirtsleeved arm a taut extension from his shoulder. He couldn't quite reach the fixture.

'Wait,' she offered. 'I'll get the stool.' She brought it from the kitchen. 'You want me to do it?'

He stepped away, grateful. 'If you would. You know how I am with this kind of thing.'

She climbed up. She undid the delicate fasteners and passed them to him. When she handed him the light shield it slipped. 'Watch out!' he yelled. He caught it. 'You let go too soon.' His voice was harsh.

She hurled the lightbulb into the sink. It rolled around, unbroken. 'Do it yourself! I was trying to help you with your job.'

'It's not mine any more than it's yours.'

'Damn! You were doing it and I came by. I wanted to be with you. Now look!' She stalked from the room, crying angry tears. From the living room she heard him climb the stool, heard the grind of glass as he screwed the globe in place, and wished it would drop in the sink and crash. She stood up, paced into the next room. Would they never get through this – this murk of anger and mixed connections?

When the children returned from the movie, she listened to their recounting, jealous of their laughter.

They had a call from Annie's school. Her class was planning next year's annual. Was there a picture maybe, and one of Annie's poems they might use for a memorial page?

'That's very nice. Yes, we'd like that,' Laura said. She searched through Annie's work, conferred with Trace and the boys about the choice of a poem. She took last year's school picture from its frame and drove to Annie's old school.

In the office, she said, 'I'm Mrs Randall. I brought this poem and picture of my daughter.'

The clerk looked at her quickly. Her glance slipped from Laura's face. 'I'll copy these right away.'

'Thank you.' Other clerks were busy in the office. The silence hung heavy. They don't know what to say to me, Laura thought. Their silence angered and puzzled her. They could at least try, not act as though I wasn't here.

Back home, putting the picture back in the frame, she noticed a smudge on the forehead. From the school's handling? From hers? It was the only copy, their most recent picture! Frantic, she searched the house for her old set of pastel chalks, tried to match the colors, restore it. The spot still showed. She had only made it worse.

At dinner – she and Trace were alone – she told him what had happened. Her voice shook, telling him. He continued eating, lifting food to his face like an automaton. She reached for the photo she'd left on the buffet. 'Look. Can you tell? Can you see the place?'

'No.' But his eyes were veiled, remote.

'You're angry,' she said.

'No.'

'But you look so – far away. I said I'm sorry. I feel like I've killed her again. This was our best picture of her.'

'Don't be silly,' he said. 'You haven't.' But the expression on his face didn't change.

After dinner she saw him holding the picture, tilting it against the light. 'It hardly shows,' he said. He hung it back on the wall and walked away.

On Sunday they went to church. As Laura went by Matt at the end of the service, he put an arm round her shoulder. 'Hard times?' he said.

Tears welled in her eyes. 'Yes.'

'Something new come up?'

'No. Just being here. And school starting. And it's fall. I always loved fall.' She looked at him, helpless. 'I don't mind crying. I just wish I could choose when, choose the places.'

'I hope you would choose this place.'

The next day she called him. 'I'm going to see my mother soon. I'd like to talk with you again before I go.'

She went to his office. He took a sweater and some papers

off the easy chair so she could sit down. He sat in the chair opposite, tipped back against the wall of books. 'How are things?' he said. 'You're going to see your mother? How does that seem?'

'I've wanted to go. But I'm scared, too. Wondering how she'll be. She's not strong at all. How she'll be with me.'

He nodded, turned a pencil in his hand. 'You're not making any connections, are you? Wondering whether if you'd brought your mother here things might have been different?'

The question startled her. 'No, I don't think so. Maybe I haven't allowed myself to. But I haven't.'

Again he nodded. 'Just wanted to be sure,' he said.

'I do wonder how it will be between Mother and me, the first time together since Annie died. And I'm a little scared of going home, leaving Trace.'

'Is he doing okay?'

'I guess. He and Annie were having a bad time with each other. She told him he'd never paid any attention to her when she was growing up, all he thought of was his work. It was an exaggeration, but there was truth in it too.' She looked up, wondering whether to speak of her own anger. But Matt's face had taken on some extra pain and she thought of his own adolescent daughters. 'I know how that can be,' he said. 'Fathers get busy.' He set the pencil on the desk. 'How about you? What about you and Annie?'

She leaned forward, her handkerchief twisting in her hand. 'It wasn't like that at all with us. We were very close. We always had been. Oh, of course we had some tension between us. She was mature for her age, independent. We had struggles over that, especially this year—' Her voice caught, and she stopped.

'Was that hard?'

'Yes. We knew she had to establish her independence, but yes, it was hard.' Her eyes were stinging again and she blew her nose.

'Was Annie like you when you were sixteen?'

'Oh no. I was much less mature. Much less sure of myself. Not nearly so adventurous.' Her pride in Annie swelled in her voice – she wondered if Matt heard it.

'I used to see her down here with the other young people,' Matt said. 'She seemed to have a lot of self-confidence. Her maturity was very noticeable. Something else, too.'

'What was that?'

'She'd be talking to the other kids, asking them stuff. Somewhere, Laura,' he spoke slowly, 'she'd learned to care a lot about people.'

'I know. She was good at that.'

'Where do you think she learned it?'

She smiled, grateful. 'Some of it, I suppose, from me. I think I was a good mother.' Suddenly her voice broke off and she put her head in her hands, sobbing. 'But I have this awful feeling, what if she needs me? I don't want her to be scared and lonely.' She gulped in air, appealing to him. 'Matt, do you think she's all right?'

He reached over and put a hand on her shoulder and she felt some comfort from his hand run through her body. She reached up and pressed the hand into her shoulder and then she sat up.

'Laura,' he said, 'the memorial service – I've thought about it a lot. You remember the feeling there, so thick you could hold it in your hand?'

'Yes.' She drifted back into the memory of it. 'It was almost as though nothing could ever go wrong again, as though whatever could happen, it would be all right.'

'Yes,' he said. 'A very few times in my life I've had that feeling. To me those times are like promises, premonitions, if you will. I don't go for the streets of gold, the heavenly choirs,' he shook his head and chuckled. 'I've been a minister too long for that. But the feeling in the room that night,' his brows drew together, remembering, and his hands rested, quiet, in the hollow of his lap. 'If it's anything like that, then Annie . . .'

She nodded, tears streaming down her face. 'Then Annie's okay, isn't she?' Images of the child in the night came to her.

'Scareyitis?'

'Yes.'

And an older memory, of herself standing in the dark by her mother's bed, waiting for her to waken.

'I got scared of the shadows. The walls were creaky . . .'

'Climb in with me a few minutes.'

When she went back to bed, the shadows on the walls would be lovely pictures and the sounds of night friendly company.

'There are some lines from Emily Dickinson,' she said, though by now it seemed only an afterthought. '"Parting is all we know of heaven, and all we need of hell."'

'Sure,' he said. 'There's that. But sometimes I can believe more than that. That night was one of those times.'

'Me too,' she said. But then, 'You don't think,' it was her reservation, she had to tell him, 'we're deluding ourselves because we want so much for it to be so?'

He leaned forward, hands cupped together. 'No, I don't. That's like saying because I'm hungry there mustn't be any food.'

She sighed. 'That's nice. I like that.' She sat back for a minute and closed her eyes. Then she moved forward in the chair. 'Thank you, Matt.' She got up.

He stood, put his arms out and they embraced. 'When you go, you don't go alone,' he said.

'I know. Sometimes I even feel she's with me.' Her chin moved against his shoulder.

'That feeling's a gift too. Believe in it.'

'Thank you,' she murmured again.

'Thank you for coming.'

At home she told Trace, 'I went to see Matt. We had a long talk. He was very helpful.'

Trace was reading the paper. 'Mmm-hmm,' he said. 'Good.' He didn't look up.

She went to him, tore the paper from his hands. 'Did you hear me? He was very helpful.'

His face whitened in astonishment. 'Of course I heard you. I'm glad Matt was helpful.' He looked down at the paper, peaked on the floor. 'What do you want from me, Laura? Do you want to tell me about it?'

'Some human feeling, that's what. You're so damn distant! I tell you something that obviously has a lot of emotional weight for me and you go on as though I was a radio announcer telling the weather!'

'Distant?' he shouted. 'Every time I make a move, make a suggestion, I feel like you slam doors in my face.'

'That's crazy,' she said. 'Like when?'

'Well, in the car on the way home, for one,' he said. 'I was trying to get people to talk about what we wanted for Annie's memorial service and all I got was icy put-downs, as though I had no business asking, had butted in on someone's private preserve.'

'It was all so academic, Trace. We didn't want to talk hymn choices. We wanted some expression of feeling.'

He jumped out of the chair now and began to pace. 'Feeling! I try to express a feeling and you overwhelm me with yours. I can't compete with your grief. I have my own grieving to do. I can't always be sucked into the quicksand of yours. Sometimes I feel we'll all drown in the quicksand of your grieving.' He paused, his face white and still. 'Now, do you want to tell me about the visit with Matt?'

'Are you kidding? After that? No, I don't. I wouldn't want to subject you to any unnecessary emotion.'

'You can skip the sarcasm,' he said through clenched teeth. 'Believe me, it's counterproductive.'

She left the room, shaken, hollow at the pit of her stomach. Not only for her mother's sake but for her own, and Trace's too, she must get away from here for a while. Next week, when they all drove Philip to college, she'd fly on to see Rachel.

13

It was Philip's last night at home. Laura and Trace, Bart and Paula and Philip went out to dinner. They talked about the weeks ahead. Bart and Paula were excited about moving into their own place. They'd be all settled by the time Laura came back from visiting Rachel. They'd found an apartment, the first floor of a large frame house close to the school where Bart would be teaching junior high social studies, a position he'd acquired almost at the last minute when the previous teacher needed an earlier than anticipated maternity leave. Paula would use their car for her job doing home interviews in the town's social service network. Philip talked about his return to college. He was going to be taking courses in urban planning and joked about being at a college surrounded by dairy farms – 'crowd behavior in a cattle barn,' he said. Laura spoke about her wish to return to art projects. She had that assignment to complete for the Walter Stone Company and later might take a course at the college.

After dinner they came back and sat in the living room. Bart and Philip told high school stories – how the advanced placement history teacher's hearing aid went out of commission and how the students, knowing this, would stand to recite and mouth words with no sounds. They told of study halls with poker games in the back rows and of an exasperated teacher screaming, 'Piss pot!' at a disruptive student. Paula, who'd gone to private school, a more decorous setting, gasped in horror as the boys recounted their adventures.

Then the jokes and stories tapered off. The knowledge that this was their last night together seemed to settle over them all.

'I hope you guys write me,' Philip said. 'I'm going to miss you.'

'We'll come up,' Bart said. He sat on the sofa with his arm round Paula. 'We'll all come for the weekend.'

'Good,' Philip said. 'But wait till I invite you.' They laughed.

All during the evening Trace had said little. Now Philip turned to him. 'How about you, Dad? How are you going to be?'

He was sitting back in the blue corner chair, his face half in shadow. At first he appeared not to have been listening. Then he said, 'Oh, I'll be fine. As soon as my classes get underway. Except . . .' He brought the tips of his fingers together unsteadily. They waited.

'Except what, Dad?' Philip said gently.

'Except,' his voice shook and he seemed to inhale sharply, 'I wish things had been better between Annie and me.'

There was a murmur of assent and then they were silent in the face of his vulnerability, honoring his pain, the helplessness any of them felt at the irretrievability of lost time, of opportunities to be, again, what any of them would have wanted to be to their daughter and their sister. Laura, listening in the silence, closed her eyes, felt her compassion move toward him, hover, pull back, felt the memory of her daughter's anger, and her own: wait, it was a long time coming.

At college, they helped Philip carry in his things. In the cindery driveway, they stood in a circle, on the edge of leaving. 'Remember, come and see me. I'll write you.' He hugged them, each in turn, his eyes bright. He left first, going off toward the campus center. At the bend of the path he turned to wave.

At the hotel by the airport, Laura and Trace got out. They would stay overnight before Trace went on to a meeting in Chicago and Laura went on to visit her mother. 'We'll see you back in Woodbridge.' Bart and Paula drove off.

In their room, Laura threw herself face down on the bed,

exhausted. Trace stretched out beside her. 'How are you?' he asked.

'Tired.'

'We've been through a lot these last days, Philip leaving.'

They rested, and after a while he began to move his hand over her shoulders. At first it felt only soothing, then she began to awaken, the surface of her body first, then deep inside her the desire for him opened slowly, like a flower, and she turned over and drew him down. His eyes questioned, wanting to be sure, and she nodded, yes. This time it was she who unfastened his shirt, loosened the buckle of his belt. They moved to one another. On the nightstand the sweep of the minute hand went round and round and over the bed a pair of fauns danced on a muted tapestry in a gold frame that glittered in the slanting light of late afternoon.

They lay against one another for a long time. She sighed deeply, content. 'I wondered if it would always be sad for me, thinking of her,' she said, her voice light. 'It wasn't, not at all,' and she lifted herself on one elbow and kissed him again.

They got dressed and went down to dinner, past the coffee shop, to the dining room with its dark panelled walls and candles flickering in columned glass shades.

A small combo played for dancing, and after dinner they got up and danced, drifting in one another's arms. Laura raised her head. 'Do you remember our wedding night, dancing in the hotel after dinner?'

'Yes.'

She recalled leaning into him, tense, wondering, the corsage of white gardenias quivering on the shoulder of her velvet going-away suit.

'So much has happened,' she said.

He acknowledged it. 'Yes.'

They danced a while longer, then returned to their table and drank the rest of their wine. 'Ready?' he said.

They went upstairs and made love again and went to sleep. In the morning Trace flew to Chicago and Laura flew to Massachusetts to see her mother.

Virginia Thayer would meet her at the airport.

* * *

The plane began its descent over the Connecticut Valley, the golds and reds of trees mingling in a blurring haze of flame, the river a dark band, its current hidden beneath a surface that seemed ageless and still. On either side of the river lay a fringe of trees, then barns, the broad brown fields of rural Connecticut, the fields and towns of western Massachusetts.

Laura sat forward in her seat. Home. Every fall she got homesick for New England, tried to make a trip. One October she'd driven here with Annie, driven through tapestries of red-gold trees, through the smell of Concord grapes and apples heaped in baskets along roadside stands.

Every summer she and Trace came with the children who, as they got close to their grandparents' home, would call out the familiar places – 'The ice cream store. The lookout tower! The school Mom went to.' Arrived, they'd spill onto the grass. Rachel and Will would hurry from the house. 'Well, here you are!' Hugs all round, then the children would run through the house and yard, finding favorite places – an attic stairway that pulled down from the ceiling, the sleeping porch high among the elm branches, a window seat in the upper hall beneath whose hinged lid a cache of treasures awaited, including an old stereopticon and attendant pictures, boxes of dominoes used for building a snaking parade which when touched with a finger would fall in a rippling chain reaction.

The wheels touched down. The plane roared along the ground and stopped. People got up and began moving into the aisle.

Inside the terminal Laura walked down the ramp. Near the electronic arches a crowd waited. 'I'll be wearing a tan trenchcoat and a red scarf – RED BADGE OF COURAGE,' Virginia had said. 'As you pass me I'll hum "Londonderry Air".' Over the phone they'd laughed. As adolescents, they'd read a book in which spies in trenchcoats hummed songs outside the gates of foreign embassies; it was always raining. 'I'll know you,' Laura said.

But it had been a long time. She scanned the crowd. An arm shot up, waving a red scarf. She started to run.

'Ginny!'

'Laura!' Their arms were round each other, Laura's chin over Ginny's slim shoulder in the tan trenchcoat. They stood back, holding one another at arm's length.

'I don't believe it!' Laura said.

'You look wonderful!' They both said it, and fell against each other again.

'Let's get your bag,' Virginia said. 'Have you had lunch?'

'No. Coffee. Three times.' Laura laughed again.

'Can we stop on the way to Hadley? Or do you want to get right on to your mother's?'

'Let's stop. I talked with her last night. She's not expecting me till mid-afternoon.'

They got the bags and the car and worked their way out of the airport cloverleaf onto the road toward Hadley.

'Do you remember Van's, the hangout after dances?' Ginny waved toward a large building advertising china and glassware at wholesale prices. 'That's where it was.'

'I came only once, with Alex Barlow, after a senior dance. Only he was a junior.' She went on, remembering it all. 'I liked him all right. He invited me and I wanted to go but I was embarrassed to be seen with a younger man. Then we won the Spotlight Dance.' She broke into a laugh. 'I was mortified.'

'We had fun, though, in those days,' Virginia said.

'Yes, we did, Though I always felt just on the edge of social success. It looks all right to me now, looking back.'

Virginia slowed the car, turned off the road to a low colonial building, a long white porch with a row of pillars and a huge plaster cow straddling the peak of the roof. 'No class,' Virginia said, 'but it's the old Dutchland Farms. They still have good food.'

'I remember. Hot fudge. In your own pitcher. I brought Annie here once.' In spite of her intention, her voice broke.

'Would you rather somewhere else?'

'No, this is fine.'

In the restaurant they ordered salads and coffee. Laura leaned back in the chair, studying Virginia. She had been an 'Irish beauty', black hair, clean skin, blue eyes. Now gray tendrils curled forward onto her cheekbones. The rest of her hair was dark, drawn back into a coil at her neck, the line of her cheek still taut, a strip of pale rouge under the cheek-bone. Her eyes picked up the blue of a lapis-lazuli necklace knotted against a white cashmere shirt. Rust-colored lipstick – Virginia had always been able to keep her lipstick on. Chic was what Virginia was. Slender. She always had been. Both of them had been thin as poles; they'd had names for each other – 'Ginny McSkinny' was Virginia's. 'You do look wonderful,' Laura said.

'So do you. God, it's good to see you. I've thought about you these past couple of months. Ever since I read about it. Ever since we talked.'

Laura nodded. She could feel her eyes begin to smart. Their salads came, and the coffee. 'I want to talk about it,' she said. 'But first tell me about you and Tom. I feel so far behind on news of you.'

Virginia told about moving back to Hadley, a year ago. 'That time I saw your mother?'

Laura nodded.

'She gave me your address and I lost it.'

'She told me about your visit. I'd not known about your Tommy, until then. I wrote you, asked Mother to send it on. Even though it was so late, years late. Did she?'

'It doesn't matter. Maybe it got lost. We were coming and going so much in those early weeks.'

Laura stretched out her hand. 'I'm sorry, about Tommy.' She hesitated. 'I'm afraid this brings it all up again for you.'

Ginny nodded, her eyes bright. 'Thanks. Still, it's nothing like it was, like it is for you.' She paused, then went on, 'I kept thinking I'd call your mother and find out when you were coming for a visit. We were away when your father died. I somehow missed learning about it.'

They talked on. Virginia had lived in New York, then Boston. Then Tom thought he could conduct his business from a smaller town. 'Less frazzle,' she said. 'And with the Interstate he can get to Boston in an hour and a half. We love being back.' Several years ago she'd gone into advertising, writing copy, thinking up catchy slogans for companies. 'I do it freelance. My latest project was helping push a new soap product.' Virginia wrinkled her nose. 'Mrs Clean, that's me. Not the greatest social usefulness, perhaps. But

I love what I do.' She picked up the water glass, drank, put it down on the mottled beige of the table top. 'What about you? Any yen to get back into art, stuff like that children's magazine? At least I knew what you were doing after college.'

'A little. I haven't been able to think about it much.' She felt her heart race; she would put it off a little longer. 'Your family? You have, what? Three other children?'

'Three daughters. Linda and Jane Anne have government jobs, in Washington. Susie is halfway through Wellesley.'

Laura told her about Bart and Philip, how Philip was in his second year of college. 'Your children are a little older than ours,' she said.

'Tom and I married right out of college. We had Tommy right away.' Virginia looked up, acknowledging. They had come to it.

'He was the oldest?'

'Yes.'

'Trace and I talked about that, how it would be a different loss, the oldest one.'

'Yes, it was as though we'd lost ground, had to start over.'

'And with us, we got there too soon, to our time alone.' She had been turning her glass in her hand and she put it down suddenly and reached in her purse for a handkerchief. 'I wasn't through yet!' Her voice was harsh. She blew her nose. 'Sorry,' she said.

'Why?'

'I don't want to blither all over the restaurant.'

Virginia's look was tender. 'I suppose they're going to have to get canoes to get the people out?'

Laura laughed. 'Sure.' They had finished their lunch. 'Can we go? We can talk in the car.'

On the way out she remembered something. 'Tell me about Fred.'

'My brother? Oh, sure. I forgot you'd dated him.'

'Just a couple of times. I had quite a crush on him, actually. But he was two years older and there was *lots* of competition.'

Virginia sighed. 'Fred's had quite a saga of his own. I think he's doing all right. He comes through town from time to time. I'll tell him you asked about him. He'll be pleased.'

The idea of Fred Thayer's caring a whit about her inquiry, even remembering her, distracted Laura but they had reached the car by now and got in, and the thought of Fred stayed outside in the open parking lot, the breezy sunshine of a fall afternoon.

In the car Virginia opened the windows and let the cool air blow over them. For a while they rode in silence, except for sounds of the moving car, of leaves skittering along the roadside. Then Laura closed her window partway and turned to Virginia. 'I'd like to ask you some things.'

'Sure, go ahead.'

She took a deep breath. For weeks she had made lists in her mind. What was the hardest part? When did it get better? Did she have anything to recommend about what they should do, how to go about helping themselves heal? Other questions. Did she believe in life after death? Did she have any feeling of being in touch with her child? What had Tommy's death meant to her relationship with Tom? There were things she wanted to tell Ginny, too, about the closeness of friends, the memorial service, how wonderful the boys had been, and Matt, and Paula, and how there had been, well, portents, somehow, of Annie's early death. And about Annie herself, what a wonderful daughter, what a wonderful person, and with none of the problems of lack of self-confidence that had plagued Laura's adolescence. All these thoughts came tumbling over one another, jostling against each other like a crowd coming out of a movie, and she saw the image of her daughter, her brown eyes laughing, her hair round her neck, her long legs striding up that path on the Colorado mountainside; Annie on the couch with Roger's foot in her lap, her hand passing back and forth over his ankle, Annie's tenderness after Will's death, coming to put her arms round her – 'Mom, I miss Grampa too.' The image shifted. The crowd coming from the movie – they were all sixteen years old and they all had Annie's face and beyond them the sidewalk and the streets were empty of people and cars went back and forth, black cars, old, never stopping, and the road was covered with rain.

'Ohh!' She uttered a long shuddering cry and sat back

against the seat cushion and put her hand over her face and pressed the heels of her hands against her cheekbones. 'Oh Ginny! Sometimes I wish I were dead!'

She felt, then, Ginny's hand on her arm, steadying, calm, as the car continued to move through the October afternoon. 'It's all right, babe. It's all right, Laurapolora.'

14

The car stopped in front of the familiar house, the white clapboards – Will had resisted aluminum siding. 'I want wood,' he said – the green shutters, the porch, the flagstone walk. 'Do you want to come in and say hello to Mother?' Laura asked.

'Not now. I'll come over some afternoon,' Virginia said. 'I want you to meet Tom, too. If your mother goes to sleep early you could come for a drink.'

They got Laura's bag and set it on the grass, hugged one another. 'Call me.' Virginia's gaze probed Laura's face. 'For anything. We'll talk.'

'I will. I want to. Thanks.' She picked up the bag and started for the house, up the walk, onto the porch, its lattice sides covered with honeysuckle vines. She didn't hear Virginia drive away.

The inner door was open. She opened the screen door, went in and put her bag on the oriental rug in the hall. 'Hello?'

Carlena hurried from the kitchen, gray hair in bunches round her face, one of Rachel's aprons, too long for her, covering the front of her squat shape.

'Laura!' she said, a loud whisper. 'I didn't hear you come. Your mother's asleep.' They kissed one another. Carlena held on to Laura's hand. 'How are you, dear? I'm so sorry. I pray for you. Every night I say a rosary.'

'Thank you, Carlena. We're doing okay.' She could feel

tears start. 'I'll just go look at Mother, then take my things up and unpack.'

'Let me.' Carlena picked up the bag and started up the stairs.

Laura shook her head. 'You'll spoil me,' she said.

She went on through the living room, round the corner into the dining room, now Rachel's bedroom as well. Her bed sat in the alcove under the window, beside it a table with a tray of medicines, a glass, a pile of books and magazines. Around the mahogany bedpost wound the cord of a heating pad and the extension line of the telephone Rachel always kept close at hand. It lay on the blanket, like a toy phone slipped from the hand of a sleeping child.

Rachel was asleep, the collar of her paisley robe turned up against her hair. Her face was toward the window, the rise of her cheekbone visible. Beyond the window the leaves of sassafras trees and lilac bush moved in the gentle air, the pullied clothes line travelled into trees.

'Mother!' The word came involuntarily. Rachel didn't stir. Her mouth was open. She was snoring. She would hate that, or would have before her health began to fail and all barriers of privacy and reserve slowly eroded away.

Then, with a loud intake of air, Rachel turned. She opened her eyes.

'Mother!' Laura leaned over, her hands on her mother's shoulders.

'Darling!' Rachel blinked, her eyes focusing, her tongue coming forward to lick her lips. 'When did you come? I didn't hear you.'

'A few minutes ago. Virginia brought me.'

'Virginia?' Rachel looked uncomprehending.

'My friend, Virginia Thayer Shaughnessy.'

'Oh, yes.' Rachel looked around the room. 'Where is she?'

'She dropped me off. She'll come back another day and see you.'

'I'd like to see Virginia.' Her voice was still thick. 'Did you have a good trip?'

'Yes, it was all right.'

'How was the weather?'

'It was fine.'

'It's been nice here, too. Though I don't get out much.'
Rachel shifted her weight in the bed. She drew in her breath
and grimaced.

'Something hurt?' Laura asked.

'Arthritis. It aches all the time.' Rachel's sigh hung
between them like a loose tether. 'Carlena?' she called.

Carlena bustled to the door. 'Yes, dear? I know, it's time
for your medicine.' She went back to the kitchen, returned
with a glass of water, uncapped one of the bottles on the
bedside table and shook out a pill. 'Here you are, easy now.'
Rachel raised her head. Her hair, flattened from lying on
the pillow, stood away from her head like a stringy brown
halo. She swallowed and, looking at Laura, smiled wanly
and fell back on the pillow. 'Would you like some tea? Carlena can make some.'

'Yes, but I can do it.'

Carlena was already running water into the kettle. 'You
visit with your mother,' she called over the sound of the
water. 'She's been counting the hours till you came.'

Laura sat back against the hard wooden chair. 'How are
you, Mother?' She said it calmly but panic gathered in her
chest. Why all this chatter? When would her mother speak
of Annie?

Rachel sighed. 'I'm not at all well. That fall I took – I still
feel it. The angina acts up. But Carlena takes care of me.
We get along. The doctor comes every week or two. I talk
on the phone.' Her hand moved toward the phone, then
moved away. 'I can't get out much, you know.' She looked
out the window. 'Of course I haven't driven for a number
of years. Father didn't think I should.'

'Of course not. Not lately.'

'When the insurance comes due I'll probably sell the car.'

Laura swallowed, struggled for breath. She'd come
expecting solace for her heart's pain. Her mother spoke of
insurance. A feeling as of a lost child beset her. If her ulti-
mate haven failed, what then?

'Laura dear,' Rachel spoke slowly, 'I am not unmindful
of Annie.' Her face crumpled and she turned away.

'Mother!' Laura pressed her cheek against Rachel's,
the salt of Rachel's tears on her lips, slipped her fingers

between her mother's, felt the ridges of rings – the gold wedding band, the diamond solitaire, her grandmother's wedding ring. 'Mother,' she said again. Then, seeing a handkerchief on the pillow, she wiped her mother's tears and then her own and sat back.

They looked at one another, a sudden awkwardness between them. They had waited so long to be together and now, what was there to say?

It was Rachel who spoke first. 'Did she go quickly?'

'Oh, yes.' Had they not even told her *that*? Or had Rachel forgotten? 'She lost consciousness right away. She never came back.'

Her mother's hand in hers relaxed. 'So she didn't suffer. I'm glad about that. I've wondered.'

Laura shook her head. 'I'm sorry we didn't tell you before. I thought we had.' It was bad enough, even knowing. She had gone over it and over it, deciding each time to believe what the doctors had told them – in a fall like that, it is the first blow. But to have wondered all these weeks . . . 'No, she didn't suffer.'

Rachel nodded. 'I've thought of something else.' She looked down at the ridge her legs formed under the rose-colored blanket. 'She didn't have to get old and sick.'

Carlena brought in the tray with tea, the rosebud cups, a plate of cookies.

'Oh, look,' Rachel said, 'Carlena made us tea. Thank you, dear. That was nice of you to think of.'

Laura looked at Carlena, alarmed. 'Will you have some with us?' She picked up a cup.

'Not this time, dear. You be with your mother. I got work to do.'

Laura poured the tea. 'Can you sit up?' Rachel propped herself on an elbow and with Laura's help swung her legs in flowered flannel pajamas so she could sit on the edge of the bed. She reached for the teacup. 'Let's see, what day is this?'

In a few minutes Rachel's eyelids became heavy. She lay back and dozed. Laura gathered the tea things and took them to the kitchen. Carlena stood by the sink, holding a potato under a stream of water.

'How's Mother doing?'

'She's good today,' Carlena scraped the potato with a knife. 'Some days she's not good at all. She's much better with you coming. You're sure good for her, I can tell you that.'

'Oh, Carlena.' Laura's hand slipped on the tray she was holding. The question asked itself again, should I have taken her with me? The images of Rachel's hurt and anger last spring came flooding toward her. 'Is it a lot for you, caring for her?'

Carlena laid down her knife. 'You couldn't have done it, you girls. It keeps me hopping. She wants a lot, your mother. She's got a heart of gold. But she wants a lot of attention. Get me this. Get me that.' She shook her head. 'You couldn't have done it.'

Grateful, Laura put her hand on Carlena's shoulder, as though acknowledging the transfer of weight that had already taken place. 'Do people come by?' she asked.

'The neighbors drop in. But they forget. The minister comes. Your Aunt Ella and Uncle Jackson come – they're awful good to her. But they don't do things the way she likes.' She held the potato under the water again. 'Tell you the truth I can't blame her. Ella comes in, she talks on and on. Your Uncle Jackson, he sits in the corner and snoozes. She thinks they'll never go home.' Carlena put the potato in the pan of water and picked up another one. 'She misses your father. She can't get used to it, and you, Laura, she's so sad for you.'

Laura went upstairs to unpack. Instead she lay down on the bed and closed her eyes.

Her childhood room. Her bed. Her bookcase and closet. Lillian's bed next to hers, for all the years except that one when she was sick and they wouldn't let Lillian stay because she might catch it. And they left her here, alone, her neck so sore she couldn't move to sit up, couldn't even turn her head.

Her illness. She'd heard the story so many times – stopped on the street corner when she and Lillian are out shopping with their mother. 'Which was the one?' Her mother's posture shifts. She moistens her lips, her shoulders settle back. 'This one,' she says.

It slows them up. She gets tired of waiting. She looks at the shoes in the store window, on one side satin shoes with silver buckles and high heels, on the other side the sturdy shoes with laces they always have to get for school. Some day, when she grows up . . .

Her mother is telling the story. 'When they took her to the hospital we thought she'd never come home. Her heart couldn't stand a general anesthesia, they had to use a local. We heard her scream.'

At this part Laura cringes inwardly. She does not remember. She remembers other things that can't have happened, memories of doctors sharpening knives like the knife her father used to cut the Sunday roast.

Over and over she has played the scenes through to herself, trying to find the missing parts. Why can't she remember? She remembers some things. Her baby brother, playing there on the foot of the bed, his tiny feet making bumps in his nightgown. Remembers the evenings after they've given her her supper and gone back downstairs and she hears them laughing, and wonders when anyone will ever come upstairs to be with her again. Remembers cutting out those paper dolls and folding the tabs of purple dresses down over the shoulders of girls with wavy yellow hair and standing them against the pillow and pretending they were children to play with.

Her mother is quoting the doctor from Boston. 'You realize that child has no right to be alive.'

How it has all stayed with her, colored her childhood, turned to what it couldn't have been, like the memory of the knives and the operating room. How she capitalized on it, back then. Telling her friends when they talked of ballet and elocution and she needed something to make her a star. 'I almost died,' she said.

Their attention turned to her. She had won a place, competed with the girl with the perfect golden curls.

And with Lillian, her ebullient older sister, a sparkling, precocious child. 'Still waters run deep,' Rachel said, characterizing her quieter second daughter. 'A blessing too – such a good child. When she was so sick she did just what they told her. If she'd acted up, if she'd fought them in the operating room . . .' The message was clear: to fight is to die.

There was another message, too, from those months of recuperation, which Laura had believed with all the fervor of her childhood passion, her terror at the pain and separation from home: it was Rachel who had saved her, Rachel alone who could keep her from dying. From her bed by the hospital window she would watch for Rachel's tall figure to emerge from the bordering grove of pine trees – 'My mother is coming!' Rachel who brought her comfort, love, assurance of life in the loving hands with which she held her close, soothed the fevers from her body with cool washcloths, her hands a blessing. 'Savior, like a shepherd lead us,' Rachel sang, her voice soft and clear, sweeter than any birdsong, 'much we need thy tender care.' At last she would drift off toward sleep, Rachel's hand a blissful assurance of life.

Laura sat up. Why did she think of it all now? Was it just that on this, her first time home since Annie's death, the ghosts of this room returned? Or was it more? When Rachel had announced she wanted to come and live with them and Laura, in desperation, had said, 'Mother, I'm sorry. I can't,' Rachel had reminded her, 'I took care of you when you were sick,' and then, 'You'd never have made it without me.' An unspoken contract reneged on? A debt flouted, unpaid?

That she had recovered was Rachel's validation, too. Rachel who had cared for a sickly mother and could never make her well; she had died aged seventy after years of being a semi-invalid. 'My angel mother,' Rachel would say. 'You're named after her, you know.' Laura, who remembered her grandmother only as a saddening shadow that drew her mother away from her.

It was an intricate business, this legacy of mother to daughter. There had been other things, too, from that hallowed, frightening, grace-filled time. 'We feel you were saved for a reason,' Rachel would say.

Although at times it seemed a burden – who could be

worthy of such a miraculous reprieve? – she had cherished the promise. When she grew up, she would marry, raise children, as her mother had. It was always her wish.

She had done it, too, been a wife, and a mother. 'Saved for a reason'? That was reason enough while the children were small.

There was another reason, something else she'd dreamed of being.

She went to the closet, drew from the high shelf a large white box, set it on the bed and removed the lid. Inside were tubes of paint, pencils, some sketchbooks and loose pages, the blue metal paintbox her parents had given her when she was eight. She took out the paintbox, opened it to reveal the bright coins of color – red, green, yellow, blue – the brush, its black point stiff, lying in the channel beside them. The white enameled lid was grooved to hold puddles of water and paint. The paintbox and sketchbooks had been companion of many Sunday afternoons as she sat at the dining room table, oblivious of the sounds of family in the next room or of the thickening dusk. 'That's lovely, dear,' Rachel would say, standing over her shoulder watching her paint flowers on a fluted fan, or pastoral scenes with trees and a hill and a path winding along the hill. Maybe a house or a few animals, stick figures of children playing in the yard. Basking in her mother's approval, she had said, 'When I grow up, I'm going to be an artist.' Sometimes, heroine in her own drama, she would stand in front of her bedroom mirror and, blood tingling with the possibility of creating worlds, say it to her own reflection, 'When I grow up, I'm going to be an artist,' and she would turn her face this way and that, observing how shadows changed at different angles, how the bridge of the nose obscured the corner of the eye, how one side of the mouth foreshortened as she turned her head to the side.

Wryly, she stood up now and went to this same mirror. But what she saw wasn't the wide-eyed child who'd found in her own hands and in her mother's blessing the vision of a future worthy of a fateful beginning, but a middle-aged woman, her face drawn, deeply shadowed, eyes swollen from mourning for a dead daughter. Startled, her voice harsh, she asked of the face in the mirror, 'Is this it? Is *this* the reason you were saved?'

Rachel sat propped against a pillow in her chair at the end of the table. They had finished dinner. Carlena was busy clearing up the kitchen.

'Is Bart serious about Paula?' Rachel asked.

'Yes, he is,' Laura said.

'Are they going to get married?'

She hesitated. She'd like to tell her mother about their living together, but how would Rachel take it? 'I don't know.'

They moved on to other things – Rachel's friends, the visits of Ella and Jackson, the pattern of Rachel's days. 'I read a lot,' she said. 'I like a few things on television. I go to bed early.'

'Do you sleep the night through?'

'No. I wake too early.'

'Then why go to bed so soon?'

Rachel looked off at the black glare of the window. 'I get tired. There isn't much to do.'

When her mother fell asleep, Laura went upstairs, began putting clothes in drawers and closet.

In the back of the closet she came upon two old prom dresses. The rose lace – that had been a favorite. She slipped it from the hanger, held it against herself and swirled once round the room. There was another favorite, aqua taffeta with tiers of ruffled skirt. Useless to anyone as hand-me-downs, they had stayed here for the 'dress-up' play of visiting granddaughters – Annie and her cousins.

At first Annie had loved putting on the dresses, asking Laura to tell her about the parties, the boys who accompanied her when she wore these glamorous clothes. She would listen, eyes wide, then hoist the dresses up so the long skirts didn't drag, parade around the house, the tarnished chain-link purse hanging from her wrist.

The last few years the dresses had hung unused. The questions about Laura's adolescent social life had stopped. Any mention Laura made of chaperoned hayrides, of dancing class with programmed instruction and parties that ended at ten o'clock, of dates that culminated in a shared fudge sundae at the drugstore were met with derision. 'Dancing class!' Annie said. 'The Stone Age!'

'It wasn't so dull,' Laura protested, and, thinking of the solitary gyrations of the young in what currently passed for dancing, 'We even touched each other when we danced.'

Annie raised her eyebrows. 'There are other ways to do that,' she said.

Annie had had her first boy friend in sixth grade. 'The dashing Keith Mitchell.' It was Laura's phrase. She'd seen him at a school concert, taller than the others, dark, his hair shaggy over a handsome face. He announced the program. Afterwards she asked Annie, 'Who was the announcer? I thought he was quite dashing.'

Annie laughed. 'You and everybody else. That's Keith Mitchell. He's president of the Student Council.'

One late afternoon there'd been a ring of the doorbell. Laura went. A boy with dark hair, a canvas newspaper bag slung over his shoulder, asked, 'Is Annie here?'

'Annie—'

Annie emerged from the den. 'Keith! Hi!'

He smiled, awkward, his thumb running under the strap of the canvas bag. 'I finished early. I was going by your house. I thought I'd see if you were here.'

Laura retreated to the kitchen. A half-hour later Annie came back. 'It was the dashing Keith Mitchell,' she said, her voice shimmering with excitement. She went toward the phone. 'I gotta call Janet.'

The friendship between Annie and Keith prospered. In Junior high they went to basketball games. He would come over and they'd sit on the steps outside, or walk round the block, hand in hand. Once they were gone for two hours. It was dark when Annie came in.

'Have a nice time?' Laura asked.

'We were in the back yard, talking.'

'Why don't you invite him in? You could talk in here.'

'Mother!' Annie said. 'We're not doing anything.'

She had believed Annie then. Of course she wasn't 'doing anything', as she said. Later, with Gordon . . . Perhaps they should have known. Not that Annie had lied to them; they had never asked. When they did learn, she and Trace had been so enlightened, modern, accepting, trying to wrench themselves into another world, caring more than anything to keep talking, trying to understand, stay close. She had tried—

Anyway, her own thought interrupted her, I thought you were glad she was adventurous, especially since she had so little time.

I was. But it was hard. I accepted it. I did well with it. And she never gave me credit.

A sob caught her off guard. She sat down on the bed, gripping her knees. Was that always the way it was, mothers and daughters pulling away from each other until each learned to stand alone and they could be friends again? For some it took a few years, for others, decades? A slow struggle or a quick one and then healing, new strength? Were she and Annie on their way when Annie's death cut across it all, left it unfinished? Fright cupped at her stomach. Did she love me? Was I a good mother? She began to summon images of Annie's approval, pack them close lest anything slip between them. Annie's 'Nice' on seeing the pastel drawing she was working on that day on the cabin porch. Annie on the phone last winter when, visiting Rachel and Will in Hadley, Laura had called home, discouraged, dismayed with herself, needing to talk to someone, and Annie had said, 'Mom, Mom, it's okay. I love you.'

Did she want Annie's blessing? Or was it her daughter's forgiveness she craved? For what? For still being alive, for winning? She opened her mouth and gulped in air. Do you forgive me for letting you die?

'Ohh!' She swung her feet to the floor and turned on the light. Ten thirty. She wished she could talk to Trace. He was at that meeting in Chicago. Virginia?

She found the number in her purse and went to the phone in the upper hall. 'Ginny, it's Laura. Sorry to call so late.'

'Not late at all. Tom and I were just talking about you. How are things going? How's your mother?'

'She's okay. She's asleep. Downstairs. I mean she sleeps downstairs. I guess she's okay. I don't know.'

'You don't sound too great. Is it rough being home this first time?'

'Oh, yes.' She looked at the wall, the light coming in from the street. 'Yes. Yes it is. Those dresses—' she broke off in a staccato gulp of air.

'Dresses?' Virginia said.

'In the closet.'

'Listen, Laura, you want me to come over?'

She swallowed. 'Sorry, Ginny, I'll get hold of myself. Not tonight. But soon. Tomorrow?'

'Tomorrow's fine, but I'd be glad to come now.'

'No. There's Carlena. Mother might wake up.' She took a deep breath. 'I feel better already. But come tomorrow. About three?'

'I'll be there.'

In the night, Rachel fell. Laura didn't hear her. The deep sleep into which she'd fallen prevented it. Carlena heard her, from her room at the top of the stairs, went down and helped Rachel back to bed. The next morning she was stiff and sore. Carlena called the doctor. She came back from the phone. 'He thinks we should get an x-ray, just in case. He'll send an ambulance.' Aside, she whispered to Laura, 'He wants blood tests too. He don't like her falling.'

Rachel hadn't broken anything. The doctor wanted her to stay overnight, for observation. He came and talked to Laura while the nurses wheeled Rachel to her room. 'There's some deterioration in the blood vessels,' he said. 'She has a recurrent bladder infection; it may require catheterization. Her medicine keeps her heartbeat steady.' He slipped his glasses back into the pocket of his coat. 'There's nothing critically wrong, just some deteriorations of age.'

Laura winced. 'Of course. She's lost a lot of ground since I saw her last.'

'None of us is getting any younger.' He was about to go.

She spoke quickly. 'Since my father died she's been lonely. Do you think she's all right, my mother – getting good care?'

'She misses your father, of course. Yes, she's getting good

care. If you girls were closer it would be easier for her. But she does pretty well.' He hurried away.

You girls, Laura thought. Why not Howard too? Why was it always daughters? And, with a lurch in her heart, what if there wasn't a daughter to help parents grow old?

In the hospital room Rachel sat against the raised mattress, the piled pillows, her hair combed back, the water bottle and the box of tissues on the green bedside table. 'Well!' she said when Laura came in. 'We never know what next, do we?'

'I'm glad nothing's broken. How're you feeling?'

'My leg aches. No worse than usual. My arthritis bothers me all the time.' She launched into a long account of the wait, the discomfort of the x-ray table. 'I suppose I'll have to ask Carlena to sleep downstairs with me so she'll hear me get up. You can help her bring a cot from the attic.'

'Those cots aren't very comfortable. You have a bell by your bed if you need help.'

'I know, but I forget to ring it.' Rachel's voice was querulous.

'Mother! Wouldn't it be simpler to remember the bell than drag Carlena's bed downstairs?'

A look of disapproval settled on Rachel's face. 'My mother and I never had a cross word,' she said. 'Anyway, when my mother was sick she always had somebody with her – my father or a nurse. Sometimes *I* slept with her.' Her gaze glanced off Laura and she stared into the hall.

'We'll work something out.' Laura picked up a newspaper from the dresser. 'Want to see the paper?'

Rachel held her hand out stiffly. 'I guess so.'

Laura stood. 'I have to make a phone call.'

'What for?'

'Virginia was coming to the house this afternoon. I might meet her somewhere instead.'

'You're going to leave me?'

'Just while you're having a nap. Now that I know you're okay.'

'Oh.' Her mother returned to the paper.

Laura found a phone booth in the hall.

'Fine,' Virginia said. 'Why not come here? There's someone here who'd like to see you.'

'Oh?' She didn't inquire. She went back to the room. The orderly had brought an extra lunch. She and her mother ate, saying little.

Rachel began to settle herself for her nap. 'Don't stay too long,' she said.

Laura gathered her things and hurried down the hall.

In the car at last, she put her forearms on the steering wheel and rested her head against them and took several slow, deep breaths.

Then she straightened up, started the car, hoping that Virginia's friend, whoever it was, wouldn't interfere with their visit.

15

At Virginia's house, she lifted the knocker, let it fall.

The door opened. A man stood there, medium height, dark hair, pressed denim jeans, a tan corduroy jacket over a navy blue shirt.

'Laura!' Blue eyes searched her face. He held out both hands, grasped her hand eagerly and drew her into the house.

'Tom?' She was startled at the intensity of his welcome. She had never met Ginny's husband but had imagined a man of more ceremonial restraint.

'No.' A chuckle came from deep within his throat. 'Guess again.'

'I-I don't know,' she began, but something in the blue eyes, almost a deepening of color, a warmth half joking, half pleading, recalled to mind . . . 'Fred?'

He laughed, an arm light on her shoulder. 'Ginny didn't tell you I was here?'

'She said "someone". She didn't say her brother!' She said it almost accusingly, as though she should have been forewarned. 'What brings you here? How are you?' Expecting a stranger, she had encountered Fred, of all people. Not that there would have been anything different to *do* about seeing him again. Fred, whom she'd admired from afar, the handsome older brother of her best friend, always surrounded by girls, always out of reach. Obliquely, she looked at him again. His face was lined by the passage of years but still had the same intriguing lift at the corners of his mouth, the smile that implied something unexpected and wonderful could happen at any minute. The eyes were darker perhaps but they held the same sparkle. 'How are you, Fred?' she repeated the question. 'Are you living in Hadley, of all places?' The last she had seen of him he was about to go as a pilot to Vietnam, and maybe as a farewell to his old home town – she could never figure out why – he had invited her to a first of the season high school football game. She was a senior and he had two years of college behind him. After the game they had gone to Charley's and danced in the dim light and she remembered now the feel on her skin of her excitement and apprehension, and for the moment forgot completely the devastating truth of her life.

'No, I don't live here,' he said. 'I'm something of a transient, Laura. In fact,' he looked at his watch, 'I have to leave right now for an appointment in Springfield. I was hoping you'd get here before I left. Ginny says you'll be here for several days. Perhaps we can get together, catch up a little bit?'

'I'd like that,' she said hastily, then thought, nothing too demanding, please. Do I want to hold up a full half of a conversation?

He was watching her face. 'Maybe the four of us, you and Ginny and Tom and I, could have dinner some night.' His expression softened and he said, 'Ginny told me about your daughter. I'm sorry.'

'Yes. Thank you.' There it was. He knew. She would have wanted him to know. 'It depends on how my mother does, but I'd like to, if we can.'

Ginny came down the stairs then, slender and lovely in cream wool slacks and a blue silk shirt, a necklace of knotted gold rope.

'Laura.' They hugged. Fred moved toward the door. 'Good luck with the interview,' Ginny said. 'Hope you land the job.'

'Goodbye.' His glance swept them both, and he closed the door.

'He's looking for a job?' Laura asked.

Ginny laughed. 'He's in the travel business – designs

brochures, sales videos, that kind of thing. He's checking out a new account.'

'Has that been his work?'

'One way or another. He says it supports his habit, which is travel. The more exotic the place, the better. He just got back from Iceland. Before that it was the Galapagos Islands.'

'He doesn't live here. Where?'

'He has a home, a small house on the Cape. But he's not spent much time there since his marriage broke up.'

'Oh, I'm sorry,' Laura said, thinking back to the face that greeted her at the door, a vulnerability she'd not remembered in the Fred Thayer she knew.

'It's been a while,' Ginny said. 'His wife was a set designer. They lived in New York, then Paris. I think his coming and going was too much for her, or for them. She found someone else who could be around. They have one child, who's with her mother.'

They were still standing in the hall. Ginny put her arm round Laura's shoulder. 'Come on in,' and they entered the living room together.

'Oh, what a lovely room,' Laura said. Modigliani prints framed the doorway. The room was filled with light, yellow and ivory and white fabrics, green plants on a glass-topped table, over the mantel a painting of large abstracted flowers – a single yellow lily by a blue iris. On the mantel was a triptych of family pictures and a tiny antique fire engine, its driver in a gilded helmet.

'Thank you. Sit down. What can I get you? Tea? Wine? A glass of milk?'

'Nothing, thank you. Well, maybe a glass of water. I can't stay long.'

Ginny left to get the water and Laura sat, her mind still awhir at the unexpected meeting with Fred.

She had not always admired him. They'd first met in a Saturday art class, even before she knew Ginny. Their storage cupboards had been next to each other – Taylor, Thayer. At the time he'd seemed an obnoxious braggart, affecting artistic mannerisms. She was twelve. He was fourteen and probably trying out roles for himself. By the time she reached high school Fred was entering his senior year. He'd played Sky Masterson in the school production of *Guys and Dolls*. She'd been one of the girl friends of the gamblers and with yearning in her heart had watched Fred move through the play. Did Ginny know? They spoke of casual crushes, other boy friends, but somehow anything other than the most casual talk of Fred seemed out of bounds. Ginny must have known about that date. Or, suddenly shy, had she wanted to keep it just for herself? A brother is, after all, seldom a romantic figure.

Ginny returned from the kitchen, water in hand. 'How is your mother?'

'She didn't break anything – I told you that. She'll go home tomorrow. But she's frail. Very frail.' Suddenly, she put her face in her hands. 'I really can't think of losing her, not yet. Not someone else.' She reached for her handkerchief. 'Oh, excuse me. I'm such a shambles these days. People will think I have no stamina at all!'

'Nonsense. Who cares what people think?' and then, hesitant, 'I hope you don't mind that I told Fred.'

'Oh no. I'd want him to know.' She sighed. 'That's always part of the issue, isn't it? Whom to tell? How soon? I can't bear to be with anyone for long, if we're going to be friends at all, without telling them. It's almost like my name. "I'm Laura Randall. I have two sons. I had a daughter but my daughter was killed."'

Ginny nodded. 'That goes away, that need to tell everybody. I still remember the first time I didn't. By then we had Linda, so it was a couple of years, and someone said to me, "Do you have children?" and I said, "Yes, I have a daughter, Linda." Before that I always had to add, "I had a son, too, but he died." I used to wonder whether it was my anger, that I wanted other people to suffer too. Or my need to keep him alive, not have him forgotten, dismissed so quickly. So quickly.'

Laura, who had been staring into her lap, looked up at the repeated words. Ginny's eyes were wet and Laura stood up and went to her and they put their arms round one another. Ginny pulled a tissue from the cuff of her shirt and wiped her eyes. 'I still want to tell people sometimes. I look for an excuse. If someone says, after I tell them about the girls, "All daughters? No sons?" I'm quick to jump at it – "I had a son but he died in an accident as a child."' She wiped her eyes again. 'I guess I'm still angry,' she said.

They were sitting at opposite ends of the sofa now. Laura picked up a pillow of needlepointed violets and held it against her pale yellow sweater.

'Tell me about her,' Ginny said. 'About you. Whatever you want.'

So Laura unburdened herself of some of the things she'd wanted to say to Ginny in the car on the way home but had been too overwhelmed to begin, about what a wonderful child Annie had been, such a confident adolescent – 'not like me', at which Ginny shrugged her skepticism. 'You were fine,' she said. Laura told her about Bart and Philip and how they'd been so helpful during the first terrible weeks, and about the memorial service, and the friend who sang 'One day at a time'.

'That's how she lived, Ginny,' Laura leaned forward, 'almost as though she knew she didn't have much time.' She lifted her head in a gesture of pride at Annie's courage. 'Sometimes, though,' she looked at her friend, and stopped.

And began again. 'There's something else, Ginny. I hardly know how to talk about it.'

'Go on,' Ginny said.

'We were going through some hard times, Annie and Trace and I. She was very adventurous, very determined to do things her way. Sometimes that caused us a lot of pain, kept us on edge. What new thing was she going to try, what punches would we have to roll with next? So that when she died, that was all gone. There was a part of me,' she stopped and inhaled deeply. 'I can hardly bear this myself, let alone tell you.' Her fingers worked at the welting on the pillow, kneading the velvet cording in and out.

'Go on,' Ginny said.

'There's a way it's easier, having her gone!' She blurted it out, pulled the pillow even tighter against the sudden cramping in her diaphragm.

'Good for you!' Ginny said, and reached over to put a steadying hand on Laura's knee. Then she sat back. 'Listen. Tommy was born with a mild case of cerebral palsy. You'd hardly notice it – a slight drag when he walked. But we had to massage his leg every day, do exercises. It was a nuisance. At times I resented it. It took a lot of time, he fussed. Then he died and I didn't have to do it any more. Of course I'd have given anything to have that task again.' She spread her palms, empty. 'But I didn't. It was hard to allow myself that freedom. I'd invent jobs to do, or I'd sit, every morning and evening when we used to do the exercises, and dwell on my grief, how much I missed him. As though to use that freedom was to be guilty of his death. You see? If Annie's death has some aspect of ease in it for you, that's a side effect. It's *after* the fact. It doesn't make you an accomplice.'

'Oh, thank you.' Laura pressed her handkerchief against her eyes. 'Tell me again.'

'Dear Laura, listen to me. *It doesn't make you an accomplice.* You didn't wish for it. *She's* not holding you responsible. Don't you do it either.'

'Thank you.' Her voice was a whisper. In her mind she looked for Annie, saw her face, the brown hair curling round it, the eyes clear, direct, bright. Annie would understand, wouldn't she?

'Thank you,' she said again. 'I'll try to believe it.'

'Something else, Laura. When you start to do things on your own, maybe things you couldn't have done before, remember that you didn't bargain for that either with her death. Keep the order straight. You acted second, not first.'

Laura shook her head and smiled. 'I may ask you to tell me that again later. Though I do know what you mean. I finally bought some new clothes a few weeks ago. At first every time I put them on it seemed I had abandoned her, turning toward a future she won't share. Then I thought, the hell with that, there's nothing in my future she won't share. Though I sure wish the terms were different!' She lifted the pillow against her face, then put it back on the couch and patted it into place. 'Well.' She looked at her watch. 'Mother will think I deserted her.' She eased forward and stood. 'I can't thank you enough. I feel,' she touched her chest, 'well, tons *lighter*, I guess.'

They hugged one another. 'Will you come over sometime and see Mother?' Laura asked.

'Of course. But tonight, how about going out for a late supper with Fred and Tom and me? After visiting hours.'

She hesitated a moment. Would Rachel mind? But Rachel would be going to sleep. She'd be safe with Ginny and Tom. And yes, it would be nice to see Fred. 'I'd love to.'

'Good. Come over here when you're through. We'll be ready.'

She'd been gone longer than she'd intended, a couple of hours at least. Hurrying along the corridor toward Rachel's room she saw at the end of the hall a bent figure in a paisley robe, a white-clad nurse on either side. It was her mother. The robe reached to just below her knees. Beneath the robe her legs, white and thin as bones, angled in toward her feet. Laura stopped, remembered how as a young woman Rachel had been proud of her legs, remembered a day long ago when Rachel and Will had just come from a wedding. Rachel was wearing her rose chiffon dress and the black satin shoes with the sparkling beads. She extended a leg in front of her, pointing her toe. 'Not bad,' she said. Her father stepped over and swung an arm under her mother and lifted her off the floor. 'Daddy! She's all dressed up!' Laura said. They twirled round, the rose-colored dress flaring out like a tent. When he put her down, her mother's face was pink as the ruffle circling her shoulder.

At the end of the corridor the three women were proceeding at a slow, painstaking pace. Laura started toward them, apprehensive. Would Rachel be angry, feel neglected? When she reached her mother Rachel said, 'Hello, dear. You see I'm walking.' She turned from one to the other of the nurses. 'This is my daughter, Laura. She came all the way from Tennessee just to see me.'

Back in the room they eased Rachel onto the bed. 'They'll be bringing supper soon,' the nurse said. Rachel lay back against the pillow and looked at Laura. 'I'll feast my eyes on you,' she said. But a haziness drifted onto her face and her eyelids lowered. She opened them again. 'I'm tired. You don't mind if I doze off?'

'Of course not.'

The sound of the supper arriving woke Rachel. She looked at the food – broth, chicken, canned beans, bread and butter, a half peach afloat in syrup, a small steel teapot with a teabag beside it. She picked up the teabag and dangled it into the pot. 'They don't know how to make tea,' she said.

Laura sat by her while she ate, each bite a journey over the napkin, up the slope of her chest, past her chin to her mouth.

Rachel pushed the tray away. 'That's enough.' She looked at Laura. 'What about you? You could get supper in the cafeteria.'

'Thank you. After visiting hours I'm going out to supper with Virginia.'

Her mother looked puzzled. 'Virginia?'

Laura leaned forward into the residual smell of canned beans. 'My friend, Virginia Thayer. You remember her?'

'Oh yes, I guess I do. Remember me to her. You haven't seen her in a long time, have you?'

'Not until yesterday. She brought me from the airport.'

'I see.'

They talked of other things, of Rachel's fall, of whether Carlena would need groceries from the store. Rachel's attention came and went. She recognized it herself. 'I'm sorry I'm not any brighter tonight, dear.'

'It's no wonder, Mother, after a day like this.'

Rachel closed her eyes again. Laura watched her, a sadness coming over her. You are going from me. There are things I need to say to you. Shall we manage it, you and I?

When she was sure Rachel was asleep, Laura picked up the newspaper and read through it, seeing familiar names – Thibedoux, Ferriante, Alger. She had known many of them in school. They were running the city now.

When the voice came over the loudspeaker, 'Visiting hours are over. Will all visitors please leave,' she kissed her mother's forehead, touched her hand. The pattern of Rachel's breathing shifted but she did not waken.

In the corridor Laura stopped at the nurses' station. 'My mother's asleep,' she said.

The nurse looked up, startled.

Laura went on, took the elevator down, and went out into the night.

*   *   *

Light from the stone fireplace played on Delft tiles along the wall, flickered on a set of hanging copper pots, shone in miniaturized tiny fires – reflections on the glass of the hurricane lamp, the empty wine glasses – at the Country Pedlar Inn where Ginny and Tom, Laura and Fred sat finishing their coffee.

'I've always liked this place,' Fred said, the sweep of his hand taking in the restaurant, its deep alcoves and candlelight.

'I have, too.' It had been Laura's suggestion they come here, readily agreed to by the others. 'Trace and I had our wedding rehearsal dinner here.'

'Did you?' Fred's eyes lingered on her, as though somewhere in his mind he was trying to imagine that event.

'We missed each other's weddings,' Ginny said. 'How could we have let ourselves grow so far apart?' She reached for Laura's hand. 'No more,' she said.

Laura took the hand offered her. 'No more.'

The evening had gone well. Laura liked Tom, straightforward, courteous, watching his wife's pleasure in her girlhood friend.

It had been Fred who'd greeted her, again, when she'd arrived at the door after leaving Rachel. He had exchanged the corduroy jacket and denim pants for a navy blazer and gray slacks. 'Come in, Laura.'

They stood in the hall. 'Ginny and Tom will be here in a minute,' he said, and then, his voice heavy with the weight of it, his blue eyes steady on her, 'How are you, dear? It must be hell for you, losing your daughter.'

'Yes. Thank you, Fred. It is. I guess I'm doing okay.' She could feel the tears start to rise and she turned, grateful for the clattering of shoes on the stairs – Tom and Ginny.

Ginny leaned forward, the tie of her red silk blouse falling forward onto the hand she extended. 'Laura, this is Tom.'

He shook her hand. 'How do you do?' He was a tall man, dark-haired, dark-suited, his necktie a proper stripe.

'How do you do?' she answered. 'I'm so happy to meet you after all this time.'

'Virginia has told me so much about you,' he said, his tone slightly formal. 'I hope your mother is doing well.'

'I think so.'

'I do extend my condolences – your daughter . . .' He stumbled, awkward, uncomfortable in extending sympathy for a loss with which he was so familiar. Why the stiffness? Suddenly she remembered Trace, his matter-of-fact tone, describing the events around Annie's death.

'Thank you,' she said.

Ginny took her arm, 'Let's go,' and they went to the car, the men following along behind.

During dinner much of the conversation had been reminiscences of Laura and Ginny's adolescent years in Hadley. The men listened contentedly, every once in a while asking a question or making a comment.

'Of course you were here too.' Tom shifted his attention to Fred.

'Yes. But I was older. Two years seems like a lot of time when you're sixteen and full of your own importance.'

'You *were* quite the star,' Laura said. 'I think half the sophomore class had a crush on you. I did.' She laughed, startled by her admission.

Fred's smile was benevolent. 'I liked you a lot too, though you were my sister's friend. We even managed a couple of dates, as I recall.'

'We did. A Joni Mitchell concert with some friends. And then the ball game.'

'After the game we went to Charley's and danced – right?'

'Right,' she said, pleased that he remembered and even now recalling the sweet seduction of the music and how well she and Fred had danced together.

She gave a theatrical sigh. 'And then you went off to college, lost to me forever.'

'I thought about you though,' he protested, the glow in his eyes soft. 'You'd be surprised to know how often.'

She smiled. 'Could have fooled me.' But the words warmed her nonetheless.

She picked up her coffee cup, drank, put it down again onto the green, gold-rimmed saucer. Her eyes caught Ginny's, blue-gray in the candlelight, her dark lashes casting feathery shadows on her cheek. 'It hardly seems that long ago, does it? All of that, those high school years?'

'No.' Ginny was reflective. 'Though so much has happened.'

'Yes,' Laura said. She means Tommy, she thought. I mean Annie. Will it always be that way?

Fred interrupted her reverie. 'Ginny says you're a painter.'

'Not quite.' The remark startled her, and she launched into a vague wandering speech about her interest in painting but not knowing whether she'd be able to, about being fearful of being home alone all day but not wanting to run from that solitude either.

Fred was thoughtful. 'You have good friends, I'm sure. I mean in Tennessee – where is it you live?'

'In Woodbridge.'

'Your husband teaches there. They must have art courses. Maybe you could take a class.' He said to Tom, 'That's where Laura and I first met, in an art class.' He turned back to Laura. 'I think it was before you and Ginny were friends.'

She nodded in agreement.

He chuckled. 'It's a wonder I didn't scare you off from the whole family. As I remember I was a terrible snob at the time.'

'Snob?' Ginny laughed, and pushed her dark hair back from her face. 'About what? Your superior artistic ability? You were good, I know, but not that good, not then. Were you?'

'I think I was affecting a jaundiced view of the world – a junior cynic. Probably covering up my insecurities.' He smiled ruefully, bent his napkin back along the fold.

'You?' Laura said. 'I thought you knew it all.'

'So did I,' he said.

'So what are you doing now?' she asked. 'You live on the Cape? I was there once, years ago. I thought I'd love to go back there some day and paint. All that sky, and water, and sand, and those wonderful, slatted, beat-up lobster pots.' When was it she had been there? Long ago, with Trace, before any of the children were born.

'Come down some time and take a crack at it,' he said. 'We sure have lots of painters – summer, winter, spring or fall. Come anytime.'

'Thanks,' she said. 'Maybe I'll get back there some day. I was always going to take the children. Now . . .' The familiar lump rose in her throat. The next thing she would be crying. Not here, please, she admonished herself and rummaged in her purse for a tissue or a hankie. Where was it? She never went anywhere these days without a handkerchief. A folded white linen square appeared at her elbow. 'Here, take mine,' Fred said.

'Thanks,' she said.

'Well.' Tom shifted in his chair, realigned the meal check and signed the charge slip on the small pewter tray. 'We seem to be almost the last ones here. Perhaps we better go.'

He went to get the car. Ginny retreated to the Ladies' Room, Fred and Laura stepped out onto the veranda, breathed in the night air. Laura looked back at the lighted windows of the inn, remembering the occasion of the rehearsal dinner, so long ago, on an evening in early fall, an evening much like this.

Fred followed her glance to the lighted windows. He seemed to read her thoughts. 'It's a lovely place,' he said. 'Your husband, how is he? Do you talk a lot?'

'Yes. Yes and no. He puts a lot of energy into his work.' She took a deep breath. 'I need to put more into mine.' Chagrined, she suddenly remembered. 'I asked you what you do and never gave you the chance to answer. I'm sorry. I'm so preoccupied with my own stuff these days. So what do you do? Travel? You were so good as Sky Masterson I thought you might try the theatre.'

He looked startled. 'You remember that?'

'Always.' She closed her eyes, hugged herself in her turquoise corduroy suit. 'You were a dream to all of us girls. A matinee idol. We vied for who would stand next to you at the final curtain calls.'

He smiled. 'Well, maybe I should have gone on with theatre, though that's not a very predictable life either.'

'Predictable?'

'You know, steady job, regular hours, what some women want in a husband. Never mind that they themselves choose a precarious profession, like set design,' he added wryly.

She hesitated, then said, 'Ginny told me your marriage didn't work out. I'm sorry.'

His smile was sardonic. 'No, it didn't. I'm not sure how much schedule had to do with it. I tried city government but I couldn't stand the bureaucracy. Everything else seemed to keep me on the road. I flew a plane, carrying small freight. For a while I ran an import business. We lived in a lot of places before we finally gave up on the marriage. I've always loved travel, so when the marriage failed, I turned to that.'

'You have a child?'

'Yes, but she's given up on me, I'm sure. She's in California. I never see her.'

You travel, Laura thought. You could easily arrange to see her. But she felt reluctant to venture further into his private world and she did not say so. Instead, she said, 'I'm sure that could be a fascinating life, travelling a lot.'

'It is. I'm always looking for new destinations. And I do a lot of my own advertising.' He paused. 'It occurred to me, when you were talking,' he inclined his head toward the restaurant, 'about wanting to get back into art, would you want to try your hand at travel brochures? Watercolor sketches for a cover? Ginny says you've done that kind of work.'

'Really, Fred?' she said, and caught her breath at the timeliness of the suggestion. 'Yes, I might like to. Yes. Thank you. I might like that very much.'

'We'll talk about it. You'll be here a few more days?'

'Yes.'

Tom appeared then with the car, and Ginny emerged from the Ladies' Room and they all got in and drove off.

At Tom and Ginny's they said goodnight and Laura switched to her own car. 'It's been a wonderful evening,' she said. 'I can't thank you enough – all of you.'

The house was quiet when she let herself in. She got ready for bed and turned out the light and, in the dark, again and again, played the evening through, until finally she fell asleep.

Trace stopped at the post office, picked up the few days of accumulated mail, and drove on home. In the old days,

193

which now meant anytime previous to his daughter's death, he would have gone to the office, checked over mail and messages, done a few hours of study or gone over notes for a class. But he was tired from the meeting – a subcommittee of the American Philosophical Association which oversaw selection of scholars for endowed lectureships, in which he'd once had a great interest but which now seemed arcane and uninteresting.

He unlocked the door and went in. The house was quiet. Usually he welcomed solitude but somehow the silence in the house seemed ominous, lurking, as though something was waiting, ready to do him harm. It had almost the musty air of a house that had been shrouded and quiet over a season and now everything must be freshened again. But Bart and Paula could only have been gone for a day or two at most.

Or maybe they hadn't moved out yet. They'd be at work now, of course, but maybe they were still packing up, getting ready. He had a wild hope and, suitcase in hand, he hurried through the house to where the bedrooms opened off a corridor, set his suitcase down and walked the several feet of corridor to the doorway of the room Bart and Paula had occupied.

His heart dropped. They were gone. The guest room aspect was restored – the quilt coverlet in place, the dresser cleared of everything but a ceramic flower holder, a silver-backed hand mirror, and a tray with small glass carafe and inverted water glass. The desktop, too, was clear. He opened the closet door. It contained a few seasonal garment bags pushed to one side, and an array of empty hangers. Bart and Paula had moved out.

Then he went by Philip's room, now atypically bereft of disorder though the bulletin board still had banners and buttons from various high school events, and the poster of the Grateful Dead still hung over the desk. He shook his head. He had never come to terms with names music groups supposedly for people's enjoyment gave themselves and this one seemed singularly inappropriate now.

Back in the hall, he hesitated at the doorway to Annie's room. The door stood ajar and he caught a glimpse of blue and white bedspread but he went on and, picking up his suitcase, took it to the room he shared with Laura, set it up on the bed, and unpacked.

That done, he went downstairs, picked up the paper, for which he had had delivery resumed, went carefully over the mail – a few financial statements, some solicitations for funds, a letter from his congressman, *Newsweek* and the *New York Times Book Review*. And then several cards of sympathy and condolence. At first there had been a stream of such mail; now they still received two or three a week from people who had just learned of Annie's death. They cherished these messages, some of them full letters, some only a signature on a printed card, but evidence that someone in the human family was reaching out to them. And remembering Annie. That as much as anything, Trace thought, putting the card with the roses and the butterfly back in the envelope for Laura to see; another mark on the face of the earth that this daughter had not vanished without some note being taken of her going, of her having been here.

For how could it be that at one moment a life was in full sail, heading into a future full of promise and expected occasions, the multiform trivia and substance – parties, trips to the store, conversations with people, donning of clothing and choice of food, lovers, arguments, birthdays – that impress a person's life on the wax tablet of being, and then, in a moment, in some freakish accident of fate, it is gone? Finished. The present stops, and there is no future at all. In all of his studies of good and evil, of metaphysics and eschatology, Trace had never stood on the edge of an abyss like this one.

And how had it been for her? She was safe now. Had there been a choice? Even unconsciously, had she chosen to leave? Going back with Bart to the scene of her fall, he had tried to satisfy himself she had in no way encouraged this death, been less than full-hearted in trying to save herself from falling – if there had, indeed, been time for her to do more than be carried along by the runaway horse. He knew she was angry with him. And, yes, she had a right to be. But he had banked on the future, that they would forgive one another this period of tumult and mutual hurt feelings. He saw her standing angry in the kitchen that night he said he couldn't go to the art reception and she'd hurled the accusation at him, 'You're never here for me! You never have been, not since I was a little girl!' He saw her lovely face distorted with rage, and longed to see it again – just that way if need be. 'I'm here for you now,' he said into the empty room, 'where are you, for me?'

After a while he stood up from the chair. He looked at the clock – almost six. He supposed it was time he got himself some supper. He went to the freezer and opened the door. He knew Laura had stocked it with dinners he could heat in the microwave. Yes, there was a stack – chicken in various forms, two boxes of fish Florentine, some pasta combinations.

Suddenly it occurred to him that maybe Bart and Paula would like to join him, or maybe he could take them out to dinner. They could catch up with each other, he'd find out how the move had gone.

The more he thought about the idea, the better it seemed. He dialed the number they'd so recently put in the family phone book. Four rings, a click, and then Bart's voice, 'Hi, you have reached 442-3720. We can't come to the phone right now, but please . . .' Trace could guess the rest of it, but he listened anyway, somehow reassured by the prosaic reality of his son's voice. When the beep came to leave a message, he hung up. He didn't want them to think he was meddling in their lives, or 'intruding on their space' as the young would say.

Now what? He felt at a loose end, lonely. Later, after the rates changed, he would call Laura at her mother's. He thought of calling Philip. But trying to reach a college student when you didn't know his schedule was like trying to find a particular title in one of those book warehouse sales.

He was almost through some frozen yoghurt following a rather dried up chicken Dijon when he had another thought. Would this be a possible time to talk with Kate about her thesis? Before he'd left she'd asked if they could meet soon. He looked at his watch. Not quite seven. Reaching her might be as difficult as he'd imagined reaching Philip would be.

But he called and, yes, this would be a good time and she'd meet him at his office in ten minutes.

As it happened, Dave Ignatius was also in his office – light on, door ajar. 'Hello. Welcome back,' he called as Trace came in.

'Thanks.' He saw Henry Bowen was in talking with Dave and he went into his own office and sat down, any disquiet he might have felt about meeting a young woman in a solitary setting eased. He couldn't imagine any blurred areas of propriety between himself and Kate but one could hardly be too vigilant these days, with all the sensitivity about sexual harassment. 'Don't touch!' was the going dictum. Not that he had much impulse to reach out with more than a handshake to anyone with whom he was not on very close terms. And even then . . . Once more the ghost of his daughter rose before him. 'Don't hug me. You know you don't feel like it.' He'd not argued with her, though his heart recoiled, his arms ached to hold her, to have all this tension between them banished, gone away.

He was still lost in the pain of that moment when he heard a knock. 'Dr Randall?'

'Come in, Kate. Sit down.' She came in, papers in hand, wearing jeans and a long blue sweater and those huge white shoes everyone wore. She sat down, pulled her glasses from her sweater pocket, unfolded them, pushed the bows behind her ears and then, with her index finger, pushed the glasses up her nose. The gesture undid him. It was so like Annie. She'd worn contacts much of the time but often her glasses, too, and something about the way Kate moved the metal arch of the frame up the ridge of her nose then slid her finger back down reminded him so strongly of his lost daughter, of whom he'd already been thinking, that to his great chagrin and embarrassment his eyes filled with tears and he started to cry. 'Oh, Kate,' he said.

'Dr Randall!' she exclaimed. 'Have I done anything to upset you?'

'No,' he said. 'No,' reaching for his handkerchief, his voice muffled in an attempt to blow his nose. 'Excuse me, Kate. I'm terribly sorry.' He looked up and the compassion in her eyes bathed him in a faint hope of forgiveness for all he had done wrong not only to Annie but in his whole life. 'It's just that you – you remind me of someone,' he said and immediately thought, so what kind of an excuse is that for losing control in front of a student? 'You reminded me just then of my daughter,' he said. 'I'm sorry.'

She shook her head, tears in her own eyes now. 'Dr Randall, I am honored. Please don't feel bad.' She moved a hand toward him and drew it back. 'I've been thinking about you a lot. I don't know how you stand it.' She swallowed hard. 'What I want to say, what I've been thinking I want to say, is that your daughter was very fortunate to have you for a father. I've never had a teacher I thought was so,' she was struggling for the right word, 'so *attentive* to his students as you are. Why, in class you take every question, no matter if it's dumb, with great respect and seriousness.' She stopped talking now because she saw she wasn't making him feel better, he was in fact crying more freely, except that he was smiling at the same time and she sat back in her chair and lowered her eyes so he wouldn't be embarrassed – if indeed he was – by seeing her watching his distress.

He blew his nose again, a large, trumpeting sound, and said, 'Well!' and she looked up and he had, in fact, stopped crying. Having watched him these few weeks since college began and seen his face look haggard and drawn and watched him walk around staring at the ground, always answering politely if you said 'Good afternoon' to him in passing but always so, well, so sad, she thought he looked . . . less burdened, maybe, and wasn't he even sitting up straighter in his chair?

'Dr Randall?' she said.

'Yes, Kate?'

'If you don't mind. I mean, well, would you let me give you a hug?'

'Oh, please do.' He stood and, awkwardly, he held out his arms and she came and wrapped her arms around his shoulders, her face against the side of his head while sobs rolled over his tall, sturdy frame, seeming as fragile now as canvas stretched over twigs. 'Oh, Kate,' he said, and after a moment he moved back and his face, though tear-stained and flushed, was smiling. 'I do thank you, my dear.'

They sat down in their chairs then, opposite one another. He pulled his handkerchief from his pocket again and wiped his face, and Kate did the same to her face with a bunch of tissues she had stashed in her backpack.

'Well,' he said, and they smiled at one another, each through tears. 'Thank you, Kate,' he said, continuing to mop his face. Then he said it again, 'Thank you, Kate,' and breathed a great sigh. 'Now, shall we talk about the golden mean?'

Rachel came home from the hospital. They re-ensconced her in her bed under the dining-room window. Fred called. He was leaving town again, might not get back until after she'd left, but he'd send her some pictures he'd taken in Iceland, along with a few of his past brochures, so she could see the kinds of things he had in mind, how they were usually blocked out. Would that be all right?

She was disappointed not to see him again, but yes, that would be fine. She could mail sketches to him.

'When are you coming back?' he asked. 'Maybe I could arrange to come up.'

'I don't know,' she said. 'I'm sure before too long.'

'Well, let me know.'

Virginia came over. The minister came by. Ella and Jackson came, Ella sitting by the bed and talking, her voice ceaseless. Rachel grew drowsy and fell asleep. Laura talked with her aunt, the soothing vacuity of their talk a balm after all – stories of obscure relatives, the moving of furniture from one house to another, Ella's bi-weekly trips to the bank. But after a while her aunt's meticulous soft-spoken ways irritated her; Laura wished they would leave.

At last they were going. They stood by the door.

'You go back tomorrow?' Ella's hand rested on Laura's arm.

'Yes.'

'Need a ride to the airport?'

'No, thanks. My old friend – you knew her as Virginia Thayer – is taking me.'

'C'mon, Ella,' Jackson cleared his throat again.

'In a minute.' She had turned to answer him and now turned back. 'You doing all right?' she asked.

'Thank you, yes, I'm doing all right.' Go, she thought, please go.

'Bless you.' Ella reached for a handkerchief. 'Mother able to help you much?'

'Sometimes yes, sometimes no.' Ella's face was a mirror of concern. She expects me to cry, Laura thought. 'I'm really all right.' She edged ever so slightly closer to the door where her Uncle Jackson waited.

'C'mon, Ella,' he said again. He turned to Laura. 'Take care, honey.'

Laura sat by her mother's bed, feeling restless. She'd be going home tomorrow. One more day. So much unsaid. 'How's Trace?' Rachel had asked. 'Fine.' Never a word about how hard it was sometimes for them to talk with one another, how distant and abstracted he often seemed. She still hadn't told Rachel about Bart and Paula. They had talked of Annie some, remembering particular days. But speculations about death had never seemed the thing to speak of. Perhaps it was too close for Rachel herself, old and failing.

Rachel seemed irritable too. People didn't call her. Or when they did, sometimes they talked too long. Didn't they know she got tired? And Ella and Jackson, she was glad to see them and they'd been helpful during Will's illness but really it took Ella so long to do anything, to say anything – those endlessly dragged out farewells, and Jackson there coughing, clearing his throat, trying to nudge her along.

She shifted in the bed. 'This blanket,' she fumed. 'It's so heavy on my leg.'

Laura adjusted it. 'That better?'

'Maybe, a little.'

Carlena came with Rachel's medicine, a glass of water. Rachel swallowed the pill.

'Finish the water, dear,' Carlena urged.

Rachel grimaced, did as she was told. Carlena left, taking the glass with her. 'She never lets it run cold enough,' Rachel complained.

Laura looked out the window, acknowledging her growing restiveness, irritation. Is this the best we can do? she thought. Maybe this pettiness was for lack of anything more interesting to think about. Was this the time to tell her mother about Bart and Paula?

But why? Rachel was old. She would surely be upset. Really, she probably need never know. They could spare her that, spare a possible bad scene. Why tell her? Finally, she acknowledged it to herself – because it sticks in my throat. Because *I* need for her to know.

She leaned forward. 'Mother, there's something I'd like to tell you. It's important to me but it may be hard for you to hear. Do you mind if I tell you?'

Rachel put down the paper she'd been desultorily reading. The complaining look changed to one of compassion. 'Of course not, dear. What is it?'

'It's about Bart and Paula.'

'What about them?'

'Well, they've been living together.'

'You mean – together?'

'Yes.' She added quickly, 'It's all right with us, Mother. It's not what we'd have wished for, but it's all right. We love Paula very much. She seems such good news in Bart's life, and in ours.' She stopped. What was she trying to do, anesthetize Rachel into concurrence?

Rachel appeared to be thinking. 'They don't want to get married?'

'No. At least not now.'

Laura waited. Her mother's face was sober, almost expressionless. Then she said, very slowly, 'Well, I suppose it's more important that Bart find the right girl than what they do about the legalities of it.'

'Mother!' It was Laura's turn to be startled. 'That's very fine of you. I'm proud of you!'

'Well,' Rachel looked a bit nonplussed, 'I try to keep up with the times. I guess I'm a little surprised at myself.' She raised her chin. 'I do know things change.' Then, as though she might have gone too far and be thought a transgressor, she added, 'Of course you do understand I'd rather . . .'

Laura's laugh was light. 'Yes, I understand.' But it was a

blessing, a burden put down, and suddenly she was talking about things that had been lying waiting, except it seemed as though their time might not come and she would go back to Woodbridge with the words unspoken. About Paula, and Annie, about the memorial service and her talk with Matt. And when she had finished all that, she said to Rachel the last thing, the most dearly needed, the most hoped for: 'I believe we shall be with her again.' And she cried, because such a thing is not lightly said. In a while she asked, 'Do you?'

'These last years,' Rachel said, 'I've thought that's almost too good to be true.' She was quiet and the trees in the back yard blew, crossed branches with one another, straightened again. 'But my father believed it,' she said. 'And my mother . . . Did I ever tell you about my mother, dying, calling her sisters' names?'

'Tell me.' Laura had heard it before, and it always moved her, and she needed it now more than ever.

'Well,' Rachel said, and she told how her mother, dying, had called out the names of her two sisters who had preceded her in death. 'Rebecca had died years ago, but Lilly,' and here Rachel always paused, her voice thinning out, as though the story demanded the utmost reverence, otherwise one did not deserve such a gift. 'Lilly had died only a few days before and they hadn't told her, sick as she was. "And Lilly, too!" she said. "And aren't they beautiful!"'

Rachel's voice broke then, and she reached for Laura's hand and they sat in the presence of the story while the afternoon light came in through the window and fell on the dining-room table, illuminating everything – sugar bowl, place mats, scratches, spilled grains of salt.

'If there's anything to it,' Rachel said, 'I like to think, there was Will, waiting for her.'

Laura did see Fred again. In the morning, Virginia called. A client was coming through and needed to see her. 'I'm so sorry, Laura. I was counting on it. Tom is tied up too. Would it be all right if Fred . . . ?'

'Is he back? I can get someone else.'

'He came in this morning. He wants to do it. He'll be there at ten.'

Fred came and she kissed her mother and Carlena good-bye and left the house and they set out for the airport.

They talked about her visit home and about where he'd be going next. 'I'll send you that material,' he said.

At the airport she insisted he drop her off, not wait. She got out and he helped her with her bags. They stood on the sidewalk. In the distance the trees were still gold, but already some were turning to a burnished brown, and at the tops of the hills the horizon line was dark and sere.

'Thank you, Fred.' She held out her hand. 'I'm awfully glad I saw you.' She smiled. 'Apart from possible work, I mean.'

'Me too.' He took the proffered hand in both of his. 'Take care of yourself, dear. Tell your husband hello. I hope he knows how fortunate he is.'

The look in his eyes, wistful, tender, startled her, and she leaned forward and kissed him lightly on the cheek. 'Thank you, Fred. You take care too.' She picked up her bags and went on into the airport, nearly missing the door.

16

Bart and Paula invited them to dinner and to see the apartment. 'The furnishings are early attic,' Bart warned over the phone. 'Supplemented with a few choice pieces from the Salvation Army.'

The house was in an area of once resplendent mansions now largely converted to apartments and university rooming houses. Bart led them up the partitioned stairwell.

'It smells wonderful,' Laura said, inhaling the fragrance of garlic and thyme.

'It's Paula's clam sauce,' Bart said as they emerged into a light airy space of large rooms, windows with low sills and reaching nearly to the ceiling. In the living room a couch covered with an Indian paisley bedspread faced a fireplace with gas logs and above it a wide cream-colored mantel on which they had set a piece of driftwood, a cobalt vase, a small sculpture of hikers on a mountain, a few photos. A Georgia O'Keefe poster – an adobe church on a sandy plain, mountains in the distance – hung over the mantel.

'Well, what do you think?' Paula came from the kitchen. She was wearing jeans and an oversized white shirt and a denim apron covered with stenciled shapes of cooking spoons. She hugged Laura and Trace. 'Welcome to our abode. You see we're expecting you.' A wave of her hand took in the dining table covered with a blue cloth, places set for four, salad bowls and wine glasses in place, a cluster of candles in the center of the table.

A timer dinged. ''Scuse me. Time to drain the pasta.'

Paula returned to the stove, lifted the pot, drained it into the sink.

'It's lovely,' Laura said. 'It takes me back. Remember our first apartment?' she asked Trace.

He was examining books in the bookcase. 'Whose is *The Letters of E.B. White?*'

'Mine,' Paula said. 'Dinner's ready.'

During dinner – linguine with clam sauce, salad, garlic bread, cabernet – Laura reported on her visit with Rachel. 'I saw my old friend Ginny, too, and her brother.' She laughed. 'I used to have something of a crush on Fred. I hadn't seen either one of them in years. He may throw some business my way.'

'Art business?' Paula asked.

'He has a travel agency. I might design some travel brochures.'

'Great, Mom,' Bart said. 'Maybe you and Dad could get some free trips.'

'I don't think so,' she said, and thought, maybe me? By myself?

They were finishing the cherry cobbler when she said, 'I told Grandma about your living together. I hadn't told her before.' She recounted the conversation, her delight at Rachel's response. 'I didn't know how she'd take it. I was really proud of her.'

There was a moment of portentous silence. Then, 'That's great,' Paula said, but her voice was flat.

'If my grandmother can hack it,' Bart was looking at Paula, his face grim, 'then surely your mother . . .'

They were glaring at each other. Laura looked at Trace who returned her glance, passed his fork over his already empty plate.

Paula flushed. 'My mother doesn't know we're living together,' she said. 'She's coming to visit next month.'

'Paula wants me to move out,' Bart snapped.

'Just for those few days,' Paula said.

Bart said, 'Good God, Paula! Doesn't she read the papers? Doesn't she look around? We're old enough to know what we're doing.'

'And I'm old enough not to unnecessarily hurt my

mother. I'll tell her when I'm ready.' Paula's hand came down flat against the blue cloth. 'For one thing, I want her to know you better first.'

Bart sighed. 'Paula, it's not going to make any difference. From what you say she wouldn't approve of your sleeping with Mahatma Gandhi unless you were married.'

'Ugh,' Paula said. 'No competition, sweetheart.'

Bart was not amused. He leaned forward, looked intently at Paula. 'Let me tell you something. If I leave, I'm gone.'

'What's that supposed to mean?' Paula's gaze was steely.

'Think about it.' He pushed back his chair, turned to his parents. 'Want to see the rest of the apartment?'

They toured the apartment, the tension easing as they moved from room to room, laughing at the old-fashioned plumbing, enthusing about the back porch even though it overlooked garages and the alley, an overflowing dumpster at the bottom of the outside staircase. 'They pick up tomorrow,' Bart said. 'It usually looks better than this.' Back inside, he proudly pointed to the smoke alarm. 'I put that in right away,' he said. 'These old wooden buildings are pretty close together.' In the bedroom a spring and mattress were stacked on the floor and covered with a puffy quilt in an abstract design of bronzes and gold. A photo of Annie and Bart and Philip stood on Bart's dresser. Laura lingered before it a moment, felt Bart's arm round her shoulder, reached for his hand.

Nothing more was said about the coming visit of Paula's mother but in the car on the way home, Laura pulled her jacket close about her. 'That was a pretty grim scene about Paula's mother coming.'

Trace shrugged. 'They'll work it out.'

'In a way it surprises me,' she went on. 'So many kids are living together now. It's the exception to get married first.'

'We were certainly creatures of another era.' He smiled. 'I'm sure they'll manage it somehow.'

But she wasn't through with it yet. 'I can see why Bart would be upset – almost as though Paula's ashamed of him.'

'That has nothing to do with it. Her mother just wants to protect her daughter.'

'Don't we want to protect our son?'

'That's different. Girls get pregnant, after all.'

Laura bristled. 'That's a sexist comment – from another era. I'm sure that's not at issue here. I can't believe her mother would turn against her.'

'Quit fretting about it. If he's chased out he can help me clean the gutters.'

'Clean the gutters!' Laura exclaimed. 'There's a principle at stake here. Honesty.'

'Calm down, sweetheart. Mothers are irrational. You know that.' He reached over and put a hand on her knee.

'I know.' She pulled a tissue from her purse and wiped her eyes. 'Maybe I'm afraid of losing Paula from the family.' She was silent for a minute. They were approaching the house. 'If her mother only knew how fortunate she is to *have* a daughter,' she said.

'There is that,' he said.

In his dream Bart reached to her again, and again. It wasn't a horse she was riding, and she was only a little girl. They were children. He had taken his telescope out on the roof to watch the stars. He'd left the window up and didn't see her come out, wearing her long yellow nightie. He heard her cry out and saw the yellow bundle rolling past him down the slope of the roof. 'Help!' she called. He reached for her but she was too far away. A rise of the roof at the bottom of the slope kept her from falling to the ground. By the time he reached her she was crying with fright. 'You're supposed to be in bed!' he shouted. 'What are you doing here?'

'I saw out the window that you were here. I just came out,' she stammered. 'Don't tell Mom!'

He hadn't. And she'd been none the worse for her fright. But he had never been able to get his telescope out again without thinking of that night, and how he almost reached her but couldn't.

'Bart, wake up. You're sobbing! What is it?' It was Paula's voice. She was sitting up in bed, shaking his shoulder. Coming to, he saw the dip of her breasts at the neck of her white gown and he buried his face against her. 'I should have taken that horse!' he cried.

'No, Bart. No!' She cradled him against her and rocked back and forth in the bed. 'No,' she crooned. 'No, my love, no.'

Laura had been home a week when a large envelope came from Fred. It was postmarked Dennis, so she knew he was back on the Cape. Several travel folders fell out when she opened the envelope, along with a yellow packet labelled 'Iceland' – photos of dark mountains and running brooks, long stretches of sea coast edged with beaches of black sand, pictures of steam rising from the earth, of a stylized Norse figure in front of a long low greenhouse. The accompanying note was cryptic. 'Anything here for a cover picture? It's not everybody's cup of tea – or stein of grog. Great seeing you. When are you going back to Hadley? Love, Fred.'

She smiled, reread the note several times, sifted through the pictures, put it all on the table in her workroom. She would go back soon, surely, to see Rachel. Would she let Fred know?

With Philip gone and Bart and Paula moved to their own apartment, the house seemed empty and still. In the mornings, after Trace had gone, she often wandered aimlessly, drifting from room to room. She had work to do apart from Fred's – she'd finished only three of the pictures for Walter Stone. The central figure was a young girl. She'd used her memory of Annie as a starting point for the girl and after a few minutes of stroking with pen or brush her hand would start to shake, and she'd quit.

Except for Trace, and her weekly trips to church and the grocery store, she saw few people. Her best friend, Julia Prentiss, had been in Scotland on sabbatical with her husband since mid-summer. Sometimes she met a friend for lunch, or talked on the phone, but she shrank from group gatherings and if she went to lectures or other events at the college she left as soon as the main event was over. 'I feel everyone is watching me,' she told Trace after one such return. 'They're feeling sorry for me, waiting for me to break down – which I will, as soon as anyone says anything sympathetic and kindly.'

'Is that so bad?' he said. 'People want to be helpful. They'd understand.'

'I feel like such a spectacle,' she said.

'You can't drop out for ever,' he said one evening after a lecture on South-East Asia. 'Why don't we stay for the reception?'

'*You* can stay,' she snapped, casting her eyes downward as they left the row of auditorium seats. 'I'll even come back for you if you give me a call.'

'I could get a ride with someone, I'm sure,' he retorted, as they wove against the crowd that surged toward them. Once outside he pulled at her arm. 'You could at least be civil,' he said.

'What do you mean?' The street light shone on his face, the anger in his eyes.

'People spoke to us. My department chair, Ben Stoddard, was trying to say hello. You just charged on out.'

'Sorry.' But she wasn't. She was in a panic to get away from the crowd, to get to the safety of home.

One morning, in her wanderings after Trace left, as she passed the door of Annie's room her eyes fell on the desk. She went in and stood before it – the slanting front, the three drawers below, on top an incense holder and a framed photo taken on a family vacation. They were all sitting in a rowboat, smiling. But whoever it was who had taken the picture – had held the camera at a slant, so it looked as though they were about to be dumped into the water.

She lowered the writing surface, dropping it down on its hinge. In the cubbyholes were old letters, notepads, a ceramic candle holder in the shape of a frog, the velvet box containing Annie's high school ring. Beneath the cubbyholes were folders of school papers, spiral-bound notebooks, a sketchpad with *Anne Randall* drawn in dark, heavily-ornamented script, some journals and diaries. Some of these Laura had looked through before, putting aside an initial scruple that she was invading Annie's privacy. She and Trace had talked about it, agreed it was a needless concern; their need to know anything they could of Annie, fill out their picture of her brief life to whatever fullness they could, far exceeded any need to protect the privacy of one who was beyond any need of protection.

Laura picked up the sketchpad and turned through the pages to watercolor washes of pastoral scenes, a sketch of a caterpillar undulating over spikes of grass, a sailboat riding on stylized waves. On one page Annie had drawn a sketch of a girl's face, the outline of her head the hook of a question mark and in a puff beside her, in quavering letters, the word HELP! Help? What was that about? She closed the sketchbook, took out one of the diaries.

Riffling through the pages she stopped at the word 'Mom'. The entry was dated; it was four summers ago when Annie was twelve. 'Today Mom and I went shopping for a bathing suit. I want a bikini. Mom is skeptical.' Laura remembered the afternoon, standing outside the curtain of the dressing room until Annie called, 'Okay. Come in.' Annie was newly modest then, her body already a series of turning curves. She'd gone from child to young woman in a matter of months without an awkward twitch or clatter. The entry continued, 'I tried on one I loved – purple, with three pink roses, two on the bra and one on the pants. Mom thought it was too suggestive. I thought it was pretty. Anyway, what's so bad about' – and here she'd misspelled it – 'sugestive?' There followed a cartoon face, eyebrows drawn together, a downturned mouth. Then, 'I still love her though,' and her name, 'Annie,' and a P.S.: 'I got one that's pretty cute – navy blue with yellow flowers. In fact I love it.'

Laura held the book against her chest. Memories so sharp, so fresh. Such a dear daughter.

Next she picked up a large manila envelope marked 'Photos'. She recognized the envelope. This would be harder. It was a group of nude photos of Annie that a girl in her photography class had taken last spring. The girl had come to the house, taken the pictures in Annie's room. Annie had shown Laura the contact sheet, small photos of Annie sitting, lying on her side, standing spread-eagled, arms over her head, her smile exhilarated and unabashed.

They'd talked about the pictures. 'What will Jennie do with them?' Laura had asked.

'Develop the best ones and submit them to the teacher.'

'Will they be exhibited in the class?'

'Sure, I suppose so.'

'Is that all right with you?'

Annie laughed. 'Sure, why not?'

Laura opened the envelope and took out one of the enlargements, a side view of Annie sitting on the bed, one knee raised, an arm encircling the knee, the beginning curve of her breast visible under the bend of her arm.

She pored over it a long time, her hunger for her daughter lingering on the lines of Annie's body, the texture of her skin, the dark hair fanning out over her shoulders. She put it back in the envelope. She'd look at the others later. Not now.

She turned to the leather notebook, Annie's last journal, and opened it on an entry from last spring. 'Sad times,' she read. 'Everything seems hopeless. Gordon's in a down mood. I feel tense and trapped. So many things I want to do but can't.'

Perhaps she should quit. She'd like to find a happier place first. She jumped ahead a number of pages.

The entry began pleasantly. 'Gordon thinks I'm lucky. He thinks Mom is neat. He thinks Dad is STRANGE but o.k.' Laura winced – how would Trace feel? – and went on. 'I guess I should be glad they care about me. But dammit,' Laura turned the page, 'I want out. Bart and Philip are lucky, getting out of this prison. Dad is a zombie and Mom is so emotionally all over the place I want to run for cover. I'm sick of parents who want to be friends. Fuck off, will you! Get off my back! Both of you. Pleez.'

Her throat tightened. She closed the book and stood up, her body stiff. *How could Annie!*

She walked from the room, went and sat on the couch in the living room, closed her eyes and read the words again and again, in burning bright letters, in the darkness of her head.

*   *   *

Trace came home. 'Hi.' He kissed her lightly, brushed past her into the house.

She followed him into the den. He was putting things in the drawers of his desk. Then he started looking through the day's pile of mail.

'Trace,' she began, 'I read something in Annie's journal today . . .'

'Oh?' He continued to flip through the envelopes.

'Trace, I read some disturbing stuff in Annie's journal, from last spring.'

'Un-hunh.' He was slipping his finger under the flap of an envelope. Order forms fell out on the desk. He scooped them up and put them in the wastebasket.

He didn't look up when she left the room.

In the bedroom, she slammed the door shut. 'Damn!' She paced to the window, and back. 'Damn!'

She looked at her watch. Almost six. Surely Bart and Paula would be home by now. She went to the phone and dialed their number.

Since they'd moved she'd avoided calling them much. Sometimes, lonesome for them, she'd suggest calling, 'just to see how they are?' 'I wouldn't,' Trace would say. 'They need their independence.'

But this time . . .

Bart answered. 'Hello?'

'Bart, can I come down for a few minutes? I need to talk to somebody.'

'Sure, Mom. Come ahead.'

When she went through the living room Trace was sitting in a chair reading.

'I'm going out.'

'Oh?' He looked up. 'Now?'

'Yes, now. Give you some peace to read the damn mail!'

'Laura, what on earth?' He was on his feet, the paper on the floor.

'I'll tell you when I come back – if I come back!' Her voice shook.

He moved toward her. 'What in the world?'

She moved away. 'I'm sorry. I'm upset. I'm going to talk to Bart and Paula. I'll be back, never fear.'

213

'I wish you'd tell me—'

'I tried to tell you. I tried.'

'When? What?'

'I said, twice, "I read in Annie's journal . . ." You said, "I see," and went right on reading the mail. You didn't even hear me!'

His jaw tightened. 'I'm sorry. I've had a rough day. I've got a big seminar coming up. I'd like to hear about the journals. Can you tell me now?'

'It's too late now! I needed you then! It's no wonder Annie gave up on you – always in your own head!'

His face whitened. He followed her into the hall.

She went out and slammed the door. She had never walked out on him before.

Bart answered her knock, Paula close behind him. 'Come in, Mom. What is it? What's the matter?'

'Ohh!' She went in and sat down, dug her hands into the Indian spread covering the sofa.

'You're shaking,' Paula said. 'Tell us.'

'I was reading in Annie's journals today.' She looked up. Their faces acknowledged a quicksand danger. 'I came to this place and –' She broke off, stifling a sob. 'Oh! Do you think Annie loved me? Did I drive her away? Do you think I was a good mother?'

Bart sighed. 'Of course, Mom. Of course she loved you.'

'I can't stand it if she didn't!'

Bart and Paula looked at each other. Paula said, 'Can you tell us what you found?'

'Well, I read a lot of stuff that was fine, things we'd talked about. Then,' again she broke off, gulped in air, 'I know children, adolescents, have mixed feelings about parents. But having her gone, and then finding it . . .' She put her face in her hands. 'It talked about Dad being a zombie and me being emotionally all over the place and then it said, "I'm sick of parents who want to be friends. Fuck off, will you! Get off my back!"'

Bart snorted. 'Mom, don't be silly. She was just mad about something.'

Paula said, 'It was her age. I felt that way about my folks sometimes. Kids do. It doesn't mean that was her general opinion. Didn't you ever feel that way about your mother and father?'

The question startled her. She thought back. 'No. Not that I remember. Nothing like that.' Panic rose in her chest again. 'If she didn't love me . . .'

'Of course she loved you, Mom,' Bart reiterated. 'Stuff like that is no big deal.' There was a touch of irritation in his voice. He walked over to the fireplace, stretched his arm along the mantel. 'She talked to Philip and me when we were home last spring. She was worried about how you were going to get along when she went to college next year.'

'She was?' Laura sat back, flooded with gratitude and relief. 'Thank you for telling me!' She reached for a handkerchief. 'That about my being emotionally all over the place – I guess I am.'

'Whatever that means,' Bart said. 'You cared about us a lot. Is that a sin?'

She shook her head. 'I'm sorry to be such a mess. I miss her so! When I was home with my mother, I kept thinking what it would be like to be old, and no Annie.'

Bart had turned his head away and when he turned back there were tears in his eyes. 'We'd all counted on her being here,' he said.

'I know.' She stood up. 'Thank you. I feel much better. I just had to talk to someone.' Impulsively, she said to Paula, 'You, a young woman, it's so great to have you close. But I'm sorry I bothered you both.'

'It's no bother at all,' Paula said. 'You want to stay and eat with us?'

'No, thanks. Dad's home.'

'He is?' Paula said. They looked surprised, alarmed.

She couldn't tell them. 'He was busy,' she said. The alarm stayed on their faces. Quick, change the subject. 'I meant to ask you, Paula. When your mother comes, we'd like to have you all over to dinner.'

Paula's eyes shifted to Bart, then back again. 'Thanks, but I suggested she wait until spring. Bart raves so about the Tennessee spring. I'll go up there for Christmas.'

Laura glanced at Bart. He was gazing intently at his shoes. He looked up. 'I'll be here,' he said. 'Just Paula is going.'

She searched their faces, remembering the argument. 'Is that okay with both of you? I know when we were here . . .'

Again they exchanged glances. 'It's fine,' they said in unison, reserved, but none of the hostility she'd seen that night at dinner.

'Well, thank you,' she said again. Christmas – she didn't want to think about it. Christmas without Annie. 'Thanks for everything.' She hugged them and started down the steps.

'Maybe you and I could have lunch some time,' Paula called after her.

'Oh, I'd like that,' she said, tears springing to her eyes again.

'Tell Dad hi,' Bart said. 'You sure you're okay?' as she was leaving.

'I'm fine. I'll talk to you later.' Quick, get in the car before you lose it and tell them what it's like living with someone who half the time doesn't know you're there.

She drove a few blocks, pulled over to the curb, shut off the motor. Calm down, she told herself, taking some deep breaths. Sure, it was rough finding that diary entry of Annie's. But Bart and Paula were reassuring, not even thrown by her outburst. Annie was right. She was 'emotionally all over the place'. She had probably over-reacted with Trace. She could have waited until he'd looked through the mail, not sprung her story on him when he first got home. She saw his face, white, frightened, as she slammed out the door. He must have thought she was crazy. He would be waiting. She started the car.

He was on the phone in the kitchen when she went into the house. As she passed by she planted a quick kiss on his shoulder, the nubby grain of his Oxford-blue shirt. He waved a hand, said something into the phone and hung up.

'So do you feel better? How are Bart and Paula?'

'Yes, I feel better and Bart and Paula seem okay.' She opened the refrigerator door to get out things for dinner. 'Who was that on the phone?'

'Kate Morton.'

'Kate Morton?'

'My graduate student.'

'It's an odd hour to be calling you. Dinner time.'

'She didn't call me. I called her.'

She held the door, looked at him. 'Oh?'

'She and another student are helping with my seminar on Descartes. She'd asked me some questions this afternoon. I thought I'd answer. Since I had the time.' The words were measured, slow.

She was tearing lettuce into a salad bowl. 'Have I met her?'

'At the department Open House last spring. Tall, dark hair. She was wearing a bright pink dress. Some kind of a shawl with fringe.' He moved toward the cupboard. 'Shall I set the table?'

The hubbub of lunchtime diners filled the restaurant, along with the smells of gumbo and apple crisp. Laura, seated across from Paula in a sunny corner booth, offered her the roll basket. 'Here, have another.'

'Thanks. I love these biscuits.' Paula took one, broke it open, buttered it, took a bite, and put the rest on her plate beside the nearly finished quiche and fruit salad. A waitress came and tipped the pitcher sideways to refill their glasses of iced tea. Ice as well as tea tumbled into the glass. The waitress moved on.

'Bart tells me they serve iced tea all year round here. In the north it's a summertime drink.'

'That was a surprise to me, too,' Laura said. 'Along with the predilection to sweeten it. So if you want unsweetened tea you often have to ask for it.' She lifted her glass in acknowledgement, set it down. 'How about some dessert?' She gestured toward a tiered cart against the wall. 'Have you tried chess pie yet?'

'No more for me, thanks. I'll finish up my fruit and get back to work.' Paula smiled, looking across at Laura. 'But it's very nice being with you. I love having our own place, but I miss seeing you and Mr Randall.'

'We miss you, too,' Laura said. 'And I apologize again for bursting in on you the other night. I was a real basket case.'

She shook her head. 'You were sweet to take me in. And it was dear of you to call me and suggest this get-together.'

'I'd been meaning to,' Paula said. 'I miss my mom, and I know you . . .' She paused. 'Not that I'm any substitute.'

'Not a substitute, no,' Laura said, 'but a wonderful presence in our lives, someone who,' she hesitated, groping for words, 'who partakes of some of the same life she did, though several years further down the road.'

'I'm so glad I had a chance to meet her that time you came to college,' Paula said.

'She liked you a lot. She was looking forward to your being here,' she smiled wryly, 'hoping you and Bart would be an escape hatch from the terrors of living with us, I think.'

'Oh, Mrs Randall. I'm sure you had your tensions. But all in all, Annie was a lucky young woman to have parents like you.'

Laura was wistful. 'Sometimes I think she saw that.'

Neither of them spoke. The murmur of voices, the sound of silverware scraping against dishes was an easy backdrop to their silence. Then Laura said, 'Your mother, not coming till spring. Is that really all right? I know there was some tension between you and Bart about his staying in the apartment when she comes. He was so adamant – though I can see his point, too.' She ran her finger down the side of her glass, clearing a path in the moisture. 'I guess whatever shock Trace and I might have experienced we used up long ago.' She looked up at the young woman across from her. 'You know Annie was sexually active – at sixteen?'

Paula nodded, her eyes registered sympathy. 'Bart told me. That is young, though a lot of young people are active at that age. He also said she was very responsible, using birth control. Still, I'm sure it was hard for you. I'm sure my mother guesses that I have been too, though I was older. But to live with someone advertises it to the world and you can't deny it any more.'

'Sometimes young people live together for company and safety. No particular sexual involvement at all.'

Paula laughed. 'I know. My mother finds that hard to fathom too. And she'd never believe that of Bart and me.'

'Would you want her to?'

'No. Besides, we couldn't maintain the demeanor. And we have one bed.'

Laura chuckled. 'That *is* a giveaway.'

'As far as delaying her visit, yes, it's okay. She works in a college bookstore and it's a busy time with the fall classes getting underway. It's fine with her as long as I come at Christmas, which I've planned to do all along.'

Laura was reassured. 'Good. I was afraid pressure from Bart had made you do something you really didn't want to do, or not do something you did want to do – have your mother visit.'

'That is part of it, but only part. We talked about it after you left that night – why he was so "adamant" as you put it. We talked for a long time about what was going on with him.'

'Like what?' Laura asked. 'If you can tell me. I don't want to intrude.'

'Well, for one thing, it was your first time to visit us, and he wanted everything just right.'

'It was a lovely dinner, Paula, and fun to inspect your place, look at the yard.'

'Which looks like a junk shop before trash pickup day,' Paula interjected.

'And it was wonderful to be with you and Bart, though I noticed that except for the flap about your mother's visit, Bart didn't say a lot. Does he talk to you much about Annie?'

'Quite a lot.'

'I'm glad. He's not talked much to us. And I've worried about it.'

The waitress came. 'Anything else I can get for you, ladies?' she asked in a bright voice.

Laura and Paula looked at each other, shook their heads. 'No thank you.'

They were getting ready to leave when Paula stopped her slide out of the booth and turned to Laura. 'There's one more thing.'

'Yes?'

A shadow crossed Paula's face. Her eyes looked troubled. 'He blames himself, too, that he wasn't able to save her.'

'Oh, Paula! How could he?' Laura's heart clamped in her

chest. 'The horse had run off. Bart wasn't even there.'

'I know. So does he. But he can't seem to be free of it, the idea that somehow he could have saved her life. That maybe you blame him.' And then she added softly, 'Or that he might have been the one.'

Laura could feel the pain of such speculation twist in her gut. Dear Bart. 'No, no, no,' she murmured. Could he have handled a runaway horse? Or, if he had ridden that horse, might it not have bolted? If they had lost Bart, what then? To choose, even in fantasy, between her children appalled her. In horror she drew back, walled off such thoughts, cast them away. 'He mustn't think that,' she said. 'No, no. You mustn't let him think that.'

Now Paula's eyes were grave. 'Please don't tell him I told you this,' she said. 'I probably shouldn't have. But if he sometimes seems a little distracted or whatever, well, that may be part of the reason.'

Distracted? Laura thought. It wouldn't be surprising. His father wrote the book on distraction. She reached across the table to take Paula's hand. 'Please know that no way on earth would Trace or I think of blaming Bart at all, not at all. I've been so grateful that he was there, to be with her, his tenderness . . .' She remembered in the car on the way to Boulder Bart's telling how he had covered her with his jacket, patted her back, told her she would be all right. Remembered his words, 'I didn't want her to be alone.'

They were gathering up their things now, resuming their leaving.

Outside, they embraced. 'Say hi to Mr Randall,' Paula said.

'Give my love to Bart.' Hungrily, she watched Paula move off, then got in her car and went home.

17

Woodbridge readied itself for Christmas. Ropes of red and silver foil festooned the street lights on the main street of town. 'Little Drummer Boy' and 'Rudolph the Red-Nosed Reindeer' scratched away on store PA systems. The symphony, a mix of town and gown musicians, prepared its holiday concert. The ballet troupe attempted *The Nutcracker* once more. The first snow fell.

Philip, arriving for Christmas vacation in the old beat-up car he'd bought for two hundred dollars from a fellow student, went first to Bart's and Paula's house. It was evening and there were lights on in the ground floor apartment where the owner lived but no lights on upstairs. He parked and went up on the porch and rang their bell anyway. He'd seen the place before they moved in but couldn't remember the layout of the rooms.

No one answered. In a ground-floor window a child's face peered round the edge of a window shade. Philip smiled and waved. A small hand appeared beside the face, waved a starfish wave. The child disappeared. Philip turned and went back to his car and continued on home.

He was uneasy as he approached the door. His mother's grief was so raw – he could tell that on the phone – and how would it be for him, going into that familiar house with Annie gone? Of course they'd all been here at the end of the summer, but this would be confronting it all over again.

He rang the bell and heard his mother's voice, 'It's Philip!' and the rush of feet. The door opened and they were both there and he hugged them, one at a time, and it was really all right that his eyes were wet with tears.

Then the three of them went out and examined the car in the light from the street lamp. 'It had two new tires and a tankful of gas!' Philip exulted. They all agreed what a bargain it was and then of course his mother needed to be reassured that it was safe to drive and his father wondered what kind of mileage he got and had he done anything about insurance and if he hadn't they'd put a rider on their policy to include him. Which he knew was a big expense, he being under twenty-one, but also that right now they would do anything for him that they could, as he would for them.

'I went by Bart and Paula's,' he said when they got back in the house. He didn't say why – to be some kind of a buffer against coming home. 'The baby downstairs waved at me but no sight of Bart and Paula. Anybody know where they are?'

Laura put down the familiar panic. Ever since Annie died, any uncertainty on the whereabouts of anyone close to her could set it off, even though there was no reason on earth she should know, right now, where her son and Paula were. They could be at the store, visiting friends, delayed at work. 'Paula's going to her mother's in Ohio in a couple of days and she said something about finishing her shopping. You can call them later. They know you're coming.'

Just then there was another knock at the door. A key turned and they heard Bart's voice. 'Hi! I see he made it. That's some crate you've got out there. You have to push it to get it home?' He came in, laughing, he in his heavy mackinaw filling the door, his arms outstretched to his brother, and there was Paula behind him, pink-cheeked, wearing her purple down coat. They all hugged.

'How about some coffee, or beer?' Laura asked. And to Philip, 'Have you eaten?' No, he hadn't eaten – or at least he was ready to eat again. She went into the kitchen, put the heat on under the still warm stew, and allowed herself a few tears. How Annie would have loved this homecoming.

With Philip here, they bought a wreath for the front door, and a Christmas tree. 'Maybe,' Laura said to Trace as he came in from taking the tree from the trunk of the car and leaning it against the shed wall until it was time to bring it in, 'maybe we'll get through this season after all.'

He hugged her. 'Sure we will,' he said.

All fall she had dreaded the coming of Christmas. All the familiar family rituals of Advent wreath and tree and gifts, of special food, of going to church on Christmas Eve and coming home to spiced tea and Christmas cookies – it would all be a mockery, fraught with pain. They had talked briefly of going somewhere away from home, but knew their sadness would follow them. Somehow, they would slog it through.

Christmas was on Tuesday. On Friday Paula left. Bart brought his suitcase and moved back into his old room with Philip – 'for old times,' he joked. 'Besides, I get better food here than batching it on my own.'

Two days before Christmas, Trace and Bart and Philip put up the tree. Trace brought down the box of ornaments from the attic. Piled on top were the stockings, each with its name. Laura fingered them, the appliqued felt and tiny sequins, the white squared letters of the names. 'Please, let's not hang the stockings this year.'

She lifted out the box containing the Christmas creche she'd had since childhood. It was one of Annie's favorite Christmas things. Since she'd been a little girl she'd always helped Laura set it up on the mahogany buffet. She unpacked the pieces – Joseph with his knicked arm, Mary in a faded blue cloak, the baby Jesus now a blurred oblong of wax, his halo a dingy gold – and arranged them, wordlessly, a fierceness in her hands.

On Christmas Eve they went to church and, in the luminous darkness, sang.

They came home, sat together in the darkened living room, the white lights of the Christmas tree blinking off and on, like new constellations demanding attention.

Finally, they spoke of it.

'All fall I tried to study,' Philip said. 'She was all I could think of.'

From his chair in the corner Bart nodded, his face a mask of pain. 'I know what you mean.' Then he said, 'A guy I

223

work with has a sister who was in Annie's class. She came in last week. She'd ridden with Annie a couple of times. She said sometimes a horse will just take off and if they sense a person is scared . . .' His voice broke off and Laura, remembering her conversation with Paula, thought, don't do this to yourself, there's nothing you could have done.

Philip turned toward Trace and Laura. 'How is it for you guys?'

There was silence for a minute, then Laura said, 'I've dreaded Christmas. I wished it would never come. Who would hang the Angel of the Lord?' She laughed then. Annie had named it that years ago, a small red felt angel with worn gold wings. Always she had hung it as high as she could reach, its passage up the tree reflecting year by year her growing stature. It hung now, close to the top. Laura had put it there, asking no one, claiming it for herself as her prerogative. They had probably seen her do it. They had not spoken of it. She got up and touched it now, turning it to catch the light. She sat down.

In the quiet that followed Trace said, 'It's been hard, of course. But I almost feel she's here, come to be with us.'

They looked at him, surprised. They would not have expected such a sentiment from him, such an intuition. 'There's a young graduate student in my department,' he went on. 'Sometimes she reminds me of Annie.'

Kate? Laura wondered.

On Christmas afternoon Paula rang. Bart came from the phone. 'She sends her love. She's having a good visit.' He sighed in resignation. 'She was going to look for a good opportunity to tell her mother. She hasn't found one yet.'

Laura called Rachel. 'How are you, Mother?'

'I'm all right. Ella and Jackson are here. How are you?'

They talked for a while, then Rachel said, 'Howard has some science meeting in New York. He's coming to see me on his way. When are you coming?'

Laura remembered the acrimonious discussions in the fall about when she would go to visit Rachel and was glad not to have to repeat that. 'I'll come after New Year's, after Philip goes.'

The phone rang again before she got out of the kitchen. It was Ginny, calling from Hadley. 'I knew this would be a tough Christmas. Tom and I are thinking of you.'

'Thanks,' she said. 'It was dear of you to call. How are you?'

'Fine. Fred's here too. He sends his love.'

'Oh! And mine to him. Tell him I'm working on his drawings.'

She heard murmurings at the other end of the line. 'Here, you tell him.'

'Laura?' Fred's voice came on. 'How are you, dear?'

'We're okay. Our boys are here. Thanks for sending the material.'

'How does it look? Anything that catches your eye?'

'I've started some sketches. Just started, though. I haven't done much of anything lately – getting ready for Christmas.' And I hadn't the heart for it, she thought to herself.

'No hurry. When are you coming up?'

'Sometime next month.'

'I'll try to get over while you're here. I'll check with Ginny.'

'That'd be great.' They said goodbye and she hung up, her hand light on the phone. She realized she was smiling. She stood for a moment by the window. Outside, the neighbors' Christmas lights sparkled in the darkening night. The sounds of carolling children drifted up the street. The season, though so colored with sadness, still offered its tender mercies, its promises of hope, its gifts of the love of family and friends. Didn't it?

'How's Grandma?' Philip asked when she returned to the living room. He sat slouched against the sofa, his red shirt pulled taut by the book he held propped open on his chest, his hand spread across a glossy green page.

'She's doing all right. Very well, in fact. She's surprised us all, how well she's managing with Grandpa gone. She's quite a gutsy woman, my mother.'

He laughed. 'Good.' He shifted the book and tilted it toward her. 'Look. Argonne Woods.'

'Argonne Woods!' she repeated. 'What book is that?'

He flipped the cover over to show her the title, *American*

Wilderness. 'I just discovered the picture.' He returned to the photo – deep woods, the winding river in the distance, in the foreground a few sprigs of white trillium and wood violets. He read the caption, '"Argonne Woods. One of the last stands of virgin timber in the east." Our old hangout,' he said.

Years ago Trace had taken them to Argonne Woods. He'd gone there when he was young. After the first time they were all hooked. They went every spring, to stay a weekend in a log cabin by the river, its edges blurred by burgeoning green and the occasional cloud of woodsmoke sent up by a controlled Park Service fire. It was one of Annie's favorite places. 'When I get married,' she'd said, 'I'm going to Argonne Woods for my honeymoon.' They hiked in the woods, the ascents and glades and lookout points familiar to them year by year. In the evenings they played Monopoly and Hearts, gathered at the round table beneath the flared metal cone of the single hanging light, and promised that next year they would remember to bring a brighter light bulb.

She sat down on the sofa by Philip. 'We didn't go last year. Annie didn't want to. She said she was too busy.'

Philip looked away, regret etching his face. 'She would have,' he said softly. 'She wrote me, begging me to get off school and come. She said with Bart and me both gone it would just be too sad.' He sighed. 'I was busy. I didn't think I could take the time.' His voice caught in a sob. 'Every day since she died I've wished I'd said, "Yeah, let's go." I thought there would be time.' He moved his hand deliberately over the page, as though to erase in the lushness of these trees the memory of his sister's wish ungranted.

Laura put her hand on his shoulder. 'I didn't know,' she said. 'She didn't tell me.'

Trace came into the room, wearing his new shirt from Paula and Bart. 'Nice?' He turned round for their approval.

'Yes. But look, Trace. Argonne Woods.'

He came and looked over Philip's shoulder.

'It was one of Annie's favorite places in the world,' she said.

'Where did we get this book?' Philip asked.

226

'I bought it,' Trace said. 'Last week.'

Laura looked at him. 'You didn't tell me.'

'I would have. We've been so busy.' He sat down. 'You were able to get through to Mother? How is she?'

'She's well. I told her I'd come up in a couple of weeks. I talked to Ginny too. I'll see her and Tom. And Fred,' she added impulsively.

'Fred?'

'Ginny's brother. I told you about him. An old flame – sort of.' Was she teasing him? He seemed not to notice.

'Fine,' he said and picked up a new book, a study of political systems, and began to read. She looked at him in wonder and consternation. Had he not heard? Was he so secure – or uninterested – that the mention of revisiting an old flame aroused no touch of concern or speculation? But he was lost in his book. Should she be glad of such trust? And who was this Kate Morton?

She picked up *American Wilderness*. It fell open to the picture of Argonne Woods and she tried to re-enter that world, with all of them there, walking the trails together.

After a few minutes she put it down. Bart and Philip had gone outside to trade notes on car maintenance. The house was quiet. She leaned back in the chair, eyes half-closed, watching the sparkle of tree lights, the flicker of ornaments as the slight motion of warm air rising moved them against the deep green of the pine. Her eyes travelled up the Christmas tree to the red felt skirt, the bent gold wings of the Angel of the Lord, turning in the light. Where are you, my darling? Suddenly the words cut through her heart. She felt overcome by a feeling of unutterable loneliness. Slowly she stood up and moved toward Annie's room. Trace seemed not to notice her leaving. In Annie's room she stood for a moment before the louvered doors of the storage closet, then opened the door and took from the shelf, where she had put it five months ago, the box of Annie's ashes, brownwrapped in its mailing paper. She sat down on the bed and cradled the box in her lap, her body leaning forward to surround it with her own warm flesh. Tears fell on her skirt, made dark splotches on the wrapping paper of the box.

Moments passed. She looked up, toward the open closet

door. There on a lower shelf were some old books – children's books, a Bible, an old *Farmer's Almanac*.

Her grandfather had given her the Bible when she was recovering from her childhood illness, along with a Bible story coloring book. She remembered some of the pictures in the coloring book – one of Jesus and the children, his face turned sideways and the shepherd's crook in his hand, the children in white gowns reaching below their knees. Another picture of an angel by a wall and a huge stone. She remembered sitting up in bed, coloring the angel. Her mother stood beside her.

'What color are the wings?' she'd asked.

'I don't know,' her mother said. 'Gold, maybe?'

She remembered pushing through the crayons and looking for gold, then finding it and coloring in the wings.

18

Laura found Rachel frailer but in no apparent crisis. She was confined to bed most of the time. The doctor's prediction that she might require permanent catheterization had been borne out: a flannel-covered bag was hooked to the side of the bed. When Rachel got up once or twice a day to walk round the room or sit at the table, the bag went with her.

'Is it uncomfortable?' Laura asked.

'No, I'm used to it.'

After that they did not speak of it.

At supper, Rachel sat propped up against pillows, her shoulders listing to the side, her head tipped so far it almost touched her plate but she did not know it – a small curled woman, her mouth working round bites of food, her hand on the teacup so unsteady Laura looked away lest her mother read the fear in her eyes.

After supper they talked for a while, but soon Rachel said, 'I'm tired. Help me back to bed.' Laura passed her arm round her mother's shoulders, guided her as she shuffled the few steps back to bed.

Rachel lay back, her eyes closed. When she opened them, her glance brushed over Laura. Then, not speaking, she reached for the evening paper, its pages fanned out on the bed. She had already been through it once. She began to turn the pages slowly but her eyes didn't move. When she finished, she turned back through it again, stopping at each page, her eyes not moving over it at all.

Laura got up and went into the kitchen where Carlena was finishing the dishes. She picked up a towel but Carlena took it from her. 'No, no, I'll do it.' She looked at Laura. 'There now, dear, you mustn't cry. Your mother's had a good life. She's not suffering.'

'Is she always like this? Reading, not seeing?'

'She's good in the mornings. You'll see a big difference in the morning.'

Carlena was right. The next morning Rachel was much brighter. She asked about Trace, Bart and Paula, Philip.

They spoke of Rachel's friends, Laura prompting, going down the list one by one.

'Alice?'

'Alice has bad diabetes, you know. Her foot doesn't heal.'

'Mabel?' Mabel Olmstead had long been a favorite of Laura's. She'd often visited her when she came to Hadley.

'Mabel is in the Cramer Home.'

'Oh. Does she like it?' Rachel had talked once of trying Cramer Home herself. It was after Will died.

'I think she likes it. She has friends there. She misses Barney, of course.'

'Sometime I'd like to visit her. And Eloise?'

'Oh, I guess I didn't tell you. She's gone to live with her daughter in Connecticut.'

Laura looked up quickly. Was there censure implied in this comment. Rachel's face seemed untroubled, free of resentment or guile.

'I didn't know that.' She hurried on, 'How about Marjorie?'

'I never hear from her. She's way out in the country. Joe is still living. I guess they're all right.'

But when they had finished the account of family and friends, there seemed little to say. Rachel dozed off. Laura drank the last swallow of cold coffee, observed how the trees edging the back hill were still winter-gaunt. How the trees had grown over the years since Rachel and Will had built this house on what was pastureland in Will's father's farm. Now the street was lined with houses, the last lots bought years ago. 'We were first,' Rachel said. 'We could have had any lot we wanted. I wanted to face toward the hills,' and she would look up at the dark horizon beyond the last row of houses. 'I will lift up mine eyes unto the hills,' she would say, giving a Biblical blessing to their choice, all those years ago.

Laura looked at Rachel, sleeping now, and hungered with a hunger reminiscent of childhood for her mother's presence. Rachel was so frail – these few days together could be their last. How to make the time blossom before it slipped away?

It was Rachel herself who provided a key, inadvertently, from her simple physical need. She was cold. 'Will you get me another blanket, dear?' she asked, and Laura, for once circumventing Carlena's ever-present helpfulness – she was in another room and didn't hear – went upstairs to find one. And so began a succession of memory-evoking objects – by which memories they extended, sanctified, their time.

The blanket she chose was a handwoven wool coverlet of cream and deep blue. Her great-grandmother had woven it as part of her trousseau, weaving the name of her beloved, 'Dewitt, Dewitt', round its four borders.

'Here, I brought this one,' she said, unfolding it and spreading it over Rachel, releasing the smell of mothballs into the air.

Rachel's face brightened. 'My grandmother wove this before she was married.'

'It was so romantic,' Laura said. 'Lillian and I loved to go up there when we were playing house. When did you get it? I don't remember its ever not being there.'

'My father was her first child,' Rachel said, her hand moving back and forth over the cloth, her dry skin scratching against the soft wool. 'She gave this blanket to my father when my grandfather died.'

Laura turned it round in her mind. She had not known that part of the story. 'Do you think of him often, your father?'

'Yes. I think of Will, too. Sometimes I get them mixed up, which is which, putting them in the wrong place – Will in the house in Troy, my father here, taking care of Mother and me.'

Laura looked at her mother, the wistfulness in her face.

In some way emboldened by the blanket, she ventured, 'I like to think that in some way they are still loving you, caring for you.'

Rachel's face contorted with emotion. 'I hope so,' she said. She looked off into the distance and after a minute Laura said, 'What are you thinking of?'

Her mother turned back. 'I was just thinking of the color of Annie's hair.'

Laura's eyes filled with tears. 'Yes,' she said.

'Darling.' Rachel reached out to her and she laid her head on the edge of the bed and her mother stroked her hair. 'You think of her every day,' she said.

'Yes,' her voice muffled against a lift of the coverlet. 'It's like the air I breathe. Or the lenses of my eyes.'

The next day she brought to Rachel's bedside a string of carved amber beads. She held them in the morning sunlight. 'I remember these. What did you wear them with?'

Rachel shifted her head against the pillows. 'I don't know. I think I had those when we were first married. I haven't worn them in years. Where did you find them?'

'In a jewel box in your drawer. I used to open it sometimes when I was putting away your handkerchiefs. These beads were such a symbol of glamor to me. You dressed up in them to go out with Father.'

Rachel smiled. Laura continued, 'I remember when you turned forty. I would have been eight. I thought forty was so old.' She waited, watching Rachel's face.

Rachel was gazing out the window. She appeared not to have heard and Laura wondered whether she was tiring her mother, whether being together in this way, recalling old stories, enriching though it was for her, was too much for Rachel.

'Mother?'

'I'm listening, dear. You thought forty was old.'

'Do you mind me talking on this way?'

'Mind?' Rachel turned, her expression tender, luminous. 'I don't mind anything you do, dear. Don't you know that?'

Laura drew in her breath. Mother, there have been times. Is it all right with us now?

'Well, what about forty?' Rachel said.

'Forty?' She had forgotten in the flow of peace that seemed suddenly to bathe the room. Then she remembered. 'Just that I thought forty seemed so old and then soon after your birthday you and Father went somewhere and you had on a long yellow silk gown, and these beads, and you came in to kiss us goodnight and you looked so beautiful.'

Rachel was smiling again. 'It's . . . in . . . the . . . eye . . . of the . . . beholder,' she said, recalling a word at a time. 'My father used to say that, beauty is in the eye of the beholder.' She picked up the amber beads. 'When I was forty, Howard was still an infant. I've often wondered . . .'

'Wondered what?'

'I thought of being a writer. In college I wrote for the magazine. But when I finished raising children, it seemed too late. Women weren't doing so much, the way they are today.'

Laura nodded, knowing all too well. 'It's still hard to get going on a new career. But it was a different time, Mother.'

'I wrote a few things as you were growing up, some poems from time to time. I'm sure you'd think they were old-fashioned and sentimental. I threw most of them away. I did one when my mother died.'

'Did you save it?'

'Yes.'

'Do you know where it is? May I look?'

'It's under some notebooks, in the drawer of my desk that's nearest her picture. Go and see.'

Laura went to the desk in the living room. There, under the notebooks, was a single sheet, rippled with time, cream-colored at the edges: 'My Mother's Dress'. She brought it to Rachel. 'Shall I read it aloud?'

'I guess so. If you want.'

She began.

> For mornings Mother always wore
> A print of lavender;
> She had gray hair and smiling eyes,
> The color suited her.
> But when the dinner work was done,
> The house all clean and bright,

233

> She changed the morning lavender
> For soft and dainty white.

Halfway through, Laura stopped and looked up. Rachel's face was flushed. 'Go on,' she said.

> Now Mother's earthly work is done,
> God called her home to rest.
> And so she changed her gown to white.
> I know, of course, it's best.
> But oh, I miss the lavender
> My earthly eyes could see,
> The dear familiar morning dress
> She wore at work with me.

'That's lovely.' Laura looked at her mother again.

'I told you it was old-fashioned.' But Rachel was pleased, her eyes shining. 'My angel mother,' she said.

They were quiet together. 'When you were so sick,' Rachel said, 'I prayed to God for your healing. But it was my mother's face I saw.'

Laura closed her eyes, half looking for the woman in the pale dress and dark hair of the photograph by her mother's desk – her grandmother Laura.

'I wish I remembered her,' she said.

'You remind me of her sometimes. Do you know, I still miss her,' Rachel said, surprise in her voice, 'after all this time.' Her hand brushed against the cream-colored paper, brittle, fragile with age. 'I wonder,' she said, 'if you'll ever write about me.'

'The thing is, Ginny,' Laura set the glass down on the wicker table, 'we don't seem able to talk much any more, Trace and I. If I start to talk about Annie he gets impatient or he turns away.'

They were sitting in Ginny's sunroom, a pitcher of Sangria and a plate of crackers and cheese on the table in front of them, the wicker planters, the shelves of green plants and violets around them. Since Ginny had met her at the airport several days ago and taken her to Rachel's, they had talked almost daily on the phone. Now Laura had come for a visit while Rachel napped. 'Take your time, dear,' Carlena had said. 'Your mother and I will be fine.'

Ginny picked up a cracker, topped it with a thin slab of Havarti. 'Maybe it's too close to him, all that pain.'

'It's hard to believe he even cares.' The vehemence in her voice surprised her. 'That was the thing with him and Annie, too. She felt he never *listened* to her. She and I talked a lot.'

'So in some ways he wasn't there for her?'

'In some ways he wasn't. He knew that, and he knows it now, and it's terrible for him.'

'Does he talk about it?'

'Not much. I wish he did. He talked about it once when the boys were home.' She remembered it. 'Actually, when he does, I don't know that I'm much help. I want to be sympathetic but sometimes I think, you brought it on yourself, now live with it. It's almost,' she drew her shoulders forward in a shudder, 'as though I want him to suffer, as though I'm blaming him all over again for what's finished.' She reached in her purse for a handkerchief and blew her nose. 'I suppose we set each other off, too. He told me once, "You always outclass me with your mother's grief."'

Ginny nodded.

'In a way he's right,' Laura went on. 'I sometimes feel like I'm the one who's most deeply hurt. I put more into raising her, so the lion's share of grief is mine. Sometimes we're with people and it comes up about Annie's death and someone asks Trace a question about how it happened and he tells them, one detail after another, hardly any feeling in his voice. I want to scream. I want them to ask *me*.'

Ginny sighed. 'We shield ourselves, Laura, sometimes to protect ourselves from feeling. Sometimes to preserve our illusions. You. Trace. Tom. I. We have to, at first. Then, little by little, we braid it into our lives. Do you mind if I tell you something about Tom and me?'

'Please do.' But she thought, not me. I have not shielded myself, I who have walked into the middle of this death, kept myself open to its nuances and its pain.

'You know our Tommy was killed by a car?'

'Yes.'

'But you may not know the circumstances.'

Laura shook her head.

'He ran out of the play yard, into the street.' She paused. 'The play yard had a gate, and Tom had left the gate open.'

'Oh, Ginny!'

'It was awful for him, of course. But I blamed him too. We talked about it. I tried to forgive him – he felt so terrible. But in between times I'd find myself thinking, you did it. You're responsible for it. It's your fault.' She put her hand to the throat of her red blouse and swallowed. 'But three weeks before Tommy was killed, *I* had left the gate open. I found him toddling along the curb, beside the road. It terrified me. I thought, what kind of mother am I? How could I have been so careless? I was too ashamed to tell Tom – and it could have warned him.

'After Tommy was killed I kept pushing all that out of my mind. I couldn't acknowledge it. It was as though the memory would come toward me and then veer off. The incident wasn't real. No one must know about it, least of all me. What had happened was Tom's fault, not mine. I had to blame someone. I couldn't blame myself. And he *had* left the gate open, the critical time.'

She sat back in the chair, her hand playing over the intertwining cords of white wicker. 'I struggled with it for months. Then one day I told Tom. We talked, cried all over again, forgave each other for whatever there was to forgive by then. But for a while I had this myth I needed to keep believing – that I was a better mother than that. Even that I was the good parent, almost like being the good child.'

During the last of this recital Laura had been turning her watchband round and round, twisting the links of the chain, turning them back. Now she stopped. Images flooded through her mind – Annie smiling, Annie coming to put her arms round her after Will's death, Annie's face when she asked, 'Is it all right if I take your drawing to school?'

But there were other images, too. Annie's cool 'No, thanks' when Laura offered to share again a cooking project they used to do together; Annie's defiant 'Why not?' when they wouldn't let Gordon stay overnight; the figure of a girl hunched over a desk, writing angry words in her journal.

She looked at Virginia. 'I have had my own myths,' she said.

They were finishing dinner when the phone rang. Carlena jumped up. 'I'll get it.' She returned in a moment. 'Some man for you, Laura – don't sound like your husband.'

She hurried to the phone. Bart maybe? A moment of panic. He'd seemed pretty low the last time she'd seen him.

But it was Fred Thayer. 'Laura, Ginny told me you're here. Why didn't you let me know?'

'Fred! How nice to hear from you.' Her relief was audible, magnified her pleasure at hearing from Fred. 'I did think about it,' she said, apologetic. 'Maybe because I haven't done anything about Iceland.' It was true. She'd made a few attempts at pencil sketches, but nothing seemed promising. It was even hard to get to the last two panels for Walter Stone, and she did know what that required – the darker gouaches, some ink outlining, blocking in the text.

'Forget Iceland,' he said. 'What about Cape Cod?'

'Cape Cod? Where are you?'

'I'm in Northampton,' he said. 'I've been working here several days and have more still to do. But what I called about . . . I'd really like to see you again and I had this wild idea.'

'Wild idea?' she said, bemused. 'Tell me.'

'I have to drive down to Dennis tomorrow for a home-owners' meeting – we do this once every winter and hope we don't get snowed in – and I wondered if you'd like to go with me. I remember that you love the Cape. It would be a long day but we could make it. The meeting will be a couple of hours in the early afternoon. You could hang out at my house, maybe bring your sketching stuff, or a book to read. The town isn't much for browsing in mid-winter. I invited Ginny too, but she can't come. What do you think?'

She was quite speechless at the suggestion and at first didn't say anything.

Then he said, 'I thought it might be a nice change for you – if your mother could spare you for a day.'

For a moment she closed her eyes, imagining. It would

be wonderful to fill her lungs with sea air and, yes, to leave for a full day the necessary cares and anxieties of the sickroom. And to be with Fred. Yes, to be with Fred. So much to talk about, so much unspoken history to share. 'Hold on a minute.' She hurried into the dining room where Carlena was settling Rachel back onto her bed. 'There you go. Let me put this pillow under your head.' Rachel lifted her head obediently, sank down again.

'Who was it, dear?' she asked Laura.

'He's still on the phone,' she said. 'It's Ginny's brother, Fred. He's invited me to drive down to Cape Cod with him tomorrow – he has a meeting. We'd go early and get back pretty late at night. Would that be okay?' Even as she asked she realized how much she wanted to go, was prepared to deal with Rachel's protest if it was forthcoming.

'But it's winter,' Rachel said, puzzled.

'I know,' Laura said. 'He's going down for a meeting. Just for the day.'

'I guess it's all right,' Rachel said, her voice trailing off.

Carlena patted the pillow and spoke into Rachel's ear. 'We'll be fine, dear.' Her mouth closed in a tight line and Laura wondered whether a day-long trip with a man not your husband stretched Carlena's moral code.

'I'll bring you some salt water taffy – if I can find any off season,' she said and turned, uncertain whether Rachel acquiesced or not, or even understood.

She picked up the phone, feeling an ominous tug at her heart. She had only a few more days, and here she was, leaving Rachel. Or was it just the passing of time, the prospect of inevitable loss? 'I'd love to go, Fred. When shall I be ready?'

They left just as the sky was beginning to lighten. 'I'm dressed for the North Pole,' Laura said. She was wearing plaid wool slacks, her heavy Irish sweater over a coral turtleneck, fleece-lined boots. She carried a coat over her arm. 'I have a wool cap in my pocket,' she said, patting the bulge in the coat.

Fred laughed. 'The weather prediction is good. Unless there's a lot of wind, it can be very pleasant on the beach, even in January.' He had wool slacks, too, and a down jacket, and a cap stuffed into the well pocket of the car door.

On the way they talked – of the weather first, that it was a nice day, nothing untoward predicted. He asked about Rachel. 'I think she's doing all right,' Laura said. 'Sometimes, like last evening, she dozes a lot.' It was true, her mother had seemed unusually torpid last night, coming in and out of awareness, mumbling a few words, then going back to sleep. 'Other times she's as alert as you or I,' and she found herself telling him about the coverlet, the beads, the poem about her grandmother.

'That's lovely,' he said, and she nodded, remembering the quality of that afternoon.

They recalled high school days. Fred, too, had not kept up with his classmates. 'I travelled so much, and we lived abroad for a while. Until the divorce. After that I bought the Cape Cod house. I keep an apartment in New York, but I consider the house my home. I've always loved the ocean.'

'Me too,' she said. Then, 'Your divorce, how long ago?'

'About ten years. I was still in the import business then.' He sighed. 'I really worked at it, flying all over. I made a lot of money, too. But I suppose you'd say it cost me my marriage, though I'm not sure that was all of it.'

'Nothing is ever all of it,' she said wryly.

He nodded. 'I suppose.'

They stopped at a Friendly's restaurant near Worcester for breakfast. When they turned onto the Cape it was still mid-morning, the sun bright, only the slightest residue of old snow clinging at the bases of seagrass and the stubby pines that tilted against the dunes.

As they approached Dennis, he said, 'My meeting is at two. I keep some food in the house – wine, frozen stuff. Most of the restaurants are closed now, but there's a place where they sell fried clams to go. How about it?'

'Sounds wonderful.'

He pulled up at the Clam Shack and came out carrying a large brown bag. He set it on the floor by her feet. She saw the top of a quart box mounded with fried clams and a second box, covered, cylindrical. 'Clam chowder,' he said, laughing. 'Might as well OD while we're here. And down in there somewhere is a box of coleslaw – an attempt at a well-balanced meal.'

'Great. I'm willing to let the food pyramid go for the day. I mean,' she looked out the car window at the wide sky, bright blue, a few scudding clouds, and against the horizon dunes and grass and the blurred gray line of the sea, 'it's another world.' She turned to him, put her hand over his as it rested on the steering wheel. 'Thank you,' she said. 'I didn't know how much I needed to get away, just to see . . . this.'

His smile was warm. 'You're welcome. Thank you for coming.'

They drove in silence the additional half-mile along the beach road. 'Here we are.' He pulled in beside a gray-shingled house, one of several on a grassy overlook about one hundred yards from the beach. They got out and she went to stand on the promontory and took deep breaths of air and held her face to the sun and felt some of the strain and sadness of the past months ease away and felt her eyes sting – not from pain but from joy, and she thought, this is one of life's perfect moments. And then the reminder – but your daughter . . . And she thought, yes, my daughter, and went back to rejoin Fred who was going in at the side door, the brown paper bag in his arms.

He put the bag down on the table. 'This is it.' They were standing in the kitchen in a stream of sunlight from the wide glass windows, the skylight overhead. 'I put that in,' Fred pointed up to it. 'A little solar heat and a lot more light.'

'It's lovely,' she said, looking past a dining area and into a living room – the walls stark white, curtains of a blue and white swirling abstract print framing the windows, a few soft chairs, a sofa, a fireplace.

'It works, too,' Fred said, watching her eyes light on one thing, then another. On either side of the fireplace were walls of books, a few nicknacks and photos scattered among them. Over the fireplace a Winslow Homer-like picture of fishermen at sea. Beneath the glass covering, a coffee table held a profusion of shells. At the far end of the room a door stood open. 'Bedroom and bath,' he said. 'Two more bedrooms and a bath upstairs, and a spray shower by the back door to wash sand off your feet.'

He got out plates and bowls and silverware. 'Coffee?' he asked. 'Wine?' He took a bottle from a wooden wine rack in a corner of the kitchen.

'Yes. Please. Both.' She was feeling a little uneasy, wished Ginny could have come. Or was it uneasiness at leaving Rachel? She looked at her watch. Not quite twelve. 'Is your meeting far from here?'

'No. Five minutes. Did you bring your drawing stuff?' He eyed the huge purse she carried. 'Or you might want to take a nap – we started out so early.'

'I brought a small pad and some pastels. And a book. But I may just sit on the porch and absorb atmosphere while you're gone.' She glanced out the window – the sun was still bright on the water.

He smiled. 'I spend a lot of time doing just that. One of the joys – and hazards – of the place.'

'Hazards?' she said.

He had been pouring wine and he turned the bottle to stop the drip and looked up. 'It gets lonely,' he said, the vulnerability in his eyes again. 'C'mon, you ready?'

They ate lunch from paper plates and assorted bowls for salad and soup, drank wine from goblets and coffee from heavy crockery mugs. 'Not exactly the Four Seasons,' Fred said, lifting another crusty, fragrant clam from the cardboard box.

'It's wonderful,' she said, licking her fingers, then wiping them on her napkin before picking up the wine glass again.

He found an unopened bag of Pepperidge Farm cookies in the cupboard. 'Dessert.' He broke it open and offered it to her, then sat down, his look thoughtful. 'Your husband,' he said. 'You said he's very busy. Is he a nice guy? You love him? You have,' he hesitated, 'other children?'

'We have two sons, wonderful young men. And my husband . . .' The image of Trace sustained her, quelled the uneasiness she had felt. There was a shadow, too. She would speak of it. Fred was obviously no stranger to domestic tension. 'But we've had some hard times. Our daughter's death has meant different things to us. Sometimes we're not much help to each other.'

'Couples split up over things like that, you know.'

A surge of anxiety rose in her chest. 'I know.'

He looked at his watch, pushed back his chair. 'You want to have a walk on the beach before I go?'

They walked down the slope of sand toward where the ground levelled out and then walked along, following the shoreline. The incoming tide had left a chain of small shells and beach detritus. Below that lay the ribbons of silvery threads, like lines on a musical staff, deposited as the tide went out. The air was cool. A breeze whipped in off the water, capping the waves with spume and white froth. Further up the beach the blackened hull of a boat tipped on its side into a low dune. Gulls swirled overhead, landed, took off again. A few sandpipers jigged along on their short legs. High on the shore a row of houses paced along, their open porches for the most part empty of the chairs and chaises that would occupy them when summer came.

'Wait.' Laura ran to the water's edge, close enough to the incoming tide to reach down and put the palm of her hand on the water. She backed off quickly as the wave advanced.

'I just like to touch the water,' she said, returning to him.

He laughed, and reached for the wet hand she offered him. 'We'd better turn back. I'll have to be leaving soon.'

They turned, began to walk hand in hand along the beach.

Again she took a deep breath of the salt air. 'Do you know,' she said, 'that a few months ago I wouldn't have believed in this moment, not ever in my life again.'

'What do you mean?'

'I thought I would always be sad. There might be exceptional moments I'd be happy. But now it seems possible it could be the other way around.'

'It will be,' he said, 'if you let it.'

Something about the tone of his voice made her wonder. 'Oh?'

He shook his head. 'I've been through some things in my life too, Laura. Said some goodbyes.'

She thought of the divorce, of his daughter, of Ginny saying, 'It was awful for him.'

'Yes?' she said. He didn't answer her but the tenderness of the moment made her want to bring him some word, some gift of disclosure shared, and she said, 'It's part of the problem, isn't it?'

'What is?'

'Letting go. Being willing to let go.'

Again he didn't respond and this time she was relieved because maybe she'd been pressing him and she was glad he felt free not to go on. It was probably her way, to want to tell all, but not his, and she didn't want to frighten him out of her own need – make of him something he was not, some perfect father figure to whom she would bring all things and lay them at his feet and he would bless them. Only the blessing wouldn't last. She would have to find more gifts to bring him, a constant stream, so he would pay attention to her and not to anyone else at all.

So she was left with her own prescription and it reverberated in her head – 'Letting go. Being willing to let go.' She was learning that, wasn't she? To let go of her sadness, her preoccupying grief for Annie. But as they approached his house she felt a mounting sadness, as if some huge cloud was trying to push its way into the center of her consciousness. It was as though time pulled apart and collapsed back on itself, like an accordion bellows, except the moves were distorted and without frame.

'I can't get it straight in my mind,' she said.

'Can't get what straight?'

'My daughter's accident. When it happened – the time all runs together for me. The fact that it happened to her first and then I learned about it.'

They had reached the house. She turned to him, her head a buzz of confusion.

'Laura?' he said, a puzzled expression on his face.

'I'm sorry,' she said, agitated, feeling the cloud coming closer, about to envelop her. 'I know I'm not making sense. You go on to your meeting. I'll be fine.'

'You sure?' His eyes searched her face.

'Yes. Yes. I may go inside and take a nap. Or I might do some sketching.' With a wave of her hand she took in the bright afternoon, the porch with its two rockers still in place.

'Good. I won't be long. A couple of hours maybe.' He hurried down the porch steps and out to the car, and she went inside and closed the door.

19

Inside the house, Laura walked through the living room, pushed open the bedroom door and, taking a blanket from the top of a blanket chest, she unfolded it and lay down on the double bed and spread the blanket over herself and closed her eyes. But after a few moments she remembered with almost a kinetic memory having performed these same gestures on the day of Annie's accident, and in a turmoil of anxiety she sat up in bed, slid her feet back into her boots, wrapped her heavy sweater round her shoulders and went out onto the porch. She sat down in one of the rocking chairs and buried her face in her hands.

In her mind she hovered again at the day of the accident. Why did those mid-afternoon hours run together? She remembered going up to the cabin to take a nap and looking out from the porch to see if she could spot the riders. They had already gone. She remembered Trace rushing in and the drive to Estes Park, then to Boulder, and the long wait while Annie lay in some secret room.

But the time between, the hour or two when she was resting, lying on the bed reading – she could not find that anywhere in her memory. When she thought of the accident, it was always happening while they were racing into Estes Park. That was where her mind kept putting Annie's fall – while they were driving in their anguish to meet her.

But that was wrong. Annie was already mortally hurt. Strangers had called an ambulance. The ambulance had already taken Annie and Bart on ahead. Why did she keep getting it in the wrong order, keep having to take the event and put it back in place, like a child who keeps cutting ahead in line?

She drew her knees up against her chest, dug her heels against the edge of the chair and rocked back and forth. Tears sprang to her eyes. Words began to form out of the swirling images in her mind.

It was hers. It wasn't yours. It was her body, not your body. You are two people, not two parts of one. Her life was hers. Her death was hers. You cannot have it, not even as a way of keeping her can you have it. So let her go.

Tears streamed down her cheeks. Why this confusion? Why had she fought that so hard, so fused herself in her own mind with her daughter that she could not even allow her to die away from her hovering emotional presence? That a blow to Annie's body must be perceived as a blow to her own – some doomed attempt to preserve the illusion that they were one? Because if they were two, Annie might leave her and she would be abandoned? The irony of it was clear. Annie *had* left. Still she had persisted in thinking of them as one. What was the terror so great that she would try, against the facts, against her own knowledge, again and again to rearrange the truth, to preserve some myth of her own making, so that she experienced Annie's death as a tearing away at her own being?

She heard a sound of low wailing, hiccuping sobs, helpless, like a child abandoned. It was her own voice.

In a bright hospital room lights shine from the ceiling. A doctor stands in a white coat, a white hat covers the top of his head. He wears a mask over his mouth.

Why is she here on this table? What is he going to do? Her neck is sore. Why did they bring her here and let strangers wheel her away to this room?

They are putting green cloths on her body. They are bringing bottles and tubes. The light is bright and coming closer. There is a long needle in the doctor's hand.

She opens her mouth and screams.

Rock. The chair creaked on its hinges back and forth, on the wooden floor of the porch. She clutched her knees more tightly against her chest. A gull flew across her line of vision, cawing at the air.

So had she learned in that operating room, the months of recovery from her illness, a lifetime uneasiness, a fear of being separated from those she loved? And not only separated, but violated in some way? That needle, the image of knives. 'Her heart couldn't stand a general anesthesia. They had to give her a local.' No wonder she had repressed the memory of it – a legacy of terror.

But there were rewards from that time.

Her mother is coming toward her down the hall, her maroon flannel robe sweeps behind her. She sits down on the edge of the bed, strokes Laura's cheek. Outside, Lillian calls, 'Mother?' 'Not now,' Rachel says. Lillian goes away. Her mother's hand soothes her burning forehead, reassuring her, promising her that she will not die. As long as Rachel is there, she will not die.

Rock. Rock. Had she made some Faustian bargain with her mother that they would always be special to one another because Rachel's love, her care, her will, her very presence had made the critical difference and saved a child who, according to the doctors, had 'no right to be alive'. But it was never to be forgotten, this debt, and at any time it might be called in. It had worked fine for most of her life. Her job in another city, her marriage to Trace had put enough distance between Rachel and herself for the delicate balance of closeness and independence to be maintained. But when Will had died and Rachel had wanted to move in with her, some unconscious wisdom, her own desperate need for survival, had raised a barrier as impenetrable as lead and she had said no. It had taken her forty years.

It was no wonder Rachel was upset. To her infinite credit she had adjusted and gone on, the river of her love diverted round the rock of Laura's defection to come right back – 'I don't mind anything you do, dear. Don't you know that?' Rachel, who had translated her fear that her invalided mother might die into adulation – 'my angel mother', with whom she had never exchanged a cross word.

And had this struggle for independence, always present from parent to child but compounded in her case and

Rachel's by the special circumstances of their life together, had it swung down like an acrobat monkey swinging down from the rungs of a ladder to imbue Annie, too, with this burden of a mother's love almost too demanding, too enriching, to bear? Because it *was* enriching, a gift for intimacy that, with all its dangers, bestowed some luminous aura, like the legendary jewel in a fairy tale, which contains such extraordinary power for evil and for good that people risk killing and being killed to keep it in their possession.

And if she had unwittingly handed this legacy to her daughter – the cloud that had driven her inside and then out onto the porch darkened now, hovered close – was that part of the reason, as well as Trace's distance, his abstractedness, that Annie had been so adventurous, so determined to forge her own ground? Had it even – in a moment of panic Laura considered it – driven Annie to ride away to her death in order to escape, win a freedom she could find in no other way?

Rock, rock.

She held the thought, like a tissue pattern against a piece of cloth, against her knowledge of Annie's life. Then, with relief, she put it aside. It did not fit. Annie had left – there was no denying that – but not out of pique or some desperate search for freedom, any more than the trauma of her own childhood illness was Rachel's will for her. She remembered Ginny's words, held like a banner against the irrational fear that her relief at being spared some of the tensions of life with Annie had caused Annie's death. 'You've got it in the wrong order,' Ginny had said. 'It's a side effect. It's *after* the fact. It doesn't make you an accomplice.' Like the creak of the rocking chair, it didn't rock because it creaked, it creaked because it rocked.

And another thing. Perhaps Annie's lunges into independence had been a sign of health, of a transmitted strength that also passed from mothers to daughters, from women to women. After all, Annie had had no invalid mother, no long childhood illness to bond her to some script of undue accommodation to a mother's wishes.

The strength passed from daughters to mothers, too, she acknowledged, eyes stinging again, remembering Annie's courage on ferris wheels, the bittersweet memory of Annie's words when she told her, finally, that she and Gordon were making love: 'I feel very good about myself as a woman.'

The patterns of mothers and daughters – her grandmother Laura, her mother, herself, her daughter. Stories of infinite complexity, but the outlines constant, like those transparent pages in the World Book encyclopedia they'd bought for the children, in which the muscle system overlaid the page for the nervous system, which overlaid the page for the bone structure, which overlaid the page for the circulation. Somehow a congruence was achieved, distinctive, the outline always the same.

Yet they were all symbols to explain the unexplainable, like the bread and chalice that Matt offered at the memorial service – a cup of wine, a piece of bread to share. Like Rachel's hand on her back, soothing away the fear. The sound of Rachel's voice in the night as she sat by the bed, singing, 'Through the darkness be Thou near me, keep me safe till morning light.' The sight of Rachel walking through the pine trees to visit while she lay in her hospital bed, eyes turned to the window.

She stopped rocking, wiped her face with her hand. The massive threatening cloud that had pursued her had broken up, become patches of light and dark. She looked at her watch. It was past four. She had been sitting here for more than an hour. Fred should be coming back soon.

She sat quiet, trying to see it all, let it find its place. The feeling startled her at first, the low contractions deep in the womb, and then she remembered this same sensation in the waiting room in Boulder, and she wondered, what is being born this time? Something began to come clear. The clouds were moving again, driven by the wind. There was a hill, some figures on a hill. In a rush of recognition and returning panic she stood up. There was another journey she had to make and she did not want to make it alone. Just then she heard Fred's car pulling in beside the house and she ran to the end of the porch. 'Fred!'

He bounded up onto the porch, his face distorted with consternation. 'Laura, whatever . . .' He took her hands in his. 'You're freezing. Why aren't you inside?' He put his arm round her shoulder and led her into the house, over to the sofa where light from the skylight brightened the blue twill cover, and they sat down.

'I'm really all right, Fred,' she said, steadying her hand on the knees of her wool pants. 'But I need you to be with me. I'm awfully glad you came just now.'

'I'm right here,' he said. 'What is it, Laura? Are you sick? Do you need a doctor?'

She shook her head. 'I just need you to be with me,' and she took his two hands in hers and sat forward on the sofa so her knees pressed against Fred's. Closing her eyes tightly against tears, she saw the slope of a hill like the hills in the woods behind Hadley where she used to walk with her family on Sunday afternoons. On the hill were two figures. At the bottom of the hill ran a clear stream, rocks breaking the surface and watercress growing in the lee of the rocks. The figures were herself and Annie and the narrow stream at their feet was like the River Styx, the stream between the living and the dead. And though there was no sound the words played in her head:

You have been here long enough. You must leave her now.
    Are you sure it's time?
It will never be easy, but you're ready.
    Can I look back?
Yes.
    I will still be her mother?
Always.
    And the sadness will stay with me?
Yes.
    Can I go back if I want to?
For a while, yes. You'll be with her one day, you know.
    And I am not abandoning her?
Look at her. Does she look frightened or troubled?

She looked. There was no fear, only a tender smile on her daughter's face. Gripping Fred's hand even more tightly, she watched as the older woman let go of the young woman's hand, walked down the last stretch of shallow slope and stepped over the brook to stand on the other side.

'Oh, it's so sad,' she said. She was crying softly. Her grip on Fred's hands relaxed and she pulled a handkerchief from the pocket of her shirt and wiped her face. 'Well!' she said, and sighed. But there was a lightness in her voice, for the relief of it. Then she began to tell him . . .

She looked up from her story and he was watching, his blue eyes steady and warm, and she told him how it had been hard to separate from her own mother but that such closeness had its gifts and she had wanted it all, all of it, the closeness and the freedom, too, for herself and Annie. And maybe they might have had it, who could know?

'So I'm glad to realize all that,' she said. 'Or begin to – I'm sure it goes on and on.' She wondered, what must he be thinking? 'I'm grateful to you, for staying with me.'

He looked down at his hands, red marks still on them where she had gripped him so tightly. 'Try and get away,' he said, but his eyes were kind.

She shrugged, laughing. 'But you let me go on, you didn't intervene, or pull back, or try to make it anything different. You didn't leave me, not for a second!' And she bathed in that knowledge, as in sunlight. And for a moment all the empty places of her life seemed filled to the brim, secure and bright. 'I'll wear this moment for the rest of my life,' she said.

'Laura, dear,' he was mystified, 'I don't know what I did.'

'You didn't *do* anything. You just *were*!'

'I'm glad I could help you,' he said, still puzzled. 'I'm sure you were a good mother.'

'Thank you,' she said, and it was for the whole gift of his presence she thanked him.

She stood, almost light-headed. Her body felt fluid and spare, like a dancer's. 'Come with me to the beach again?' she said.

They jumped down from the veranda, went to the beach in an easy loping walk. She stooped down and splashed her hands in the water and passed them over her face.

He looked surprised, startled, almost amused. It had been an impulse, a moment of playfulness. Nothing to explain. She slipped an arm round his waist as they returned to the house. 'I must go down to the seas again,' she began, trying to reassure him she had not gone completely mad.

But by the time they reached the house, their arms round

one another, legs brushing together as they walked, there was another feeling between them and in the shadow of the veranda she turned to him, noticed for the first time the way the hair curled forward over his ear and that the roots of his beard had, just below his mouth, started to gray. The look in his eyes was unmistakable, an invitation, a longing, and he put his hands on her shoulders and she leaned into him, her face against his cheek.

'Well, how was the meeting?' she said.

'The hell with the meeting,' he said, and wrapped her in his arms.

Bart dragged himself up the stairs, opened the door to the apartment and went inside. He'd seen the car; Paula must be home already.

'Hi,' came her voice from the bedroom. She walked out, buttoning a baggy shirt over her jeans. 'I was just changing.' She looked at his face. 'It's Friday. Let's radiate a little joy. It's the weekend!'

'Right.' He slumped down in the chair, his long legs stretched out in front of him over the worn carpet, let his briefcase slide to the floor. 'I wasn't meant to be a teacher. I'm just putting in time there. My energy is shot by ten in the morning.'

She came and sat on the arm of the chair, swung her legs across his lap and stroked his cheek. 'Junior Hi is a notoriously hard age to cope with. Are the kids raging out of control?'

'No.' He snorted. 'That's what's so crazy. They seem to like me. They pay attention, ask good questions, do the work. Mr Randall this, Mr Randall that. I'm the one who's the washout.'

She rested her head against his. 'Can I get you a beer? Do you want to go out to dinner? Or rent a video? We could have a nice cozy time at home.'

'No.' He hitched up a little so they weren't at such a crazy angle to the floor but made no move to embrace her. 'Nothing appeals to me – that's the problem.'

She continued to stroke his cheek. 'You're depressed.

252

Maybe you could talk to someone, help you sort all this out.'

'Naah,' he dismissed it. The thought of unwinding all his stuff with a stranger was the last thing he felt like right now.

She sat up a little, turned to face him. 'We could get married,' she said, faking a coy look, fluttering her eyelashes.

He uttered a sigh. 'I'm not ready for that, either.'

'We talked about a six months trial. We've already been together more than six months – if you count the month at school.' She looked at the calendar on the wall. 'Six months and five days.'

'And you haven't told your mother yet.'

'If we got married, she'd never need to know.'

'That's a lousy reason for getting married.' His voice took on an edge.

'Just kidding,' she said. 'How about that we love each other – is that a good reason?'

He gave her an appreciative squeeze but his expression didn't change.

'It's about Annie?' she said.

'Sure. I keep seeing it all in my head. Her horse riding off into the trees, the wrangler turning to follow her, calling "Hold on". And I just sat there.' His voice faltered. 'Stupid oaf,' he said.

'What makes you think you could have made any difference?'

'Maybe not. But I could have at least tried.'

'The wrangler was the expert, you weren't.' She was getting impatient now. They had been through it so many times, always the same questions, the guilt he couldn't seem to shake. Besides, she was tired and hungry and she feared he was going to be this way all weekend. 'I'll put the water on for pasta,' she said and got up from his lap. He put his head back and sprawled back on the chair, his eyes closed. There was a great big hole in his heart, an Annie-sized hole, and he didn't know what to do about it.

He heard, down below, the hum of conversation, the laughter of the baby. The baby was about to have a birthday. He was not quite one year old and had just started to walk.

The thought of the child cheered him, and he stood up and went to the kitchen. 'Sorry to be such a grouch,' he said. 'Shall I make some of my razzle-dazzle sauce? Do we have stuff for salad?'

She looked up from the pot of water. 'Well, what cheered you up? Or maybe I shouldn't ask – just be glad.'

He came and stood behind her, put his arms round her waist. 'I was just thinking of little Jimmy. We're invited to his birthday party, aren't we?'

'Yes, a week from tomorrow. After dinner we could go buy him a present.' She tilted her head to look up at him.

'Good. And maybe take in a movie,' he said. 'Sometime this weekend I want to call Dad, see how he's doing.'

'We could invite him over.'

'Good,' he said.

When they got home from the movie it was late. The house was quiet. It was probably late to call Trace. They would call him tomorrow. They went to bed and made love and fell asleep, not anticipating that as the night grew colder, thermostats would kick in the heating elements in the old house, including a wall heater downstairs near a pile of loose papers in Jimmy's room.

'Come in.'

Philip pushed the door open and walked into his advisor's office. 'Hi, Mr Krantz.'

Charles Krantz stood and extended his hand. 'Glad you could come by, Phil. Sit down.' He reseated himself in his chair.

Philip took the chair on the other side of the desk. 'I got your note,' he said.

'Yes, I know conferences don't come up for another month or so, but I thought maybe you and I should get together sooner. How are things going?' He looked down at a paper on his desk. Phil couldn't see clearly what it said, but he read, upside down, what looked like 'Office of the Academic Dean'.

'Not real great, I guess.' Philip crossed one leg over the other, felt his ankle jerk against the leg of his chino pants.

'I know from talking with you in the fall that you had a family tragedy over the summer.'

Philip nodded his head, yes.

'It's very understandable that your work should slip.' Krantz looked back at the paper. 'You had almost a 4.0 last year and it could be hard to keep that up under any circumstances.' He looked back at Philip. 'But your work has suffered pretty badly, Phil. Some of your professors are quite concerned. Work not completed, and not your usual quality when it does come in.'

'I don't know what to say.' Philip uncrossed his legs, sat forward. 'It's just hard to make myself believe it's important. That is, I know in my head it's important, but that lasts me about twenty minutes. Then I think, "What's the use?" and give up.'

Mr Krantz nodded. 'Is there anything we can do to help you? You have friends?'

'Yes.' Though that had changed, too, since last year. He'd seen his bio lab partner his first day back in the fall. Bob had called to him across campus, 'Hey, Phil,' and come toward him on the run, feigned a punch at his side. 'Good to see you. How was your summer? Cut up any cadavers?'

It was an old joke, but not this time. 'It was terrible. My sister died.' He didn't know what kind of response he'd expected from Bob – some sympathy, surely, some understanding.

Bob had dropped his hand from Phil's shoulder, backed away, his face a blank. 'I'm sorry. Well, see you around,' he'd stammered. And then, 'Gotta run.' He'd turned and loped away. After that Philip watched who he told about Annie, and when he did tell, he broke it to them more gradually.

He realized Mr Krantz was looking at him, expecting an answer. 'I – I don't think so,' he said finally. 'Am I in danger of flunking out?'

Mr Krantz frowned. 'You may have some incompletes,' he said.

Philip hesitated. 'I've thought of taking off a semester, getting a job, something like that.'

'That's a possibility, of course,' Krantz said. 'But I

wouldn't rush to do that. Give yourself a little more time. See how things go. You might want to talk to someone over at Health Services. And come in and see me any time.'

'Thanks, sir.' He left as quickly as he could.

He unlocked his bike from the bike rack and set off up the hill – no particular destination, just a need to go somewhere, no matter that it was getting dark or that he'd hardly slept for two nights and only fitfully before that. No matter that he was way behind on his Darwin paper and hadn't even begun the reading for sociology of cities.

He passed the tree where he used to sit and look out over the valley. A couple of times last year he'd brought his girl friend Sarah up here and they'd studied together, talked, laughed – in that other lifetime before Annie died. He could scarcely remember how it felt in that carefree time when the most serious issue was getting papers in on time or whether or not to smoke a joint with Sarah.

They had written over the summer. She was working on a ranch in Montana. He wrote her after Annie died. She sent back a damn sympathy card, with only her name.

She'd tried to cheer him up since they'd returned to campus, tried to distract him, make him think of something else. She probably would have had sex with him if he'd wanted – they'd come close last spring. But the relationship had cooled and there wasn't enough to ignite it again. She tried to be understanding, but her own stuff got in the way. 'Death scares me,' she said once. 'I try not to think about it.'

'Well, lots of luck,' he said, and he didn't call her again. She didn't call him, either, which told him she was content to drop the whole thing.

With the spring coming, he was haunted by the thought of Argonne Woods and how last year he'd thought he was too busy to go. Well, he certainly wasn't now. Not that he didn't have work to do, just that he wasn't doing it.

He heard the sound of the train. He'd always loved that before – there was a train track not far from their house in Woodbridge. Now it frightened him. How easy it would be to ride down the hill and onto the tracks. In high school he'd played chicken a couple of times – see who could stay on longest with a train speeding right toward you. Sometimes now when he heard the wail of the train whistle he thought of riding onto the tracks and not getting off.

He jerked himself to attention. He wouldn't do that, would he? He'd thought a lot about death since Annie died. What, if anything, was on the other side? He'd even had dreams of seeing her again.

He shivered. It was cold and he swung round in a loop on the empty street and headed back for the dorm.

Inside the beach house – the light was dimmer now with the approach of early evening shadows – Laura and Fred shed their wraps, turned to one another again in a recognition that they had a new world to negotiate. He moved toward her.

'My God, Laura.' Fred pressed his lips against hers. She opened her mouth to him, slipped her tongue under his, her arms round his neck, felt the presence of his body hard against hers, felt weightless, as though he carried the weight of gravity for them both. His hand was easing her heavy sweater from her shoulder. 'We don't need this,' he said gruffly and she let her arm drop so that first one sleeve and then the other fell away from her and the heavy cardigan tumbled to the floor.

'Oh, Fred,' she whispered, raising her arms again to encircle his neck, press her lips to his, her body aflame. But then with a groan she pulled back and shook her head lightly against his shoulder and said, into the warmth of his flannel shirt, 'I can't.'

'No, I don't suppose you can,' he said, and kissed her again.

Again she returned the kiss, this time her hand playing along his neck, moving up through his hair.

But she drew back from him, looked up into his face, his eyes bright with the intensity of desire. 'I can't' she said.

'Please,' he whispered.

Again she shook her head, then reached round to disengage his arms from her body, dropped down into the nearest chair and covered her face with her hands. 'It's too much,' she said through her fingers. 'Too much has happened. I can't take it all in.'

She heard rather than saw him sit in the chair opposite her and then she opened her eyes and saw him gazing at her with a look of such unguarded hunger and tenderness that she closed her eyes again against the urge to go to him, yield up the day to whatever might happen. And why not? She had trusted him with her most intimate story and he had been worthy of that trust, had heard her out, honoring whatever she had to say with absolute attention. He had helped her move into a present that felt alive and hopeful, so that she felt renewed, her body light with new life, now so drawn to the man who sat before her that to move toward him in an ardor of love-making seemed the most natural thing in the world and to do anything other than that would deny the power and beauty of this whole afternoon.

As though reading her mind he said, 'Life has few enough such moments, Laura.'

Again she felt her body stir, the blood rise. It would be an adventure, to go to him. Would Annie approve? Her adventurous daughter, hardly more than a child, telling her, 'I feel very good about myself as a woman.'

But there was another face she saw – dark eyes, gray hair falling over his forehead, the eyes luminous above her, the body moving against her own. So many years of shared history. Moments strung along the turning chain of years like strands of DNA moving in elliptical circles, the dance of life.

'Thank you, Fred. I'd like to, but I can't.'

'No one need know,' he said, his eyes pleading.

She knew she could trust him – his silence, his genuine care for her. For a minute she closed her eyes, watching the play unfold. 'I would know,' she said.

He shrugged, turned away, then stood and walked over to the fireplace, stared into its black cavern.

She went to stand beside him, put her hand lightly on his arm. 'I'm sorry,' she said. 'I'd like to go to bed with you, but I couldn't bear the aftermath – the guilt, the secrecy, the pain to Trace if he knew.'

'Would you have to tell him?'

'It would cost me too much keeping silent. I've always told him everything.'

'Lucky bastard,' he said.

She looked at him, startled.

'Sorry,' he said. 'I'm jealous of him and I've never even met the guy.' He was staring into the curios and photos on the mantel. He seemed to hesitate then reached to take a small framed picture from a shelf and handed it to her. '*My* daughter,' he said. The picture was of a girl of nine or ten, braids lying against her shoulders, a sailboat barrette at the end of each one. She was wearing a white blouse and dark jumper with a school emblem on the pocket.

She drew in her breath. 'Oh, Fred. When was this picture taken? How old is she now?'

'Fifteen. She was four when we were divorced. For a while I would go and get her, take her places. Then Lucy remarried and they moved away. I send her presents at birthdays and Christmas. But I haven't seen her for a long time.'

'I remember she's in California. You could be in touch with her if you wanted. You fly out there.'

'Yes, I could find her. But I'm afraid it's too late. I'm afraid she won't have anything to do with me. She'll blame me for not being a better father all these years.'

'For you there is still time,' she said softly, not knowing whether he heard.

They gathered up their things and got ready to leave. Laura stopped in the middle of the room, engulfed by a surge of tenderness for this now hallowed spot. 'In a way I'd like to stay for ever.' Fred stood at her shoulder, his down jacket slung over his arm.

'You could always change your mind and stay. Just overnight,' he teased. 'We could call your mother, tell her the weather was bad down here.' He started to open the door. 'Oof,' he said. 'As a matter of fact, look at this.'

She stepped to join him. Off to the west the sky had darkened to an ominous steel gray. A driving wind entered the room and flung the curtains against the wall.

Fred closed the door. 'Better check.' He moved to a small black box on a shelf near the refrigerator. 'My weather channel,' he said.

He pushed a button and a voice came on in the crackle of static. 'Severe storm watch along the New England coast until 2 a.m. Travelers' advisories posted for Cape Cod and the eastern seaboard.'

Fred's face clouded in worry. 'I don't know, Laura, whether we should venture out.'

'Are we safe here?' she asked. 'The house, I mean.'

'Oh, yes. Nothing about hurricanes. Some snow probably, and rain, and a lot of wind. Once we got off the Cape and a little inland we'd be okay. But it would be rough going for a while.' He cocked his head toward the stairs. 'We could stay here. I'd sleep upstairs. Leave you safely down here.' He smiled, acknowledging the possibility of more intimate arrangements.

Again, that inner startle of wonder and desire. The adventure of the whole thing. And it was stormy outside. At best it would be an uncomfortable drive.

'You could call your mother,' he went on. 'I'm sure she'd agree it would be wise to wait.' He looked toward the refrigerator. 'I have food in the freezer. Wine.' He gestured toward the stairwell, lined with bookcases. 'We have books to read, jigsaw puzzles. I could even put on some music and we could dance for old times.'

She smiled. 'For old times.' She remembered them dancing at Charley's. So long ago. And now, this reconnection with Fred – it was a gift, defying time. 'Okay. I'll call.'

Carlena answered.

'Carlena, it's Laura.' She didn't have time to say more.

'Oh, Laura. I been frantic. Your mother's in the hospital. She's in a coma.'

Laura sat down on the window seat, felt the blood leave her head. 'Tell me.'

'She's been sick all day, throwing up. Then I couldn't wake her up. I called the doctor. He sent an ambulance. He said call the children. I called the others. I couldn't reach you.'

'I'll be there, Carlena. We're starting out now.' She hung up the phone. 'My mother. She's in a coma, in the hospital. We'll have to go.'

Commiseration etched his face. 'Of course. We'll take it

slow. After we get off the Cape it should be fine.' He held
his arms out and she came to him, rested in the circle of his
embrace. 'I'm sorry,' he said.

'I know. Thanks.'

At the door, about to leave, she thought of Trace. He
should be alerted in case he had to come to Hadley. 'I'd like
to call my husband. He should be home now,' she said to
Fred who was standing peering out into the storm.

'Go ahead.'

She rang the number, but he wasn't home. She tried the
office, but he wasn't there, either.

Trace hurried into his office but the phone had stopped
ringing. He hoped it wasn't the dean who was usually pretty
upset if people didn't keep their announced office hours.
Something of a stickler for administrative detail, that man.
Which was probably one reason he was a dean and hadn't
stayed with the more imaginative world of scholarship.

Trace put the poem down on his desk – a lined sheet of
paper he'd found under a drawing pad in the middle drawer
of Annie's desk. If Laura had been home, he probably would
never have wandered into Annie's room like that. When
she was home, she seemed to take over most of the grieving,
just as she did the shopping and cooking.

But with her gone and Bart and Paula moved into their
own place he'd got lonely and, wandering around the
house, had found himself in his daughter's old room. It
didn't look the same since they'd moved the waterbed out,
put in an old double bed they'd had in the attic, swapped
Annie's orange paisley throw for an antique crocheted
spread that had belonged to Laura's grandmother. He'd
gone along with all that though he'd thought it a little hasty
of Laura, changing it so quickly. She hadn't even asked if
he was willing. He'd felt it would be childish, cowardly, to
ask for delays – 'Please wait. I'm not ready yet.'

Inside the room, he'd sat down at the maple desk chair,
opened the middle drawer first, leafed through a stack of
letters, some blue buckram-covered notebooks, a box of
slides, a few report cards. He'd not happened upon the
journal that Laura had had such a fit about. It was no

abhorrent scandal to him that his daughter had expressed herself in that burst of fuck off. Not that he cared for such terms. He thought the angry expletives of the young entirely too limiting to the language, and the easy way out, besides. In his youth girls went to some trouble to say the forbidden words. 'I went to the dam to get some dam water. The dam keeper said I couldn't have any dam water.' And so on. 'I told the dam keeper to keep his dam water.' Fifth grade. A daring sequence. At least it had some varied images in it, some grammar. Different from fuck you. Fuck off. What the fuck. And so on *ad infinitem*.

He wasn't looking for anything special, he told himself, leafing through the contents of the drawer, maybe just some sign of her, some reminder of the particularities of her life. And there it was, that piece of paper, sticking out from the pages of a drawing pad she'd evidently used in last spring's art class. Was it calling to him? He pulled it out, and read it. And read it. And read it, gratitude pouring from his body like sweat.

Laura couldn't have found the poem or she'd have told him. It gave him some satisfaction that he'd found something of Annie's first. Though he'd share it with her as soon as she got home. She'd be touched by it, as he was. They would be glad together.

His daughter's gift to them – to him, maybe especially to him, alone in the house for nearly two weeks. That crazy notion always came when he was alone, whether that squabble he'd had with Annie the day before she died had somehow made her less willing to fight for her life, even caused her death. As a philosopher, a student of reason, he knew better. As a grieving father, he didn't.

It was a simple matter – Annie wanting to take the car. He didn't even remember what she wanted it for – to take Roger on some errand or go to Estes Park for a magazine and some shampoo. She'd asked Laura, who'd said, 'It's all right with me if Dad doesn't need it.'

Well, he did need it. There was a prominent scholar in the area and it was his last chance to drive over and have a talk. 'I'm sorry, I've arranged a visit to a philosophy colleague in Colorado Springs.'

'Dad! Did you ever hear of vacation? I give up!' she'd said, her eyes blazing with anger, her face almost as red as the shrimp-colored T-shirt she wore, and stomped out the door. It was the next day she died. It was that 'I give up!' that kept running through his mind.

So what was comforting about the poem, in addition to the fact that it was a lovely poem and quite astonishing, really, was that she had written it *before* that exchange, though goodness knows she'd been cross at him enough those past months. But if there was any unconscious sense of impending death, at least it had preceded the argument about the car. What fragile things we cling to, he thought.

He looked at his watch. Where was Kate? She was never late. If anything, she came early, was almost embarrassingly eager to talk with him. He looked at the poem again. It had nothing to do with Aristotle but he wanted to show it to her anyway.

He heard her footsteps coming down the hall and there she was, her presence somehow always more than he'd expected – the way his heart lifted when he saw her. 'Come in, Kate.'

'Sorry I'm late. I knew some of the doors were locked after six and it took me a while to find one open.' She shrugged off her heavy jacket and put her books down on the low filing case that doubled as a table by the extra chair. She was wearing jeans, that same blue sweater that matched her eyes. A gold chain with some kind of symbol he didn't recognize hung round her neck. With a characteristic gesture she flipped her hair back over her shoulders and sat down, picked up a manila folder from the pile of books and looked up at him. 'I have a bone to pick with Aristotle,' she said.

He was amused. 'You wouldn't be the first,' he said. 'What's your complaint?'

'He's so unreadable! Of course I knew that before, but this last chapter,' she flung her hand toward the dark green-covered book on top of the pile. 'Does he "suffer in translation", as they say?' She wrinkled her nose and her glasses slipped another half-inch down her face so she was looking at him over the top of them.

'I wish I could let him off the hook,' Trace said. 'But he's difficult in the Greek too – a poor stylist. There's even a question whether what we have is notes one of his students wrote down rather than his own work.'

She sighed in resignation. 'Well, I don't feel so bad then. I thought maybe it was just me.'

'Not at all. You're in excellent company.'

'I know that,' she said, her quick smile acknowledging her pleasure in being with him.

He felt his face flush. 'Well, thank you,' he stammered, forgetting all about the poem.

But when they had gone over together the most recent section of her work and she had jotted down on her pad the material she would aim to cover before their next conference his equanimity was fully restored and it seemed the most natural thing in the world to say to her, 'I have something I'd like to show *you*.'

'What is it?' Her eyes scanned his desk, the nearby table.

'This,' and he pulled out Annie's poem, written in her own hand on a piece of lined notebook paper.

She took it, a question in her eyes. 'Yours?' she asked.

'My daughter's.'

'Oh.' A look of sadness crossed her face and she took the paper, held it up to catch the light. As she read, she softly spoke the words into the stillness of his small office and he sat back in his chair and listened as she read:

> I'm quite a child, you know
>> lost in between the popcorn and the lace
>> and never in my life have I
>> approached you without
>> first retreating.
> All the better, I believe
>> for you, at any rate.
> You wait, you'll see just what I mean
>> when I shatter into thousands.
> You've never been so scared
>> in all your life,
> And never so rewarded.

She stopped and he watched as, silently now, she read the lines again. When she looked up there were tears in her eyes. 'It's beautiful,' she said. 'It's a little uncanny too, isn't it? When did she write it, do you know?'

'Not exactly. Before we went away. It was tucked into a drawing pad in her desk. I found it there. This afternoon.'

'Ohh. Thank you for letting me read it. It must be very precious to you.' She leaned forward, handing him the paper but reading it again even as she did so. 'Do you know who it's written to? Who is the "you" in the poem?'

He took it from her, his eyes scanning the now-familiar words. 'I've wondered that, of course. Obviously someone important to her. Gordon maybe, or her mother. But,' he spoke softly because he had not yet fully claimed it, and its value as preceding her fall would be the same in any case. But then it was as though he looked through a lighted scrim and saw his daughter nodding, encouraging him with her smile, and he knew that what his mind had been struggling with, playing with, all afternoon was true, that Annie cared for him this much, was even promising gifts from this so terrible event and he said, his voice strong now, 'I think it's to me.' He looked at the young woman in the chair opposite his. 'Do you think so, Kate?'

'Oh, yes, I do, Dr Randall. From what little you've told me, that's what I guessed. I think it's to you.'

20

It was almost midnight when Fred and Laura reached the edge of town. A light snow was falling.

'Want to go right to the hospital?' Fred asked.

'Yes.' She directed him through the darkened streets. 'Up that hill.' They had come here times without number when Will was sick, more recently to visit Rachel.

He pulled up at the brightly-lit door. A sign indicated 'Visitor Parking' in an adjacent lot. The lot was almost empty.

'You go on in,' Fred said. 'I'll park. I'll find you.'

She hurried into the large vestibule. The hospital was hushed. A woman sat at a desk behind a sign – 'Information.'

Laura went to the desk. 'My mother, Rachel Taylor, was brought in this afternoon in a coma. I just arrived from out of town. Could you give me her room number?'

The woman nodded sympathetically, addressed her computer screen. 'Three hundred and seven. Take the elevator down that hallway,' she pointed. 'Get off at the third floor. Turn left.'

'Thank you.' Laura hurried to the bank of elevators, pushed the button.

Fred came in the front door. His eyes scanned the room. When he saw her he came over.

'Third floor,' she said. 'Three oh seven.' The elevator came, the door slid back and they got on.

'Any word?' Fred wondered.

'I didn't ask.'

At the third floor they got out, walked to the left, following the door numbers. 'Three oh three . . . three oh five . . .' Down the hall a nurses' station stood in an island of light. A woman bent over a book. She didn't appear to notice them.

'Three hundred and seven,' Laura said.

'I'll wait here.' Fred squeezed her hand, and Laura, heart pounding, entered the room.

A low light illuminated the area around her mother's bed. Rachel appeared to be sleeping. Laura stepped to the bedside. Her mother's color was good, her breathing regular.

'Mother,' she whispered. Her mother stirred, but didn't waken.

Laura want back out of the room, beckoned to Fred and they approached the nurses' station.

The nurse looked up. 'May I help you with something?'

'I'm Laura Randall, Mrs Taylor's daughter. I've just come from out of town. I was told she was in a coma. Can you tell me . . . ?'

The nurse nodded. 'She has come out of the coma. Her condition is stable at the moment. We've taken some blood. The results will be available in the morning.'

'So she's . . . all right?'

The nurse addressed them both. 'At present. Why don't you go home and get some sleep? We don't expect anything to develop over the next hours.' She looked down at her chart. 'We have your phone number. We'll call you if there's any change for the worse.'

'Oh, thank you,' Laura said and they moved away from the desk. 'I'll just go tell her goodnight,' she said and slipped once more into the room – still the quiet breathing – and put a light kiss on her mother's forehead. 'See you tomorrow,' she whispered and went out to rejoin Fred.

In the car, she put her head back against the seat. 'Ohh,' she breathed, and allowed herself some quiet tears of relief.

The windows of the house were dark as they approached. Fred turned off the motor, put his hand over hers. 'Do you want me to come in with you? Will you be all right?'

'You don't need to, thanks. Unless you want to sleep here. What will you do?'

'I'll go to Ginny's. I know where the key is.' He opened his door. 'I'll walk to the door with you.'

'Thanks.' She got out, waited for him to join her.

Hand in hand they proceeded up the flagstone walk, covered now with a thin layer of snow. The wind had died down but a light snow was still falling. When they reached the house Laura put her key in the lock, turned to look back.

Beneath the white dome of the street lamp snowflakes fell, drifting stars of light.

'When I was growing up I loved to look at the snow under that light,' she said. 'I'd stand at the front window and imagine it was a fairyland and I was a princess, dancing in the falling snow.'

He put his hands on her shoulders. 'You *are* a princess,' he said gravely, and kissed her. He passed his hand over her head in the knit cap and said, 'Goodnight. I'll call you tomorrow.' He went down the walk, got in his car and drove away.

Laura went in, hung up her coat. She crept up the stairs, got ready for bed and climbed in. The sheets were chilly and for a long time she lay awake, thinking of Rachel, and of Fred, playing through the events of the day, her heart full from its richness and for the journey safely made. And yet . . . And yet . . . What if they had stayed? She drifted off to sleep holding to herself the memory of Fred's arms round her, her lips to his.

The smell of smoke reached Bart as he slept, became a dream of fire. Then the shrill *beep beep* of the smoke alarm.

'Paula!' He grasped her shoulder. 'Paula! Wake up! There's a fire!'

'What? What?' She came to slowly. 'What's the noise?'

'The smoke alarm. Wake up!'

Immediately, she was out of bed, her feet on the bare floor, reaching for her robe hung over the nearby chair. 'Where is it? I don't see any fire.' It was true. The smoke was seeping up through the floor, curling along a wall. 'It's coming from downstairs,' she said.

'I know it.' He was jumping into his pants, pulling a sweater over his pajamas, groping with his feet for his shoes. He banged on the floor, shouting, 'Fire! Fire!' through the crack in the floorboards.

'That's Jimmy's room,' she said. 'He won't understand.'

'Damn!' he said. 'You call emergency. I'm going downstairs,' and he was off, his feet clattering on the stairwell as he went.

In the entrance hall, he pounded on the door of the apartment below. 'Fire!' he shouted. 'Ray! Susan! Your place is on fire!'

He remembered that their bedroom was in front of the house, two rooms away from Jimmy's. The smoke might not have reached them yet. They probably didn't have smoke alarms anyway. He'd suggested it to them once – 'An old house like this could go up in a hurry.'

'Yeah,' Ray had said. 'We should do something about it.' Bart guessed they hadn't, any more than they'd cleaned up the back yard or taken the barrels of debris out of the basement. 'Feel free to store stuff down here,' Ray had said when they first moved in.

'Thanks,' he'd said, and vowed to himself, not this guy, thank you. Not with all the junk you have down here.

He banged again on the door. No response. 'I can't wake them!' he called to Paula who came running down the stairs.

'The fire truck's on its way,' she said.

'Keep knocking here.' He ran out of the entrance hall and onto the front porch and banged on what he thought would be the bedroom window. 'Ray! Susan!' he called. Should he break the glass? Try their door once more. He ran back inside. The smell of smoke was coming through the door. He tried to open it. Locked, of course. 'Stand back!' he said to Paula and ran against the door, hitting it with his shoulder. The wood creaked, but nothing gave way. He pounded again. 'Open up! Open up! Your house is on fire!'

'What's going on – lost your key or something?'

They turned. Through the open front door they saw Ray, his head out the front porch window.

'Your house is on fire, dammit. Open the door,' Bart shouted.

'What the hell?' Ray disappeared. In a minute the door opened. Ray stood there in his pajamas, the smoke billowing from behind him. He seemed in a daze. 'We better get outta here. Susan!' he hollered.

But Susan had streaked past him, running toward the back of the house. 'Jimmy!' she cried out. She disappeared into the smoke. Bart couldn't see her. But he heard her ratcheting cough. 'I can't see!' she cried out. 'Jimmy! Jimmy!'

Taking a huge gulp of air, Bart lunged past Ray and into the smoke. It was dense now. He wasn't familiar with the layout of the hallway and rooms back here. The dim figure of Susan was outlined against a doorway. He saw her stumble, grab for a door jamb, fold over, clutching at her chest.

He heard another cough, from a back room. 'Ma-ma!' a voice called out, then a cough and silence. Jimmy. Behind the door.

He groped for a door handle, burst through the door. 'Jimmy! Where are you?'

No answer. A crib. Where was the crib? Bart swung his hands at waist level, touched a wooden bar – the crib. His eyes stung, his throat was burning, it was impossible to see. He reached into the crib, fingers spread wide, touched a lump of what must be Jimmy, and with a single motion scooped up the child and in a lurching run plunged down the hallway and into the living room where fire was eating now against the wall, sucking at the couch where Susan and Ray, coughing, disoriented, were trying to push the smoke back with their hands, trying to reach the room where their son lay sleeping. 'I've got him,' Bart yelled. 'Get out!' and he burst through the front doorway as the wail of the siren turned the corner and a fire truck slammed on its brakes at the end of the walk.

A man in fireman's gear and carrying a hose rushed up onto the porch, taking in the sight of Bart clutching the child to his chest even as he turned his head aside to cough, and the man and woman supporting each other as they tried to clear their lungs of smoke. 'Anybody else in there?' the fireman shouted.

'No!' Ray called out and then, coughing still, he turned

to Bart who was bending over Jimmy, now screaming in fright but his sleepsuit untouched by fire, his lungs apparently unharmed. 'Is he okay?' Ray shouted.

Susan reached her arms to take the child and Bart, tears streaming down his face, handed the baby over and stood there while Jimmy's screaming turned to quiet sobbing, and then, freed of the baby, he sat down on the top step of the porch and coughed a few more wrenching coughs and put his head down on his knees and sobbed.

He was there when Paula found him, a few minutes later. She had been trying to comfort Susan who sat in a rocking chair on the other side of the porch rocking Jimmy in her lap, crying hysterically. 'We might have lost him,' she sobbed. 'I told Ray to get smoke alarms!' she said. 'If it hadn't of been for you folks,' and then she cried again, and buried her face against the baby.

The firemen ran their hoses into the house, played them over the flames. The fire was quickly extinguished. 'Most of the damage is from smoke,' the fireman told Ray. 'It was the heater started it. That wall heater. Looks like there was papers close by.'

'I guess so.' Ray shook his head, bewildered. 'I guess so. We didn't know a thing about the fire till our tenant upstairs pounded on the door.'

The fireman shot a look at Bart. 'You're a good neighbor,' he said. 'That smoke was pretty bad. The baby could've died. You're a good neighbor,' he said again and couldn't understand why Bart, the hero of the evening, couldn't seem to get a grip on himself. 'They should try a fireman's life,' he muttered. 'It's always crisis time for us.'

There were questions to answer, forms to fill out. The senior fireman on the truck did a close inspection of the house to be sure nothing was left smouldering, urged Ray and Susan to get smoke alarms, 'especially with that baby not right close to you', and to 'get some of that trash out of the cellar'. He assured them it was safe to stay in the house, that there'd been no serious structural damage. They'd have to get a house cleaning company to get rid of the smoke smell, and maybe they'd have to replace a few baseboards and do some painting, but all and all they'd been pretty lucky. 'Could have been much worse,' the fireman said as he remounted the hook and ladder and the fire truck moved off into the darkness.

Ray and Susan, still carrying Jimmy, and Bart and Paula went back inside and into the kitchen which appeared to be untouched. 'Would you like some coffee?' Susan asked. 'I don't think this baby will go back to sleep right away,' looking fondly at her son who seemed quite cheered by now, looking around, taking everything in.

Bart and Paula looked at each other. 'Sure,' Paula said.

So they all had coffee and went over where each of them had been when they realized the house was on fire and what each of them had done in response and Ray and Susan expressed again and again their profuse gratitude to Bart, which Bart acknowledged with quiet deference, he was glad he'd woken up, and anybody would have done the same thing once he saw what the situation was.

The eastern horizon was beginning to glow with first light when Bart and Paula went upstairs and climbed back into bed. 'Thank goodness it's Saturday,' Paula said, and hugged Bart with a desperation born of near catastrophe, and went to sleep.

But Bart stayed awake for a long time while a gratitude too deep for words planted itself in his consciousness and grew and grew until it seemed to fill his chest with a sweet buoyancy he'd not experienced since that awful day when he'd been immobilized by God knows what – and maybe it wouldn't have made any difference anyhow. But his ability to act had sure as hell made a difference today. He heard again the words of the fireman, 'You're a good neighbor,' and he got up and sat by the window. This mood would probably slip from him soon enough; he didn't want to cut if off by sleeping. And he said, to a face he longed for but could not see, 'I saved his life, Annie,' and she said, from somewhere up in the fuzzy front pine tree where the morning sun was just beginning to turn the black spikes to green, 'I know you did, Bart. I watched the whole thing.'

'I'm sorry I couldn't have done the same for you,' he said.

'You think you could have?' she said. 'Who was God before you?'

'You tell me,' he said.

He could have sworn he heard her laugh.

When Laura woke in the morning, Carlena was already up, eager to tell her part of the story of Rachel's crisis. So while Laura drank the steaming coffee, ate the breakfast Carlena had set out for her, Carlena talked on.

'She complained of nausea early in the morning. I gave her tea and toast. But she couldn't hold anything down. She acted real confused. When she went to sleep I thought, that'll do her good. But when I couldn't wake her up for her noon medicine I called the doctor. He ordered the ambulance.' She stopped for breath but continued to hold Laura's attention with her eyes. 'Once she was settled I called a taxi and came home so I could call you children. I was frantic that I couldn't reach you.' She looked up and saw the anguish in Laura's face and hurried on, 'Of course I knew you'd be home by evening – time enough, whatever happened.' Another pause. 'I tell you I was scared. But when I called the hospital at ten thirty last night they said she had improved. I asked could I speak to her and they said no, she was asleep.' Laura nodded and Carlena said, 'Your mother's a tough cookie. She may come out of this just fine. And she's had a good life. Remember that.'

'Oh, I know, Carlena. I saw her last night. She was sleeping then.' In a rush of feeling she said, 'Thank you for taking such good care of her.'

Carlena's eyes filled with tears. 'She's a good woman, your mother. A heap site better than some I've taken care of.'

Laura took the last draught of her coffee and set the cup down. 'I'll call the hospital.'

When she reached the floor nurse, she said, 'I'd like to know the condition of Rachel Taylor.'

'Mrs Taylor's condition is much improved. She's awake and has taken a little nourishment.'

'That's wonderful!' Relief tingled in her hands. 'That's very good news. This is her daughter. I'll be down to see her.' She put the phone back on its cradle, said to Carlena, who stood waiting, arms crossed over the bib of her flowered apron, 'She's much better – she's even taken some food.'

Carlena beamed. 'What did I tell you! Your mother's some strong lady.' They hugged one another.

'I'll call Lillian and Howard.'

Carlena nodded her approval. 'I called them late last night. They're waiting to hear.'

After Laura had talked with them, shared the good news and promised to keep them informed, she called Trace.

He answered the phone. 'Trace Randall speaking.'

'Hi, Trace.'

'Laura! How's everything going? I miss you.'

Unexpectedly, she began to sob. 'I miss you too.'

'What is it? Is Mother in bad shape?'

'No. That's just it. She's in good shape. But she wasn't.' Then she told him the story of Rachel's sudden illness, her trip to the hospital. 'I wasn't here. I'd gone to Cape Cod for the day. With a friend.' She waited. Would he ask more? Did she want him to?

'That's nice,' he said. 'By the way, did Bart call you?'

'No.' Her hand tightened on the phone. 'Is something wrong?'

'Not now. There was a fire last night downstairs in the house where they live.'

'A fire! Was anyone hurt?'

'No. Thanks to Bart. The fire was in the baby's room. The parents were asleep two rooms away. They might not even have noticed until it was too late. Bart woke them up. There was a lot of smoke. Heavy smoke. The mother was almost overcome. Anyway, he ran in and got the baby.'

'Oh, Trace, he could have been killed. How did he know?'

'The baby's room is right under his. The smoke came up through the floor, set off their alarm.'

She sat down in a nearby chair, her hand trembling. 'Was there a lot of damage?'

'Smoke damage. Some water damage from the fire hoses. Everyone's okay.'

Laura felt as though a huge hunk of cotton stuck in her throat, nearly choking off the air.

'How did it start?' she asked.

'Some papers near a wall heater is what the firemen said.'

'And Bart and Paula are okay?' In her mind she saw Bart doing a football run into dense smoke and running back out, the baby held against his side.

'They're fine. We didn't talk long. Bart was obviously dead tired. But he wanted me to know. He said, "Tell Mom too, will you?"'

'Thanks,' she said. 'I'll call him later.' They exchanged a few more words and hung up.

Laura leaned her head back against the wall. Her heart raced. Another disaster. It was too reminiscent. If we had lost him, too . . . But we didn't. Bart and Paula were safe. And the downstairs family – relief for their safety, too. They would remember it always. The parents would tell the child of his narrow escape. It would become part of his personal drama, something to tell about when boys – or men – vied with one another for heroic stories. But Bart . . . How she used to worry about them, scaling rocks, walking along the knife-edged ridges of mountains. But fire? Fire in your own home. While you're asleep in your own bed. Well, he was all right, thank God.

And close behind her pride in her son and relief that everyone was safe came another feeling, unbidden: why not Annie? Why couldn't Annie have been saved? As quickly, her mind recoiled in aversion. Would it always be this way? Would she never again feel unmitigated joy at the good fortune of another? It was the old question – is the cup half empty or half full?

When she got to the hospital a little after nine, Rachel was sitting up, propped against pillows, her hair a matted halo. 'Oh, hello, dear,' her voice trailing and weak.

'Mother!' Laura hugged her, her face against the soft cheek. She stood back, smoothing the hair along Rachel's forehead. 'You gave us quite a scare.'

Rachel's smile was wan. She was drowsy. 'I don't even remember . . .' The words were thick on her lips. 'When . . . did . . . you come?' but before Laura could answer, her eyes closed again.

'Mother?'

Rachel didn't answer. Alarmed, Laura went out into the

hall and stopped a nurse. 'Could you check my mother?'

The nurse came in, jostled Rachel's arm, called into her face, 'Mrs Taylor! You all right, dear?'

Rachel opened her eyes and smiled, trusting, like a child. 'I'm all right.' Her eyes closed again.

The nurse stepped away from the bed, lowered her voice. 'She really had us worried for a while. Her housekeeper said she'd had some kind of digestive upset. Too much loss of body fluids. It takes the potassium and they just go under. As soon as we started her on IVs she began to rally.' She looked back at Rachel. 'She'll be ready to go home in a day or two.'

The nurse left the room and Laura sat down in the chair. She should be jubilant that Rachel had passed this crisis, and she was. And certainly she was glad the fire in Woodbridge had had such a happy ending. But all her elation of yesterday, her sense that her life was moving into new realms, no longer weighted by consuming grief – where had it all gone? She closed her eyes, trying to recapture the feeling and saw, as on a moving screen, a silhouetted couple walking along the beach.

She sighed when she got home, how would it be for her and Trace? When she tried to tell him about her journey of self-discovery, would his look grow distant, his attention wander? How much would she tell him about Fred Thayer?

She was gazing out the window when she heard a rustle at the door. 'Laura?'

She turned. It was Ginny and Fred, with a bouquet of flowers – forsythia and pussy willows, shrouded in green tissue.

'I was just thinking about you,' she said.

'I called Carlena,' Ginny said. 'She said things are much better. I'm so glad.' She kissed Laura's cheek. 'Fred said you had a good day, even with a stormy drive home. Sorry I couldn't go.'

'We did have a good day,' she said. 'Fred was a wonderful help to me. It would have been a good day with you there too.' Her eyes met Fred's. 'But different,' she said. 'A different proposition.'

A look of mild alarm came on Fred's face.

Ginny went out into the hall in search of a vase and his look changed to a conspiratorial smile. 'Watch your language,' he said.

'Just an expression,' Laura said, 'and it *was* a wonderful day.'

'Now that the crisis has passed,' Fred looked toward the bed where Rachel was peacefully dozing, 'may I take you to dinner tonight?'

'Yes,' she said before she had time to think about it. 'I'd like that. After visiting hours?'

Ginny came back in, brandishing a vase. 'They have a closet full of these,' she said.

By the time they got to the restaurant, the dinner crowd had mostly gone. The tables and booths that ringed the large area of hardwood floor left clear for dancing were occupied by young couples having snacks and drinks, occasionally rising to dance to music provided by a trio of musicians flanked by an array of palm, on a raised platform at the far end of the room.

They ordered drinks, then dinner – light pastas with salads and a bottle of wine, noted the food, the decor, the dancing skills of two couples who bounded to their feet whenever the musicians struck out with some rapid-fire rock music.

All but finished, Laura sat back against the padded banquette, her wine glass in hand. 'This is such a respite for me, Fred. A place to be quiet, collect my thoughts.'

'Which are?' He looked at her tenderly, reached in his pocket. 'A penny for your thoughts,' and offered her a coin on his extended palm.

She took the coin, and his hand as well.

'For starters, how much I'm enjoying being here with you.'

He smiled. 'That's worth two pennies at least. But I don't want to let go of you.'

'Nor I of you,' she said. 'I'll miss you when I go home.'

'I'll miss you too.' He leaned toward her. 'I missed you all day today, except for that few minutes at the hospital.

Now that your mother's improving so, I could wish we'd not made that phone call last night.'

She smiled. 'I've thought of that. Carlena would have worried. She wasn't too sure it was proper for me to go off with you yesterday. If I'd stayed away overnight . . .'

'You're a grownup,' he said. 'You don't have to answer to Carlena. Or –' He broke off.

'Or anyone else – is that what you were thinking?'

'Wishful thinking,' he said, and smiled. 'How is it going to be for you, going home?'

'I don't know,' she said. 'I want to tell Trace about my experience yesterday afternoon, the whole sequence of that revelation about how I was holding on to Annie, overlapping my life and hers, partly as a way of holding on to her. But I don't know that I can make him see it.'

'Does he have to?'

The question startled her. 'What do you mean?'

'Just that experience, especially inner experience, is so much our own. It's hard to really share that. Maybe the poets have the best crack at it, but they must feel people aren't getting it a lot of the time.'

'What's the use of sharing your life with someone if they can't know what's going on for you?'

'They can. There are degrees and degrees. And extenuating circumstances, like how much a person is preoccupied by his own needs. Some people do better than others. I'm not saying a person can't learn, or can't improve. Women are probably more adept than men at really listening, taking in the subtleties of what someone is saying.'

She nodded. 'I know. But you, yesterday . . .'

He shook his head. 'I was blessed to be there for you, Laura. Believe me,' his voice took on an earnestness and his eyes darkened, 'I would consider turning my life over into your hands if you were free – and would have me. But even at that there would be places where we would be alien to one another.'

'You would?' she said, startled, touched by what she had just heard. 'We've only known each other a little while.'

'We've known each other all our lives,' he said. 'We just found out about it lately.'

'It seems that, doesn't it? And of course we knew each other back in high school.'

'"My salad days, when I was green in judgment,"' he said. 'I should never have let you get away.'

She smiled, wistful. 'Who knows?'

The musicians, who had taken a break, were starting up again. 'We'll try something for the old folks,' the bass player said. 'Something slow and sweet.'

Laura looked around, laughed. 'That must mean us. We're the oldest people here.'

But some of the young folks, too, were getting up to dance to the strains of a Cole Porter song, and when three couples had stepped into the circle of light and begun dancing, Fred put down his glass and said, 'Shall we?' and she stood and followed him out onto the dance floor and moved into his arms.

'It's not exactly Charley's, is it?' he said.

'No, and we're not the people we were then, either.'

'No, we're not,' he said, holding her close and they danced on, wordlessly, turning as the music carried them along.

They drove home in silence. At the door she said, 'I won't invite you in. It's very late. I think Mother's coming home tomorrow. But it's been wonderful being with you this evening. I'll be going home myself in several days.'

'I suppose so,' he said, a sadness in his voice, and he took her face between his hands and kissed her. 'I'll call you,' he said, and stepped down from the porch.

She went inside. The house was quiet. There was a note on the message pad in the hall. 'Your son Bart called. He asked that you call him back. No matter if it's late.'

She looked at her watch. Midnight.

Hastily, she put in the call. Paula answered. 'Hello?'

'Paula, this is Laura. Bart called. Nothing wrong?'

'No. Everything's fine.'

'I understand you had some excitement there last night.'

'Yes, but he wants to tell you. Bart,' she called. 'It's your mother.'

He came to the phone. 'Mom! Where you been? Hospitals throw you out before midnight.'

'I've had a late dinner with a friend. But I'm so glad you're all right. Such a brave thing, Bart.'

'Oh yeah, the fire. Dad told you?'

'Yes, this morning. It must have been awful.'

'It was pretty horrendous for a few minutes. But everyone is fine. We don't even have much mess to clean up. But that's not what I called you about.'

'Well, what then? Nothing wrong?'

'Hardly. Paula and I are going to get married.'

'You are! That's wonderful! When?'

'Not right away. We just decided. Sometime in the next year.'

'I couldn't be happier! Does Dad know? Have you told Paula's mother? Or Philip?'

'I'll call Phil. I haven't reached Dad yet. I guess he's at a meeting or something. Paula called her mom tonight. She's coming down to visit real soon. And guess what?'

'What?'

'I don't have to move out.'

Paula came on the phone. 'Hi, Mom,' she said, laughing. 'We're real happy. Are you surprised?'

'I'd hoped, of course. But I didn't know. How about your mother?'

'She's excited. My brother was married two years ago. But she's never been the mother of the bride before.'

A sudden pang – the mother of the bride. 'No, I guess not,' Laura said.

'Maybe when she's here we can all talk colors.'

'Wonderful,' Laura said. A few more exchanges and they hung up and for a moment Laura stood quietly in the hall, letting the joy sink in. A new milestone for them all. How excited Annie would have been, and yes, it would be sad not having Annie there. But she wouldn't think about that now. Because it was wonderful news about Bart and Paula. Sometimes the cup was filled to overflowing.

21

Rachel came home. She seemed in good spirits, even stronger from her brush with death. She spent long stretches on the phone, describing her health crisis and recovery. 'And the funny part about it, I don't remember a thing from the time I threw up my breakfast until I saw Laura's face in the hospital.'

Laura called Trace again. Rachel was home and doing well. What was the news from Woodbridge?

He'd talked with Bart and Paula; yes, it was wonderful about their planning to marry. He was busy with work. He and Kate had had several good sessions with her thesis. 'She's invited me over for some of her mother's raspberry cordial.'

'Are you going?'

'Yes, I'm going.' His laugh seemed self-conscious, or was she imagining it?

'Any word from Philip?'

'A letter came. He seemed kind of down. He's finding the term difficult, having a hard time concentrating.'

'Do you think he's all right?'

'I imagine so. Probably feeling depressed when he wrote.'

'We can call him when I get home.'

'How's Trace?' Rachel asked when she came from the phone.

'Fine. Busy. He's talked with Bart and Paula at dinner. He's had a letter from Philip.' No particular point in telling her mother about Kate and the raspberry cordial.

283

'How is Philip?'

'A little blue – maybe a mid-winter slump.'

'No wonder.' Rachel looked out the window, then back at Laura. 'Would you do something for me while you're here?'

'What is it?'

'I've enjoyed Ginny's flowers.' She looked over at the crescents of yellow flowers, the stalks of pussy willows, still fresh and lovely, spilling from the glass vase. 'But now I'd like to share them . . . with Will.' She looked up, her eyes questioning and vulnerable. 'Would you take them to the cemetery? Is that foolish?'

Laura leaned over, kissed her mother. 'Of course it isn't foolish, and I'll be glad to take them, right now.'

'Let me see them up close once more before you go.'

Laura brought the vase of flowers over to Rachel's bed and watched as her mother touched the yellow blossoms, ran her fingers up a stalk of pussy willows. 'There. Thank you. Now you can take them.'

Laura emptied the water from the vase and put flowers and vase on a newspaper in the back seat of the car and drove the mile and a half to the cemetery. She drove through the open gate, then slowly along the serpentine road that wound between the plots marked with gravestones of granite and marble – rose, gray, white veined with blue. In the center of each plot was a large stone bearing the family name – Stedman, Forbes, Dowling – around it a village of small headstones, the names of their dead.

There it was, Taylor, incised in the granite block. She parked beside the road, took the vase and cluster of forsythia and pussy willows to the nearest faucet, filled the vase, set the bouquet into the water and, kneeling down, set the jar on the earth in front of Will's headstone – William A.

She sat back on her heels, her knees pressed against the hard ground. Beyond Will's headstone were the graves of his parents, Cassie and Charles Taylor. A black iron cross for the Spanish-American War. A small stone marked 'Baby' for the child of Cassie and Charles who had died at birth, before Will was born. Beyond that, the grave of a maiden aunt. But closer, on this side of the large central stone, only

Will's headstone broke the wide corridor of brown winter grass. There, beside it, would go Rachel's. When? Not soon, she hoped, not soon. But not too long a time, either, for Rachel's sake.

The water in the jar caught the light, recalled a single tea rose rising through water in a clear glass vase. The memorial service for Annie. Will. Annie. Rachel's life hanging by a thread as easily interrupted as a beam of light.

It was then the thought came to her. Annie! She saw the box, wrapped in brown paper, on the shelf in the closet in Annie's room. Annie's ashes. Perhaps this is what they should do. When her mother died, bury Annie's ashes close to those of her grandmother, consign them together to this already hallowed ground. They could incise their name, Randall, beneath Taylor on the large stone. There would even be room to bury the ashes of the rest of the family, if they wanted it, if it would help to think of it that way – herself, Trace, the boys.

Her mind flew back to that afternoon when she and Trace had brought Annie's ashes home.

'I wonder what we'll do with them eventually,' she'd said. And Trace's answer, 'When the time comes I think we'll know.'

There, opposite Will's, would go Rachel's stone. And, beside it, a third? Her chest knotted and she bent forward and pressed her forehead against the hard earth. 'Anne,' she moaned. 'Anne.'

Driving away from the cemetery, she passed the Cramer Home, a rambling brown clapboard structure. On a sudden impulse she stopped the car, parked along the curb and got out. The home was an old Victorian house, with leaded glass panels on either side of a large oak door, and a deep porch, lined with rocking chairs, running across the front.

She rang the bell. A woman in a white uniform came to the door.

'I'm Laura Randall. Could I see Mabel Olmstead?'

'Why, yes. Come in.'

She entered a large carpeted vestibule hung with gold-framed paintings and flowered drapes, clusters of soft chairs and sofas slipcovered to match the drapes. A poster labelled 'February Birthdays' with names pencilled in hung over a small writing desk.

'This way.'

She followed the woman down a corridor panelled in dark wood, a brass handrail extending along the wall.

The nurse stopped at a doorway. 'Mrs Olmstead, here's somebody to see you.' She nodded and left as Laura entered the room.

In a large chair in a corner of the room, a pink blanket over her lap, a crocheted shawl covering her shoulders, a small woman looked out over the shimmering circles of her glasses. 'Why Laura Taylor! I do declare!'

'Mabel!' Laura stepped forward and hugged her, her face against the white curls. 'I'm glad to see you.'

'Pull up a chair and sit down. You're in town to see your mother. Say, wasn't that a scare she gave us? How is she today?'

'She's doing well. Better, I think, than before this happened.'

'A little excitement is good medicine for us old folks.' Mabel's shoulders lifted under the shawl. 'We run out of things to toot our horns over. Your mother'll be talking about that for weeks – almost as good as a new grandchild. How are your babies? I suppose they're all grown up.'

'Yes, Mabel, my babies are grown up.' Was it possible she didn't know about Annie?

'Of course I heard about your daughter. I'm so sad, dear. It doesn't seem right that folks like us should stay and she should go.' Mabel's voice quivered and Laura reached over and touched her tiny knarled hand. 'Thank you. Tell me how you are.'

'I'm doing well. They're awful good to us here. There's lots to do. I have friends. I go to the dining room for my meals. Sometimes when Buddy and Ellen come they take me for a drive.'

'Do you see them often? Are they still in Boston?'

'Yes. They come. Seems like you get to Hadley about as often. We talked about my going down there. But I've lived in Hadley for forty years.' She looked up, as though to share the astonishment of so much time. 'Buddy calls me. I call him. Children have to live their own lives, you know.'

They chatted on, about Mabel's neighbors, about people they'd both known. Then Mabel said, 'Say, let me show you.' She turned to the table beside her, crowded with books, a box of tissues, a water glass, a small radio, and pulled out an old photo album. Crumbs of disintegrating paper fell from it as she brought it to her lap. 'I was looking at this just this morning. It's got pictures of your mother and father in it.' She lifted the corners of the dull black pages, one by one.

'Here!' She turned the book so Laura could see two snapshots, almost alike – six young adults crowded on a sofa, six others standing behind them. She'd seen pictures of these same twelve people in her parents' photo album. 'We were the Couples Club,' Rachel had said. 'We were all young and poor, so we made our own fun – we had parties once a month.'

In Mabel's pictures they were wearing costumes – a man in a pirate suit with a patch over one eye, a woman in an old-fashioned wool bathing suit, the white braid squaring off the neckline of a darky middy blouse over ballooning dark knickers. In the back row were her parents, her mother wearing the Indian dress from her days as a Camp Fire Girl, her father in a white apron and high chef's hat. They were all laughing, their arms round each other. Barney Olmstead stood by her mother, his cheek against hers, grinning for the camera.

A wonder crossed Laura's mind. Years ago, a teenager, falling in and out of love, she had asked Rachel, 'Do you think there's one man for one woman?'

'No,' Rachel said. 'I've known other people I could be happy with. Mr Olmstead, for one.' It had startled her then; Mr Olmstead was little more than a stranger to her though a good friend of her parents. Looking at their faces now, she wondered, had they ever spoken of it between them, her mother and Barney Olmstead? Did they have it in their shared possession, a jewelled cache of fantasy and high regard?

'Mother used to tell me about those good times,' she said.

She looked at the faces again. Mabel said it first: 'So many of them are gone.'

A nurse came to the door. 'Would you like some tea for your guest?'

Laura stood. 'Thanks. I've got to go. I was just coming by and thought I'd stop.' She kissed Mabel goodbye and left, with a final glance at the photo album on the table.

At home Carlena was boiling water for tea. 'I thought you'd be here sooner,' Rachel said. 'Did it take that long to do the flowers?'

Laura shook her head. 'I stopped at the Cramer Home to see Mabel.'

'How is she? What did you think of it? I haven't been there since she moved.'

'It's attractive. They evidently get good care. She goes to the dining room. Buddy and Ellen come to see her. Interesting things going on. It seems like a fine place. She seems very happy.'

For a yearning, tender moment she hovered on the edge of a question – Mother, is it all right, your not coming to Woodbridge? Do you forgive me? But she didn't ask. It would be for her own sake only and it might revive an old hurt.

But Rachel wasn't looking at her. Her eyes were scanning the room – the folding screen with white chrysanthemums her own mother had painted, the buffet stacked with books and pictures and trivia of her life with Will, the doorway onto the porch where roses covered the trellis every June, the china closet, the window looking out toward the lilacs and the pulleyed clothes line. Her gaze came back to rest on Laura. 'But it's not like being in your own home,' she said.

Laura's heart lifted in gratitude. Her mother had answered the question without her asking.

It emboldened her, her mother's contentment. There was something else that came to her, formed out of the inchoate blundering pain of the past months.

'Mother?'

'What is it, dear?'

She drew closer, felt the tears start.

Rachel stroked her hand. 'Was the cemetery that hard?'

'No.'

'Then what, dear?'

'It's about Annie.'

'What about her – that lovely child?'

Her voice caught on the jagged edges of her breath. 'I feel as though I failed.'

'Why?' Rachel was uncomprehending.

'Because,' she was crying now, but could not stop, 'mothers are supposed to save their children. You saved me, and I couldn't save her.' There. She put her head down, sobbing.

She felt Rachel's knarled hand on her neck, stroking gently, as of old. 'Darling. That was a totally different thing. Yours was a sickness. Annie's was a violent death – over right away. She had a beautiful life, dear. Not as long as we'd hoped, but very full for her years.' Rachel's hand lifted Laura's hair, smoothed it back in place. After a while she said, 'I want to tell you something, dear.'

'Yes.' Laura looked up. Her mother's eyes were luminous and clear.

'I have a feeling I may not live long.'

'Is it a new feeling?'

'The last few days. Since my hospitalization.'

'The doctor says you're doing very well. You seem very alert, full of cheer.'

'Do I? That's good.'

Laura reached for a handkerchief. 'I'll miss you, whenever you go . . . And I feel like saying to you, "Give her my love", and Father too.'

'Don't think I won't,' Rachel said.

The next day Laura called Trace's office. It was late afternoon. At first no one answered but then someone picked up the phone and a woman's voice said, 'Hello.'

'I'm sorry, I'm trying to reach Mr Randall's office.'

'This is Mr Randall's office.'

'Who is this?'

'This is Kate Morton.'

'Oh. Well, this is Mrs Randall. Is Trace there?' She drew

in her breath. Was this girl taking over Trace's office, or what?

'He just went out for a minute – wait, here he is.' She heard Kate say, 'It's your wife.'

'Hello? Laura?'

'Hi. I didn't think I was going to reach you. How are you?'

'I'm fine. Just a minute.' She heard, 'Goodbye, Kate. Let me know when you're ready to confer again . . . Thank you, yes. You, too.' He returned to the phone. 'How are you? How are things going?'

'Fine.' She heard the reserve in her voice. Did he?

'Any thought as to when you'll be home? I miss you.'

'Mother is doing well and I'd planned to come tomorrow, if you're not too busy.'

'Of course not. When does your plane get in?'

'Three twenty-seven in the afternoon.'

'Good. I'll be there.'

'I'll see you then. Trace . . .' What did she want to ask? Do you love me? Are we right for each other? Who is Kate Morton to you?

'Yes?'

'Nothing. I'll see you tomorrow.'

In the evening she sat by Rachel. When it was time to go to bed she held her mother in her arms, her body light, like a child's.

'Wake me before you go,' Rachel said.

In the morning, bustling around the kitchen with Carlena, she ate an early breakfast. Then she woke Rachel. 'I'm going, Mother. I'll see you later.'

Rachel was confused, hardly awake. 'You'll see me later? When?'

'When I come again.' She stroked Rachel's hair, put her cheek against her mother's.

'They're here,' Carlena called.

'Coming.' She kissed her mother once more and went to the front hall. 'Goodbye, dear.' She hugged Carlena, picked up her suitcase and hurried to the car, where Ginny and Fred waited to take her to the airport.

* * *

They neared the airport. Laura, sitting in the back seat with Ginny, watched the New England countryside go by, sere and brown, though patches of snow still lingered among the roots of trees on the northern side of the hills.

They'd been engaging in small talk most of the way, about some mutual friends Ginny had been with, about Fred's return to Northampton but then on to Cancun. 'I may get to Tennessee,' he said. 'If I do I'll call you.'

'Please do,' she said. 'We could drive to Nashville, take in the Grand Ole Opry.'

'I was there a few years ago,' he said. 'If I'd known you were there . . .'

'Well, come back.' Their eyes met in the rearview mirror, in glad acknowledgement that they'd enjoy being together again.

'And keep in mind the Iceland brochure,' he said.

'I will, as soon as I get back home.'

She took a sidelong glance at Ginny, and thought how, in a bittersweet way, the equation among the three of them had changed since her visit to Hadley last fall – her first time after Annie's death. Then it had been Ginny she turned to, her lifeline to sanity, her most trusted and confided-in friend, and while Ginny was still a deeply cherished friend it was more to Fred her thoughts flew now when she was roaming her inner landscape for signs of hope, the possibilities of moderating her sadness with some kind of life-giving joy. Did Ginny know? She herself had said nothing to Ginny to indicate the depth of her friendship with Fred. She doubted that Fred had. In fact Ginny had seemed quite puzzled when she'd called about taking Laura to the airport. 'Fred wants to come along. Is that okay?'

'Sure,' she said, glad that Ginny couldn't see her face. 'Is he back from Northampton?' When last she'd spoken with Fred, he'd had a critical meeting at the time she'd be flying home.

'He's changed some plans. He'll be here. I told him I could do it myself,' Ginny said, a touch of irritation in her voice.

As they turned onto the access road the mood in the car grew heavier, perhaps shadowed by the prospect of her leaving, the seriousness of Rachel's condition.

'You don't know when you'll be back,' Ginny said.

'No. I'll see how Mother does.'

'You'll be glad to be home,' Ginny said.

'Yes. To see Trace.' But there was an undertow of anxiety there too, which she did not speak of.

At the curb by the departure gate, Fred parked, turned to Ginny. 'Will you wait with the car? I'll help Laura in with her bag.'

'Sure.' Ginny stepped from the car, hugged Laura. 'I'll call your mother from time to time. Remember, I'll be thinking of you.'

'Thanks. Thanks for all your help.'

Fred picked up her suitcase and they went into the terminal.

There was a short queue at the desk. 'Go ahead,' she said. 'I'll be fine now.' But he waited, inching forward with her as the line moved. She got her boarding pass and they walked toward the departure gate.

At the gate the boarding calls were about to begin. 'Go back now,' she said. 'Ginny will be waiting.'

He put his arms out and she came to him. 'Thank you for everything,' she said.

'Thank you,' he said, his voice gruff against her hair.

'For what?'

'For your trust. For being with me. For letting me know you all over again. And one more thing. Last night I wrote a letter to my daughter.'

'Oh, Fred.' She stood back and looked into his face. His eyes were filled with tears. 'Oh, Fred,' she said again. 'Thank you,' and kissed him, and, since the flight manager was now calling her row, she went up the ramp, turning to wave, and stepped into the plane.

She found her seat next to a window and sat down. At the edge of the field a large truck, its light whirling, was trying to position itself – kept backing and moving forward, backing again, edging forward. Finally it got into position and drove onto the edge of the field, moved toward one of the planes. Some kind of service truck? Fuel, maybe, or food for the journey.

She looked back at the aisle filled with boarding passengers. A flash of plaid caught her eye. In the waiting room she had seen a brown-haired young woman in a plaid jacket – bright red, greens, yellows. Annie had had just such a jacket. This same young woman had entered the plane, was coming toward her down the aisle, checking the overhead numbers. A momentary panic seized her. The empty seat beside her – could that be the girl's seat? And if she came here, what then?

But well in front of her the young woman hesitated, checked her flight pass again against the number overhead, slipped into a row and dropped down in front of the high seat back, out of sight.

Shaken, Laura looked at the space where the girl had been. In her mind she hovered there, willing some kind of blessing on this stranger and glad, for now, for this distance between them.

As the plane took off, she sat back, watching the blurred world going by.

By now Fred and Ginny would be well on their way back to Hadley. The fact that Fred had written his daughter filled her with gladness. It had not occurred to her that she had given anything significant to him. She had taken so much – all the attention, all the listening, the being with, that he could offer.

What if there on Cape Cod she had made the other choice? The body's hunger, fed by a trust born of sharing the deep heart. Wasn't that what made the offering of the body a natural outcome, once the possibility had really presented itself? I have told you everything else about myself. Now let me tell you this. It is my most intimate secret. Enter it with me. I trust you.

There was more. Curiosity. Who will I be with you? The shyness – I am afraid. What if you find me unlovely? Never the other anxiety – what if I find you unlovely? The adventure. The mystery. The play in three acts. An outward sign of an inward and spiritual grace.

She thought of that picture of her mother and Barney Olmstead, smiling, cheek to cheek. It was beyond her comprehension that her mother might have been unfaithful to her father. But what wanderings of mind and triphammers of the heart might have been part of those years when Rachel and Will and Mabel and Barney were such good friends?

And she – did she hold on to her marriage out of habit? The thought of leaving frightened her – to be without a partner, or to take on the labor and risk of finding another. Yet if the marriage was only habit she did not want it, hard though it would be to reshape her life. As the would-be inheritor of her daughter's courage, should she begin again altogether?

And what of Trace? Had he turned to Kate for comfort and understanding? Those evenings when she couldn't reach him – was he with her?

Her mind flew back to her early days with Trace. Newly engaged, they had found some test in a magazine. 'Is he/she the one for you? Would you rather A. Go for a ten-mile hike? B. Attend a classical music concert? C. Work on fixing up your house?' How they had laughed at the transparency of the test, revelling in their compatibility. There would be nothing they couldn't handle together. And so it had seemed through the years. She remembered being with Trace at a concert – she was pregnant with Annie so it was a long time ago – at the bandstand down by the river on a summer evening, the air sweet with the smell of honeysuckle. For one number a quintet of men stepped away from the chorus, rearranged themselves and sang *a capella*, 'If I fall in love, it will be for ever', and moved to tears by the poignant truth of the words, she had reached for Trace's hand. That was who they were, so sure of one another. Well, there were no tests to prepare you for the death of a child.

They were high above the clouds now. She dozed. When she woke up they were readying to land. She reached for her coat and crowded into the aisle, began to move from the plane. He'd be there, at the end of the jetway, standing away from the wall, head slightly forward, smiling, not caring that he was making himself conspicuous in his eagerness to meet her. Brown eyes. A lift to the left eyebrow.

'Trace!' She began to walk faster.

22

At home, he stood by her while she flipped through the pile of mail. She came to the letter from Philip.

'I told you about that,' he said, reading it over her shoulder. She read aloud, 'I haven't been sleeping real well lately. I try to study and my mind wanders and nothing sinks in.' She folded the letter. 'Oh, dear.'

'I got concerned and called him,' Trace said. 'He's evidently gone somewhere. Probably taken a break for a few days.'

She looked at him, surprised. He had called Philip? Usually it was she who initiated calls to the children, unless it was some business matter or a birthday. But he had done it on his own. 'Did you?' she said.

'I left a message with the school switchboard asking him to get in touch with us. I haven't heard. We can call again.'

They rang the number of his college house. No one answered. Panic started in her chest and she tried to put it down. 'Oh, I hope he's all right.'

She made some tea and they sat down to talk.

'Tell me more about Hadley,' Trace said. 'You were there a long time – at least it seemed a long time to me.'

She put her hands round the cup, warming them. 'So much has happened, where to begin?' With her mother? With Fred? Her own tortuous journey of discovery, rocking in that chair by the oceanside?

'Things have happened, Trace, while I've been gone. I've done a lot of thinking. It will take me a while to absorb it –

some things about my mother, Annie, me. Some things about ambivalence, not having to be perfect, just being grateful for love.' She told him about her talk with Rachel. 'I guess I felt a failure because I couldn't save Annie. Of course it was crazy, but the mind does crazy things. Anyway, the talk with my mother was like an absolution. I realized how grateful I am to her, even though it's been hard to be a separate person. But the blessings . . .' She looked up to be sure he was listening.

'Yes. Go on,' he said.

'I wouldn't trade them for anything.'

He nodded, thoughtful. 'Some of us have the opposite problem,' he said.

'Like what?' she said.

'Independence can be over-valued. It takes a while to learn that. And sometimes it's too late.'

She reached over and took his hand.

He drew from the sideboard a folded sheet of paper. 'I found this in Annie's desk one day when you were gone,' and he handed her the paper.

She read Annie's poem, looked up. 'It's almost as though she knew.' She read through it again. '"All the better for you, I believe",' she read and looked up. 'Who do you think it's written to? Who is the "you" in the poem? Obviously someone she loved very much.'

'Maybe both of us?' he said. 'A collective you?'

It was a generous gesture but it didn't fit. She looked at the words again. She had been a primary person in her daughter's life, hadn't she? Yes, and all the more reason for this to be for Trace. Maybe inadvertently this had been Annie's gift to her father, since they would have no time to fix things up in person. Could she let Trace have it, even if that meant her being on the outside this once? 'I think it's for you,' she said, and folded the page and handed it back to him.

'Maybe,' he said, but the glow in his eyes spoke his gratitude.

There was something she had to know. 'Your project with Kate, how is that?'

'The basic work will be done soon. It's taken lots of time.'

Lots of time. Plenty of time for anything. Still, she didn't think . . . 'Did you talk to her, about Annie?'

'She reminds me of Annie in some ways. I told her that, so she wouldn't be scared if I seemed to have invested more than the usual academic interest in her success.' He hesitated. 'She's talked to me some about her parents, and herself.' His color heightened. 'She said I helped her a lot.'

She noted the blush. What did it mean? His pleasure in his success at helping a young woman with her life quandaries? Something else? She might never know. 'Are you in love with her?' she asked.

Slowly, the implications of her question dawned on him. His face changed from incredulity to recognition. 'No, I'm not, Laura. You weren't really worried about that, were you?'

'A little,' she admitted. 'People sometimes do . . . find other people they're attracted to . . . think it would be better . . .' She stumbled over the words.

'I know. But I love *you*. You're the one for me.'

She put her arms round his neck and kissed him.

They were in the kitchen, clearing up their few dishes, and she said, 'Something came to me while I was away.'

He put his inverted cup in the dishwasher, turned to her. 'Yes?'

'I don't suppose my mother will live much longer.' Her eyes filled with tears, telling him. 'When I was at the cemetery it occurred to me, whenever it is that my mother dies, what would you think of our burying Annie's ashes next to hers?'

She could feel in her own body how the thought of it stood at the gate of his mind, and then how he stepped back to allow it to enter.

'It is a good idea,' he said. 'I would be willing.'

They didn't hear from Philip. They called Bart. No, he didn't know anything. Laura tried to silence her anxiety, hold it in check. He had gone off on camping trips before, taken his bicycle and a backpack and gone off into the woods. But usually he told someone he was going, and where.

It was Trace who thought of it first. The third day after her return he called from the office. 'I wonder if Philip went to Argonne Woods.'

'Oh.' Her mind went like a lasso, swung back over Christmas. She saw the glistening page, the green-black leaves, the book spread open on Philip's lap – 'She wrote me about it. She asked if I could get off school and come.'

'It will soon be that time of year, won't it?'

They left as soon as he could get home and pick her up. It was a three-hour trip. The tree limbs were still bare but a few tight buds were visible along the black stalks of winter.

'It's very likely this could be a wild goose chase,' Trace said when they were within a few miles of the woods.

'I suppose so.' If Philip wasn't here, with what would they engage themselves, needing to find him?

They got to the familiar sign – the rough frame, the letters burned into varnished wood, 'Argonne Woods'. A smaller sign suspended by two small wrought-iron hooks read: 'Open for season March 30'.

The road forked and they took the fork marked 'River Cabins', passed the entrance to the Dogwood Trail, the road leading to the fire tower, the path going down to the boat dock, and came to the cluster of cabins set in among the tall trees.

There, against the brown-stained logs of the cabin, its wheel chained to a sapling by the door, stood a bicycle. Blue saddlebags straddled the bar.

'It's Philip,' she said.

'Looks like it,' he said.

Still, they weren't sure. They got out of the car, walked across the caterpillar softness of moss furred up through parchment leaves, round to the back of the cabin. He was sitting on the porch, reading, a can of soda on the weathered table beside him.

'Philip!' Trace shouted.

He looked up. 'Mom! Dad! What're you doing here?'

Giddy with relief, they looked at one another, then back to Philip. 'We were just looking for you,' Trace said.

Philip shook his head, shaking loose from his disbelief. 'Well, come on in.' He moved toward the rail. 'You'll have to come in this way, the front door's padlocked. I'm an unregistered guest.'

'Philip! You mean you broke in?' Laura said.

'I didn't break in, Mom. I just . . . let myself in. We kids learned the secrets of this place long ago.' He reached over the rail and gave her his hand and she put her foot on the edge of the porch and swung herself up and over the rail. Trace followed and they stood there. Philip began, 'I just came out here. I thought I could study here where it's quiet. I thought . . .' But his shoulders heaved and the three of them came together, their arms round one another, the sounds of the river and the woods mingling with his sobs. 'Thanks,' he said, snuffling into his sleeve.

They stepped apart.

'Well, come in,' Philip said.

At first they couldn't see anything in the darkness. Then their eyes picked out the shapes of fireplace and table, a white porcelain sink, the shine of stove burners, stacks of white dishes piled against a dark wall. Philip groped for the light switch. 'I don't turn it on much,' he said. 'Saves on the utilities.'

His sleeping bag covered the cot in the main room. On the table by the cot were more books, and a white envelope. Even in the dim light they could see the envelope bore Philip's name and his school address. It was in Annie's writing.

'It's the letter she wrote me last year, about coming here,' he said.

Laura nodded, her eyes fixed on the white paper. How could it be, Annie's letter here and she herself gone?

Laura drew her eyes away to look around the cabin again. Through the doorway she saw the two bedrooms, the partition between them going halfway to the ceiling. They used to throw pillows back and forth over the partition, she and Annie in the one room, Trace and the boys in the other, laughing and scrambling over the beds.

'How long you planning to stay?' Trace asked.

Philip looked at his watch. 'I could get back before dark if I start soon.'

They helped him pack up, load his bicycle baskets.

Together, they drove to a diner and had ham sandwiches and coffee, steaming and dark in heavy glass mugs. Philip talked about school and they talked about Woodbridge and Laura told about being in Hadley with Rachel. 'There's a question I want to ask you,' she said gently. 'When Grandma dies . . .' Yes, it was all right with him.

They drove him back to the cabin. The sun had shifted, throwing its light on the grooved log wall, the winter-dingy window, the steps where they had often stood, lined up together, while some kind passerby took their picture.

Philip unchained his bicycle, hugged them goodbye. 'I did get some stuff done. It's not like I wasted time.' He straddled the bike, one foot braced against the earth to keep from falling, the other on the pedal, ready to push off. 'I don't know what I hoped to find here anyway.' There was a touch of laughter in his voice. 'Maybe you guys – I don't know.'

He pedalled off. Laura and Trace got in the car and drove out of Argonne Woods and home. It was after dark when they got there. As they drove in, the headlights picked up tiny crescents of deep rose against the bark of the tree. The redbud was starting to come out.

23

Sooner than anyone other than perhaps Rachel herself had expected – it was four days after the trip to Argonne Woods – a call came from Carlena. 'Laura, your mother died an hour ago. The doctor was just here. But I knew.' She was crying. 'Forgive me, dear. I never get used to it.'

Laura's hand tightened on the phone. 'Tell me.' She listened and in her mind was an image of the ocean floor being pulled away beneath the waves, like a rug. 'I gave her tea. She drank it. I was in the next room. All I heard was a sigh. I came back and she was gone.'

Tears flooded Laura's eyes. She sat down in the rocking chair in the kitchen and rocked back and forth, listening to Carlena, holding the phone against her cheek.

O, thou that takest away the sins of the world, grant us thy peace, and to her a safe passage and a glad reunion. 'Rebecca . . . Lilly! And aren't they beautiful!' Will . . . Annie . . . 'Give them my love.' *And at our life's end a sweet repose. God be thanked for her. Receive her unto her own.*

Mother! She is coming now through trees, and she is coming into the room at night, to take away all cares with the touch of her hand, and she is standing luminous and still in the yellow silk dress and the amber beads, and she is fading away into the night, she who slipped from earth an hour ago. And who will succor us in the long darkness? Who will hold our head in her lap and keep us safe from hunger, cold, desertion and the fear of death?

You in whose stead the passion of lovers yearns in the lust of the body for another home to fuse into home everlasting but no more home than you . . . You the home expelled from in the breaking of the waters . . . The dream of return grows dim and wise and is, in time, forgotten in the brain or, if not forgotten, protected from, for there is pain, still, in the frayed edges of our leaving, in the jagged torn flesh of our separation and the imperfect closing over of that wound whereby we who were one become two – at birth first, and then again and again. And she torn from me, too, and then again before I was ready. What shall save us (now daughter, now mother), we who in the middle of our life are told that our mother dies and having neither mother nor daughter, turn to our-self in pain and sorrow and know as a desperate surprise that we shall prevail. Once more, we shall prevail. And who may abide?

'Yes, Carlena, yes. I'll be there tomorrow.'

Bart and Paula were in the next room. The four of them had eaten dinner together but Trace had gone to a depart-ment meeting. Bart came into the room – he had overheard. There were tears in his eyes. She stood and he put his arms round her. She leaned into him, crying. 'It's quite a thing, to lose your mother.'

He nodded, his breath a sob. He was already feeling it in the arms in which he now enfolded her.

Paula came to the doorway. She and Laura hugged one another. 'Want to come and sit on the couch with us?' Paula asked.

They went and sat together, one on either side of her, and they talked about Rachel.

They heard Trace's car drive in the driveway. He walked into the room. Laura stood. 'Trace . . .'

He stopped.

'Carlena called a while ago. Mother died this evening.'

'Oh!' They held one another, his arms round her pressed tight. 'Ohh,' he said again. His chest rose, trembled, once.

They called Philip. He would meet them at the airport in Massachusetts. Bart and Paula went home to pack. Laura went into the white-walled room, her daughter's room, and got the box of ashes and put it in her suitcase.

At the house in Hadley they all gathered – Lillian and Richard, Howard and Irene. Lillian and Richard's children had come with them from Michigan. Over the phone, talking about funeral arrangements, Laura told her brother and sister, 'We want to bury Annie's ashes next to Mother's.' It had been a grief for them, too. They were satisfied to share it now.

The service would be the day after tomorrow. They went and looked at the body of their mother, their grandmother. They talked with the neighbors, talked with the lawyer, talked with the minister. He told them, 'She did not understand why she should live and Annie should die.' They nodded. Who could understand? 'But later, she was able to put those questions aside.'

They roamed around the house. They talked with each other. Laura and Howard and Lillian would return later, for the disposition of the household.

They had given the newspaper a list of Rachel's associations. The obituary appeared on an inside page, at the top of the column of death notices. 'When our father died' – they spoke of it – 'his picture was on the front page.' He had been a city luminary. Not so for her. 'You are my life work,' she had said.

Laura called Ginny's number. No answer. Fred would be in Cancun. It was just as well. She would get in touch with him later.

The funeral director called with a question: 'Do you want her wedding band to stay with her?'

Laura had taken the call. The idea was abhorrent to her. Destroy their mother's gold ring in a fire? 'No, we'd like to have it.'

She reported the conversation to Lillian and Howard, who agreed. In the disposition of their mother's jewelry, it was the wedding band she chose. She slipped it on her finger, above her own. It fitted her finger perfectly.

The hour for the funeral came. They were seated in a side room reserved for the family. The service was brief and uninspiring. It didn't matter. The occasion spoke for itself. Laura remembered the service for Annie, how carefully they had planned it. There had been outrage and tragedy to moderate. Here there was only grief, and thanksgiving.

At the cemetery they gathered again, huddled, waiting, as the cars pulled slowly along the road. A slight wind blew, turning the green leaves to silver.

Trace and Laura stood together.

'Are you sure you want to?' Laura whispered.

'Yes. I can do it alone if you'd rather.'

'No. If you do it, I want to be part of it.' It would not have been her choice, to do it themselves, lower the box of their daughter's ashes into the ground. He had suggested it. 'Is it a common custom?' she'd asked, uncertain. 'It's sometimes done,' he said. She didn't want to press him. If it was important to him, if it would help him, she would not demur. But she didn't want him doing it without her.

'I'll tell you when it's time,' he said.

The service proceeded. The minister was reading from a service book. 'We are here to commit to the earth the ashes of Rachel Taylor and of Anne Randall.' He was facing Rachel's grave. Laura watched, the scene blurred to greens and browns, a slur of red and pink and yellow where the flowers were, near the two mounds of earth, the piles narrow and high. The breaks in the surface of earth looked small, no wider than the spread of a man's hand. The boxes were there, a small carrying loop affixed to the top of each. Her heart raced, hurt; her fingers were chilled in the wind, though the sun shone. Philip and Bart stood close; Howard and Lillian and the others, too. She heard sobbing.

The minister's voice halted, he looked up. Trace touched her elbow. 'Now.'

They stepped forward away from the others, across the unmarred grass, past the headstone for Will, past Rachel's ashes, the mound of earth, to the second grave, the second pile of dirt, the second small box, the outer wrapping now removed and an inner wrapping, white, covering the stiff square container.

Trace started to kneel. She followed him. 'All right,' he whispered. He moved a hand slowly forward, waiting for her to move with him and together they picked up the box and carried it the several inches to the deep place in the earth and together they began to lower it, their arms pressed against one another's, hand to hand, wrist to wrist, forearm to forearm.

The hole was deeper than she'd thought. She was almost to her shoulder and she felt no solid earth stopping the descent of the box. Panic invaded her heart. She might have to drop it, let go too quickly. It was the trap door again, falling away. She could not bear the thought of it, the box dropping, thudding into the hole.

She whispered to him – she was shivering, sick to her stomach, 'I can't reach down any further.'

Immediately, his voice was there, the pressure of his elbow steady against her arm, his shoulder inching forward. 'It's all right. I've got it. You can let go.'

And so she did.